Bumper Book of

NANCY DREW®

Stories

The Clue in the Crumbling Wall
The Mystery of the Tolling Bell
The Clue of the Black Keys

Carolyn Keene

WOOLWORTHS

This edition produced exclusively for F W Woolworths by
Carnival Books, an imprint of the Children's Division
of the Collins Publishing Group 1988.

Nancy Drew and *Nancy Drew Mysteries* are trademarks
of the Stratemeyer Syndicate, registered in the
United States Patent and Trademark Office

ISBN 0 00 194491-6

Printed and bound in Great Britain

CONTENTS

The Clue in the Crumbling Wall

The Clue in the Crumbling Wall was first published in the UK
in hardback in 1972 by William Collins Sons & Co. Ltd, and in
paperback by Armada in 1978 by Fontana Paperbacks.

Nancy pressed herself against the wall

·1· *Strangers in the Garden*

GREAT drops of rain pelted the sidewalk, as Nancy Drew raced madly towards home, her golden hair flying in the stiff breeze.

"Thank goodness, you're home safe!" Hannah Gruen cried in relief as Nancy came through the door.

For twenty minutes, the torrential rain blotted everything from view. When it ended, Nancy gazed ruefully from a window at her garden. She was dismayed to see the tall hollyhocks snapped off near the ground. Clumps of painted daisies were flattened in the mud.

"My lovely garden is a wreck," she said to the housekeeper, "and—why, my goodness!"

The girl dashed outside. Mrs Gruen followed, to find out what the trouble was. Nancy stared in consternation at the flower border.

"My beautiful new rose bushes!" she gasped. "They're gone!"

Where four choice bushes had been planted only the week before, there now appeared four gaping holes filled with water.

"I suppose the wind—" began Mrs Gruen.

"I'm sure it wasn't the wind, because the bushes would be around somewhere, and they're not," Nancy objected, already searching the garden. "I planted them very deep, anyway. I'm afraid they've been stolen!"

"But who would take them?" asked the housekeeper.

"I don't know, but good rose bushes are scarce this year and ours were rare."

"The police should be notified," Hannah Gruen said with determination, and went into the house to telephone to them.

Nancy continued to gaze round the garden. Except for the rose bushes, no other shrubs or plants were missing. It was very mystifying, and even more so when Mrs Gruen appeared to say that the same kind of loss had been reported by other people. An investigator would be sent to the Drew home to make an inspection.

"There's no doubt that your rose bushes were stolen, Nancy," the woman added grimly.

"And I'm afraid they won't be recovered," sighed Nancy.

"Unless you search for them yourself," Hannah Gruen said with a twinkle in her eye. "As a detective, I'd certainly favour you over anyone on the River Heights police force!"

As Nancy and the housekeeper busied themselves gathering up debris from the garden, they heard the familiar song of one of River Heights' well-known characters.

"Here's old Mehearty coming down the street!" Nancy laughed, shaking off her sombre mood. "Do you want any clams today?"

"I do not," Mrs Gruen said with emphasis. "But if I know Mehearty, he'll probably talk me into buying some anyway!"

The old man, once a sailor, had received his nickname from Nancy when she was a little girl. He often addressed other people as "me hearties," and sang nautical songs with these words. Little Nancy had mixed the whole thing up and called him "Mehearty man." Her nickname had stuck to him. Mehearty was a good-natured, lovable person, full of yarns of the sea. An injury on board ship had kept him on land for many years. He dug clams in the near-by river and sold them for a living.

The man's cart bell tinkled merrily, and a moment later the jolly, weather-beaten old fellow rounded the corner of the driveway, wheeling his little wagon. Spying Nancy and the housekeeper, he began to carol:

> "Clams by the bushel,
> Clams by the lot,
> Clams for the kettle,
> Clams for the pot."

"None for us today," Mrs Gruen called, starting towards the house.

Old Mehearty smiled his most winning smile. "Real cheap today," he coaxed. "Ye can't turn them down, me hearties. My clams are nutritious, my clams are delicious, my clams are delectable, my clams are respectable!"

Nancy laughed, but Mrs Gruen said seriously, "I'm in no mood to buy clams, respectable or otherwise, right now! We've just discovered that four of our best rose bushes have been stolen."

"Ye don't say!" The old man's blue eyes roved to the gaping holes in the flower border. "Now that's what I call bad luck, ma'am, but ye can turn it into good luck if ye've a mind to."

"How, may I ask?"

"By buyin' Mehearty's good Muskoka River clams!"

"And in what way would that help?"

"Why, ye might find a pearl in one of 'em," the old fellow chuckled. "Then ye could use the money to buy a dozen rose bushes!"

"Did anyone ever find a pearl in one of your clams?" Nancy inquired curiously.

"Just ask Jasper Hawkins on Pinewood Point!" the old man boasted. "'Tweren't a very big pearl nor a very valuable one, but a pearl just the same. Jasper sold it, too."

"Upon second thoughts," remarked Mrs Gruen, "I believe I could use a dozen or two of your clams, Mehearty. Nancy, please run inside for my purse."

"I wish we could find a pearl," Nancy remarked, smiling, when they returned to the house.

"Then suppose you help me open the clams," the housekeeper suggested, handing the girl a sharp knife. "Maybe you'll find a pearl. I've heard that somebody in River Heights once found a large one in a Muskoka River clam."

Nancy nodded and worked cautiously. Soon she had a pile of empty clam shells, but no pearl.

"Bother!" she exclaimed impatiently. "I don't believe Mehearty's clams contain anything but meat! I'm glad this is the last one!"

Cutting it open, Nancy glanced carelessly inside. As she was about to toss away the shells she saw something in one of them. It was a small white object!

"I *have* found a pearl!" she cried, holding it out for the housekeeper to see.

The woman stared at the pearl. "Yes," she acknowledged, "and it may be worth money!"

"I'll take it downtown to old Mr Weatherby and ask him," said Nancy eagerly.

Sam Weatherby was a dealer in curios and odd jewellery. Bubbling over with excitement, the girl removed the pearl, washed it, and took it to the old man's shop. Once there, she was annoyed to have to wait fifteen minutes while an unpleasant man bargained with the shop owner over the price of an antique watch charm he hoped to sell. At last the customer pocketed some money and turned on his heel, remarking:

"I might as well have given it to you!"

"That was Hector Keep, the lawyer," Mr Weatherby remarked to Nancy after the man had left. "How he loves to argue! If all my customers were like him, I'd have to close up shop. Well, what can I do for you?"

Removing the pearl from her handbag, Nancy asked the curio dealer to estimate its value.

"Well, well," the man said, examining the object carefully. "Pretty nice. It's worth a fair sum. Where'd you get this?"

"From a Muskoka River clam."

A look of astonishment spread over the man's face. In a few moments he mumbled:

"I once bought a river pearl from Jasper Hawkins, but I never expected to see another one so good."

"You'll buy mine?" Nancy asked eagerly.

"I will, and pay you a good price, too, if you'll bring me the shells from which it was taken. I want to display the pearl with them." The dealer smiled. "I suppose now we'll have a rush of folks diggin' clams!"

Nancy replaced the pearl in her purse and hastened from the shop to get the desired shells. So intense was she upon her good fortune that she failed to observe a strange-looking young man who had been standing outside the shop, and who now followed only a few paces behind her. Unaware of impending trouble, Nancy carried her handbag lightly under her arm.

Presently she passed a department store on a street thronged with shoppers and gazed into the windows. The man drew closer to Nancy. Then, so suddenly that she scarcely knew what happened, he jerked the handbag from beneath her arm and fled!

· 2 · *Heath Castle*

NANCY soon recovered from her astonishment. When she whirled round, the bag-snatcher already was running down the street. She dashed after him, trying to avoid pedestrians.

"What's the matter?" asked a man she side-stepped just in time.

"My bag——"

He took up the chase with her. As word spread, other people followed. But the thief was fleet-footed. Nancy caught a faint glimpse of him as he dashed into a lane and over a fence, but not enough of a glimpse to identify him. She noted that he was very young, and wore ill-fitting, bulky clothes.

Nancy stopped. "Not a chance to overtake him now," she said unhappily. Then she added, "Well, there goes my pearl!"

Nancy walked on down the street. The Central

police station was located at the next corner, and on impulse she went in to report her loss.

"We'll do what we can to help you," the desk sergeant assured her. "Two thefts in an hour from one person. That's quite a record!"

Nancy left, doubtful that the stolen bag would be recovered more readily than the rose bushes. At home she was surprised to find a young policewoman in uniform talking earnestly to Hannah Gruen.

"Nancy, this is Lieutenant Masters. She's just been put in charge of juvenile delinquency." the housekeeper introduced her. "She was sent to investigate the theft of our rose bushes, and has mentioned several facts that will interest you."

"Have you no idea who may have run off with your rose bushes?" asked the Lieutenant.

"Not the slightest."

"I may have a clue. They probably were taken by an eight-year-old child."

"By a child!" Nancy exclaimed.

"Yes, the case is a strange one with mysterious angles."

"Please tell me about it."

"The girl in question has a passionate love for flowers and an amazing knowledge of them. In recent weeks she has taken seeds, plants, and even shrubs to satisfy her longing."

"I've already told Lieutenant Masters that we'll not prefer charges against a child," Hannah Gruen explained to Nancy. "I feel that her parents are more to blame than she is."

"Joan's father is not living," the young officer resumed. "Her widowed mother is ill and very poor."

15

"Then please forget that we ever made a report of the affair," Nancy requested.

"No. I'll see that the bushes are returned to your garden. It is best that Joan do that. Mrs Fenimore will insist upon it, anyway, for she is greatly distressed by her child's strange behaviour."

"There must be a reason for such queer actions," commented Mrs Gruen.

"There is," nodded the policewoman. "If I had more time, I'd probe the mystery of the Fenimores."

"Mystery?" questioned Nancy alertly.

"I'm on my way to their house now," Lieutenant Masters smiled, pleased to note Nancy's interest. "Why not come with me? Then you can hear everything first-hand."

"I'd love to go."

Later as Nancy and the officer went up the flagstone walk, the policewoman called attention to four rose bushes newly planted beside the sagging porch.

"Are these yours?" she asked.

"They look like the ones we lost," Nancy admitted. "But, please, I don't want to get a child into trouble—"

She broke off, because a little girl in a faded pink dress had just come round a corner of the house. Seeing the woman in uniform, she stopped short and then turned as if to run off.

"Don't be afraid," the lieutenant said kindly.

"Did you come to take me away?" the little girl asked.

"Indeed we didn't, Joan. But I'm afraid we'll have to send you off to a special school unless you decide to be good."

"I am good," Joan said, tossing her blonde, tangled curls. "Just ask my mother!"

"In many ways you are very good. I know you work hard and you take care of your mother. But why do you dig up shrubs and plants that don't belong to you?"

Joan's gaze roved to the telltale rose bushes. She hung her head and did not answer.

"I'm sure you don't really mean to be naughty," went on the policewoman. "Why do you take flowers?"

"Because they're pretty," Joan said with a trace of defiance. "We can never buy anything nice."

Sinking down on the porch steps, the child began to cry. The young policewoman comforted her. Soon she gained an admission from the little girl that an older boy, Jeddy Hooker, who lived next door, had suggested that Joan help herself to the rose bushes.

"I don't know why I did it," the little girl sobbed. "I wish my Aunt Florianna would come home. Then we could have nice things."

In an undertone, Lieutenant Masters explained to Nancy that Aunt Florianna, whose real name was Flossie Johnson, had been missing for many years. The woman, a talented dancer, had disappeared while on a vacation trip.

"Joan only knows about her aunt from her mother," the lieutenant added. "Mrs Fenimore wasn't married when her sister disappeared. Since Mr Fenimore's death she has been ill and has had very little money. It's too bad Florianna can't be found, so that she might help her."

"It's a shame," said Nancy soberly. "Did she run away deliberately?"

"Come inside and let Mrs Fenimore tell you the story herself," the policewoman suggested.

Joan's mother was resting and apologized for this.

"Please pardon such an ungracious way of receiving you, but my illness——"

"I'm sorry you're not feeling well," Nancy replied. "Perhaps it would be better if I came some other time."

"No, no."

"If you feel strong enough, Mrs Fenimore," said Lieutenant Masters, "I wish you would tell Miss Drew about your sister's disappearance. She was asking me whether you think Florianna dropped out of sight deliberately."

"I can't believe it of Flossie—that's what I always call her. She took the name of Florianna when she became a dancer," explained the woman. "She went away for a month's rest and was never heard of again."

"If Aunt Florianna would come home, we'd live in a castle," Joan blurted out. "We'd have beautiful gardens and everything nice. Aunt Florianna would be rich."

At Nancy's look of surprise, Mrs Fenimore explained that the dancer had been engaged to a wealthy manufacturer named Walter Heath. Five years after her strange disappearance he had died, leaving Heath Castle and the rest of his estate to her.

"There is a provision in the will which keeps me from collecting my sister's inheritance," said Mrs Fenimore. "You see, Mr Heath tied up the property by stipulating that if Florianna did not return to claim the estate within five years, the grounds were to be converted into a county park."

"Where is the property located?" asked Nancy.

"Several miles up the Muskoka River. The place is called Heath Castle. Once it was a very beautiful estate with walled gardens and sunken pools. Now I'm told it looks more like a jungle."

"Legally the property still belongs to Florianna?" Nancy inquired.

"It does for the next three weeks. After that she loses all claim to it. Oh, I do wish for Joan's sake my sister would come back."

"Mr Heath tried to trace Florianna before his death," Lieutenant Masters revealed. "But the detective he engaged failed to turn up a single clue."

The story deeply interested Nancy. She shrewdly guessed that the policewoman had hoped to intrigue her with details of the case. Confirming this suspicion, the young woman officer suggested that the girl might find it worth her while to visit Heath Castle soon.

The circumstances which had caused the petty theft continued to trouble Nancy, however. That night at dinner she told the story to the housekeeper, regretting that her father was not at home to hear it. The following day she repeated it to her friends, Bess Marvin and George Fayne. The two girls, who were cousins, were most interested in the part dealing with Heath Castle.

"What are we waiting for?" George cried enthusiastically. "Why not go there right away and explore the place?"

"Will it be safe?" asked Bess cautiously.

"It won't be an easy trip," Nancy warned her friends. "The estate is several miles from here and I'm told the undergrowth is like a jungle. The best way to get there is by motor-boat up the Muskoka River."

Twenty minutes later the three girls were heading upriver on a small, rather old motorboat they had rented at Cambell's Landing.

"Listen!" George said suddenly. "What was that?"

"A motorboat!" Nancy exclaimed. "Oh, now you can hear the engine plainly. But where is it?"

As she spoke, a small blue and white painted craft shot out from one of the river's many hidden tributaries. Until that moment it had been screened from view by overhanging bushes.

"Look out!" Bess cried in alarm.

The man in the oncoming boat had not seen the girls. At high speed he raced straight towards their little craft.

Desperately Nancy spun the wheel. There was not enough space to clear.

With a splintering crash, the two boats collided!

·3· *A Runaway Boat*

THE speeding boat which had struck Nancy's craft veered sharply away and raced downstream.

"Hey, wait!" George shouted angrily at the reckless pilot. "You've damaged our boat! Nancy, go after him! Don't let him get away!"

Nancy, however, was busy with another problem. When the crash had come, she had seen Bess lose her balance, strike her head on the side of the boat, and topple into the water.

If Bess were unconscious, there was no time to lose! Nancy instantly turned off the motor, located the spot where her friend had gone down, and dived in. Grasping the stunned girl under the shoulders with her left arm, she struck out with the other for the boat. George leaned over and helped pull the unconscious victim aboard.

"Is she—?" her cousin began in a terrified voice.

"I'm—all—right," Bess said weakly. "Our boat—" She tried to point.

For the first time the others realized that water was filling the craft at an alarming rate from a small hole in its side.

"Quick, George! Bail!" shouted Nancy.

George picked up an old, battered tin can and started to work. Nancy leaped forward, crumpled up a newspaper lying on the bottom of the boat, and stuffed it into the hole. Looking in a tackle box near her, she discovered a burlap sack, which she rolled up and added to the paper. In a moment, the influx of rushing water was stopped.

"Good!" panted George, sitting down. "Now we can chase that other boat!"

It was not in sight, however, and Nancy wisely decided it would be useless to try to pursue the speedier craft. She turned her attention to Bess.

"How are you feeling?" she asked.

"Oh, all right, I guess, but—but I'd like to go home."

"I wish we hadn't lost that fellow," said George. "If I ever see him again—" she added angrily.

"Would you recognize him?" asked Nancy.

George confessed that she would not, and inquired if the other girls would. Bess had not noticed him, but Nancy replied:

"I didn't see him very well. But I believe I'd know him if we ever meet again. At any rate, I'm going to keep my eyes open for both him and his boat."

Discouraged that the trip to Heath Castle had been a failure, Nancy took her friends home, then went to her own house. The following day found her still without a clue to the identity of the unknown boatman. Though she described his blue and white craft to several persons, no one was able to identify it. Then suddenly she thought of someone who might.

"Old Mehearty," she told Hannah Gruen. "I believe I'll hike down to his place on the river and chat with him."

Taking Bess along for company, she proceeded towards the river. As the girls approached the docks, they observed a dark-haired, beady-eyed stranger coming up the boardwalk. Instantly Nancy was struck by his resemblance to the man who had crashed into her boat. She stopped to speak to him, inquiring if he were not the one who had caused the collision.

"No, I'm not!" the man snapped. "I don't even own a boat!" Glaring at the girls, he walked on hurriedly.

The unpleasant encounter disheartened Nancy and she was silent until they reached Mehearty's little home. Then her spirits revived. The place was very quaint. Once it had been a small, well-appointed yacht. Now it was a beached wreck, weathered by sun and rain. Its only claim to any former glory was the flag which flew proudly from the afterdeck.

"Anyone home?" Nancy called, cupping her hands.

"Come in, come in!" invited the old sailor in a loud voice.

The room was small and cluttered, but very clean. Mehearty's bunk was neatly made, and on a shelf above it was displayed an amazing array of sea shells.

"I collect 'em," the sailor explained, following

Nancy's gaze. "Some o' those shells came from Puget Sound and some from the South Pacific." Hobbling over to the shelf, he pointed to a curious-looking specimen. "That's called the washboard clam. It's one of the biggest of our river clams."

"How interesting!" the girls exclaimed.

Pleased by their attention, the man showed them other shells which were too large to stand on the shelf. One, measuring three feet across, had come from an island in the Pacific.

"My, think what a pearl one might find in a clam that size!" Nancy laughed, then told of her own loss, saying she was glad the pearl was not large. "Mehearty, what would you say is the largest one ever discovered?"

"Well, now that's a poser. The largest pearl I ever heard tell of weighed about three ounces. There's probably bigger ones yet to be found."

"That's incredible!" said Bess.

Amazed at the variety in his collection, Nancy asked Mehearty if he had obtained the many different kinds by going to the various places where they could be found.

"No," the clam digger laughed. "Mr Heath gave 'em to me."

The name startled Nancy.

"Not Walter Heath?" she inquired alertly.

"No. Ira Heath—Walt's father," Mehearty answered. "He gave me the shells when he had his button factory on the inlet."

"A button factory near here?" Bess asked in surprise. "That's news to me."

"The factory's been closed for years. It was shut

23

down when the supply of fresh water mussels gave out. They use 'em, you know, to make buttons."

Nancy and Bess were learning a great deal, and they wanted to learn more.

"What became of Mr Heath?" Nancy inquired.

"Ira was born in England and went back there on a visit," Mehearty revealed, lighting a corn cob pipe. "He died there. His son Walt was left in charge here, and he stayed on at Heath Castle."

"His father built the castle?" inquired Bess.

Mehearty nodded, warming to the story. "Yes, Heath Castle was built to look like one o' them fancy English places."

Nancy was becoming more eager every minute to see the estate.

"But for me," went on the clam digger, "the place is too lonesome. No houses close by. The old gent built it 'bout a mile up the river from the button factory. Since Walt died 'bout five years ago, no one ever goes near the castle, or near the factory on Harper's Inlet, either."

"Harper's Inlet?" Nancy repeated thoughtfully. "Someone must have been there yesterday."

"That's right," agreed Bess. "We saw a motorboat come out of the inlet. It crashed into our boat and threw me in the water."

"Funny," commented Mehearty. "I don't know what business anyone would have at the factory. Who was the fellow?"

"That's what we came to find out," Nancy said.

She gave a complete account of the accident. Mehearty could not identify the man from her description, but he promised to watch for such a person.

"I'll keep an eye out for that boat, too," he added thoughtfully. "Can't figure why the fellow would be prowling up the inlet. Fishin's no good there. Maybe I'll run up and have a look."

Satisfied that Mehearty would be able to locate the boat and its mysterious pilot if anyone could, Nancy and Bess thanked him and left his quaint yacht home.

"How about going to Heath Castle now?" Nancy suggested to her friend.

"Sorry," Bess replied, "but I can't go today. Let's do it tomorrow. Then maybe George can go with us."

Nancy agreed, and the girls separated. When she reached home, a surprise awaited her. While she and Mrs Gruen had been away from the house, four rose bushes had been planted in the garden.

"Joan must have brought them back!" Nancy declared. "Oh, I'm so glad, for I'm sure she wouldn't have taken them if that boy Jeddy Hooker hadn't urged her to."

She was pressing dirt firmly round the bushes when her father drove into the garage.

"Hello, Nancy," he smiled fondly. "How's the garden?"

"Rather successful today," she laughed. "Four rose bushes that were taken yesterday are home again. I wish all mysteries could be solved as easily."

As they went into the house together, Nancy told him about the boat accident, the Fenimore problems, and the mystery of Florianna.

"Dad, tell me all you can about Ira Heath and his son Walter," she asked. "Did you know them?"

"Only by reputation. For years they operated a very

successful button factory. Then the business went to pieces."

"I already know that part," Nancy said. "What about Heath Castle? After Ira and Walter died, who took charge of the place?"

"Hector Keep, I believe."

Nancy's mind flew to the unpleasant customer in the curio dealer's shop.

"Isn't he a lawyer?" she asked.

"Yes," Mr Drew agreed soberly, "but I'll confess that Keep's type of law never appealed to me. I consider him a shrewd, calculating man."

"Is there any reason why he should allow Heath Castle to go to ruin?"

"None that I know of."

"Do you think Mr Keep did everything to find Florianna?" Nancy asked thoughtfully.

"So far as I know, he did. I can't see any reason why he shouldn't have."

"Did you know her?"

"I saw her perform many times. I admired her dancing very much," Mr Drew replied, smiling in reminiscence. "Why she should have disappeared at the height of her career has always puzzled me."

"Apparently she left no clues behind," remarked Nancy.

"The case was a strange one," her father said. "I guess Walter Heath was pretty broken up over it. I've always wondered——"

"You've wondered what, Dad?"

"Well, it occurred to me that Heath Castle might provide a key to the mystery. I've no real reason for thinking so—it's merely an idea I have."

"And I have a similar one!" Nancy cried jubilantly. "Two Drew minds can't be wrong!" she laughed. "Tomorrow I'll go there and ask those crumbling old walls to give up their secret!"

·4· *The Haunted Walk*

THE following morning found Nancy, Bess, and George at the entrance to Heath Castle.

"How do we get in?" asked Bess.

"Over this locked gate—Commando style," laughed George. In her eagerness, she tripped as she sprang from the automobile.

Nancy and Bess, following their chum, gazed with misgiving at the sharp iron spikes of the high, rusty gate.

"I don't like the idea of climbing over that gate. There must be an easier way to get in," Nancy said, her gaze roving along the crumbling, ivy-covered wall.

"I'll not attempt to climb over any part of it," announced Bess with finality. "I have on a good dress."

"Then you'll be left behind," George told her cousin tersely.

She and Nancy examined the stone wall. Some distance along, it was a bit lower than the gate and offered good toe holds. It was not difficult for the girls to grasp the vines and pull themselves to the top. Bess finally decided to follow. Leaping down lightly from the wall, the three friends started through the dense growth of trees and shrubs.

27

As they progressed, Bess felt rather uneasy. Beneath the canopy of leaves it was damp and cool, but there were many strange noises to unnerve her.

"Listen!" she commanded tensely. "What's that?"

Nancy and George could hear the sound plainly, but for a moment they could not identify it. Then Nancy smiled.

"The cooing of a pigeon!" she explained. "Come along, or we'll all have the jitters."

Before long, Bess had a bad case of jitters, bordering on real fear. She walked directly into a spider's web. She shuddered and brushed it from her mouth.

Just ahead, stretched a long avenue of oak trees which gave prospect of leading to the castle. Tramping through waist-high grass, the girls came first to a vine-tangled, fern-matted bower. Two handsome stone vases lay on their sides, cracked from being filled with water which had frozen during the winter.

"What a shame this place is being neglected," Nancy commented, pausing a moment. "Mr Keep ought to take care of it. If Florianna should come back, she would hardly recognize it, I'm sure."

"I wonder where this leads?" Nancy said, staring at a slippery, moss-grown stone walk.

On a rotted post nearby was a rustic sign with carved letters. The Drew girl stepped closer to look at the words.

" 'The Haunted Walk,' " she read aloud.

"I wish we'd gone the other way," Bess complained. "This is no fun."

"I think it is," Nancy replied. "It's so mysterious here! It's so——"

For an instant, a pair of penetrating, human eyes

seemed to stare at her from behind the evergreen. Then the eyes blinked shut and vanished completely.

"It must be my imagination," Nancy told herself, but she was not completely convinced.

"Let's go back to the car," Bess proposed suddenly. "We've seen enough of this place."

"I haven't," corrected Nancy. "I'm getting more curious every minute."

Further on was a summer-house and a stone wall. It occurred to Nancy that if someone really had been observing them he might have scrambled over it to avoid detection. She announced her intention of climbing up to make sure.

"Don't do it!" Bess pleaded nervously. "After all, we've no right to be on this property. Let's go."

Nancy was not to be deterred. While Bess and George watched uneasily, she scrambled up the vine-covered wall. Weathered stone crumbled beneath her fingers. Before she gained a hold on the ledge, she slipped and nearly fell.

"Do be careful, Nancy," Bess warned her. "There are sharp rocks just beneath you, and goodness only knows what's on top of that wall."

Indeed, Nancy was in danger. Agile though she was, she did not have the strength to swing herself on top of the wall. Her arms were tiring, and she could feel the soft rock loosening under the pressure of her fingers.

"Can't make it," she gasped.

George started to reply, but the words froze on her lips. Bess, too, was struck speechless with terror.

On the ledge overhead was a huge, venomous snake, its head raised. It was about to bury its fangs in Nancy's upstretched hand!

· 5 ·   *Beyond the Wall*

NANCY could not see the snake. Bess was so horrified, she could not speak. It was George who found her voice, crying out sharply:

"Let go, Nancy! Quick!"

Startled, the Drew girl let go and dropped to the ground. Picking herself up, she gazed questioningly at the girls.

"Just s-see what was heading towards you!" Bess quavered, still shaken from the close call her friend had had.

Dramatically she pointed to the huge snake. At the sight of it, Nancy shuddered involuntarily. Though a bite from the copperhead would not have been fatal, it would have been painful and required medical attention.

"Oh, George, you saved me!" she thanked her friend appreciatively. "I should have been more careful. Guess I'd better not climb the wall."

"Please, let's go back to the car!" Bess declared with feeling. George set out as guide.

"I hope you know where you're leading us, George," Nancy said sometime later. "It seems to me we're moving in a wide circle."

George paused to catch her breath. Her gloomy silence confirmed Nancy's suspicion.

"George, are we lost?" she asked.

"I don't know about you," the girl answered ruefully. "Myself—yes."

"It's going to rain any minute, too," Bess said, sinking down on a mossy log. "Oh, why did we come to this horrible, gloomy place? Imagine anyone building a home here."

"If the roads were opened and some shrubs cut down, the estate would be lovely," Nancy commented. "I'd like to live here myself."

After resting a few minutes, the girls took a vote on what to do, and decided to continue on through the woods. Nancy was chosen leader, and proved a better pathfinder than George. Before long, she came to some trampled grass.

"Now I know where we are!" she cried jubilantly. "We're near the estate boundary."

A few yards farther on they saw the wall itself and scrambled over it, reaching the shelter of the car just as the first raindrops splashed against the windshield. Fortunately, Nancy was able to get to the paved highway before the side road became a mire of mud.

"Let's wear old clothes next time we go to Heath Castle," she said to Bess and George, as the girls parted company in River Heights.

"And take along snake serum, axes, and lunch," advised George pointedly.

Alone, Nancy suddenly recalled that she had invited Lieutenant Masters to dinner at the Drew home that evening. At seven o'clock she arrived, not wearing a uniform, but looking very feminine and pretty in a blue lace dress.

As dinner progressed, Nancy knew from her father's chuckles and the quick repartee that he was enjoying their guest immensely. After a time, the talk became more serious as mention was made of several famous court cases. Nancy brought up the problem of the Fenimores and the mystery of Florianna and Heath Castle.

"I thought that mysterious place would interest you," young Lieutenant Masters said, smiling. "By this time I suppose you've been to the courthouse, too, and read the Heath will."

"Why, no," Nancy confessed. "So far I've confined my investigations to the estate. Have you read the will?"

"No, I've never had time to examine it."

"Why not do it together?" Nancy proposed eagerly.

To this the policewoman promptly agreed, saying that at ten o'clock the next morning she would meet the girl at the courthouse.

Since Nancy was familiar with legal terms, having read many of her father's papers, the Walter Heath document was easy for her to decipher. Hector Keep was named as sole executor.

A quick reading confirmed the story that the entire Heath estate had been bequeathed to Florianna, also known as Flossie Johnson. In the event of the estate not being claimed by her within five years of Walter Heath's death, the property was to go to the county for a park.

One clause in the will held Nancy's attention. It read:

"It is my belief and hope that Florianna still lives and will claim the property within the allotted time. She will be able to identify herself in a special way, thus insuring that no imposter can receive my estate."

"I wonder what that means?" Nancy mused, pointing it out to Lieutenant Masters, who was equally puzzled.

"I haven't the least idea," said the officer.

They re-read the document, but it gave no clue to the special means by which Florianna might establish her identity. Thinking that the dancer's sister, Mrs Fenimore, might know the answer, they drove to her cottage.

The invalid, her face pale, was sitting on the shabby front porch. She was trying, without much success, to patch a sun suit of Joan's.

"Good morning," Mrs Fenimore greeted the visitors wanly. She stared anxiously at the policewoman. "It's —it's not Joan again?"

"No, it isn't. I'm happy to report that your little girl is behaving very well. We came to ask you a few questions about your sister."

The invalid relaxed but spoke wearily. "I'll tell you everything I can. Long ago I gave up hope that she will ever be found."

"Then you believe that your sister may not be living?" Nancy interposed soberly.

"No, Flossie must be alive," Mrs Fenimore replied with quiet conviction. "Otherwise, in all these years I would have had some word of her death."

"Tell us about your sister," urged Lieutenant Masters kindly. "She was younger than you?"

"No, Flossie was seven years older. Our parents died when we were very young, and we lived with an aunt who was pretty strict. I never minded Aunt Matilda's scoldings, but Flossie was highly strung. She took dancing lessons secretly, and when Aunt Matilda punished her for it, she ran away.

"For several years Flossie danced wherever she could get an engagement and studied during her spare moments. She changed her name to Florianna. Oh, she worked hard! She was determined to get on in the world."

"You saw Florianna often, after she became famous?" inquired Lieutenant Masters.

"Only now and then. But she wrote to me every week without fail. I was so excited when she became engaged to Walter Heath. It was a secret, so of course I told no one."

"You have no idea why your sister went away?" asked Nancy.

"She needed a rest. That's all I know. Flossie didn't tell anyone her plans." The speaker's voice had become soft and dreamy.

"Could anything have happened between Florianna and Walter Heath to make her unhappy enough to disappear?" speculated Nancy.

Mrs Fenimore shook her head. "Florianna never hinted of such a thing. She was beautiful and talented. He was handsome, wealthy, and very kind. They adored each other. No, I'm sure he had nothing to do with her disappearance."

Mention of the deceased estate owner reminded Nancy of the real purpose of her call. Accordingly, she asked Mrs Fenimore about the strange identification clause in the Heath will.

"I wondered what that meant when I read it," the invalid replied. "The only thing I could figure out, was that Walt and Florianna must have shared a secret."

"Do you think Hector Keep might know what it was?" Nancy asked.

Mrs Fenimore's face darkened. "Please don't mention that man's name!" she requested sharply.

"Don't you like him?"

"I detest him. All these years he's pretended to search for Florianna."

"Pretended?"

"Well, I can't prove it, but I'm sure he's not honest. From the beginning he assumed that Florianna was dead. He made only half-hearted attempts to find her. Now he doesn't even try, and——"

Mrs Fenimore suddenly slumped in her chair. Both Nancy and the policewoman jumped forward to catch her as she fainted.

"Water!" said the lieutenant tersely. "This has been too much for her!"

Nancy flew to the kitchen of the little house, returning a moment later with a glass of water. The policewoman had laid the inert victim on the floor of the porch, and was taking her pulse. Now she whisked a tiny first-aid kit from her pocket, crushed a tablet from it in the palm of her hand, and held it to Mrs Fenimore's nostrils. In a moment the invalid revived and was given the water to drink.

"It was foolish of me to faint," she said as they assisted her to the couch in the living-room.

"Perhaps we'd better not talk any more today," suggested Nancy.

"I'm all right now," Mrs Fenimore insisted, "I'd like to talk. Isn't there something we can do to find my sister?" she asked pitifully. "The time's getting so short. In less than three weeks the estate will go to the county. I don't care about myself, but Joan needs so many things that Florianna could give her."

"Surely there must be some clue to her whereabouts," Nancy said thoughtfully. "A clever person should be able to find your sister."

"If only someone would make an honest effort!" Mrs Fenimore's voice became pleading. "Won't you help me, Miss Drew?"

"I'm afraid it's too big a job for me."

"Oh, no it isn't!" Mrs Fenimore insisted. "I've read about your work. You're the very one to find my sister."

"I hardly know what to say," Nancy demurred, glancing towards the policewoman.

Lieutenant Masters gazed at the girl with a challenging smile.

"Why not say yes?" she asked softly. "From the first, I've known that this was a case for you. If you work fast, you may find Florianna in time to save Heath Castle."

· 6 · *Exploring the Inlet*

NANCY promised Mrs Fenimore that she would do everything she could to trace her missing sister. Secretly, she wondered whether she would be able to find the dancer in time to save Heath Castle for her.

"May I see a photograph of your sister?" she requested.

"I have a number of excellent ones," Mrs Fenimore replied eagerly. "They're in the drawer of that table."

At her direction, Nancy got them. There were six, taken years before when the dancer was at the height of her career. Several were inscribed with her name and a greeting. The face was a distinctive one. Carefully Nancy noted the perfect features, the beautiful dark eyes, the straight nose and firm chin.

"Florianna doubtless has changed a great deal since I last saw her," Mrs Fenimore remarked. "I can't seem to realize that ten years have slipped by."

"Your sister is lovely," Nancy commented. "Joan looks a little like her."

"Yes, she does. And certainly my daughter has Flossie's vivacious ways," the woman replied. "She's quite a little actress. Maybe some day—"

As the invalid looked dreamily into space, Nancy was afraid that she might faint again. Fortunately, Mrs Fenimore controlled herself. Lieutenant Masters, fearing the conversation had upset the woman, said they must leave.

"Please try not to worry," the Drew girl urged Mrs Fenimore. "I'll start working at once on the mystery."

When she and the woman police officer reached the automobile, Nancy declined a ride, saying she would like to walk and think about how she would start solving the strange case. The lieutenant wished her luck.

"Call on me any time I can help you," the young woman urged, as she drove off.

Nancy wandered up the street. Children were coming home from school to luncheon. Some of them smiled in a friendly way at the girl, but many were rude.

"It's too bad Joan has to live in this neighbourhood," Nancy thought. "I wonder—"

At this moment she spied the child playing with an older boy in a vacant site. They were tossing a ball for a stray dog to retrieve.

"That boy looks familiar," Nancy thought. "Where have I seen him before?"

Suddenly the boy, in a fit of temper, hit the dog with a stick. Joan screamed.

"You ugly, mean brute!" he shouted. "You're chewing my ball to pieces!"

Nancy paused. "Stop that!" she ordered. "Is that a nice way to treat a dog? He hasn't hurt your ball. He was only playing."

The boy, who was ragged and dirty, gazed at her with hard, unfriendly eyes.

"Is he your dog?" he asked impudently.

"Why, no."

"Then it's none of your business if I hit him! I'll do it as often as I please! So!"

Nancy started to reply, but it was not necessary. The dog dropped the ball and slunk off. The boy picked it up. Giving the girl a baleful look, he too went on his way.

Nancy led Joan away by the hand. As tactfully as possible, she suggested that the child should find a girl playmate in the neighbourhood.

"Jeddy Hooker's the only one that lives close to me," Joan replied, skipping happily along beside her companion. "I don't like him when he's cruel like today, but most of the time he's lots of fun. He always thinks up things to do."

"Why didn't you go home to lunch?" Nancy asked.

Joan hung her head. "There's nothing good in the house to eat."

Nancy turned into a store, bought some sandwiches and milk and told the child to take them home at once for her mother and herself.

"Oh, thank you, Nancy Drew," Joan beamed. "And —and I won't play with Jeddy any more if you don't want me to."

"That's a good girl."

"And please try to find my aunt for me."

"I will," promised Nancy, starting in the other direction,

Until they were out of sight of each other, Nancy and Joan continued to turn round and wave. Nancy was sure she had made a firm friend of the little girl.

"I'm not very far from Mehearty's," the young detective thought presently. "I believe I'll go there and find out if he's seen that man who crashed into my boat."

She turned down a side street and in a short time came to the clam digger's home. The old sailor was on the shore repairing his rowboat.

"Well now, me lass, I'm glad to see ye," the old sailor said. "But I'm afeered I haven't got good news for ye."

"You mean about the boat?"

"I've looked high and low for that damaged boat," the old man told the girl regretfully. "It's not tied up anywhere along here."

"How about the inlet?" asked Nancy.

Mehearty admitted that he had been too busy to go there. "Maybe I'll go this very afternoon. I need clams and there might be some up the inlet. Ye want to come along? I'll show ye the Heath factory if ye want to see it."

The upper river was very still. As the little boat slipped into the inlet sometime later, there was no sound except for the occasional chirping of a bird.

Nancy and George whom she had invited along, watched the coves for hidden boats. There were none and there was nothing to indicate that anyone had been near the inlet for weeks.

"It don't look as if we're goin' to find your friend," Mehearty remarked after rowing a quarter of a mile up stream. "We're near Heath's button factory now. I'll anchor here."

The old man located a bed of clams in the shallow water. Asking the girls to balance his woven basket on the gunwale, he waded in to dig them out. As he tossed them, some landed in the basket, others the girls caught and threw in. All the time Mehearty sang snatches of familiar sea songs, but each one ended with:

> "Clams by the bushel,
> Clams by the lot,
> Clams for the kettle,
> Clams for the pot."

"Basket's full," Nancy soon called.

George caught the last one and examined it. The clam looked different from the others. Then she stared in astonishment at an ugly purple stain on her fingers. Her dress had been splattered with dye.

"Goodness!" she exclaimed in dismay. "Where did that come from?"

Mehearty splashed over to the boat. He looked surprised when he saw George's stained hands.

"That purple colour is a dye," he explained. "It came from this here whelk."

"So this kind of mollusk is called a whelk?" Nancy asked.

"That's right," Mehearty replied.

It was not the shell, he told the girls, but the body of the animal inside that produced the dye.

"Real dye?" Nancy inquired, deeply impressed.

"The very best. Whelks have been used for dye makin' since ancient times. Used with purpuras or dog whelks, they make the finest dye ever. This whelk is the kind ye can eat, too."

"I'll not try eating any," said George with a grimace. She attempted without success to wash the stain from her fingers. "Is it difficult to make the dye?"

"Anyone can do it. Ye break open the shells and remove the little animals. Soak 'em in salt water for a few days, then boil 'em in a lead kettle until ye have a pale green liquid."

"Green?" Nancy asked in surprise.

"Yes'm, the liquid is green, but when ye dip wool into it, it comes out purple."

"I'll buy my clothes already dyed," George said, grinning ruefully. "Whelks aren't used commercially here at River Heights, are they?"

"Never heard of anyone goin' into the business. Ain't enough whelks round here."

Mehearty got into the boat and started off again. As they rounded a bend, the girls saw a large, square building set some distance back from shore. The banks nearby were littered with discarded bits of clam shells.

"That's the Heath button factory," Mehearty identified the place. "She's sure gone to pieces since I was last here."

Nancy gazed curiously at the neglected, brick structure. Vines lay thick on the shingle roof and all the windows were broken.

Not expecting to find anyone around, she was surprised to see figures close to the factory entrance. Two men were visible for an instant. Then they vanished, and Nancy was certain they had gone into the building. Before she could mention what she had seen, Mehearty pointed to something hidden near some bushes.

"A boat!" he exclaimed. "And her prow's smashed."

The bow of the boat had been drawn up on the sand. At a glance George and Nancy identified it as the blue and white craft that had struck them.

"Oh, Mehearty, please pull in here," Nancy requested excitedly.

"Is that the boat ye're lookin' for?" the old sailor asked, resting his oars.

Without replying, Nancy leaped out, splashing through knee-deep water to the shore. George followed close at her heels.

"Hey, where ye gals goin' in such a rush?" Mehearty called after them.

Nancy paused, suddenly realizing that it might be wise to proceed with caution. Tersely she explained to the old clam digger that she had just seen two men disappear into the button factory. Maybe they owned the boat!

"Hmph!" Mehearty grunted. "Well, I'll bet ye a mess o' clams they've no right in there!"

"I want to talk to them," Nancy called. "Mehearty, will you stay here near the damaged boat? If the men come, try to hold them until we get back."

The sailor disliked such an inactive role, but before he could protest, the girls had gone.

·7· *A Mysterious Explosion*

"I'm sure those two men went into the building," Nancy stated as they moved closer to the old button factory. "One of them wore a cap like the fellow who crashed into our motorboat."

"And the other?" George inquired. "Do you know him?"

"I caught only a fleeting glimpse of him," Nancy replied vaguely.

Actually she thought that he resembled the lawyer, Hector Keep. Not being certain, she was reluctant to give a definite answer.

Twenty yards from the factory, the girls were startled at the sound of hammering. The pounding noise came from inside the building.

"Those men are in there, just as I thought," Nancy said, cautiously pulling aside the tall grass to obtain a clear view of the building. "What are they doing, I wonder?"

"Workmen sent to repair the place, perhaps," was George's reply.

Nancy offered no comment. It was entirely possible that Hector Keep had brought another man to the property either to inspect it, or to do some work, though she seriously doubted this.

As the girls moved closer, the hammering ceased. They waited several minutes, but it was not resumed.

"We may have been seen," Nancy said uncertainly. "I hope the men haven't left."

43

Directly outside the disused factory, they saw that the front door of the building was open. Nancy peered inside. A long corridor opened into several offices and led to a large work room at the back. No one was there.

As the girls started along the hallway, they heard retreating footsteps. Glancing out of one of the dirt-smudged windows, they saw two men running in the direction of the river.

"Oh, Nancy!" George cried. "They must have heard us!"

"They're going towards the boat!" added Nancy excitedly.

Already the men were well hidden by the high marsh grass. The girls ran quickly towards a rear door. As they neared it, deafening sounds of an explosion filled the air. The walls of the factory rocked and plaster tumbled down.

"Nancy!" George cried frantically.

She lurched backwards just in time to avoid being crushed by a heavy falling beam. A board struck her on the forehead, slightly dazing her.

"Nancy!" she called weakly. "Nancy!"

There was no answering cry. To George's horror she saw that a huge pile of debris had separated her from her chum. One whole corridor wall had caved in.

Nancy must be buried beneath it!

"Nancy! Nancy!" George shouted again, struggling to her feet.

The air was thick with plaster dust, but she paid no heed. Coughing and choking, she frantically pulled away boards and plaster.

In the meantime the two strangers, who had paused

in the tall grass, were just about to go back to the factory when they heard running footsteps. Mehearty, fearful upon hearing the explosion, was racing towards the factory, clam rake over his shoulder. He passed within a few feet of the men.

"Oh dear, oh dear," he kept mumbling, "I hope nothin's happened to the lassies!"

He found George still working feverishly at the pile of debris.

"Mehearty!" the girl cried. "I can't find Nancy! She must be under the wreckage!"

The old man's worst fears were confirmed! He said nothing, but began raking furiously at the pile of plaster that blocked the corridor.

At this very moment, Nancy was lying stunned on the floor of a little room some distance from where the others were working. The force of the explosion had lifted the girl off her feet and hurled her into a storage closet. Then the door had slammed shut and the ceiling above it, in falling, had sealed the entrance.

As she regained consciousness, Nancy found herself in total darkness and wondered where she was. She found a door and tried it. It would not budge, and there was no other exit. With all her strength Nancy pounded on the door and pushed her body against it. At last it yielded ever so slightly. Through the crack she shouted:

"George!"

"Nancy! Where are you?" came a muffled reply.

"Here I am! In the closet!"

They quickly released Nancy from her prison.

George embraced her friend in excited relief. "Oh, I was so scared," she said. Then soberly she added, "Why didn't you answer when I called you twenty minutes ago?"

"I didn't hear you," the Drew girl replied ruefully.

"Knocked out?" asked Mehearty, gazing intently at Nancy to be sure she was all right.

"I'm afraid I was. But I'm none the worse for it. What caused the explosion?" Suddenly she recalled the two strangers who had run from the building. "What became of those two men?"

George had forgotten about them during the excitement. Recalling that she last had seen the pair hastening towards the river, she asked Mehearty if he had observed anyone.

"Nary a soul," he responded.

Nancy, George, and the old clam digger plunged through the marsh grass towards the river bank. The damaged motorboat was no longer there.

"Those rascals sneaked away, drat 'em," Mehearty muttered in disgust. "Do ye think that makes 'em guilty, Miss Nancy?"

"Guilty on two counts," the girl replied. "Guilty of damaging the boat I rented, and guilty of causing the explosion."

"But why cause an explosion?" asked George.

Nancy shrugged. She did not want to mention any of her theories just yet, but an idea had come to her. One of the men had resembled Hector Keep. The lawyer's actions were becoming very suspicious. He actually had been accused by Mrs Fenimore of not being honest. The man certainly had neglected to take care of the Heath gardens and the factory. The whole thing looked bad for him.

"But what could be his reason for wanting to destroy the factory?" Nancy mused.

She was brought out of her reverie by George, who suggested that they go home.

"The fellow with the damaged boat is gone," she reminded her friend. "Since we came here to find him, we may as well leave."

During the trip back to Mehearty's, the clam digger and the girls watched for the blue and white motorboat, but saw no sign of it.

"I'll be glad to take ye on a trip again," the old sailor offered when they reached the dock at River Heights.

Nancy thanked the man. On the way home she was very thoughtful, and could hardly wait for the moment when she could talk to her father in the library after dinner. For half an hour she expounded her theories regarding the mystery of the Heath estate.

"But why would Keep want to damage property he's paid to look after?" asked Mr Drew, when he had heard the story. "It doesn't make sense to me."

"I'm sure there's a great deal more to the Heath case than Florianna's disappearance," Nancy declared. "Take the explosion today, for example. It wasn't just an accident. There may be something pretty sinister behind it all."

"I'll agree with you on that point," Mr Drew said soberly. "Nancy, I know it's useless to ask you to give up trying to solve a mystery—"

"Oh, it is, Dad!"

"At least I can ask you to be careful. Remember, you're my one and only daughter."

"I'll keep it in mind," she said, hugging him affectionately. "Now, about the Heath affair. Isn't it possible that someone is prowling around the property in the hope of discovering the clue Walter Heath mentioned in his will?"

"You mean the one by which Florianna can identify herself beyond all doubt?"

"Yes, Dad. If an imposter should stumble upon that clue, it would be an easy matter for him to have some woman claim the fortune."

"Not so easy as you may think, Nancy. A number of persons knew Florianna."

"But in that time she could have changed so that no one would recognize her."

"True. I follow your reasoning. Nevertheless, any person who put in a claim would have to satisfy Hector Keep and the court that it was a just one."

Nancy gazed steadily at her father. "Do you think Hector Keep would be difficult to satisfy? If he isn't honest—"

Mr Drew squirmed in his chair.

"Nancy, I don't like to think the man would take a bribe, if that's what you mean," he said. "You know my opinion of Keep. I don't like his way of handling law cases, but I can't prove he's actually done anything dishonest."

"You admit that the Heath case looks suspicious?" the girl pressed him.

"Yes, I do, Nancy. And you have my full approval to work on it; that is to find Florianna. The rest of it you should leave alone."

"I've mulled over it a lot," the girl went on. "I've even thought that maybe Florianna is being held a prisoner somewhere."

"In the castle?" Mr Drew asked in surprise.

"Who knows?" his daughter bantered. "But seriously, I hardly know where to begin my investigation. The explosion today kind of changed my plans."

"How do you mean?"

"I heard that Walter Heath made scientific experiments at the castle. If Hector Keep suspects there's a secret somewhere within those crumbling walls—I need your help, Dad."

"Well, if you put it that way," said her father, weakening. "Actually, I haven't the time to spare, but I will go to please you."

"Tomorrow morning, then."

"So soon?"

"Well, I've only three weeks to solve the mystery."

·8· *No Trespassers Allowed*

Nancy led the way through the dew-laden grass to the scene of the explosion. There was no sign of anyone near the factory. The only sound to be heard was the wild cry of a huge water fowl which rose from the nearby marsh.

"Those two fellows did a good job of destruction," commented the lawyer as the Drews cautiously entered the building.

"Here's where the wall caved in near George and me," Nancy explained, kicking at the debris with her foot.

"Looks as if it might have been dynamited," her

father remarked, after gazing about carefully. "Let's see if we can find any telltale evidence."

For the next half-hour father and daughter scrambled in and out of the rubble. Discovering nothing of importance in the corridor, they decided to investigate the large workroom at the back. It was necessary for them to go outside and climb in through a window to reach the room, because the inside doorway to it was blocked.

"Oh, it's like a ghost town," said Nancy, as she surveyed the rusted machinery and layers of dust. "To think that this once was a prosperous factory!"

"It isn't much of a tribute to the Heaths, I'll admit," commented Mr Drew.

"What was this machine used for?" Nancy asked, interested in a steel saw attached to it.

"This is for cutting," her father explained, pausing beside it. "The clam shell is placed in the machine. An operator moves a lever and down comes the circular steel saw. Presto! A little shell disc drops into the hopper. Another machine slices the disc into pieces of uniform thickness, and there you have some buttons!"

"How clever!" said Nancy.

"The buttons pass through still another machine which polishes them," Mr Drew went on. "In the last operation thread-holes are drilled through them."

"To think all this was done right here in River Heights and I never knew anything about it," Nancy said in wonder.

Mr Drew turned away. "I guess there's nothing more to learn, Nancy, either about the buttons or the mystery of the factory. If those men deliberately caused the explosion, they skillfully covered their work. We may as well leave before we're accused of trespassing."

Bitterly disappointed, Nancy was just about to let her father help her through the window, when her sharp eyes caught sight of something.

"Dad! Look!" she cried.

Sticking out from a corner of the rubble in the doorway, lay a scrap of paper, and near it were several freshly made footprints. Nancy darted towards them, and picked up the paper.

A glance sufficed to show her that the words on it might have value. The sheet had been torn in such a way that only part of the message was there. It was written in a man's hand and read:

> Dear C,
>   Some
> cret which I
> in a wall
> famous
> worthy

Nancy showed her father what she had found.

"Interesting," he commented, scanning the torn paper. "But I can't say that it makes much sense. The footprints might be a better clue."

He stooped to examine them. "Freshly made without a doubt," he said. "Evidently your two strangers have visited here since the explosion!"

"Then that practically proves they're searching for something," Nancy concluded. "Something they think was hidden and could be found only by blasting it out."

"If that's true, I'm sure it has nothing to do with Florianna," said Mr Drew.

"Maybe not," Nancy sighed. She was staring at the

torn note. "I believe I've stumbled on a worthwhile clue just the same," she said slowly. "I can guess now that one of these words is 'secret'."

She pocketed the message and reluctantly left the factory with her father, who had an appointment at his office and was already late. At home again, she spent more than an hour trying to piece together the missing words of the note. Who had written them? The paper appeared old, the ink slightly faded.

"It wouldn't surprise me if Walter Heath wrote the message," she said to Hannah Gruen. "No way to prove it, though."

"I know how you might find out," was the housekeeper's surprising answer.

"How?"

"Walter Heath was a member of the River Heights Historical Society before his death. Isn't it likely that the society would have specimens of his handwriting?"

"Hannah Gruen, you're a genius!" Nancy cried.

Luck was with her. On many of the books and pieces of furniture which Walter Heath had given to the museum she found not one, but several samples of the deceased estate owner's handwriting.

"It's the same as that in the note!" Nancy decided excitedly, comparing the script. "Now, if only I can find the missing half of the note!"

Many questions plagued the girl. Had the torn sheet fallen from some niche in the wall at the time of the explosion? Or had one of the strangers dropped it when leaving the ruins?

"Hector Keep may have the other part," Nancy speculated. "If so, I'm afraid I'll never see it."

Seeking her father's aid once more, Nancy asked him

to talk to the lawyer and try to get what information he could from him about the Heath case. Again she was to be disappointed.

"Mr Keep came honestly by his name," Carson Drew reported somewhat later to his daughter. "He certainly kept his secrets from me!"

"Didn't he tell you anything?" Nancy asked.

"Nothing worth mentioning. As soon as I spoke of Heath Castle and the button factory, he closed up as tight as one of Mehearty's clams!"

"Did you mention Florianna's name?"

"Yes. Hector Keep stressed that he was still searching diligently for her."

"I wonder," said Nancy softly.

The Heath Castle mystery was no nearer to a solution than before. Eager as the girl was to revisit the estate, she found it impossible, because her father had made her promise not to go there alone; and none of her friends would be free to accompany her until the next day.

"I know what I'll do," she thought enthusiastically. "Go over the whole Heath property by plane."

For some time Nancy had been taking flying lessons whenever it was possbile. She had not soloed yet, but hoped to do so very soon. Telephoning to her instructor, she made an appointment.

"I wondered when I was going to hear from you again," the young man said, as the two climbed into his plane. "Have you been busy solving a new mystery?"

"There's a new mystery bothering me right now," laughed Nancy. "How to work all these gadgets."

Despite her words, she started the motor and headed the plane into the wind as if she were a seasoned pilot.

Reaching sufficient altitude, she banked and headed in the direction of Heath Castle.

Nancy circled the area several times. Satisfied that she could jot down a general plan of the place, she started to leave. Suddenly the girl noticed a cloud of smoke in the vicinity of the castle. Curious, she banked the plane and flew back over the estate. The smoke was rising in a mass, but Nancy could not make out its exact origin, because the foliage was so dense.

"Someone is on the estate, anyway," she mused. "Oh, dear, I hope the fire won't do any damage."

The plane nosed downwards, reminding the girl that she must pay close attention to her piloting. For the first time her instructor spoke to her. With a hasty glance at the altimeter, she climbed to a safe height and returned home to make a perfect landing.

Upon reaching home, Nancy sketched an air map of the Heath Castle grounds. The next day she showed it to George and Bess, proposing that they start out at once for the estate.

Packing a picnic lunch, the three girls set out in Nancy's car. This time they dressed more appropriately for the trip by wearing riding breeches and stout boots. On the way, Nancy explained the latest developments in the mystery.

"Nothing must drive us away from the estate until we've investigated every nook and corner of it," she declared, as the car rocked over the bumpy road. "I'm sure we can find a clue there."

Directly ahead loomed the familiar ivy-covered boundary wall. Nancy parked the automobile beneath a cool tunnel of overhanging tree limbs.

Leaping out, the girls walked to the rusty gate. There

they stopped short, staring in dismay. Tacked to the barrier was a freshly painted sign which read:

NO TRESPASSING
UNDER PENALTY OF THE LAW

· 9 · *The Pointing Finger*

Nancy was not easily discouraged. She was aware that if they were to help Mrs Fenimore and Joan they would have to do better than Hector Keep had in locating the missing dancer. And no signs were going to keep her from hunting for necessary clues.

"It's most important that we try to find Florianna," she assured her companions. "If the fortune is saved, it probably will mean that Joan and her mother will be provided for."

"They certainly need help," said Bess. "But dare we trespass here?"

"I really have police sanction to do so. Lieutenant Masters urged me to take the case," Nancy replied.

"Then I guess it's all right," said George.

She had walked to the rusty gate to peer between the spikes. The grounds seemed as deserted as ever, but as Nancy and Bess joined her, the girls were startled to hear the sudden barking of dogs.

"Listen!" Nancy exclaimed. An instant later she added, "They're inside the grounds!"

"And coming closer," Bess said uneasily. "They must have heard our car stop here at the gate. Well, that settles it," she declared almost in relief. "We can't possibly go inside now. We might be chewed to pieces."

"I'll go first," Nancy offered courageously. "If they don't attack me, it will be safe for you two to follow."

George and Bess watched uneasily as their friend climbed the crumbling wall. On the ledge she hesitated.

"Don't attempt it!" Bess called nervously. "Please!"

Nancy spoke gently but firmly to the hounds. Then, taking a chance, she began to lower herself very gradually. One of the dogs came straight towards the girl. Her heart began to beat wildly, but she showed no outward fear.

"Well, old fellow," she murmured, "do I come in?"

To her relief the animal ceased barking and displayed only a friendly interest in her.

"It's all right," Nancy called to her chums. "Come on over."

She continued to pat the hounds and talk to them as George climbed the wall and leaped down. The dogs did not try to molest her. As soon as Bess's head appeared, however, they began to snarl.

"Don't mind them," Nancy called encouragingly. "They're only testing your nerve."

"They'll tear me to pieces if I jump down there!" Bess was so nervous that she was almost in tears.

"They'll leave you alone if you don't show any fear," Nancy assured her.

It was impossible for the frightened girl to do this. "Go on without me," she said after two vain attempts. "Those dogs just don't like me. I'll wait in the car."

"All right," Nancy agreed. "Don't eat up all the lunch while we're gone!"

She and George set off alone. The dogs remained

behind. Soon the girls located the avenue of trees which led past the ruined loggia.

"Here is a path that I'm sure will lead to the castle," Nancy remarked, as they came to a forking trail.

"Maybe," smiled George, "but this sign reads 'To the Fairie Gallerie'."

"Let's see where it goes anyway," urged Nancy.

They passed a weather-stained statuette in a wall niche; lingered a moment to gaze at a rose garden choked with weeds, then went on to a clearing. Before them rose an artistic structure. The sides were formed of slender twisted stone columns, while sprawling over them was a roof of untrimmed vines, supported by thick stalks. From one end of the shelter hung a rustic sign on which were the words:

Who enters here may fairies meet,
With laughter soft they should be greet.

"How pretty," said Nancy dreamily. "Joan Fenimore would adore it here. Incidentally, I'd love to meet a fairy who would reveal the secrets we want to know."

George, surveying the gallery closely, remarked practically, "It looks as if Father Time had taken over here instead of the fairies," adding that the stone columns looked as if they might tumble down any minute.

Nancy stooped to inspect the base of one of the pillars, saying that she was amazed stone could be damaged so greatly by weather.

"George!" she exclaimed suddenly. "Will you look at this?"

"What is it?"

"Someone has deliberately tampered with these

columns. See the marks on the stone! They've been weakened—probably with a pick-axe!"

"It does seem that way, Nancy! But why would anyone do that?"

As the girls inspected the other columns, Nancy spoke of the note she had found at the old button factory, and the words "in a wall."

"I'm sure someone is searching in various walls for an article of value," she said. "What it is, I have no idea."

"But why destroy these lovely columns?"

"Maybe the person didn't find what he wants in any of the actual walls, and is now looking in the columns. Oh, if only I had the missing half of the message!"

George was not listening very closely to her friend's words. Instead, she was gazing down the path as if transfixed.

"What do you see?" Nancy asked in a low voice. "Those dogs aren't coming back, are they?"

The other girl shook her head, pointing towards the bushes. Nancy could make out nothing unusual.

"It's an old man!" George whispered. "He's pointing his fingers at us!"

Nancy was startled too, as she saw the man amid the heavy shrubbery. Her pulse quickened, but she moved towards the figure. Nearing it, she laughed softly.

"Why, it's only a life-sized statue, George!"

Decidedly embarrassed by her mistake, the crestfallen girl went over to inspect the figure.

"That pointing finger may have a special significance," Nancy remarked thoughtfully, noting that the direction indicated was along a path. "Let's follow this and see where it takes us."

The trail had been nearly obliterated by weeds. It twisted in and out among the trees and seemed to lead nowhere. The girls were about to turn back, when Nancy spied the flash of water in filtered sunlight.

It proved to be a large, stagnant pool clogged with water lilies. George went over to inspect it.

"Why do you suppose the statue pointed to this?" she speculated. "It doesn't look like any—"

Her words ended in a little scream, as the soft bank beneath the girl's feet gave way. Before Nancy could make a move to save her friend, she had slipped into the water. It proved not to be deep, but George was soaked.

"Look at me! I'm a mess!" she cried struggling, to her feet. "Now what am I to do?"

Nancy helped her chum scramble up the slippery bank. Gazing about her, she noticed a stone house nearby. Apparently it had once been used as a tool shed.

"Go in there and get out of your wet clothes," she advised George. "I'll dry them in the sun for you. It shouldn't take long."

This appeared to be the only solution, so the wet girl disappeared into the stone house. She tossed breeches, blue riding shirt, stockings and shoes through an open window. Nancy spread them on the bank in the sun and started walking round the pond.

On the bank close by, she noticed a whelk shell which evidently had been dislodged from the bottom of the pond by George's fall. At first glance Nancy gave it no thought. Then it occurred to her that it was unusual it should be there.

After a moment's thought, Nancy stripped off shoes and stockings and waded into the shallow water.

Dipping her hands into the sand, she discovered that the bottom of the pond was thick with discarded whelk shells.

"This is strange," she mused, "finding these so far from the factory. They couldn't have come from there. And certainly the Heaths wouldn't have eaten this many."

Still trying to figure out a logical answer to the puzzle, she returned to the bank and sat down. Suddenly a thought came to her. Mehearty had said that whelks were used in making fine dyes. Walter Heath had spent much of his time on scientific experiments. Was it not reasonable to suppose that the estate owner had been using whelks to perfect some kind of dye for use at the button factory?

"Hey, why so pensive?" George called, interrupting Nancy's thoughts. "See if my clothes are dry, will you?"

Nancy obediently arose and felt George's garments. "Not yet," she reported.

"I'm getting hungry," complained George. "And Bess will be having a fit if we don't get back."

In this she was right. Hungry herself, and tired of waiting, Bess was fuming in Nancy's concealed car. As the sun climbed high overhead and the others failed to return, the girl became annoyed.

"Guess they've forgotten me," she thought.

To add to her irritation, the hounds came dashing back to the gate when she walked over to look through it. Seeing her, they bayed savagely.

"Just wait until I see George and Nancy!" Bess stormed. "I'll—"

Just then she heard a car coming up the road. Bess barely had time to hide herself in the bushes before it swung round the bend. She was glad that she had hidden herself, for she was sure from Nancy's description that the driver was none other than Hector Keep. He was alone.

To the girl's dismay he got out and walked all round, thereby spotting Nancy's car. The man muttered something that Bess could not hear. Finally he went to the double gate and unlocked it.

"He's going to drive into the grounds!" Bess told herself. "Nancy and George will be caught trespassing! Oh, I must warn them!"

Fairly beside herself with anxiety, the girl did not know what to do. Hector Keep still had his back turned towards her. The sedan, its engine running, was not ten feet away.

There was no time to think or plan. Impulsively, Bess darted to the car. Climbing into the back part, she crouched on the floor.

Hector Keep returned to the automobile. Unaware of his passenger, he drove through the gates into the estate grounds.

· 10 ·   *Nancy Explores*

"GEORGE, would you mind if I do a little exploring?" Nancy asked. "I'll be back by the time your clothes are dry."

"Don't you dare leave me in the lurch!" the other girl warned her.

Nancy smiled. "I'm not going far. But I've just found a lot of whelk shells which may indicate something important. Perhaps some bottles of dye from them are hidden nearby."

She moved off, looking about carefully for any possible storage space: a small building, a hidden enclosure. None appeared, and in her search Nancy wandered farther than she had intended.

"What's that?" she wondered when she became aware of a low rumble which seemed to shake the earth.

She stood still and waited, but there was no further sound. In the distance, a cloud of white, powdery dust caught her attention.

"Another explosion!" she murmured excitedly. "Maybe that's what happened yesterday when I was in the plane and thought I saw smoke down here!"

Cautiously she went towards the scene, but her path was blocked by a high briar hedge over which she could not climb without scratching herself severely. Following the hedge for some distance to find an opening, Nancy was startled to hear the sound of an automobile.

"Someone must have driven into the estate grounds!"

The sound drew nearer. Deciding to find out who the newcomer was, Nancy plunged through the woodland to a weed-grown clearing just as Hector Keep drove up and stopped.

Nancy drew back quickly into the shelter of the protecting bushes. The man did not see her. Parking his car under a gnarled maple, he got out and set off on foot.

"I'll follow him," the girl thought impulsively.

Hector Keep walked so fast that Nancy could scarcely keep him in sight. The lawyer seemed thoroughly acquainted with the many trails, for he never hesitated when he came to a turn.

Before long, the man vanished from view. When Nancy came to a fork in the path, she wondered which way he had gone. Fearful lest she lose track of him entirely, she pressed her ear to the ground and very faintly could make out a steady beat on the right fork. Thus guided, she hastened on.

Presently, this trail branched off in three directions. Again Nancy was baffled. When she flattened herself on the ground this time she could hear no sound.

"I've lost him!" she thought in dismay.

Choosing a path at random, she went on doggedly, so intent on her sleuthing that she completely forgot about George and Bess.

Meanwhile Bess was still hiding in Hector Keep's car. Though Nancy had been near by, she had not seen her. Deciding she had better find her cousin and her chum, Bess cautiously climbed from the automobile and started up the trail the lawyer had taken.

Bess had not gone far before she became alarmed. The dogs had begun to bark. They were coming closer to her each moment.

"They've picked up my scent!" the girl thought in terror.

The hounds bounded into view, and Bess was thrown into a panic. She shinned up a tree, hoping the dogs would pass by, but instead they took up a vigil at the foot of the trunk.

Back at the tool house, George Fayne was restlessly waiting for Nancy to return. From the window, she could see her clothes on the sunny bank of the pond. They seemed to be dry.

"I can't wait another minute!" she thought impatiently. "I'll go and get them myself!"

George went to the door of the tool house and there stopped short. A tousy-haired boy in faded overalls had emerged from among the trees. He appeared to be eleven or twelve years old. Seeing the clothes, he suddenly snatched them up and hurried off.

"Hey, you! Those are mine!" George cried angrily from the window.

The boy did not hear her; or if he did, he paid no attention.

"Good grief!" George cried out in despair. "Now what'll I do? Nancy's done a disappearing act, and I'm stranded here without any clothes!"

Unaware of the difficulties of her two chums, Nancy was intent upon another subject. The trail she had chosen had not led her to Hector Keep, but it had brought her to Heath Castle.

It was constructed of massive grey stone covered in large part by ivy. The roof line was broken by several turrets, a large one at each end of the great residence, with smaller ones in between.

"It's a perfect copy of an old English castle," Nancy decided, "only smaller. Oh, if Mrs Fenimore and Joan could only come here and get away from that dingy house they live in and that dreadful Jeddy Hooker!"

Her thoughts were interrupted by a faraway, plaintive cry. At first she thought it was the same sound which had frightened Bess on the girls' previous visit to the estate. Now she wondered. When the sound was repeated, it seemed more human.

A wild thought crossed Nancy's mind. Was someone in the castle in distress? Perhaps Florianna *was* being held a prisoner in one of the tower rooms!

"Oh, I must get inside!" she determined. "If some-one is in need of help—"

The girl began to circle the castle walls, reflecting as she looked at their stateliness that it was a pity they had to stand in the midst of a ruined garden. A massive side door of the big house stood ajar. Nancy wondered whether Hector Keep had opened it. She hesitated to trespass, then decided if someone were in trouble, it was her duty to aid the person. Without further ado she slipped into the dwelling.

The girl found herself in a long corridor which twisted and turned crazily. Large rooms lined with beautiful, panelled wood opened from it. Many of these rooms were empty, others contained a few pieces of fine old mahogany furniture. At a glance, it was apparent to Nancy that nearly everything of value had been re-moved from the place.

"Odd," she mused. "I thought the castle was left to Florianna intact."

The inside wooden shutters in the gloomy rooms were closed, giving the few sheet-draped chairs a ghostly appearance. The unexpected sight of herself in a long mirror gave Nancy a momentary fright. At the same time she heard the plaintive cry again. It seemed to come from upstairs.

Quickly Nancy found steps leading to the second storey. A search of the rooms there, including all of the many closets, revealed nothing.

"The only places left are the towers," the girl decided. "But how do I get into them?"

Try as she might, she could find no entrance to any of the turrets. Then, glancing from a window, she realized that the castle was built round a hollow square, which proved to be another tangled garden. Nancy imagined some of the bedrooms actually were the smaller turrets. The high towers no doubt were separate, with doors to them opening from the court-yard garden.

"How like olden times to imprison someone in a tower!" she thought, as she heard the plaintive cry again and hurried down the stairway to hunt for an exit to the inner garden.

The door to it lay hidden in the shadows of the corridor, so Nancy did not locate it at once. When she did, she quickly tripped the bolt so she would not lock herself out, and stepped into the sunshine.

Glancing round, the young detective discovered her guess had been right. There were entrance doors to the two high, round towers. As she opened the first one, she held her breath, wondering what lay beyond.

What Nancy actually saw was disappointing. Apparently, the tower had been built for architectural purposes only.

She turned her attention to the other tower, glad that the massive door to it was not locked.

Would she find anyone there?

She climbed the steps to a tiny room with an open parapet beyond it. There was no one there. In disappointment, Nancy looked out over the grounds.

·11· *Locked in the Tower*

As Nancy watched from the tower balcony, she saw a boy accidentally drop a garment on the grassy sand by the river bank.

"George's riding breeches!" the girl thought in dismay.

Nancy was too far away to call to the boy. She saw him dart to the water's edge, jump into a boat, and row away.

"I never should have left George alone at the tool house," she blamed herself.

Realizing that she must do something at once to help her friend, Nancy retraced her steps through the balcony to the stairway, ran down the steps, and raced to the courtyard door.

When she tried to pull it open, it would not budge. She yanked and yanked, then finally realized that someone had locked it.

She was a prisoner in the tower!

"Oh, I must get out!" she told herself.

Nancy refused to become panicky. Surely there must be some way to get out! Returning to the open parapet, she looked about her.

It was a forty-foot drop to the ground, and far too dangerous for her to attempt. Thoroughly discouraged, the girl went down to try the locked door again. As she twisted the knob, Nancy thought she heard the sound of voices. Her heart leaped! Two men were just outside. They were coming nearer.

"We'll get caught, I tell you!" one was arguing in a loud voice. "And if we are, the old man'll say he never saw us before!"

"Oh, quit your worrying," the other growled. "Just leave the brain work on this job to me. We'll find that clue yet. It's somewhere in one of the walls on the estate."

"Yeah? Which wall?" the first man asked sarcastically. "The place is full of 'em! Anyhow, I'm satisfied with what we've found already and kept for ourselves!"

"When he sees all the walls we've blasted, he can't deny we did a pretty thorough job for him!" the other snickered.

"Well, that proves a few of my theories!" the girl thought grimly. "The walls of Heath Castle and the gardens have been damaged deliberately, and because of someone who wants to find a clue! Evidently those men have found something of interest, too. It could be the missing half of the note I picked up; or something to do with Walter Heath's experiments. Or it could very well concern Florianna."

Hoping to glimpse the men, the girl returned to the parapet and watched eagerly. She did not see them, but soon she heard whistling and calls to the dogs. Then all was quiet again.

"They've gone!" Nancy thought uneasily. "Maybe I should have let them know I'm here when I had the chance. But no, they're not honest, and they probably would have ruined all my plans. I'll get out somehow!"

Nancy searched vainly on the ground floor of the tower for an exit. To add to her dismay, she was very hungry. From her watch, the imprisoned girl was amazed to discover that it was after two o'clock.

"If I ever do get out of here, George and Bess will skin me alive!" she thought.

But if she had only known! Bess Marvin just then was frantically trying to save her own skin. She was perched in a tree quite a distance from the castle and surrounded by watchful dogs that she was afraid might tear her to pieces.

She was almost in tears when she heard whistling. The dogs heard the sound, too. They pricked up their ears, then went racing away.

"Thank goodness!" Bess gasped, sliding down from her leafy prison.

So much time had elapsed that she decided it would do no good to try to find Nancy and George. Had they not encountered Hector Keep already, they surely would have returned to the parked car.

"I'll go back there," Bess concluded. "But which way did I come?" she wondered.

Hopelessly confused, she started off, unwittingly taking a trail leading towards the river. After a long walk, Bess found her way blocked by a crumbling wall. One of the stones had fallen out, creating a perfect peephole. The girl peered through it, hoping to see the road. Instead, she saw the river below her. On the nearby beach lay a pair of riding breeches.

"George's clothes!" she identified them instantly.

There was no sign of either George or Nancy. Bess could not believe that her chums had gone for a swim.

"My cousin must be in trouble!" she concluded in panic.

Bess tried to climb the wall, but the stones crumbled beneath her fingers. Once she nearly made it, only to lose her hold and fall.

"I'll go back to the car," she decided at last. "If Nancy and George aren't there, then I must go to River Heights for help."

Stumbling through the tall grass, the girl came to a path. By this time she was so beside herself with anxiety she failed to observe that it had been trampled recently.

The trail, Bess soon discovered, did not lead towards the main gate. Instead, she came to a crescent-shaped pond covered thickly with water lilies.

"Oh, where am I?" she asked herself desperately.

Then she heard a cry. "Bess! Bess!"

The girl whirled round. She saw no one. A few yards away was a stone tool house, its window hidden by overhanging tree branches.

"Bess!" the voice shouted impatiently. "Over here! In the tool house!"

This time Bess could not doubt but that it was her cousin who had called her. Hastening to the little building, she looked inside.

"I thought you never would pay attention to me!" George regarded her accusingly. "I've been stranded here for hours! Just wait until I get my hands on Nancy Drew!"

"George, you must be cold," Bess gasped in astonishment.

She slipped off the raincoat she was wearing.

"Take this," she offered. "I don't need it."

George put it on, and was relieved to find her shoes still lying near the bank of the pond. Bess told her that she had seen the riding breeches down on the beach by the river.

"Let them stay there for the time being," George decided. "First, let's find Nancy."

Finally convinced that their chum was not coming, they went in search of her.

"Let's go back to the car first," George proposed. "She may be waiting there."

Without meeting anyone, and without being molested by the dogs, the cousins finally climbed over the front wall. Nancy was not in the car.

"Let's drive to town and bring help," Bess said nervously.

"Drive, did you say? Nancy has the keys to the car."

"Oh, I'd forgotten! Well, we are in a nice mess!"

"We'll have to find Nancy; that's all there is to it. She must be somewhere inside the estate grounds."

Fortifying themselves with sandwiches from the lunch, the girls started to scale the wall again. On the ledge, they hesitated as the dogs began to growl menacingly.

"Maybe if we feed them—" George suggested.

She brought two sandwiches from the car. At sight of the food the hounds became friendly, but after they had gobbled it up, they lay panting and waiting. Each time George tried to descend, the dogs rose menacingly.

Bess would not even try. "It's no use," she sighed. "We may as well wait in the car."

This displeased George; but she did not know how to get inside the grounds. The dogs showed no inclination to leave. Whenever George went near the wall, they started barking.

An hour elapsed, and still another. The afternoon

sun slipped lower behind the trees, and long shadows darkened the woodland road. Only then did the girls conclude that Nancy must be in serious trouble. Otherwise, she would have returned by this time.

"We can't sit here and wait another instant!" George cried, leaping from the car. "Bess, we must do something right away!"

Bess agreed. "I'll go for help," she said.

·12· *The Trap Door*

As time dragged by, Nancy grew more and more desperate. She wondered what had become of George. The poor girl! And Bess. What of her? With a feeling of utter dismay Nancy realized that she had the car keys with her. She certainly had gotten herself and her friends into a dreadful muddle.

Nancy sank down on the bottom step of the winding iron staircase to try to figure things out. She stared straight ahead of her.

"This is the worst trap I've ever been in!" she decided unhappily.

Suddenly the distraught girl became aware of something on the floor in front of her. A tiny crack neatly outlined a rectangular space about three feet square.

"Speaking of traps!" Nancy muttered. "Maybe this is a trap door! A chance to escape!"

Quickly dropping to her hands and knees, she inspected the crack. Obviously, it marked the outline of an opening, but there was no ring or handle with which to pull up the trap door.

Nancy pried at it first with her fingers and then with her nail file. The slender bit of steel snapped in her hands.

"Oh, how can I get it open?" she fumed, looking round for something heavier with which to lift it.

Not a single object was in the tower. After an hour Nancy discarded the possibility of this means of escape. The room grew stuffy to her; or was it because she felt almost ill from lack of nourishment? Her tongue parched and her head aching, she slowly climbed the stairs and went out on the parapet to get some fresh air.

The sky became overcast. In a short time it was almost dark. Except for the occasional hoot of an owl and the intermittent croaking of frogs, there was not a sound. Then suddenly Nancy became aware of approaching footsteps.

Her first impulse was to shout to make her whereabouts known, as she thought someone had come to rescue her. But intuition warned her to remain silent.

Springing to her feet, she looked over the parapet. A man she was sure was a stranger to her was unlocking the door far below her. He snapped on a flashlight and entered the tower.

Nancy's heart pounded. Should she walk boldly downstairs and try to bluff her way out?

"No, I mustn't do that," she decided. "If something sinister is going on at Heath Castle, this man probably is involved."

She concluded that should he find her, all her chances to help Mrs Fenimore and Joan would be ruined.

"Maybe I can escape while the man is busy," the

girl thought hopefully. "He may have opened the trap door and gone down below."

Nancy tiptoed across the little balcony room. Fortunately she did not reach the doorway, for at that instant a light flashed through the opening. It missed revealing her presence by a fraction of an inch.

As Nancy shrank into the shadows, the man began to ascend the iron staircase. With sinking heart the trapped girl stepped back of the door and pressed herself against the wall.

The intruder went directly to the parapet. As Nancy peeked out, he began to move his light slowly up and down as if he were signalling. In the backward reflection of the rays which dimly revealed his face, Nancy knew that she had never seen this cruel-looking person before.

Though she longed to watch what he was doing, she dared not tarry. This was her opportunity to escape! Tip-toeing round the door, she started down the stairway. On the third step from the bottom, she stumbled. To her oversensitive ears the noise was loud and grating. Had the stranger heard her?

Quick as lightning she darted down the rest of the steps and reached the courtyard garden in safety. Hurrying to the arched doorway, the girl was relieved to find it was still unlocked.

She groped her way along the dark corridor in the castle. A moment later her knee bumped into a piece of furniture, striking it so hard that she nearly cried out in pain.

Another precious ten minutes was lost as she carefully felt along the dark walls for a door to the grounds. At last her efforts were rewarded. With a deep sigh of relief, she rushed into the open.

"What an adventure!" Nancy shuddered. "Now if only I can find George and Bess!"

By no means were the girl's troubles at an end. She hoped that in the dusky light she would be able to find her way out. She knew the direction towards the main gate, but with weed-grown paths, treacherous rocks, and roaming dogs, she would have to be very cautious. It was fully an hour before Nancy saw the vague outline of a wall ahead of her.

"I hope it's the one near my car," she said to herself. "Oh—"

Something was moving through the bushes. In an instant the stillness was broken by the sharp barking of dogs.

"Can I trust them?" Nancy wondered. "They may not be friendly after dark!"

She made a leap for the crumbling wall and scrambled up, reaching the top just as the two hounds arrived. The Drew girl dropped breathlessly to the other side and got her bearings.

"The car must be up there a short way," she concluded, starting off.

Five minutes later she came to the automobile. To her amazement and delight George was huddled in a raincoat on the back seat. She was half asleep.

"George!"

The girl sat bolt upright, and gave a little scream. "It's Nancy!"

"Oh, you scared me nearly out of my wits."

"Sorry. Where's Bess?"

"Gone to get your father. Oh, Nancy, what in the world happened to you?"

"Plenty! But first, tell me, how long ago did Bess leave? Would it be best for us to wait?"

"She went hours ago, but it's a long walk to a bus or a phone. Somebody ought to be here any minute, though, it seems to me."

The two girls exchanged stories. George told how she and Bess had become almost frantic over Nancy's disappearance. Fearing she might be in Hector Keep's clutches, Bess had offered to summon Mr Drew.

"After Bess left, I heard a noise in the grounds," George related, "so I hid in the bushes near the gate. Mr Keep drove out. While he was locking the gate, I peeked in his car to see if you were there. I really expected you to be on the floor, bound hand and foot!"

"I was a prisoner, all right, but not tied up," Nancy smiled—she could smile now. "Then what happened?"

"Mr Keep went straight to your car."

"He must have seen it when he came, too," Nancy groaned. "And I thought I had hidden it well. Now all he has to do is look up the licence number and he'll know who was here."

A moving path of light suddenly cut the darkness. An automobile! Was Carson Drew driving it, or was Hector Keep returning?

With bated breaths the two girls waited, wondering if they should hide or stand their ground. George, weary of the whole thing, favoured the latter, but Nancy felt this move unwise, so together they scrambled out of sight.

The car stopped. Bess Marvin alighted. "Why, George is gone!" she wailed.

"No, she isn't," her cousin spoke up, walking forward. "We were just being careful."

"We?"

"Nancy is here."

Nancy herself was running to the side of the car from which her father had stepped. In an instant she was in his arms.

"Why, Dad, you're trembling!" she said.

"Nancy, Nancy, I'm so glad to see you. You gave me such a fright. Where—"

"Oh, I'm dreadfully sorry I made such a mess of things," his daughter apologized. "But maybe you'll forgive me when I tell you what happened."

"Tell me on the way home. Bess can drive your car as far as her house, then you take it the rest of the way."

On the return to River Heights Mr Drew listened without comment until Nancy had concluded. Her closing sentence made him wrinkle his forehead.

"I'm convinced," said Nancy, "that something sinister is going on at Heath Castle and in the gardens. The walls there aren't crumbling from age, Dad— they're being tampered with for some purpose!"

"I agree it looks mighty suspicious," said Mr Drew. "And Hector Keep may be involved. But suppose you put the whole case out of your mind for a while, at least until you've had a square meal!"

Upon reaching the Drew residence, Nancy made a beeline for the refrigerator. Hannah Gruen, who had been nearly beside herself with worry, could not understand Nancy's attitude. But upon hearing that nothing worse than hunger was the matter with the girl, the housekeeper smiled.

"I guess that's youth for you," she murmured. Then aloud she added, "You poor child. I'll fix you a warm supper right away."

The woman hastened to prepare a meal. Too hungry to wait for the food to cook, Nancy helped herself to a glass of milk and a few cookies. As she ate and drank, she related the highlights of her adventure to the housekeeper.

"Oh, Nancy," Mrs Gruen sighed, "your love of mystery will yet prove your undoing! You must be more careful."

"I'm not sure that you should return to Heath Castle," said Mr Drew, coming into the kitchen.

Nancy nearly spilled her glass of milk. "Oh, Dad!" she protested.

"Why not forget the whole affair for a few days?"

"But time is so short—"

"As it happens, I'm going away on a little trip, Nancy. I thought you might enjoy coming along."

"Oh, Dad, you know I would at any other time."

"I plan to go by car, and must interview several persons along the way regarding a legal case."

"Where is the place?" Nancy inquired, still without much interest.

"Hampton."

Nancy shook her head. "If you'll excuse me, Dad, I believe I'd rather stay here and try to solve the mystery about Florianna."

"I'm sorry," Mr Drew said, his eyes twinkling. "I thought Hampton might prove of interest to you, especially since it was the town where Florianna Johnson last was seen."

Nancy could scarcely believe her ears. "Say that again, Dad!" she cried.

"I was talking with Doctor Gibson in Henryville today," Mr Drew revealed. "He looked after Florianna, you know; in fact, he advised her to take the trip from which she never returned."

"Tell me more!"

"There's not much to tell. Florianna was thin and run down, so the doctor advised her to take a vacation. He suggested she slip off to a quiet place without telling anyone where she was going."

"Did the doctor know where she went?"

"No, but her sister Vera Fenimore told him she had seen a railroad ticket in Florianna's handbag. The destination was Hampton."

"Oh, Dad, I give in," Nancy stated, trying not to appear too excited. "I'll go with you!"

"I rather thought you would," laughed Mr Drew.

"When do we leave?"

"Tomorrow morning. Better pack your suitcase tonight."

· 13 ·   *In Search of Clues*

NANCY was up early the next morning. She had been too weary the night before to attempt any packing, so she did it now and then skipped downstairs.

A few minutes later Mr Drew came down and said they ought to eat at once and be off. Nancy hoped they might stop for a few minutes at Mrs Fenimore's to gather any additional information the woman might have about her sister.

"We practically go past her house," she said.

"All right, we'll drop in for a few minutes," the lawyer agreed reluctantly. "But let's make it snappy. I must be in Hampton before noon."

Mrs Fenimore was delighted to see Nancy again. When the girl presented her father, the woman expressed pleasure that she had brought him with her.

"We're en route to Hampton," Mr Drew explained, coming straight to the point. "Nancy thought that you might be able to tell us a little more about your sister's disappearance. We understand that you believe your sister went to Hampton."

"Why, yes," the invalid replied. "I don't actually know that Florianna went there, but I did see a ticket to Hampton which she had bought."

"I've given your sister's strange disappearance considerable thought," Mr Drew confessed. "It strikes me that she must have had a definite reason for abandoning her career."

"Oh, Florianna loved her work!" Mrs Fenimore protested. "Of course, she was tired and run down, but a few weeks' rest should have put her in good health again."

"We know that after leaving here, Florianna never danced again. Now, if she still lives, she must have earned a living by some means. Did she have any special aptitude for anything except dancing? Could she teach music, for example?" the lawyer asked.

Mrs Fenimore shook her head. "Florianna was interested in nothing except dancing. Oh, yes, I might add she loved gardening. My sister was very fond of flowers and liked to grow them." The invalid sighed as she added, "In that respect, Joan takes after her aunt."

"Is Joan at school?" Nancy asked.

"Yes," replied Mrs Fenimore. "The child worries

me," she said with deep concern. "Lieutenant Masters had to come here yesterday to get a plant that had been taken from the park. Oh, I've reprimanded Joan for doing such things, but it does no good."

"I suppose Lieutenant Masters talked to Joan about it?" Mr Drew inquired.

"Yes. She insisted that she had not taken the plant, that Jeddy Hooker had given it to her. Lieutenant Masters then went next door to speak to Jeddy."

This report about Joan upset Nancy. The child had promised her that she would not play with the boy, but apparently she had done so.

"I'm sure your daughter is telling the truth," she remarked, but in her own heart she was not so certain of this. As soon as she had time, she would talk it over with Lieutenant Masters.

Since Mrs Fenimore had told everything she knew regarding her long-missing sister, Nancy and Mr Drew bade her goodbye and left the house.

"I have a theory I didn't mention," the lawyer commented as he led the way to the car. "Florianna may have married after she left home. In that event, she would have had some means of support."

"But, Dad, wouldn't she have notified Mrs Fenimore of such a marriage? She had no apparent reason for keeping her whereabouts a secret."

"Quite true. Well, perhaps we'll run into a few clues at Hampton."

Mr Drew entered the parked car. Nancy was about to follow when she observed a thin, sharp-faced woman with unkempt hair hanging out clothes in the yard adjoining the Fenimore cottage.

Nancy's attention centred not upon the woman, but

on the clothing she was pinning to the line. A blue riding shirt looked strangely familiar to her.

"If that isn't George's stolen shirt, then it's one just like it!" she told herself grimly.

Acting impulsively, Nancy walked over to the yard. The woman saw her coming and eyed her suspiciously.

"Is Jeddy here?" the girl inquired, her manner pleasant.

"No, he ain't," the woman snapped. "He's at school, same as every day."

Working up to the subject, Nancy asked her if Jeddy liked to go boating on the river.

"All boys play around the water," Mrs Hooker answered. Then, as if fearful she had revealed too much, she added, "Jeddy ain't been on the river lately, though."

Nancy was convinced the woman was not telling the truth. She was certain, too, that the shirt was the same one she herself had hung on a tree branch to dry at Heath Castle. It was a very expensive make; one not likely to have been purchased by Mrs Hooker.

"That's a good-looking riding shirt," Nancy said, trying not to show her excitement. "Do you ride?"

The woman ignored the question. "Ain't I got a right to have nice things, same as other folks?" she demanded defiantly.

"Why, certainly," Nancy answered in an even tone.

"You must be another one of those snoopy police-women! Well, I won't talk to you!" snapped the woman.

Snatching the shirt from the line, Mrs Hooker hurried into the house and slammed the door.

Returning to the car, Nancy related the conversation to her father. Though he agreed with his daughter that her suspicion was justified, he thought her method of approach hardly warranted a confession from Mrs Hooker.

"You didn't expect the woman to break down and admit her own son's theft, did you, Nancy? Now you have put her on her guard."

"I never thought of that, Dad," Nancy agreed. "I might have had better luck if I had talked to Jeddy."

At Hampton she decided to make her first call at the railroad station to which Florianna was supposed to have come. The agent in charge dashed Nancy's hopes by telling her he was a new man on the job. The former agent had moved to California two years before.

Nancy refused to be discouraged. Going outside, she interviewed half a dozen elderly taxi drivers whose cabs regularly provided service to and from the station. Not one of the men had driven a cab ten years before, and therefore could give no information regarding the well-known dancer.

"If Florianna came to this town, it seems likely that someone would have recognized her," Nancy reflected. "I'll not give up yet."

At the town hall, where all records were kept, she had no better luck, and by five-thirty she was back at the hotel.

"May I look at your old registers?" she requested the clerk in charge, telling him why she wanted them.

Obligingly he brought out one containing the names of guests who had stayed at the hotel ten years before. Florianna's name was not among them; nor had anyone by the name of Flossie Johnson signed. If the dancer ever had registered there, it had been under an assumed name.

"Have you tried the tourist homes?" the clerk suggested, attempting to be helpful. "We have a dozen of them here—several were in business ten years ago."

"Thank you, that's a good suggestion," Nancy smiled.

The following morning she went to the office of the Board of Health, where she obtained a list of all guest houses in operation at the time of Florianna's disappearance. With renewed hope, she set out to interview the owners of the establishments still operating. The experience was not entirely pleasant, for upon one occasion a woman, finding the girl did not want a room, slammed the door in her face! And nowhere did she obtain the desired information.

"It's just no use," Nancy thought, ringing the doorbell of the last house on her list. "I'm at the end of my rope."

There was a delay before anyone came to open the door of the little cottage. Finally a kindly, grey-haired woman appeared.

"If you're looking for a room, I'm afraid I'll have to disappoint you," she said before the girl could speak. "A young lady rented my only vacant one not ten minutes ago."

"I'm not looking for a room," Nancy explained with a smile. "I came to ask about someone who may have stayed with you some years back."

"I'll be happy to help you if I can."

Nancy told her listener that she was trying to locate a woman who had come to the town several years ago.

"You say the young woman's name was Florianna Johnson?" inquired the woman.

"That was her stage name. She was also known as Flossie Johnson."

Nancy waited, fully expecting her hopes to be dashed again. Instead, the owner of the tourist house smiled and pushed open the screen door.

"Come in," she invited cordially. "I think I can help you."

·14· *Encouraging Information*

"I AM Mrs Delbert," the owner of the tourist home told Nancy. She led the girl into a parlour, stuffy with old-fashioned plush furniture. "You are in a hurry, I know, so I'll tell you what I can about Florianna. She came here ten years ago this month and rented my front room for one night."

"She told you her name?"

"Not at first. She just said 'Miss Johnson.' The first night she was here she was taken ill. I nursed her for three days."

"Was the illness serious?" Nancy asked quickly.

"No. She seemed more exhausted than anything. The young woman was run down and thin as a rake. I took care of her, and at the end of three days she was strong enough to leave."

Nancy asked the old lady to describe Miss Johnson.

"I can show you her picture," Mrs Delbert volunteered. From a table drawer she produced a photograph which she placed in the girl's hand. "After Miss Johnson left, I found this lying on the dresser in her room. Read what she wrote on it."

In appreciation
To Mrs Delbert from Florianna

"This is Florianna's picture and handwriting," Nancy said, identifying it instantly from a similar one in Mrs Fenimore's possession. "Do you know where the young woman went after she left here?"

"Miss Johnson said she might stay for a few weeks on a farm near Plainville."

"She didn't give you the address?"

"No." After a pause she added, "I've always been sorry I never went later on to see her dance, but I rarely get away from here."

"So far as anyone knows, Florianna gave up her dancing." Nancy explained. "She disappeared ten years ago."

Mrs Delbert's eyes opened wide. "How dreadful! And you are trying to find her? Oh, I hope you do. She was such a lovely person."

"Is Plainville far from here?" Nancy inquired. "I'll try that place next."

"About thirty miles. There's no train service from here to Plainville. And that was a funny thing, too. When Florianna left here, she directed the taxi driver to take her to the railroad station. But she couldn't have gone to Plainville by train, for there is none."

"Maybe she didn't realize that at the time," Nancy suggested, "and later went by some other route."

Thanking the old lady for her assistance, Nancy hastened to the Hampton Hotel. At luncheon she repeated to her father what she had learned.

"You've done well, Nancy," he praised her. "You've picked up a far better clue than I expected you would."

"As my reward, will you take me to Plainville?"

The drive to Plainville was a pleasant one over rolling hills. Several towns lay along the way. At a number of them, Nancy inquired without success about the missing dancer. It was not until she reached the village of Hopewell that fortune favoured her.

At her father's suggestion, she ran into the local police station. As the girl started to tell the desk sergeant her problem, a middle-aged woman in outmoded clothes bustled in. The newcomer was Mrs Speyer, known as the town gossip. Ignoring Nancy, she pushed her way to the desk.

"Sergeant, you must do something right away!" she berated him in a rasping voice. "Such a shiftless police force as this town has!"

The sergeant listened patiently to the woman's story. When she saw that her complaint was having little effect, she threatened to report him to the Chief of Police.

"Go right ahead," the officer encouraged her. "It's your privilege."

Decidedly nettled, Mrs Speyer subsided into injured silence. She started to leave the police station, but changed her mind. Having observed Nancy at the desk, she was curious to learn what the stranger's business might be in town. Ignoring Mrs Speyer, the girl told the sergeant why she had stopped at Hopewell.

"Is there no one on the force who might remember if Florianna Johnson ever came here?" Nancy asked.

"Afraid not, Miss. Even our Chief has held office only eight years."

Mrs Speyer edged closer. "Sergeant," she said, "I can probably help this young lady. Don't you remember that beautiful, well-dressed woman who came here about ten years ago? The one that was hit by an automobile and taken to the hospital?"

"Never heard about it," the sergeant retorted gruffly, but he did get down from the desk and go off to look up some records.

"Funny thing," he said, coming back presently. "The young woman you mention is listed here, all right, but it says 'No Identification.' I guess if she had a bag, her name wasn't in it."

"No doubt she was unconscious when she was picked up," said Nancy. "But wouldn't the police have gotten her name later?"

"Not if she didn't make any claim against the fellow that hit her. And she couldn't do that," added the sergeant, "'cause he was a hit-and-run driver."

"Maybe the hospital will know the woman's name," suggested Nancy.

"I knew the nurse who took care of her," Mrs Speyer spoke up. "Her name was Emily Foster. She told me she suspected her patient didn't give her right name to the hospital authorities when she was leaving."

Here was real information which warranted investigation, Nancy decided! She asked where she could find Emily Foster.

"Oh, Emily went away years ago," was the discouraging reply. "I couldn't tell you where. She promised to write to me but she never did."

"Perhaps I can find out at the hospital," said Nancy.

Thanking Mrs Speyer and the sergeant for their help, the Drew girl left the police station. Accompanied by her father, she called in at the local hospital. The superintendent of the institution received them court-eously and upon hearing their story, placed certain records at their disposal. No one by the name of either Flossie or Florianna Johnson had been a patient.

"She may have used an assumed name," Nancy sighed. "Her nurse inferred as much."

"Florianna was trying to get away from her public for a while," Mr Drew added thoughtfully.

"You might talk to Joe," the superintendent sug-gested. "He's an old coloured man who's been with us for twenty years. A friendly fellow. And his memory for patients is amazing."

Joe was on the first floor of the hospital, scrubbing the corridor tiles. When Mr Drew described Florianna to him, a wide grin spread over the old man's face.

He told them that he remembered the girl and that she had been crippled and would never walk again.

Joe's information threw an interesting new light on the mystery. Though Nancy and her father could not be certain that the crippled patient had been Florianna, they were inclined to think she had been. If such were the case, perhaps they had stumbled upon an explana-tion for her strange disappearance.

"Such an injury would have prevented Florianna from ever dancing again," Nancy said. "That know-ledge would have crushed her pride. Wouldn't it have been natural for her to take an assumed name and drop out of sight?"

"Florianna would have done exactly that, I feel sure," Mr Drew agreed. "She never would have burdened her sister or her aunt with caring for her."

"And if she were a cripple, her foolish pride wouldn't have allowed her to marry Walter Heath," Nancy added. "Oh, Dad, I feel as if we really are getting somewhere on the case now!"

At the main desk, Nancy and her father tried without success to obtain a better identification of the crippled woman.

"Emily Foster took care of her," Nancy volunteered. "She could tell us something, perhaps. Do you know her address?"

"The one I have is old, and I understand she left the place some time ago. However, the people who live there ought to be able to tell you where she is."

Nancy was grateful for the address. While her father registered at a hotel, she hopefully hurried to the designated house which stood at the edge of the town in a secluded spot. To her disappointment, she found the residence occupied by new tenants who had never heard of an Emily Foster!

"Another blind alley!" Nancy sighed as she started back to join her father. "I never knew clues to be more elusive."

As the girl walked along the street, she became aware of someone walking a little distance behind her. At first she thought nothing of it, but after she had covered three blocks, she concluded he must be following her.

"I don't like this!" Nancy thought, moving faster.

When she had walked six blocks more, and he was still behind her, the girl decided to obtain a good look at the fellow. She pretended to drop her bag. Turning quickly as if to pick it up, she gazed directly at the man. He wore a brown suit and had a sharp, angular face marked with a mole. Realizing that Nancy knew she was being followed, he turned into a side street.

"He *was* trailing me!" the girl thought. "I wonder why."

Nancy had never seen the man before, and she kept worrying about the matter. She intended to speak to her father about it, but found that he had invited a friend to dinner. By ten o'clock, after a jolly evening, she had forgotten the incident.

Before retiring, father and daughter both sat down in Mr Drew's bedroom to discuss the mystery. Nancy at once brought up the subject of Emily Foster.

"Don't you agree she's our best lead yet?" the girl asked.

Mr Drew did not answer; in fact, for several seconds he had not been paying strict attention to what his daughter had been saying. Now, so suddenly that Nancy was startled, he tiptoed to the hall door of the room. As she watched in bewilderment, he gave the knob a quick, deft twist.

The door swung inwards. A man in a brown suit was crouching just outside! Thrown off balance, he fell forward into the room.

·15· *Behind the Door*

"So you were eavesdropping!" Mr Drew sternly accused the man who had been listening at the door, as he pulled him roughly to his feet.

"No, that's not true," the fellow stammered.

"Sit down," he ordered. "We want to talk to you. What were you doing at the door?"

"Nothing," he replied in a sullen voice. "I thought this room belonged to a friend of mine."

"I'm afraid that's rather hard to believe, for you had your ear to the keyhole when I opened the door. Tell me your name."

"It's none of your business."

"I can turn you over to the police."

"And I can report to them that you trailed me today," said Nancy.

The stranger looked worried and squirmed uneasily in the chair. "You can't prove it!"

"This man followed you today?" Mr Drew questioned his daughter in surprise.

"Yes, I forgot to tell you about it."

"Then that settles it!" the lawyer announced grimly. "We'll turn this fellow over to the police for questioning."

"No, no, don't do that! I'll tell you anything you want to know—except my name!" The eavesdropper could not know that Mr Drew's threat to call the police was only a bluff.

"Very well," nodded the lawyer. "Why were you following my daughter?"

"I followed her because I was to be paid a good wad to do it."

"By whom?"

"I'm not saying. Anyhow, I don't know the guy's name."

"What were your instructions?"

Mr Drew turned so that the man could not see him. With a quick movement of his hand and a jerk of his eyebrows, he signalled for Nancy to step into her bedroom. For a moment the girl was puzzled. Then it dawned upon her that her father probably wanted her to slip quietly downstairs and make arrangements to have the stranger trailed.

"So you won't tell us your name?" Mr Drew repeated, gazing significantly at Nancy.

"No, I won't," the man retorted.

Nancy stole noiselessly from the room. Hastening downstairs, she used one of the public telephones to call the police station. Identifying her father and herself, she said: "Please send a plainclothes detective at once. I'll meet him in the lobby here and explain when he arrives. How will I know him?"

"He'll pretend to be lame."

Nancy was worried lest the detective might not reach the hotel in time. In less than five minutes, however, a limping man walked in. The Drew girl explained and asked that he trail the eavesdropper when he should leave the hotel.

"Here he comes now!" she whispered, as the brown-suited stranger emerged from an elevator. "I'll hide! He mustn't see me!"

"I hope that's what Dad expected me to do," Nancy thought, stepping into the elevator.

Mr Drew was waiting at the door to his room. He assured his daughter that she had interpreted his signals correctly and that the stranger had been too nervous to notice her absence.

"By the way," Mr Drew asked, as they sat down, "have you telephoned to Mrs Gruen since we left home, Nancy? There may be messages for us."

The girl admitted that she had forgotten to do so.

"You'd better put in a long-distance call right away," her father urged.

The call was placed, and after a brief interval Nancy heard Hannah's familiar voice.

"How glad I am you phoned," she said at once. "I tried to reach you at Hampton, but the hotel clerk said that you had left."

"Is anything wrong?"

"Mrs Fenimore was here this morning. She wanted to see you very much."

"Mrs Fenimore?" Nancy echoed in surprise. She knew that the invalid seldom left her cottage, and only an urgent matter would have prompted the woman to undertake the trip.

"She wouldn't explain why she came," Mrs Gruen resumed. "When I told her you weren't at home, she said you must be careful."

"Careful of what?"

"She seemed to think you're in danger. Oh, Nancy, I'll be so relieved when you're home again safe and sound."

"We'll be back tomorrow," the girl reassured the housekeeper. "Don't worry about me."

Nancy called at the Fenimore cottage immediately after she arrived home the next afternoon. The woman was reclining on a couch, exhausted from the strain and worry of the previous day.

"I shouldn't have become so upset," she said to Nancy after greeting her. "But Hector Keep always affects me that way."

"Then he came here to see you?"

"I had a dreadful session with him. He asked me so many questions."

"About your sister?"

"Yes, he wanted to know if I had engaged anyone to search for Florianna."

"Did you mention my name?"

"Well, I did say you had offered to help me," Mrs Fenimore admitted, "though I felt unhappy about having told him. From the way Mr Keep acted, I'm sure he intends to make trouble for you."

"Mr Keep is worried," Nancy commented, frowning. "His remarks make it perfectly clear to me that he has a guilty conscience."

"Will you risk going to Heath Castle again?"

"I'll certainly return there if it will accomplish anything," Nancy said with determination. "But I believe the mystery may be solved in another way."

At home, Nancy took stock of the mystery. Thieves probably were prowling around the Heath grounds, looking for something important. Did it have anything to do with Florianna? Was Hector Keep up to some underhanded work in connection with it?

"And then there's Emily Foster, and the man who was eavesdropping—"

As Nancy opened the top drawer of her bureau to get a handkerchief, she spied the torn half-note she had found in the debris at the Heath factory. In the recent excitement she had forgotten all about it.

"This could be my most valuable clue," she berated herself. "I should figure it out."

She sat down at once to piece out the message, but had hardly started when George phoned, wanting to know how the solution to the mystery was progressing.

"I have a clue to your stolen clothes," the Drew girl

laughed and told of the shirt like George's on Mrs Hooker's clothesline.

"Why, the nerve of that woman!" her chum exclaimed indignantly. "I'm going there at once to demand my property!"

"You can't prove anything, George," Nancy discouraged her. "Better forget the matter for the time being, and come over here. I have lots to tell you. Bring Bess along."

"Be there pronto," George replied.

As Nancy returned to her room, she said to herself, "If it was Jeddy who took those clothes, what was *he* doing in the Heath gardens? Could that boy be connected with the mystery?"

She was still thinking this over when the other girls arrived. Nancy told them all that had happened on the trip with her father.

"Poor Florianna!" Bess exclaimed. "How dreadful for a wonderful dancer to have her career stopped that way!"

"I wish you could have found that nurse Emily Foster," George added. "But maybe she isn't even alive today. Well, what are you going to work on next, Nancy?"

"This note, or rather, this piece of a note."

She produced the bit of paper, and together the girls pored over it for some time, each with a pencil and paper, trying to fill out the lines to form a logical message. Bess was the first one to claim having pieced together the missing words.

"Listen to this!" she cried gleefully. "I have it!"

"Let's hear it," urged Nancy.

"Dear C,
Some place is the se-
cret which I hid
in a wall. I want to be
famous. If I find it, it will be a
worthy work."

George scoffed. "Nobody would write a note with such uneven lines. And we know already something is hidden in a wall."

"Well, it fills in the missing words," Bess defended herself.

"One guess is as good as another," Nancy said kindly.

For some little time the three girls continued their deciphering; at least, Bess and George did. Nancy meanwhile fell to dreaming. Suddenly she jumped up from her chair, saying:

"The solution to this mystery might lie in this very house!"

Without explaining her strange remark, she ran from the room and down the stairs. Soon she returned, carrying a large book.

"How in the world are you going to find Florianna with that?" asked George.

What Nancy held was a portfolio of coloured pictures and descriptions of famous old houses and gardens in England. Knowing of the girl's interest in gardening, a cousin of Nancy's had sent the book to her several Christmases before.

"I forgot I had these pictures," she said, quickly turning the leaves. "Girls, look here!"

"Heath Castle!" exclaimed George.

"The original one in England. Only of course it wasn't called Heath!"

"And the gardens!" cried Bess, as they looked at picture after picture.

Nancy was busy reading the description of them, when suddenly a paragraph caught her eye.

"Oh, George! Bess! Listen to this! At last I think we have the clue we've been looking for!"

· 16 · *The Search Resumed*

GEORGE and Bess studied the paragraph to which Nancy had pointed. It was a quotation in Old English, and they could not make it out. Nancy, who had learned to read the works of the old English poet Chaucer in school, eagerly translated it.

" 'I have hid my treasure in the niches of the cloister through which, all unsuspecting, the gay men and fair ladies pass each day to bathe'," she read.

"Sounds quaint," said Bess, "but how does it help us? Those words were written a long time ago about people who visited the English castle, I suppose, and walked through a cloister in the garden to go bathing."

"Why, don't you see!" Nancy cried excitedly. "Ira Heath built his estate here to resemble the one in England. Probably both he and his son knew about the cloister."

"Granted," nodded George. "But where's our clue, Nancy?"

"If the Heaths had a treasure to hide, wouldn't *their*

cloister have been a good place in which to put it?"

" 'I have hid my treasures in the niches of the cloister,' " George repeated the words softly. "Is there a cloister in the Heath gardens? I haven't seen one."

Nancy turned the page and the three girls gazed thoughtfully at the picture on it, which showed a long passageway flanked by columns leading towards a river.

"This is it," said Nancy. "Oh, I wonder if there is one at Heath Castle!"

"You didn't notice it from the air or when you were in the tower?" Bess inquired.

"N—no," answered Nancy slowly. "But there was something leading from the castle towards the river—a kind of tunnel covered with vines."

"I'll bet that's it," said George enthusiastically. "Listen!" she commanded suddenly. "Here's somebody who might be able to tell us!"

From down the street came the strains of a familiar song. Presently the singer turned into the Drew driveway. He warbled,

> "Clams by the bushel,
> Clams by the lot,
> Clams for the kettle,
> Clams for the pot."

"Nancy," George continued, "I'll bet Mehearty can tell you about a cloister at the Heath estate if it runs down to the water. That old sailor knows every inch of the Muskoka River."

"It won't hurt to ask him," agreed Nancy.

"And how are ye, me lass?" he asked, as Nancy appeared at the doorway.

The clam digger asked the girl, a twinkle in his eyes, if she would like to take another trip to the Heath factory.

"No, thank you," Nancy laughed. "No more explosions for me! But, Mehearty, I *am* thinking of going to the Heath gardens by boat. Have you ever noticed a—a sort of tunnel there, leading from the beach?"

"Never have noticed any," the clam digger replied. "How do ye figure on gettin' to the place by boat? A motorboat couldn't get near the beach nowadays, and it's too far for ye to row all the way from here."

Nancy's mind worked fast. "Perhaps some time when you're not busy, Mehearty—" she began.

The old sailor suddenly slapped his thigh and chuckled. "By the Great Horned Spoon, I allus said women'd never come right out and ask for things. Miss Nancy, me lass," he added, "I'll meet ye and those friends o' yours at th' Landin' ten o'clock sharp tomorrow mornin', barrin' rain. You rent a motorboat, an' we'll tie my little dinghy to it. When we get to th' Heath place, I'll row ye ashore an' ye can hunt for that tunnel."

As Mehearty started away, Nancy suddenly stopped him, saying she had something to show him. From the pockets of her riding breeches, the girl retrieved a few whelk shells she had scooped out of the pond in the Heath gardens.

"Is this the kind that contains the valuable dye?" Nancy asked the man.

"Sure is," the old fellow said enthusiastically. "Where'd ye get 'em?"

Nancy told him. Hearing about the number to be found in the pond, he whistled.

"Now that's mighty interestin'," he declared, deeply

impressed. "In the old days fortunes were made in whelk dye. Maybe the Heaths made part o' theirs that way?"

"I rather doubt that," Nancy said, "but I'm curious to find out about Walt's experiments along that line."

"Ye can, if ye've a mind to."

"How?"

"Old Sam Weatherby can tell ye what ye want to know."

"The curio dealer?"

"Sam worked at the Heath factory afore he went into business for himself. He knew Walt as well as anyone in town."

"Then Sam Weatherby is the man I'll see," Nancy said, grateful for the information.

"Haven't seen you for several days," Sam said as Nancy entered the shop. "Did you bring that pearl and the shell I offered to buy?"

Nancy ruefully told him she no longer had them, and why.

"That's too bad," the old man sympathized upon hearing the pearl had been stolen. "Well, maybe you'll find a bigger one."

"I hope so," Nancy smiled, "but right now I'm more interested in dye than in pearls. Do you know whether Walter Heath ever did any experimental work with whelk dye?"

The question surprised the old curio dealer, because he considered himself one of the few people who knew this fact.

"Walt Heath had an idea he could use whelk dye in the manufacture of coloured pearl buttons," he disclosed. "In that way he hoped to give his waning business a spurt."

"His experiments took place at the factory?"

"No, at Heath Castle. He never perfected them enough to use the process at the factory. But his experiments were still lucky."

"How was that, Mr Weatherby?"

"Well, he found a big pearl; at least, that's what he told me. Said he was going to present it to a young lady friend of his—a dancer."

Nancy blinked in astonishment at the revelation. Perhaps young Mr Heath had not had time to give it to Florianna before she disappeared. Maybe he had hidden it in one of the walls, possibly in a niche in the cloister wall!

"At least I'm sure of one thing," she reflected. "Walter Heath experimented in dye making. He may have perfected a very fine variety, and hid bottles of it away to keep them secret until he was ready to use them."

Nancy was sure now why mysterious strangers prowled about the old factory and the estate grounds. They were searching either for the pearl or for the bottles of dye, possibly both. One of the men she had overheard while in the tower had spoken of being satisfied with what they already had found.

Thanking the curio dealer for his information, Nancy turned to leave. An object in the show case caught her eye. Resting in a velvet case was the antique watch charm she knew Mr Weatherby had bought from Hector Keep.

"Handsome, isn't it?" the old man inquired, removing the charm from its case. "An old English family design. A genuine heirloom."

Nancy admired the piece of jewellery. Mr Weatherby also showed her a pair of earrings, a bracelet and a brooch, all bearing the same design.

"You say Mr Keep inherited all of these from English ancestors?" Nancy asked.

"That's what he said. Between you and me, I think he picked them up from a client who couldn't pay a bill."

Nancy did not disclose her own thoughts on the subject. Had Hector Keep come honestly by the watch charm and the other pieces of jewellery? The girl told herself sternly that she must not mistrust the lawyer because she disliked him.

At home, Nancy learned that during her absence a long-distance telephone call had come from Hopewell.

"He was a detective," Mrs Gruen told her, "and he wouldn't give me the message."

Nancy put in the call to the police station at Hopewell and identified herself. The detective was out at the time, but had left his report for her. The stranger he had shadowed the night before had driven to River Heights. From there he had gone on to meet another man at the abandoned Heath button factory.

"If I only knew who that person is!" Nancy exclaimed.

"I have a description of him," said the police sergeant, reading it.

From the description of the strange man, the girl was almost certain he was the same fellow she suspected had damaged the motorboat she had rented.

Nancy thanked the man, saying her father would get in touch with him later. For several hours, in fact until bedtime, she kept trying to figure out this latest angle to the puzzle. Her father was to be away overnight, so she could not discuss the matter with him. She did talk it over with Hannah Gruen, but that good woman had nothing to offer except advice about the girl using caution in her sleuthing.

Nancy was up early the next morning. She was the first of those who planned the trip to Heath Castle to arrive at the Landing. By telephone she had made arrangements to rent the same motorboat she had had before. The owner assured her it had been repaired and was in first-class shape.

George came next, then Bess. Finally Mehearty showed up in his rowboat, which he fastened securely to the larger one.

"All set," he announced. "Cast off!"

The girls enjoyed the ride upstream.

"Coming to Heath Castle," the old man announced suddenly, pointing to a wild-looking spot ahead.

In the distance, the girls could see the high turrets, and Nancy recalled the man she had seen signalling from one of them with a flashlight. His helper probably had been on the water. Presently Mehearty told her to turn off the motor; they would row the rest of the way.

The shore line was matted thickly with bushes, and only a narrow beach was visible. Above it stood a high, weather-stained wall—the river barrier of Heath Castle.

"How can we ever get in?" Bess gasped, observing the height of the wall.

"You haven't forgotten about a possible opening, have you?" asked Nancy.

The old clam digger assisted the girls into the rowboat and untied it from the anchored motorboat. His powerful strokes sent the little craft surging through the water. When it grounded on the shore, they all stepped out.

"My, my," said Mehearty. "Judgin' from them little blow holes in the sand, I'd say there are clams aplenty here."

The old man began digging. The eager girls started towards the wall. Not one of the group gave a thought to the fact that an unfriendly person might be coming there and would discover them. But about two miles down the stream, and heading for Heath Castle, was a figure in a boat, rocking back and forth over his oars as he rowed closer and closer to Nancy and her friends.

· 17 · *A Pocket in the Wall*

As the old sailor explored the beach, they turned to the high retaining wall marking the rear boundary of the Heath estate. Only the high treetops in the gardens were visible. In front of the wall grew tall briar bushes.

"Hello, what's this?" Bess cried all of a sudden.

The girl had spied something half buried in the sand. Examination revealed that it was George's lost riding breeches. When their owner saw the condition they were in, she declared she never would wear them again.

Nancy was thoughtful. "That boy who took them. He just seemed to appear on the beach out of nowhere."

She paused. Bess and George waited expectantly.

"I don't recall seeing the boy scale a wall," Nancy continued after a moment. "He must have reached the beach in some other way."

Pushing ahead, Nancy began to examine the foot of the wall. In many places, bushes and younger trees had grown out from it, anchoring their roots in the cracks between the stones.

"That boy came through here," she insisted stubbornly. "There must be a passageway, and we're going to find it!"

Her determination was rewarded. Twenty yards farther on she parted some briar bushes, and revealed several large stones which apparently never had been cemented into the wall. She pushed against the centre one. To her surprise, it moved easily.

Nancy pressed against the stone. It fell inwards, to reveal a flight of eight steps leading upwards to an arched passageway.

"The cloister!" Nancy cried gleefully.

To enlarge the entrance hole, she pushed against another stone. At first it would not move. Then suddenly it gave way, weakening a whole section of the wall. A great mass of debris came tumbling down, nearly hitting the girls.

"I hope the entrance isn't blocked," said George.

There was still an opening just large enough for a person to squeeze through. Nancy scrambled inside and led the way up the stone steps. At the top, the trio paused for breath.

Before them stretched a long, flagstone passageway. One side of it was set with square columns built of stone. Between these, grew the heavy stalks of vines which formed a solid roof of leaves. The other side of the cloister was a solid stone wall with deep insets at intervals of twenty-five feet.

"Just like the picture we saw in the book!" Nancy

cried in delight. "Oh, what an attractive walk to a bathing beach!"

"Now to find the hidden treasure!" cried George. "Come on!"

Hopefully the girls examined the insets along the wall, some of which had built-in stone shelves. In one, a statuette lay on its side; in another, a broken vase had tipped over.

"Nothing here—" Bess started to say as she reached the next one, only to break off.

Nancy had held up a finger in warning. "Listen!" she whispered.

Both Bess and George could hear men's voices. The sounds came from the other side of the wall.

"This looks like a good spot!" a man said, making no attempt to speak low. "Let's have your pick, Cobb."

The voices were strangely familiar. When had she heard them before? Suddenly she knew.

She had heard them the night of her imprisonment in the tower!

The men fell to work with chisel, pick, and sledge-hammer. Tiny stones and bits of mortar rattled down at the girls' feet

As they waited, a decorative ledge loosened itself from the wall niche. Repeated blows from the other side of the barrier threatened to send it crashing to the flagstone floor.

Unable to witness such wanton destruction, Nancy caught the ledge as it fell. She and Bess laid it carefully on the ground.

Straightening up, the Drew girl gazed at the wall niche, now disfigured. What she saw caused her to draw in her breath sharply. Where the ledge had been,

THE CLUE IN THE CRUMBLING WALL

there now was revealed a long, narrow pocket!

Scarcely daring to hope, Nancy ran her hand into the dark opening. Her groping fingers touched something hard.

A box!

"Nancy!" George warned tensely.

Directly above the girl's hand a stone chisel was poking through the wall. The men on the other side of the wall were working diligently. In another moment they would succeed in making a large opening into the niche.

Nancy did not wait to be discovered. She seized the heavy box, and with the other girls turned and fled along the cloister. For a time they could hear the two men working on the wall; then gradually the sounds died away.

"We're safe," Nancy exclaimed. "Now let's open the box!"

· 18 ·   *Poet's Nook*

Carefully she lifted out a photograph. The picture was an old one, yellowed with age, and contained traces of mould. It showed a half-pose of a middle-aged man with side whiskers. At the bottom was scrawled the name "Ira Heath", and a date.

Nancy was about to hand the picture to George, when a detail of the old estate owner's clothing caught her eye. A watch chain which hung from Mr Heath's vest pocket had an unusual charm attached to it.

"Girls, notice that watch charm!" she cried. "I saw the very same thing at Sam Weatherby's curio shop. Hector Keep said it was an heirloom of his own family."

"It certainly sounds suspicious," George said, reaching for another photograph. "Oh, here's an old-fashioned one!"

She held up the picture of a sweet-faced woman in a long velvet gown with a bustle. An inscription identified her as Ira Heath's wife Ida. The woman's dark hair was worn high, exposing shapely ears which were set off with earrings of unique design.

"Those earrings!" Nancy exclaimed when she saw them. "They're at Mr Weatherby's shop too! Oh, now I *am* suspicious!"

There were other pictures in the box, but the girls passed over them quickly as they were of no particular interest. An article that did hold their attention was a small, leatherbound diary. The fly-leaf bore Walter Heath's name, and the dates of many of the notations showed they had been made not many months before his death.

"This may be what's really valuable in this box!" Nancy declared jubilantly.

Rapidly she skimmed through the small book. Many of the pages were blank, but under one date she came to an item important enough to read aloud.

" 'Stumbled upon something which may prove to be a treasure. Whelks are right on the shores of Heath Castle. They contain a beautiful magenta dye. Am mixing it with various chemicals. So far I've produced six shades of fast-colour dye.' "

"This proves that your theory about Walter Heath's experiments was right, Nancy," George said in praise.

"I wonder what became of the dye?" the Drew girl mused, thumbing through the little book. "Mehearty said that in the old days magenta dye brought high prices. Dyed wool sold for more than two hundred dollars a pound."

"Read on," urged Bess impatiently. "Maybe we'll learn what became of the dye."

"Here's something!" she cried a moment later. "Listen to this:

" 'I don't trust the new chauffeur Biggs. Have decided to hide all the bottles of magenta dye until my experiments are complete.' "

"Does it say where he hid them?" George demanded. "Read the next page."

"There doesn't seem to be anything more. That was the last paragraph in the book."

"Oh, what a shame!" Bess wailed.

"I skimmed over the first part. Maybe I'll find other clues when I read the entire diary carefully. But there's no time now."

"I'll say there isn't!" agreed George. "Sh! We'd better duck out of here—and fast!"

From just across the stone barrier came the barking of a dog. Voices were audible, and each moment they grew louder. The two workmen were approaching!

"How about looking on the opposite side of this wall?" they heard one of the men ask his companion.

"O.K.," agreed the other. "May as well make a good job of it while we're here."

Fearful lest they be seen, the girls sped on along the cloistered walk, Nancy carrying the metal box.

"We should have gone the other way, towards the

beach," she whispered belatedly. "We may trap ourselves this way!"

Her prediction proved to be only too correct. A hundred yards farther on, the cloister abruptly ended at one of the castle walls. The door leading into the big dwelling was locked.

"Oh, what'll we do?" Bess asked uneasily. "This is awful."

The men had climbed the wall and now were moving slowly up the flagstone passageway. In a moment or two they certainly would see the girls.

"Nancy, we'll have to hide the box!" George said, listening to the approaching footsteps.

"A better idea would be to hide ourselves," Bess whispered. "But where?"

Not far from the castle wall was a nook of considerable size. In their haste, the girls had passed it with little more than a fleeting glance. Now, in looking about for a place of concealment, Nancy saw that it offered possibilities.

Above the arched entrance to the refuge had been chiselled the words "Poet's Nook," but the girls scarcely noticed this, as they slipped into the hiding place barely an instant before the two workmen came into view.

"I must hide this box so that those men can't take it, even if they catch us!" Nancy whispered grimly.

Frantically the girls looked about them for a place to hide the precious metal box. There seemed to be none. Then Nancy noticed a loose stone in the wall directly above a bench at the back of the niche. Almost without hope, she asked George to see if it would move.

The stone came out, revealing an empty space behind it. Fortunately the recess was large enough to hold the metal box. Nancy slipped it inside, and George quickly fitted the stone back into place.

By this time the men were very near.

"How about working in that Poet's Nook?" one of the men asked suddenly. "Maybe we'll find something there."

"We looked there once. That hiding place over the bench was empty."

"Sure, but if we take out the whole wall, we might find another hiding place. You're lazy if you ask me, Cobb."

"Did I ask you?" the other growled. "Swinging a pick is hard work. We're not getting too much money for it, either."

The other laughed. "What we found already is good enough pay for me. And if we find the other thing, we can live on Easy Street."

Nancy and her chums relaxed slightly, thinking that the men would not search the Poet's Nook a second time. But their hopes were dashed.

"How about it?" the first man demanded. "Do we take out the wall or don't we?"

"O.K.," the one addressed as Cobb replied. "You go ahead. I'll be with you in a minute."

PICKING up a sledge-hammer, Cobb's partner started towards the Poet's Nook. Nancy, Bess, and George sought to melt into the shadows, but they knew they could not escape detection!

"Be with you in a minute, Biggs," Cobb called. "I want to see if there's anything hidden in this niche."

Biggs! The name electrified the three girls. Hadn't Walter Heath named him in the diary as a suspicious person? Could he be the chauffeur, searching, perhaps, for the bottles of dye his former employer had secreted on the premises?

Biggs now was just outside the Poet's Nook. Nancy and her friends gave up all hope of escaping detection. Then, just as the fellow was about to enter, running footsteps could be heard along the flagstones. Startled, the man paused and looked down the cloister.

Nancy tiptoed forward and peeked out. Biggs was the one who had signalled from the tower! She was just in time to see a boy who was gesticulating wildly towards the beach.

"Hey! Come quick!" the lad shouted. "I've got something to show you!"

"Out with it!"

"Not on your life," the boy retorted craftily. "You got to pay me."

"Get out of here and leave us alone."

"Maybe we'd better hear what he has to say," Biggs urged. "It may be important."

113

"Gimme a quarter and I'll tell you," the boy demanded. "Not a cent less."

Biggs and Cobb were worried. The latter took a coin from his pocket and tossed it angrily at the boy.

"There!" he snapped. "Now what have you got to tell us?"

"Part of the beach wall has been knocked down. Someone came through the hole in it too."

"How do you know that?" Biggs demanded tensely.

"Footprints on the ground. Want to see 'em?"

The two men followed the lad and soon were out of sight. When their voices died away, Nancy stepped cautiously from her hiding place.

"I believe that boy was Jeddy Hooker!" Nancy declared excitedly. "I didn't see him very well, but from the glimpse I caught of him he certainly resembled Joan's playmate. If he takes them to the beach they'll be sure to find Mehearty."

"That's so," agreed George, who had dropped down on the stone bench in the nook. "I forgot all about him. Oh, I hope they don't harm the poor man!"

As there was no way in which the girls could warn the clam digger, they considered their own plight. It seemed pretty serious.

"We can't go back to the beach," wailed Bess, "and we can't go on because the castle door is locked."

"There's one thing we can do," announced George suddenly, rising from the bench and stalking across the cloister.

"What's that?" asked Bess hopefully.

Her cousin pointed. Between two of the columns, intertwined with vines, were steps leading down into a small, tangled garden.

"See if there is a way out through here," George replied.

She and the others investigated the little garden, which had walls on each side, too high to scale. There was not a single opening in them. The girls had been defeated again!

"We're certainly in a tight spot," said George, wondering what their next move ought to be.

Bess sat down in the middle of a weed-grown path. "I'm so discouraged I could cry," she owned up.

"Maybe a drink of water will revive you," suggested her cousin practically.

On the rear wall of the garden was an artistic fountain from which spouted a little stream. Bess walked over to it and drank freely. "It's wonderful water," she announced, "and cool. It must be from a spring."

Nancy and George cupped their hands and filled them several times. They agreed the water was unusually refreshing.

"Certainly gives you a lift," admitted Bess. "I feel now as if I wouldn't mind facing those men!"

Nancy suddenly noticed something on the crumbling wall just beneath the fountain. Parting some vines to get a better view, she stared in astonishment.

"Girls, look!" she cried. "On the wall!"

The vines had grown over a small block of cement which had been set into the stones. Visible on it was the imprint of a woman's slipper. Directly beneath, appeared a single word:

Cinderella

"Cinderella's dancing slipper," George laughed. "Whoever would do such a crazy thing?"

"I'm not sure it was crazy," Nancy replied, her mind busily fitting together two pieces of the Heath puzzle. "I'd say it's romantic. It may have been Walter Heath's way of paying a compliment to someone."

"A story-book character?" asked Bess.

"No, a beautiful dancer named Florianna. Don't you recall that note I found in his handwriting which began 'Dear C'?"

" 'C' could stand for Cinderella," George acknowledged. "It also could indicate a dozen other names."

Nancy measured the dainty little shoeprint with her hand. "Oh, I'm sure this is Florianna's!" she went on triumphantly. "It's the clue we need! And we found it in a crumbling old wall!"

Bess and George did not follow their friend's reasoning, and said so.

"I mean the clue Walter Heath mentioned in his will," Nancy explained. "He said Florianna would be able to identify herself in a special way! She could do it by means of this slipper print, couldn't she?"

"The shoe is very small," Bess admitted. "Not many girls could wear such a tiny size."

"Wouldn't anyone except Florianna know about this imprint in the wall?" asked George sceptically.

"Possibly," said Nancy. "But Florianna would be the only person to have proof she was the one he called Cinderella."

"You mean no imposter would have the shoe or other identification?" inquired George.

"Exactly."

"If you've really stumbled on a secret, Nancy, we mustn't breathe a word of it," said Bess, deeply impressed.

The three girls agreed to maintain absolute silence regarding the discovery. Carefully they covered the imprint with the vines, speculating as to whether anything of value might be hidden behind the cement block.

"We can't find out today," Nancy said. "We'd have to use tools to move it."

"It would be just our luck if Cobb and Biggs decide to smash the fountain!" George remarked. "Then we'd be too late." Suddenly she stiffened. "Listen!" she cried. "What's that?"

At the end of the cloister the castle door was opening with a groaning sound. Someone was coming out! Whoever it was would see them in another moment!

"Quick!" Nancy directed in a whisper. "Lie down here in the tall grass and weeds. It's our only chance!"

A man, slightly stooped, came walking with catlike tread along the flagstone cloister. He paused to examine the vines which Bess had disturbed near the steps. Nancy's heart stood still.

The man was Hector Keep!

The lawyer glanced towards the garden, but evidently saw no one, for he strode on towards the beach, his hands clasped behind him.

"Let's go!" Nancy whispered jubilantly, a moment later. "The castle door may be open!" As the girls made a dash for it she added, "I'll get the metal box. We'd better not leave it. It's too precious to lose."

Reaching the Poet's Nook, she hastily removed the loose stone from the wall. George held it while Nancy reached inside.

"Hurry!" urged Bess, who was standing guard. "One of those men may come back any minute!"

Nancy retrieved the metal box, while George slid the stone back into place.

"Oh, please come!" Bess pleaded, and looked relieved when the others appeared.

Stealing noiselessly along, the three girls reached the castle. The door was unlocked!

Nancy, fairly familiar with the floor plan, found the main entrance. It was locked, but another door close by opened when she turned the knob.

"This is lucky for us!" George exclaimed, going out first. She stepped on to a terrace, and there stopped short. "Oh! Oh!" she cried.

"Now what?" asked Nancy, closing the door.

Lying at the foot of the steps from the terrace were the two huge dogs the girls had met before. They began to growl menacingly.

"Well, hello, old fellows, we meet again!" Nancy said cheerily.

But her friendly attitude did not work this time. The animals would not allow the girls to descend the steps.

"You try it alone, Nancy," suggested Bess.

This was no better. The hounds were acting very strangely indeed.

"What can be wrong?" Nancy muttered, perplexed. "The other day these same dogs let me pass."

Nancy shifted the metal box under her arm and the dogs growled even more fiercely.

"Why, it's this box!" she realized. "They think I'm trying to steal something from the castle!"

Telling her friends she would return in a minute, Nancy ran back inside. It required but a minute to strip the box of the photographs and diary. Stuffing them beneath her sweater, she looked round.

"Where can I hide the box?" she thought. Suddenly her eyes caught sight of a door. "That closet will do," she told herself.

Darting across the big hall, she yanked open the door and placed the metal container on the floor. As she did so, the girl could hear footsteps not far away. Someone was coming along the winding corridor!

Nancy flew back to the terrace. The dogs growled but did not try to molest her this time. She hurried down the steps, her friends behind her. Bess was fearful, but tried not to show it.

"You girls go on ahead," ordered Nancy. "I'll keep the dogs busy until you get a good start. Then I'll follow."

Since there was no time to lose, they obeyed. Thirty seconds later, Nancy followed them.

The hounds set up a fearful barking as they leaped alongside the fleeing girl. The next minute Hector Keep's figure framed the doorway.

Nancy could not avoid being seen by him, although she covered her face with her free hand and kept on running.

"Hey, you!" the lawyer shouted furiously. "Stop! Stop!"

Nancy ignored his cries. Catching up with her friends, she urged them to a faster pace.

"Quick! The wall!" she panted, holding her treasure close inside her sweater.

CLOSELY pursued by the barking dogs, the three girls raced madly to the front wall of the estate. Scrambling safely over it, they paused, gasping for breath.

The girls debated what to do. They were worried about Mehearty and what might have happened to him. Though the beach was not more than half a mile away, they had no way of reaching it.

"We'll have to return to town and rent another boat," Nancy concluded.

Walking as fast as they could, the trio made their way to the main highway. They were a long distance from River Heights, and Bess pointed out that bus service was infrequent along this route.

The girls waited patiently for twenty minutes, hoping a bus would appear. They were almost in despair, when Nancy observed a familiar coupé coming down the road.

"Lieutenant Masters' car!" she cried, signalling. "Now we'll get a lift."

"Hop in," she invited them. "There isn't much room, but I think we all can squeeze in."

"Seeing you out here makes me think you've been to Heath Castle," the lieutenant said, a twinkle in her eye.

"We have been," Nancy admitted. "I suppose I ought to tell you everything, but—"

"But it's a professional secret. I understand," the attractive young officer laughed. "Tell me something.

120

Is there any chance of your finding Florianna before it's too late?"

"I have several very good leads," the girl answered. "In fact, George, Bess, and Mehearty and I were following one this morning."

"Mehearty?"

"Yes. The singing clam digger of the Muskoka River. I'm responsible for his nickname," Nancy explained. "He used to sing 'me hearty lad' and 'me hearty men,' so when I was a little girl I called him Mehearty man."

"And now everyone in River Heights calls him Mehearty," said Bess. "The poor old fellow! We left him on the beach. He's probably in the hands of the crooks by now."

"What's that?" exclaimed the policewoman.

The Drew girl explained what she felt to be necessary, and asked the officer if a police boat might be sent out to rescue Mehearty.

"Why, of course!" Lieutenant Masters promised. "I'll call H.Q. as soon as we get to River Heights."

She remarked to Nancy that she had expected to stop at the Drew home to discuss the problem of Joan Fenimore and her playmate, Jeddy Hooker.

"She promised me she wouldn't play with Jeddy any more," said Nancy.

"I'm inclined to think she may have tried not to," the officer said slowly, "but—well, here's the story. Jeddy really causes me more worry than a dozen other boys on my list."

"What has he done this time?" Nancy asked curiously, though she thought she knew part of the answer already.

"He hasn't been to school for three days. It does no good to talk to his mother. She's an unsuitable person to look after him."

"I'll say she is," George burst out, and told Miss Masters about the clothes stolen from her, and how they suspected Jeddy and his mother of being in possession of them.

"I think the boy is a thief," the lieutenant sighed. "Yesterday I caught him at Weatherby's curio shop trying to sell a fair-sized pearl."

"You think he stole it?" cried Nancy, thinking of the one taken from her.

"I'm not sure. When I took Jeddy home, his mother said she knew nothing about the pearl. Jeddy claimed that Joan Fenimore had given it to him, but Joan denied the story. So you see it's all very confusing."

"It's a pity Joan is involved in such things!" said Nancy, shocked. "She's too nice a child."

"Jeddy's a very bad influence on her," the police-woman sighed. "Mrs Fenimore realizes this only too well. She's willing to send the little girl away for a while if I can find a place for her to stay."

"I'll talk to our housekeeper about it," the Drew girl offered. "Maybe we can work out something. She has relatives with a farm."

"That would be ideal for a while, since the child loves nature," said the officer, as she stopped in front of the Drew home. "And now, if I may use your telephone I'll see about getting a boat to rescue that man Mehearty."

Lieutenant Masters called the police station, and talked with the sergeant on duty.

"Only one man can go. Will you girls accompany

him so that you can bring back the rented boat?"

"Yes, we'll be glad to," the three said together, and thanked the lieutenant for her help.

As it developed, Nancy was not to be included. She and her friends were about to leave the house when Mr Drew drove up.

"Don't go away, Nancy!" he called urgently to his daughter. "I have something important to talk over with you."

"Do you mind if I don't go with you?" Nancy asked the other girls.

"No, not if there's a policeman along," Bess replied, and George nodded.

"Tell me what happens," Nancy requested, as they left. "I'm dreadfully anxious about Mehearty."

The woman drove Bess and George to the police dock and there said goodbye. Soon Policeman Carney arrived in a boat, and the girls climbed in. It was a fast craft, and reached the area of Heath Castle in a much shorter time than the one which Nancy had piloted.

To the girls' relief, the rented boat was still in the river; but Mehearty was not in it. Nor was he or his rowboat visible on the beach.

"He wouldn't have had time to row home," said Bess, worried. "And we didn't pass him as we came up."

"Do you suppose those men—" whispered George grimly.

The girls told Policeman Carney they were afraid the old clam digger might have met with foul play and asked him to go ashore with them. He anchored his speedboat, and the three climbed into the rowboat it was hauling.

Reaching the beach, the searchers started an intensive hunt. They were just about to despair of finding the missing man, when George spied the form of the old sailor lying near the entrance to the cloister. For a moment she was fearful something dreadful had happened to him, but he suddenly sat up and looked at her.

"Thought ye'd never come," he muttered sleepily.

George thought he was only sleepy, until she noticed blood on his face and his shirt.

"Mehearty! You're hurt!" she exclaimed.

"I'd be proud to get knocked out any time for Miss Nancy Drew," he murmured, "and nobody can say anything against her!" Mehearty looked around. "Where is she?" he demanded.

"Home," Bess replied.

"Home?" The man blinked. "How'd she get there? Not through here?" He pointed to the cloister opening.

"No. By the road," explained George. "Come, Mehearty, we'll go back to River Heights and talk on the way. Where's your boat?"

"Those rascals what give me a bloody nose took 'er," the old sailor explained.

"Now, Mehearty, tell us what happened," George demanded, as they skimmed down the stream towards Campbell's Landing.

"I was diggin' for clams," the old sailor began, "when a couple o' men and a boy seemed to come right out o' nowhere. They asked me who was in the Heath gardens."

"You didn't tell them!" Bess exclaimed.

"Yes, afore I thought I up and said, 'Nancy Drew and a couple of her friends.' It was a mistake to tell 'em. I learned that quick enough. Right away they told me to clear out, and said they'd go after the girls."

"What did you do then?" George asked.

"I tried to argue 'em out of it, but they was stubborn as mules. Then one of 'em said something about Miss Nancy bein' dangerous and she'd better mind her own business. I up and punched him on the nose for that."

"You were nice to come to Nancy's defence," said Bess, "but there were three against you."

"Ye're right, and we had a tussle. 'Fraid I lost," the clam digger added sheepishly. "But I come to pretty soon; just in time to see one o' them rascals takin' my boat."

Mehearty told how one of the other men went through the wall with the stone steps beyond and he followed him. But the poor old sailor had got no farther than the opening, when everything went black before him.

"Later I come to," he said, "but I couldn't seem to move for a while. Somewhere in the garden I heard two men talkin'. I'm glad Miss Nancy is home safe, for one of 'em said he was goin' to have her arrested!"

"Arrested!" cried Bess. "Why?"

"I didn't hear. I guess I must have kind of gone off again," the old man replied.

"We must warn Nancy right away!" George declared, pushing the boat to its utmost speed.

Unaware that her chums were racing to caution her of trouble, Nancy had been eating a late luncheon and talking with her father at home. Eagerly she showed him the photographs and diary from the metal box. She spoke of the mysterious Cinderella footprint embedded in the crumbling wall at the Heath gardens, and gave a vivid account of her adventure with Cobb, Biggs, and Hector Keep.

"You certainly had no dull moments," Mr Drew said. "Your news dwarfs what I have to tell you."

"Is it something that will help solve the mystery?" Nancy asked eagerly.

"It may, depending upon how you use the information."

The girl squirmed impatiently. "Don't keep me in suspense," she pleaded. "What is the news, Dad?"

"It concerns Florianna's missing nurse."

"Emily Foster?"

"Yes," Mr Drew nodded. "After a long search, I've located her. And here's the best part of it all. Tomorrow morning she'll be glad to see you and tell you all she knows!"

·21· *News of Florianna*

"OH, Dad! Where *is* Emily Foster?" Nancy cried, thrilled by the wonderful news. "How did you find her? What did she say about Florianna?"

"One question at a time," laughed Mr Drew. "I talked with Miss Foster only by telephone, so I did not get any details."

"Is she here in River Heights?"

"No, I traced her by contacting various nurses' registries. Miss Foster is working on a case at Hampton. She'll be free tomorrow, and has promised to meet us at the hotel there."

The Drews planned to leave for Hampton that afternoon and spend the night at a hotel in order to be there early in the morning. Knowing she had a dozen things to do before leaving, Nancy fairly flew to the tasks.

Her first act was to consult Hannah Gruen about little Joan Fenimore. The housekeeper immediately telephoned her relative, Mrs Davis, at her farm. The woman said she would be happy indeed to take the child for a visit. Nancy then notified Lieutenant Masters, but the policewoman was so busy she said it would be impossible for her to see Mrs Fenimore that day. As a favour, she asked the girl to go in her stead.

Mr Drew, knowing that his daughter had more than enough to do, generously offered to assist. He dropped into the police station and related to the Chief what Nancy had seen and heard that day at Heath Castle. He asked that a search be made for the two men, Biggs and Cobb.

"We'll pick them up," the officer promised. "But without more evidence we'll not be able to hold 'em very long."

"By that time, maybe my daughter or I will have further evidence for you," the lawyer smiled.

When Mr Drew returned home, Nancy was ready to leave. She suggested they stop at the Fenimore cottage to extend the invitation for Joan to visit the Davis farm. To her surprise, she found the invalid in very good spirits.

"The Hooker family has moved away!" she disclosed as the cause of her jubilation. "Now Joan and Jeddy will be separated. It won't be necessary for me to send my little girl away for a visit."

Nancy glanced at her father. He shook his head, indicating that it would be wise to forget the arrangement just made with Mrs Davis.

"I wonder why your neighbour left so suddenly?" Nancy mused.

"It was strange," Mrs Fenimore replied. "Mrs Hooker never talked about leaving. Around noon today a truck drove up with Mr Hooker and another man. They loaded a lot of furniture in it. Then Mrs Hooker and Jeddy left in a taxi with their bags."

Mrs Fenimore went on to say that Jeddy had been boasting to Joan lately.

"He said his father was a smart man—that he knew how to make money without working for it. Oh, the talk frightened me."

"I've never seen Mr Hooker," Nancy said, extremely interested in the remark. "Can you describe him?"

"Cobb Hooker is a tall man, sullen-faced, and unkempt in appearance."

"Did you say Cobb Hooker!" Nancy exclaimed, startled by the name.

"Yes."

Nancy let the matter pass without comment, but asked Mrs Fenimore if there was anything more she could tell her about Jeddy and his family.

"I never knew when that boy was telling the truth," the invalid replied. "But he told Joan that he knew where there was a hidden treasure."

"Hidden treasure!" Nancy echoed, light dawning upon her. "Mrs Fenimore, did Joan ever talk to the Hookers about Florianna and the property she was to inherit?"

"Dear me, yes! The child told everybody about it. The story became almost an obsession with her."

"And Jeddy repeated the tale to his parents?" commented Mr Drew.

"I don't know. But Jeddy told Joan he'd gone to Heath Castle himself. He threatened her if she told anyone about it."

The Drews made no comment about this. Soon they got up to leave, saying they were on their way to interview a woman who might give them some information about Florianna.

"Oh, I hope she can!" cried Mrs Fenimore eagerly.

As soon as Nancy and her father left the cottage, the girl told him of her suspicion regarding Cobb Hooker.

"Until now I assumed that Cobb was a last name," she commented. "It never occurred to me that Biggs' companion might be Jeddy's father!"

"You're not sure of it now, Nancy."

"True. But Cobb is not a common name. Shouldn't we talk to the police again? Unwittingly I've given them the wrong information."

Mr Drew glanced at his watch. "Very well," he consented. "But we've not much time if we're to get to Hampton tonight."

The call at the local police station did not take long, and proved to be of great value. Cobb Hooker, the Chief informed the Drews after consulting some records, had a police record. Three years before he had served a term on a burglary charge in a distant town.

"Have you a picture of the man?" Mr Drew asked.

The photograph was brought from the files. One glance at it told Nancy that at last she knew the identity of the man who had run into her with his boat.

"And Cobb Hooker is one of the men who was in the Heath gardens," she revealed.

"If you'll make a formal charge against the fellow, we'll try to track him down and arrest him," offered the Chief.

Mr Drew did not wish to be too hasty. "Couldn't we learn more by having one of your men trail him for a few days?" he suggested.

"That's a good idea. I'll put someone on the case right away, Mr Drew," said the officer, and turned to answer his telephone.

Two hours after Nancy and her father had left town, Bess and George, highly excited, arrived at the Drew house. Upon hearing from Hannah Gruen that their friend had gone away, the girls looked relieved.

"Is anything the matter?" asked the housekeeper.

"Plenty. Somebody is going to have Nancy arrested."

"Who?"

"We don't know. Mehearty heard about it."

It was well that Mrs Gruen had been warned what to expect, because that very evening a policeman came to the door with a warrant for Nancy's arrest.

"Miss Drew isn't here," the housekeeper said, thoroughly enjoying the situation. "I don't know when she'll be back, either. Perhaps not for some time."

Temporarily safe from arrest, Nancy arrived at the Hampton Hotel with her father. The next morning they waited expectantly for Emily Foster to call.

"I'm sorry to be late," she apologized breathlessly, as Nancy advanced to meet her, "but the nurse who was to relieve me didn't come on time."

Nancy and her father liked Miss Foster at once. She was a woman of early middle age, brisk and efficient, with a friendly smile.

"Mr Drew, you said over the telephone that you and

your daughter wanted to ask me about a former patient of mine," she began at once. "I'll be glad to answer any questions I can."

"As I explained, we're seeking information about a certain Flossie Johnson. The young woman also used the name of Florianna," said the lawyer.

"I never took care of anyone who called herself by either of those names. The patient you asked me about —a beautiful young woman injured in an automobile accident about ten years ago—gave her name as Miss Flower."

"Tell us about her," Mr Drew urged. "From the facts we've already gathered, it seems fairly evident that she is the one for whom we're looking."

"She was a hospital case, assigned to me about ten years ago," Miss Foster recalled. "The girl interested me more than the average patient. She was so beautiful, so unassuming, and yet so distinguished. From the first, I felt that she had not registered under her real name."

"What made you think so?" Mr Drew inquired.

"Mostly little remarks she dropped. One peculiar thing was that Miss Flower never had visitors. No messages came for her. There were no letters. She would allow the authorities to notify no one of the accident. 'I don't want anyone to know,' she would say. 'Not until I'm well.' "

"The young woman believed she would recover completely?" Nancy asked quickly.

"Only for the first few weeks. Then the doctor told her the truth—that she would be a cripple for the rest of her life."

"How did she take it?" Mr Drew questioned.

"Very hard. She wept for days, saying the strangest

things. One remark I recall was, 'His little Cinderella will never dance for him again.' Oh, it was heartbreaking to listen to her."

Cinderella!

Nancy was so sure now she was on the right track that her mind leaped from one possibility to another. She nearly missed her father's next question.

"Where did the girl go after she left the hospital?"

"I never heard," Miss Foster admitted regretfully. "From Miss Flower's remarks, I assumed that she intended to retire to some secluded place near Hopewell."

"Yet it's unlikely the woman had much money with her," Mr Drew commented. "When she was picked up, I understand no bag was found."

"That's true," said the nurse, "but she had some money in her possession, though she couldn't have had much left after she paid her hospital bill."

"All these years she must have earned a living somehow," commented Nancy. "You have no idea how, of course?"

"No, I haven't."

"That name Flower," Nancy mused. "Florianna was deeply interested in gardening," she added, recalling what Mrs Fenimore had told her about the dancer.

"And so was Miss Flower!" the nurse exclaimed. "She was always asking me to buy her garden magazines. Why, the day before her release, I remember she cut an advertisement from the local paper—"

"Yes?" Nancy asked eagerly, as the nurse hesitated.

"Probably it has no significance," Miss Foster completed. "But the advertisement Miss Flower clipped out offered a small fruit and vegetable farm for sale—a place known as Clover Farm."

"Where is the farm?" Nancy asked, her eyes dancing with hope.

"It seems to me there's a Clover Farm at Hilton about ten miles from here. I don't know whether it's the same one, though."

Nancy turned to her father.

"Yes, we'll go there today!" he said, reading his daughter's thoughts. "It may be a vain chase, but something tells me that this time we'll find Florianna!"

·22· *The Recluse of Clover Farm*

AFTER bidding Miss Foster goodbye, Nancy and her father drove directly to Hilton. Inquiry at the little village revealed that Clover Farm was famous for its superb fruits and vegetables. Yet strangely enough, no one knew anything about the owner.

"Fact is, people never see Miss Flower," a filling station attendant explained to them. "She bought the place ten years ago, but she's never left the farm since."

"Then how does she market her products?" Mr Drew asked.

"Sends her farmhands to town with the vegetables. All her help has been with her for years. They're a loyal lot, and she's taught 'em to be close-mouthed."

Mr Drew asked how to reach the farm. He was instructed to drive on for two and a half miles before turning into a private side road.

"You'll see a big sign reading 'Clover Farm, No

Visitors Admitted'," the filling station man added. "It means what it says, too!"

Convinced that at last they were nearing the end of a long search, Nancy and her father drove on in high spirits. Presently they came to the sign the man had mentioned. A decorative wooden gate, flanked by tall hedges, barred admittance to the farm.

With assurance, Mr Drew opened the gate and drove up the winding lane. Nancy glimpsed a small, white clapboard house surrounded by flower beds. There was an orchard, and two large fields of vegetables. Suddenly, two men in overalls leaped out from the roadside. Mr Drew was forced to bring the car to a halt.

"No visitors allowed here!" one of the farmhands said curtly. "Can't you read signs?"

"We came to see the owner of Clover Farm," Mr Drew explained. "Our business with her is urgent,"

"Did Miss Flower send for you?"

"No," Mr Drew admitted, "but we have important information for Miss Flower."

The workmen hesitated. Then one of them said impatiently, "Sorry. You can't see her."

Disgusted, Mr Drew was ready to go on to the house despite them. Nancy made a last desperate attempt to gain their co-operation.

"You'll be doing Miss Flower a favour if you'll let us talk to her," she pleaded. "You see, your employer has inherited a fortune. But she must claim it within the next few days or she'll lose it."

The men's jaws dropped.

"Is that the truth?" one of them demanded.

"Certainly," snapped Mr Drew. "Now will you tell Miss Flower we'd like to see her?"

"She's not here."

Nancy and her father were dumbfounded.

"But we've been told Miss Flower never leaves Clover Farm!" the girl protested.

"She never did until last night, being such a cripple. But she had to go with that government man in a car."

"What government man?" Mr Drew asked quickly. "Did he give his name?"

"He prob'ly told Miss Flower. We didn't hear it. Fact is, we didn't see her go. She left a note."

"Did she say why she had to go with him?" asked Nancy.

"It was something about income tax. Miss Flower always thought she paid the government every penny she owed. She's as honest as the day is long. But the man claimed she'd made a false report and might have to go to prison."

"This seems very irregular to me," commented Mr Drew.

"Dad," Nancy said, looking anxiously at him, "it looks as if someone was very eager to get Miss Flower away from here!"

"Before we found her, you mean?"

"Yes. Oh, Dad, we must do something!"

"First of all, we'll check with the revenue office; that is, if I can get to a telephone."

The two farmhands invited them into the farm-house. Mr Drew busied himself at the telephone, while Nancy looked at the note Miss Flower had left. The writing showed such haste and nervousness she could not identify it as Florianna's.

The telephone call required a few minutes. When the lawyer finished it, he looked grim.

"Just as we feared," he revealed. "The Federal Bureau has no case pending against Miss Flower."

"Then it was all a hoax!"

"Yes. The man who came here was an imposter. Obviously, it was a scheme to get her away from Clover Farm."

The farmhands looked to the Drews to do something about the matter. Nancy and her father promised to stop at the police station and report the kidnapping. The description the men of Clover Farm gave of the stranger was not very helpful—he was tall, slightly stooped, wore dark glasses, and had a beard.

"Probably a disguise," Nancy concluded.

Still another surprise in the case awaited them back at the hotel!

On his way to luncheon, Carson Drew purchased a copy of the River Heights afternoon newspaper. A startling headline caught his eye.

FAMOUS DANCER
RETURNS IN TIME TO
CLAIM HEATH FORTUNE

The story told how, after a long search, Hector Keep had found the missing Florianna, who was now staying at the local Riverview Hotel. For many years, the famous dancer had been abroad fulfilling professional engagements.

"Then she isn't Miss Flower!" said Nancy, her hopes tumbling.

Florianna had married a South American dancer, José Fernandez, and had been difficult to trace because she had used her husband's name. Hector Keep was given high praise for having found the woman in time to prevent her from losing the Heath fortune.

Nancy's discouragement lasted only a moment. Then her old suspicions returned. "This can't be true!" she fairly wailed. "It must be a scheme to give the estate to an imposter—an accomplice of Mr Keep's!"

"There's something underhand about it!" Mr Drew agreed, his face grim.

"Let's hurry back to River Heights and learn what we can!" Nancy begged.

"Poor little Miss Flower!" Nancy said sadly, as the car sped along the road. "I'm sure she's Florianna! Oh, where have they hidden her?"

It was late afternoon by the time the Drews reached River Heights. Mr Drew said he had to stop at his office to attend to some matters for a couple of hours, and that Nancy should take the car to do her investigating.

"I believe I'll visit Mrs Fenimore and find out if she has heard the news," the girl decided, heading for the little cottage.

The invalid and Joan were preparing supper when Nancy arrived. The child at once invited Nancy to eat with them, but the Drew girl shook her head, plunging at once into the subject uppermost in her mind. The Fenimores had not heard the exciting announcement.

"My darling sister has been found!" the widow cried, not realizing that the claimant might be an imposter. "Oh, why hasn't she come to see me? Please take me to her at once!"

All thought of supper was forgotten by the woman and her young daughter. Joan insisted upon going along to see her famous aunt. Hurriedly they changed into their best clothes and rode with Nancy to the Riverview Hotel.

"Madam Fernandez?" the clerk at the desk repeated when Nancy inquired about the woman. "I'll see if she's receiving callers. I believe she's having dinner in her room."

"I wonder if Florianna has changed much," she speculated, adjusting her hat for the hundredth time. "Imagine her marrying a foreigner! Florianna always said she would marry only an American."

Twenty minutes elapsed. Then word was sent to the callers that they might go up to Room Thirty-two. When they knocked a few minutes later, a voice said: "Come in!"

Florianna Fernandez was reclining on the bed, her back braced by several embroidered pillows. She wore an exotic negligee which set off to advantage her dark hair and creamy white skin.

"Greetings, my dear sister," she said as the three entered. She spoke in a stiff, affected way, as if English were difficult for her. "Vera, I am so glad to see you again! This so charming child, she is Joan, of course. And this lovely señorita?"

Mrs Fenimore was so confused that for an instant she could not speak. Joan clung to her mother. Nancy filled in the breach by giving her name.

"Miss Drew?" The dancer looked perplexed, but only for an instant. "Yes, I believe my dear friend Señor Keep tell me you are a friend of Vera." Turning to Mrs Fenimore, she added, "Oh, I am so happy Señor Keep found me!"

"Florianna, you've changed," Mrs Fenimore stammered. Going hesitantly to the bed, she would have

138

kissed the dancer. The woman, however, drew back quickly as if she dreaded an embrace.

"I am a famous dancer now!" Florianna said proudly. "And you should see my husband—one of the best dancers in South America! But it is hard work. We shall return home with much gold in our pockets, and work no more!"

"Suppose you tell us what you've been doing all these years," Nancy encouraged the dancer. "I notice that English seems a bit difficult for you."

"That is because I have lived so long in South America. For ten years I speak almost no English—only *Español.*"

"Then you went there immediately after you gave up your career here?"

"*Si,* I elope with darling husband."

"But how could you desert Walter Heath?" Mrs Fenimore murmured. "He was so good to you—so kind."

"I could not marry Walt when I did not love him—no! To save him much hurt, I ran away."

"And now you return to claim the Heath fortune," Nancy interposed, disgusted at such a procedure.

"*Si, si!* Señor Keep tell me that I will be rich heiress!"

"I suppose you and your husband will restore the gardens and make the estate a show place again," the Drew girl suggested.

Florianna's pretty face clouded. "No, we do not plan so," she replied firmly. "Señor Keep will sell the castle for us. He has a buyer now, he tell me."

"But, Florianna!" Mrs Fenimore protested faintly. "Surely you will remain in River Heights! At least for a time. Joan and I need you."

"I have my career—a great star cannot be tied to her family. It grows late. You will excuse me now. We will meet again, Vera darling."

Deeply hurt at being so curtly dismissed, Mrs Fenimore moved slowly to the door, her head bowed, and the picture of dejection.

"Your hair, Florianna," she said, turning to the glamorous woman. "When last I saw it—"

"I dye it black to look more like the Spanish señorita," the dancer said quickly.

Nancy was firmly convinced from the woman's contradictory remarks that Madam Fernandez was an imposter, but she dared not say so. She did have the courage, however, to ask Florianna what proof she would be able to produce to establish her claim to the Heath fortune.

"Señor Keep have all the papers," the dancer said glibly. "If anyone doubt me, let him read this!"

From under her pillow Florianna produced a torn paper. Nancy instantly knew that it was the missing half of the note she had found at the Heath factory! She read the words:

> day the se-
> am hiding
> Will make me
> Then I shall be
> of you. Love,
> > Walt.

Nancy did not have the other half of the note with her, but she knew its contents by heart. The complete message would read:

Dear C,
Some day the se-
cret which I am hiding
in a wall will make me
famous. Then I shall be
worthy of you. Love,
Walt.

It seemed to the girl that here was proof Walter
Heath had not sold, nor used the valuable whelk dye
on which he had experimented. Instead, he had hidden
it somewhere in the old estate walls until he should
have perfected his work. Florianna, meanwhile, had
become successful. He had hoped to attain a name for
himself as a scientist and thus feel he was worthy of
her.

"You haven't the other half of the note?" Nancy
asked, returning the paper to the dancer.

"No, I lose it years ago. I do not remember what i t
say."

"By the way, did Walter Heath have a pet name for
you—a nickname?" the girl inquired.

"Oh, *st*," the woman replied glibly. "He call me
Precious."

"No particular name?"

"I do not understand what you mean."

"Never mind," said Nancy, well pleased by the
reply. "It doesn't make any difference."

She followed Mrs Fenimore and Joan from the room.
Once outside, the child said bluntly:

"I don't like my new aunt."

"Sh, she may hear you," her mother warned.

When the callers were seated in the car again, Nancy

asked the widow if she were convinced Mrs Fernandez was her sister.

"I don't know, I don't know," the poor woman replied, weeping. "Florianna is so changed. In some ways she resembles my sister; her height and weight, the tone of her voice—yes, even her face. But the black hair makes her look different, of course."

"In other words, you couldn't say after ten years that she is *not* your sister?"

"No, I'm afraid I couldn't," Vera Fenimore admitted.

"Then if she is an imposter, Hector Keep has done a good job," Nancy told herself. "I'll have to produce expert evidence to outwit him." Aloud she said, "I noticed that Mrs Fernandez had rather large feet. Her slippers must be size eight at least."

"Florianna had extremely small feet!" exclaimed Mrs Fenimore.

"So I thought," Nancy said. "I doubt that they would have changed so much."

"Then the woman is not my sister!"

"I'm afraid not. That's why she's unwilling to help you and Joan."

"Can't we expose her?"

"I'm going to try," Nancy said grimly. "But doing so won't restore your real sister to you. I still must find her."

"Didn't you learn anything on your trip?" the widow asked. "You hinted—"

Nancy did not have the heart to tell the distracted woman any more bad news. She merely mentioned having interviewed someone who thought she had met Florianna under an assumed name.

"I'll go right on working to find your sister until the last minute," Nancy promised.

"Please don't ever stop," begged Vera Fenimore pathetically. "If Flossie doesn't inherit the estate, she doesn't, that's all. But if she's alive, I want to see her again, no matter when it may be."

"I'll try to accomplish both things," were Nancy's parting words, as she left Joan and her mother at their cottage.

Deep in thought, Nancy drove towards home. Nearing the police station, she suddenly decided to go in and get a report on Cobb and Biggs. Unaware that contacting the police was exactly what Hector Keep wanted her to do, Nancy innocently walked into Headquarters.

"Miss Drew!" exclaimed the sergeant on duty at the desk. "You're the very person we've been looking for! We have a warrant for your arrest!"

·23· *In the Dungeon*

NANCY was stunned at the sergeant's words.

"Under arrest?" she gasped. "What for?"

The officer opened a drawer and took out the summons which he read aloud. Nancy learned that she was charged with illegal entry into the Heath estate, as well as damage to property and stealing.

"Who preferred the charges?" the girl asked, unable to believe what she had just heard.

"Mr Hector Keep."

"Oh!"

Nancy indignantly denied all charges save one. She readily admitted she had disobeyed a No Trespassing sign, but felt she had a legitimate reason for doing so.

"Lieutenant Masters can explain everything," she insisted. "Please ask her to come here. And I'd like to get in touch with my father, too."

Mr Drew arrived shortly, followed by the young policewoman. He consulted privately with her, Captain Walker, and the Chief of Police. Nancy then was called in to tell her story. Eloquently she spoke of what she had seen and heard at Heath Castle. She mentioned her suspicion regarding Keep's association with the two men, Biggs and Cobb, who, she learned, were still at large. The girl concluded by saying that she thought Keep made the charges against her to prevent her from working on the case.

"There's something to what you say," the Chief agreed. "Well, if Mr Keep will let me tear up these complaint papers, I'll call everything off."

But the wily lawyer could not be located, so the warrant remained intact. In the end, Nancy was allowed to go home, with a promise on her part that she would come back to Headquarters the following morning.

She and her father talked until midnight, then Mr Drew insisted that his daughter get some rest. Obediently the girl went to bed, but she could not sleep. The day's happenings had been too exciting. Hour after hour, Nancy struggled to fit together the pieces of the crazy puzzle. Several times she thought she had the problem solved, but one item kept eluding her.

"Hector Keep wanted me arrested to hinder me from

going to Heath Castle. But why? Surely not because of anything I've seen there already. Is it because of something else hidden on the place?"

The girl felt sure there was something more to it than this. Suddenly she was sure she had the answer. She could hardly wait now to get back to the police station!

Tiptoeing downstairs early the next morning before the others in the house were awake, she ate her breakfast, wrote a note to her father, and left for Headquarters. The day sergeant was just coming on duty. He grinned at her, saying that she need not have reported so soon, that she hardly looked rested.

"I didn't sleep a wink last night," Nancy admitted, "but I did get some ideas. As soon as Lieutenant Masters comes, I wish she might go out with me for a little while."

The officer said he felt sure this could be arranged. When the young policewoman came in, the girl repeated her request.

"Miss Masters, will you go to Heath Castle with me? I have an idea the mystery will be solved there this morning!"

At Nancy's instigation, several policemen were detailed to station themselves outside the Heath gardens to question anyone entering or leaving the grounds. The girl left at once with the lieutenant, and the men followed in another car.

"Just what do you expect to find at the castle?" the young woman asked Nancy curiously.

"It's my opinion that Hector Keep or one of his men kidnapped the real Florianna," Nancy disclosed to her companion. "He'll hold her until Madam

Fernandez can establish her claim to the fortune. Keep will take the lion's share of it and then he'll disappear."

"Your reasoning certainly is logical," her companion admitted.

"What worries me is whether we can get in," said Nancy after she and the policewoman had climbed the wall and set out for the castle. "I'm glad those dogs are gone, anyway."

Reassured, Nancy led the way to the front entrance. To her surprise, it stood ajar.

There was not a sign of anyone stirring about the premises. Noiselessly, Nancy and the policewoman slipped inside the castle. Hearing no one, they tiptoed along the winding corridor to the courtyard garden where the entrances to the towers were. Nancy tried the door of the one in which she had been imprisoned. It was not locked.

"Will you stand guard while I go upstairs?" Nancy asked the policewoman quietly.

The other nodded, and the girl noiselessly ascended the circular iron staircase. She was gone several minutes, and Lieutenant Masters was just becoming uneasy about her when Nancy reappeared.

"No one there," she reported. "I looked over the grounds, too, but I didn't see anything suspicious."

"What's next?" asked the officer.

"There's a trap door," Nancy revealed, pointing towards the floor. "What it opens into I haven't been able to find out."

To raise it was indeed a task, but together they finally got it up. Cautiously, Nancy and Lieutenant Masters peered into the darkness below.

The policewoman snapped on a flashlight, and they

could see a flight of iron steps leading down into a long corridor. Grilled doors opened from it.

"It looks like a series of dungeons!" Nancy exclaimed.

"No doubt the Heaths used them for storing food," the lieutenant said.

The next two rooms were also empty. But as Nancy and the policewoman approached the third, they distinctly heard someone moan. Pausing to listen intently, they heard a pitiful cry from the far end of the corridor:

"Let me out! Let me out! Please help me!"

Nancy and the young officer sped up the passageway. A small woman, crippled and weak, had pulled herself to the grilled doorway. She clung there, her eyes eloquent and beseeching.

"You're Florianna!" Nancy said quickly.

"No! No!" The prisoner shrank back. "I am Miss Flower."

"We'll talk about that later."

Nancy unbolted the door. She and Lieutenant Masters assisted the woman along the musty corridor, but it was slow work, for she had to pause often.

"Who brought you here?" the policewoman asked her kindly. "And have you been mistreated?"

"I've had enough to eat and drink," Miss Flower said. "But I've been so perplexed."

Questioned by Nancy and Miss Masters, she revealed all that had befallen her. An elderly man, who had shown an identification card of a government agent, had taken her away from Clover Farm in an automobile. It was dark when they reached their destination. She had been hurried inside a dimly lighted building and locked in the cell.

"I was told it was because of not paying enough income tax," she ended the story. "What does it all mean?"

"You are Florianna," Nancy continued with quiet conviction. "Why not admit it?"

"No, no, never!"

"Do you realize where you are now?" Nancy asked, taking a different approach.

"It was dark when they brought me here. I could distinguish nothing."

"You are at Heath Castle."

"Heath Castle! You mean—Walt—?"

"Walter Heath died a number of years ago," Nancy said gently. "He loved you to the end and willed all his property to you."

"Walt—dead!" the woman whispered. "Then to the very end he thought of me as I used to be—beautiful, and a talented dancer."

"He thought of you as you still are," the policewoman spoke up. "A beautiful character with great charm."

"But these withered, ugly legs!" she cried out. "Oh, I want to be left alone with my sorrows. I have my little farm. Take me back there, please."

"You mean you don't want Heath Castle?" asked Lieutenant Masters.

"I loved Heath Castle, and I loved Walt," Florianna said brokenly. "But I hid myself away so he never would see me as a cripple. Perhaps it is foolish pride, but it seems best that I finish out my days as I am doing."

"Your sister Vera wants to see you very much," said Nancy. "She is a widow now with a little girl who looks a great deal like you."

For the first time, Florianna was deeply moved. "Vera has a little girl?" she murmured. "Where is she?"

"She and her mother, Mrs Fenimore, live in River Heights. The child's name is Joan. She likes flowers and gardening just as you do. I can't tell you the whole story now, but they need your help."

"If I had known before—" Florianna began.

"You were too proud to write to your sister?"

"Yes, at the beginning. Then later, a letter I sent to her came back. I had no idea where she was."

"Mrs Fenimore and Joan want to leave the neighbourhood where they live. Joan would be so happy in the gardens here," Lieutenant Masters said.

"Are the gardens still beautiful?" the former dancer asked dreamily.

Nancy hated to tell the woman the truth. She tried to soften it by saying, "They have been badly neglected. But they could be re-planted. Only one who truly loved the place, though, would want to do it."

"To me it would be a challenge," Florianna said with sudden spirit. "A memorial to Walt."

She added that the castle and its grounds really were pretty large for only three people.

"What a wonderful spot it would be for under-privileged children," the policewoman mused. "River Heights has always needed just such a place, especially for its crippled youngsters."

"I'd like to help them too!" Florianna announced excitedly. "Yes, I'll build this place into a beauty spot again! I'll bring Joan and Vera here. And later we'll see about the others."

"Good!" approved Nancy. "We'll take you right to

your sister, and then I'll go to settle my score with Mr Hector Keep!"

The trio had reached the foot of the stairway. Before the crippled woman could be helped up the steps, there came a disturbing sound from overhead.

The next instant the trap door dropped into place. As the bolt clicked, a voice reached their ears.

"That'll hold you! Try to get out now!"

The footsteps died away. Then all was quiet in the dungeon.

· 24 ·   *Keep's Final Triumph*

NANCY darted up the stairway to test the trap door. As she had feared, it was locked.

"We're prisoners!" she exclaimed. "Hector Keep or one of his men must have heard us!"

Lieutenant Masters was even more worried than Nancy, but she said calmly:

"I feel sure there's no cause for alarm. Anyone trying to leave the grounds will be captured by police guards. And when we fail to show up, help will come."

"But will the trap door be noticed by anyone?" Nancy asked dubiously. Then hopefully she added, "Perhaps I can find another exit."

While Lieutenant Masters remained with Florianna, she searched the various cells. No exit could be found. The only openings were the high grilled windows. Nancy carried her discouraging report to the young officer.

"Miss Masters, have you a police whistle?" she asked, struck by a sudden idea.

The woman nodded. "Yes, and a gun, too."

"Then maybe we can get out of here! By standing on my shoulders, you should be able to reach one of the windows and signal for help."

"Hope that'll work," the officer said after blowing her whistle a dozen times. "If not, I'll try firing a few shots."

Nancy sat down on the steps beside her to wait. Florianna was far from talkative, but the girl gradually drew her out. One of the first questions Nancy asked her was whether Walter Heath had given her a large pearl.

"No, but he was going to. It was being made into a ring when I went away."

Nancy next inquired if her fiancé had had a special name for her.

"Yes, he called me his little Cinderella," Florianna said, smiling at the recollection. "Once Walt asked me to step into a block of newly made cement with one of my dancing slippers. He said he was going to set it in the garden wall opposite the Poet's Nook. I suppose it was a lover's foolish idea."

"That wasn't foolish," Nancy replied. "It was one of the most sensible things Walter Heath ever did. That footprint clue in the crumbling wall will prove your claim to the Heath fortune against an imposter!"

Suddenly Nancy felt the woman beside her slump forward. In an instant, the girl had caught her and placed her on the floor.

"We *must* get out of here!" said Nancy.

"I'll fire some shots," the lieutenant decided. "Will

you stand by the window again, Nancy?"

Once more the officer climbed to the girl's shoulders. At this moment Florianna groaned.

"Wait!" cried Nancy. "If she's coming to, the shots will frighten her!"

The officer agreed and was glad Nancy had stopped her. As the victim on the floor regained consciousness, they could hear sounds of creaking boards at a distance.

"Listen!" commanded the policewoman.

Voices and footsteps could be heard echoing through the old castle. The lieutenant blew her police whistle.

"Where are you?" called a voice.

The officer shouted that they were below the trap door in the tower.

"Who locked you in there?" a policeman demanded angrily after the three prisoners had been released.

"I'm not sure," Nancy answered. "Probably Mr Hector Keep. He must have escaped."

"Oh, no he didn't," said a voice triumphantly. "We nabbed him. Also these two characters." He revealed Biggs, Cobb and Keep, all handcuffed.

"This is an outrage!" the lawyer snapped. "You can't arrest me. I have a perfect right to be on this property. The others are trespassers."

Coolly, Nancy presented her evidence against Keep. She accused him of stealing jewellery from the estate, a claim that could be proved by photographs found in Walter Heath's box.

"And that is not the worst!" she said to him. "You pretended to look for the woman who was to inherit the estate, but you didn't try to find her because you knew she would expose your dishonesty. To protect yourself, you produced an imposter with whom you had made a bargain. When you found out I was on the trail of the real Florianna, you had her spirited away and locked in a dungeon here!"

The crooked lawyer had not yet seen Florianna, who was seated on the winding stairs in the tower. Playing her trump card, Nancy now stepped aside. Speechless, Keep stared at the crippled dancer.

"So what?" he demanded after a moment. "I had nothing to do with bringing her here! And she can't prove she's the missing dancer. Just look at her!"

"Oh, yes, I can prove it!" Florianna retorted with spirit. "The imprint of my dancing shoe is embedded in a wall at Heath Castle. Furthermore, I still have the slipper that made the imprint!"

"What's that got to do with it? The real Florianna is at the Riverview Hotel!" Keep blustered. "She has a note to prove her identity. A note signed 'Walt.'"

"Don't you mean half a note?" Nancy inquired significantly. "I have the rest."

Cobb and Biggs looked startled. "You?" cried the latter. "Where did you find it?"

"At the factory after the explosion."

The men hung their heads guiltily, admitting they had been there. Biggs added:

"Hooker here found the note in a desk Mr Keep sold. He tore it in two pieces, expecting the old man to cough up more money for the second half."

Nancy was startled to hear Cobb addressed as Hooker, though it confirmed what the girl had thought. To her inquiry if he were Jeddy's father, the man nodded sullenly that he was.

"Then that explains why the boy came to Heath

Castle!" she exclaimed. "He learned about the estate from Joan. You in turn heard from your son that Florianna was missing, so you and Biggs got together. Biggs suspected his former employer had hidden some valuable things in the estate walls and you two convinced Mr Keep he ought to hire you to look for them. When you men found them, you kept the things for yourselves."

"You guessed right, but I don't know how," said Biggs.

"I know nothing about any of this!" shouted the mortified lawyer.

"Mr Keep, it looks as if the case against you is pretty serious," said Lieutenant Masters.

"I tell you I never saw these men before," Keep insisted. "Nor that crippled woman, either. Now all of you get out of here!"

For a long second there was silence. Then slowly Florianna got to her feet. Her eyes ablaze, she pointed a finger at Keep, saying:

"Arrest that man! Arrest him for kidnapping!"

The wily lawyer's jaw dropped. Then he recovered himself. "The woman is crazy!" he shouted.

"The night you came to my farm and brought me here you wore a disguise," said Florianna accusingly. "At first I didn't recognize you. But your voice—I know your voice." The former dancer's eyes burned with hate as she added, "I shall prosecute you to the fullest extent of the law for Walter Heath's sake!"

Hector Keep knew he was beaten. There was too much evidence against him. But he would not give up the fight yet. Fairly hissing as he spoke, he looked straight at Nancy Drew and cried out:

"If you had minded your own business, there wouldn't have been all this trouble! But you needn't feel triumphant over it. You think there are treasures and money for Florianna. You're wrong. There's nothing in the estate. Not one penny!"

· 25 · *Heath Castle Restored*

THE dramatic scene in the tower of Heath Castle ended abruptly. The policemen and their prisoners went one way; Nancy, Lieutenant Masters, and Florianna headed for the Fenimore cottage.

When they reached her sister's home, Florianna asked Nancy to go in first and break the news, telling briefly of her present condition and of what had transpired during the past few hours.

"Oh, you've found my sister!" Mrs Fenimore cried, after Nancy had spoken to her. "You wonderful girl! I don't care if we never have Heath Castle. To think Flossie is alive, and we can be together again!"

In the meantime Florianna had requested that all legal matters be attended to by Mr Drew. The lawyer had lost no time in having Keep and the other men prosecuted, but his report to Nancy after an investigation was discouraging.

"Cobb and Biggs admit having found several bottles of valuable dye hidden in the cloister walls, as you suspected. But they sold them and kept the money. Since then they've spent it."

Nancy had been hopeful that Keep's dire prediction

regarding the estate money would not be borne out, but such was not the case. Mr Drew had discovered that the total Heath assets were twenty dollars and a ruined castle with a few pieces of furniture.

"How about the Heath pearl, Dad? You didn't find it?"

"No. I'll keep on trying, of course. Frankly, I don't feel hopeful about the prospect."

"The cloister walls may still contain a few treasures," the girl suggested, unwilling to admit total defeat.

"I've had the place searched, Nancy. Workmen even removed the Cinderella block of cement below the wall fountain, but there was nothing behind it. Everything's gone."

"Then what's to be done?" Nancy asked unhappily.

"Heath Castle will have to be sold for what it will bring, but I'm afraid that won't be much, considering its location and present condition. Florianna wants to keep the property, but she can't. She has barely enough funds to operate Clover Farm."

"What if I did solve the mystery of Heath Castle?" she sighed. "I wasn't able to save the estate or help the Fenimores financially. And they need help so badly."

Nancy pondered the problem, but it was not until the next day that an idea came to her.

Dashing from the house, she got out her roadster and headed for Mehearty's yacht home. The old man had barely greeted her when she excitedly propounded her scheme. Mehearty shook his head.

"Your idea's good, me lass," he agreed. "The only trouble is there's nary a whelk with dye in it left in that cove near the factory. The one that stained your friend's dress must 'a been the last one alive."

"Then you've investigated the inlet since we were there?" Nancy asked.

Mehearty nodded.

"How about the beach at Heath Castle? Did you find anything there?"

"I never really looked," replied the old sailor.

"Then let's go there right away and look!"

Once at the beach the old clam digger set to work with a will. As Nancy watched, he brought up shell after shell from beneath the wet surface.

"Whelks!" he exclaimed excitedly. "And dye in 'em, too!"

Nancy wanted to dance for joy, but she controlled herself until Mehearty had dug up several dozen of the mollusks.

"You hit it, Miss Nancy!" he cried. "No doubt of it now," he grinned happily. "The place is full o' whelks."

Nancy felt as if a great weight had been lifted from her shoulders. Now Florianna would have an income. She could keep Heath Castle and fix it up.

"There's one more thing I must do," the girl thought as she and Mehearty returned to River Heights. "Talk to Cobb and Biggs."

Nancy drove directly to the jail and asked to speak first to Biggs. Since this was his initial offence, she decided he would be more likely to answer her questions truthfully than the former convict. She told the ex-chauffeur of her recent discovery and asked him if he had found any notations with the bottles of dye. When he demurred about answering, the girl suggested that his sentence might be lightened if he told her everything he knew.

"All right. I'll tell you," he said grudgingly. "I got nothing to lose."

The prisoner revealed that certain notes had been attached to each bottle of dye. Cobb Hooker had thought them of no value, but Biggs had hidden them under a certain flagstone in the cloister walk.

Nancy, overjoyed, hastened homewards to tell her father the good news. He looked at her fondly; and how proud he was of her!

"Nancy, my dear, you've saved the day for Florianna and the others," he said, smiling. Then he added, "I'll see what I can do for Biggs."

There were weeks of uncertainty before the dye project was put into effect. Mr Drew advanced money to restore the button factory, part of which was to be used as a laboratory. Mehearty was placed in charge of beach operations and a young chemist, using the notations left by Walter Heath, gradually worked out several lovely colours from the dye found in the whelks.

During the waiting period, Nancy kept on wondering whether Walter Heath might not have made other discoveries. One idea which plagued her was why he had placed the Cinderella footprint in that particular spot. At last a solution came to her.

"The water in the fountain—it gave George and Bess and me a tremendous lift!" she thought excitedly. "Maybe it has special value!"

Again Nancy Drew had guessed correctly. An analysis of the water proved it to have unusually beneficial qualities, even curative effects in bone disorders. Arrangements were made with a bottling concern to market it.

Presently, with money pouring in from two sources, Florianna was given a free hand to establish the gardens at Heath Castle, just as they had been during her romance with its former owner.

The crippled woman moved to the estate, taking Mrs Fenimore and Joan with her. For weeks she planned and supervised. Then came a wonderful day when she was able to fill the gardens with crippled children, now laughing and happy.

One afternoon, upon invitation, Nancy, Bess, George, Mr Drew and Lieutenant Masters journeyed to the estate to view the many changes. The great gates stood open. The visitors drove up a winding road between avenues of trimmed hedge and trees. The three girls smiled when they recalled how different everything had seemed to them on their former visits there.

"It doesn't make me feel a bit creepy now," laughed Bess.

"Those burning eyes that watched me from behind the evergreen!" Nancy chuckled. "I know that they were Cobb Hooker's!"

"With him in jail, what's to become of Mrs Hooker and Jeddy?" asked George.

"She's gone to work," replied the policewoman. "Jeddy has been sent to a special school, because only last week he was caught trying to snatch a handbag. By the way, he was wearing his father's clothes."

"Just like the time when he ran off with my bag and the pearl from old Mehearty's clam," Nancy said.

"It certainly was clever of you, Lieutenant Masters, to have solved that mystery and recovered the pearl for Nancy," said George.

The visitors got out of the car near the restored loggia and paused to admire the repairs which had been made to the crumbling walls. The gardens were a mass of bloom. The lawn in front of the castle was velvety smooth and free from weeds.

"How did Florianna ever accomplish so much in such a short time?" Nancy marvelled.

Several pigeons alighted near by. One of them, startled, flew to the parapet of the far tower of Heath Castle and began to coo. George smiled and whispered to Nancy:

"You were right. Those sounds we heard the first day we came here were only pigeons cooing!"

"I guess I let my imagination run away with me when I was locked in the tower," laughed Nancy. "At that time their cooing sounded human!"

Bess called the girls' attention to the children who had come out on the lawn to play. A few were in wheel chairs, but they pushed them about with amazing skill.

"Florianna is doing remarkable work with these youngsters," said Lieutenant Masters. "She's putting new spirit into them. Joan is developing into a fine little girl, too. She's proving to be a great help to her aunt."

"What is she doing?" asked Bess.

"Florianna is giving exercises to the children to restore nimbleness to their bodies. Joan does the demonstrating. And incidentally, Joan is the delight of her aunt. She's going to be a wonderful dancer some day."

"And take up where Florianna left off," said Bess dreamily.

The callers were greeted cordially by the mistress of

Heath Castle and her sister, now almost restored to perfect health. Tea was served on the terrace. Afterwards, Florianna invited her guests to the Poet's Nook, to see the children who were lined up at the drinking fountain.

"The water is helping to build strong bodies," she said proudly. "Oh, it means so much to me to bring these boys and girls here! I'd never have forgiven myself if I had returned to a lonely life at Clover Farm."

Mr Drew had been waiting for this very moment. Taking a tiny box from his pocket, he slipped it into Florianna's hand.

"A little surprise," he explained.

The woman slowly raised the lid. Nestled in purple velvet was a ring set with a huge pearl.

"Not the one Walt meant for me?" Florianna asked, dazed.

"Yes."

"But how did you recover it? I thought Hector Keep had found the ring and sold it."

"Dad was able to trace it," Nancy spoke up. "Mr Keep failed to notice the inscription inside."

Tears filled Florianna's eyes as she read, " 'To my Cinderella.' I'll wear the ring always in memory of Walt," she whispered, her voice trembling. "Oh, Nancy, my dear friend, and Mr Drew, you've made me very, very happy!"

Nancy smiled. She was glad the mystery had been brought to a successful close. Now she could devote more time to a new one on which she was working. Already Nancy was calling it the *Mystery of the Tolling Bell*.

Her gaze wandered along the stately cloister of Heath

Castle. With the afternoon sun sinking low, the shadows in the passageway had never looked more beautiful.

"Don't thank me for helping you, Florianna," Nancy said earnestly, taking her hand. "Thank these crumbling walls. They provided the clue that brought you here. And forever they'll remain a symbol of mystery and romance!"

The Mystery of the Tolling Bell

·1· *An Unusual Pushcart*

"NANCY, aren't we almost at Candleton? I'm tired of driving."

A freckled, athletic-looking girl, with the boyish name of George Fayne, stretched wearily in the roadster which sped along towards the ocean.

Nancy Drew, who was driving, shrugged her shoulders and breathed deeply of the tangy salt air. A gust of wind blew her golden hair across her eyes. Tossing it aside, she smiled at the two girls with her; George, and George's cousin, Bess Marvin.

"A few more miles," she replied. "But it's worth waiting for."

"You mean because of the mystery at Candleton?" Bess asked teasingly. "Personally, right now I'm more interested in food and getting myself fixed up."

Opening a compact, she gazed in its mirror at her shiny snub nose. Forgetting for a moment that the mirror magnified, she wrinkled her forehead in displeasure and added:

"Maybe I ought to diet!"

Nancy laughed. "We have to eat, figure or no figure," she said. "Perhaps we'll come to a fishing village where we can get some lobster. Like it?"

"Never ate any," replied Bess, who preferred cake and ice cream to any other kind of food.

The three girls, who lived in River Heights, were en route to Candleton on White Cap Bay. They had been invited to spend a brief vacation there as the guests of

Mrs John Chantrey. For many years Mrs Chantrey had been a close friend and client of Nancy's father, the well-known lawyer, Carson Drew. He was to meet the girls in the little town.

"I think your father was smart to make the trip by plane instead of riding with us," George observed as the car swung round another sharp curve. "At least he won't die of starvation."

"This is really a business trip for Dad," Nancy said, to divert the minds of her friends from food. "Poor Mrs Chantrey was swindled out of a lot of money, and Dad is trying to get it back for her."

"How did she lose it?" George asked curiously.

"Dad didn't tell me many of the details," Nancy replied. "But he did hint at mystery, and said I might help him. Mrs Chantrey is a lovely person, and I hope we can help her. She was once very wealthy, you know."

"Now she runs a tearoom?" George inquired.

"Yes. She decided to open a gift shop and tearoom after she lost most of her money."

"I was hoping the mystery at Candleton would be about something more romantic than just lost money," remarked Bess in disappointment.

Nancy's eyes twinkled. "Oh, but there is another mystery!" she said. "Maybe you'll like that one better. Mrs Chantrey mentioned in her letter that something ghostly and unexplainable happens along the coast of White Cap Bay."

"Well, that's different," said George, interested at once. "Is your father going to work on that, too?"

"Oh, no," Nancy laughed. "He's a lawyer, not a detective! His only interest in Candleton is to get back Mrs Chantrey's money."

"Nancy, you know that your father is the best lawyer

in the state! He could solve any problem," Bess declared confidently.

"He also has an equally clever daughter named Nancy," added George loyally. "Furthermore, she has two able helpers! If the three of us can't solve the two mysteries of White Cap Bay in next to no time —"

"Look!" Bess interrupted, pointing to a sign on the right-hand side of the road. "Fisher's Cove!" she fairly shouted. "We're coming to a town!"

Driving on to Main Street, they saw two hotels and several restaurants. Nancy noticed a sign with the name Wayside Inn. An arrow under the sign pointed up a side road.

"Let's go there," she suggested. "It sounds attractive."

She turned the car and presently they came to a freshly painted, white house overlooking the surf.

"This is fine!" George approved. "Pull up under that tree, Nancy."

The Wayside Inn proved to be cool, clean and inviting. Although the hour was late, the woman in charge assured the girls she could serve them luncheon.

"We have only puffed shrimp and French fried clams left," she announced.

Nancy found her luncheon very appetizing. In addition to the sea food there were tomatoes, cabbage salad, potatoes, lemonade, and for dessert, apple pie.

"I know I've gained a dozen pounds!" Bess moaned as they paid their bill and left the inn. "I shouldn't have eaten so much."

"I feel like a puffed shrimp myself!" groaned George. "Let's walk round Fisher's Cove awhile before we drive on. A little exercise will be good for us."

Although eager to reach Candleton, Nancy agreed to the suggestion. Leaving the car under the tree, they took a path which led from the sandy shore to the main street of the village.

"Oh, look!" cried Nancy suddenly, as she came to a corner. "Isn't that attractive?"

From a side street came the musical tinkle of a bell. At first Bess and George, some distance behind her, saw nothing. But a moment later a dark-haired woman pushing a flower-decked cart came into view. Spying the girls, she moved briskly towards them.

"Wonder what she's selling," Bess said in an undertone.

From a wire stretched across the cart dangled strings of tiny red metal hearts and a little bell.

The woman, obviously of foreign birth, wore a long red and white costume with an embroidered red heart on one sleeve. As she drew near to the girls, she addressed them in a torrent of words.

"You buy from Madame? I sell all zese articles *tres bon* for beautyment. Come see." She held up a bottle of perfume, some powder, and a lipstick.

By this time quite a number of people had gathered about the cart. Many in the crowd were young country girls who seemed awed by the elaborate display of cosmetics.

"Just like ze city girls buy in New York," Madame glorified her products. "Sold only in ze best salons."

"I don't recall seeing that brand before," Nancy remarked, observing that all the cosmetic containers bore the French words *Mon Coeur*.

"It means 'my heart'," translated Madame. "Powder, lipstick, rouge, and perfume, zey come in sets. Zey bring to mademoiselle beauty and allure."

"How much?" inquired a rather unattractive, large-boned country girl.

"For ze perfume, three dollars. One lipstick, rouge for ze cheeks, powder, and ze smallest heart of perfume —you take all, I make it five dollars."

"That's a lot of money," commented the country girl.

"I give you demonstration to go wiz eet."

"All right."

Madame took the note offered her, then quickly applied the cosmetics to the girl's face. The woman's sales talk convinced other bystanders. They bought the *Mon Coeur* products freely, while the blonde country girl walked to a mirrored showcase window in a shop to admire herself. To the horror of Nancy and George, she promptly put on more of the cosmetics and sprinkled herself liberally with the perfume. Then, satisfied but conspicuous, she went down the street.

Bess had been watching Madame steadily, and could not resist the temptation to buy. "I'll take a small bottle of perfume," she decided. "Also this lipstick and powder."

"Bess!" remonstrated George. "You don't know a thing about *Mon Coeur* products!"

"My zings are of ze finest," Madame retorted angrily. "You have no right—"

"Bess, do come away," Nancy urged her friend.

Bess might have retreated without buying, but quick as a flash Madame thrust the articles into her hand and snatched the money the girl had taken from her purse.

"Is this perfume the same as in the sample bottle?" Bess asked doubtfully, observing that the contents of the vial were lighter in colour than the liquid in the opened bottle.

"Zey all ze same," snapped the woman. Giving Bess the change, she started hurriedly down the street with the flower-decked pushcart.

175

In her haste to get away, Madame cut directly across the road. The little bell jangled and the heart-shaped decorations swung back and forth.

A trap and old white horse came jogging down the street, its driver drowsing at the reins. Suddenly something frightened the mare. It gave a startled snort. Before the elderly driver realized what was happening, the animal bolted straight towards the woman and her cart.

With a scream of terror, Madame abandoned her cosmetics and raced for safety, dodging into a shop. The horse plunged wildly along the street, pulling the trap over the kerb, then back into the street again. Nearly all the pedestrians had taken cover, for no one could guess which way the frightened animal would gallop next.

The flower-decked cart stood deserted in the middle of the street, directly in the path of the runaway horse. Before Bess or George could stop her, Nancy darted out and wheeled the cart to safety. A moment later the horse flashed by. Not until they had gone another block did the driver of the trap finally recover control of his mare.

"Nancy, you might have been killed!" Bess cried out. She was trembling.

"I agree with you," Nancy replied, parking the cart under an awning. "I acted impulsively. Well, shall we get the car and go on to Candleton?"

"The sooner we get there, the better I'll like it," agreed Bess.

Without waiting for Madame to return, the three friends started to cross the street. As Nancy stepped down from the kerb a poorly dressed woman rushed up to her and seized her arm.

"You're the one!" she screamed. "I'm going to have you arrested!"

Startled, Nancy retreated a step. But the excited woman pursued her, holding tightly on to her arm.

"You're a thief, and you've got no business in this town!" she shouted in a hoarse voice. "You've ruined my daughter and taken her money! Police! Police!"

· 2 · *A Strange Customer*

NANCY pulled herself free from the excited woman. By this time Bess and George, aware that their friend was in difficulty, darted to Nancy's side.

"Police! Police!" the woman screamed again. "My daughter's been robbed!"

"Who is your daughter?" Nancy asked the woman sharply.

"You should know! You sold her that there red stuff she put on her cheeks and lips!"

Light dawned upon Nancy. "Then your daughter is the girl who bought several things from Madame with the pushcart."

"She bought them from you!" the woman accused the Drew girl. "Oh, you needn't look so innocent! I saw you wheel that cart o' yours out of the street when that horse ran away!"

Nancy explained that Madame sold the cosmetics, not she. Bess and George supported her story, but the farm woman would not listen.

"Here comes a policeman now!" George muttered in Nancy's ear.

It was not the first time Nancy Drew had found herself in a predicament. Her young life had been fairly crammed with adventure.

Nancy's mother was dead. For many years the girl had been reared by Mrs Gruen, the family housekeeper, whom she regarded almost as a parent. Because Nancy was unusually sensible, clever and talented, Mrs Gruen allowed her a great deal of freedom, particularly when she was assisting her father on one of his cases.

Nevertheless, the housekeeper sometimes felt that Nancy took entirely too many risks. She had not approved when only a few months earlier those inseparable companions, Bess, George and Nancy, had explored Heath Castle, an abandoned estate not far from the city of River Heights. Their investigations had resulted in finding the "Clue in the Crumbling Wall," but Nancy had spent many trying hours locked in an ancient dungeon before the adventure was over.

Now, as the policeman ran towards the girls, Nancy waited calmly, for she knew she had done nothing wrong.

"What's going on here?" the patrolman demanded as he hurried up to the group.

"This girl robbed me!" the woman accused. " She tricked my daughter into buying a lot of trash to put on her face."

"This woman has mistaken me for someone else," Nancy said quietly.

"Then where is the other person?" demanded Nancy's accuser.

The girls turned to gaze towards the spot where they had left the cart. It was gone! Madame must have taken it away.

"I want my money back!" the woman resumed her tirade.

"See here," said the policeman sternly, "you're creating an unnecessary disturbance. What is your charge against this girl?"

"That she sold my daugher a lot of worthless rubbish!"

At this moment a man stepped up to the group, introduced himself as Professor Atkins, and said he had seen the whole episode from down the street. Smiling at Nancy, he told how she had saved the flower-decked pushcart and had not received so much as a thank-you from its owner. The woman turned pale.

"I—I guess I've made a mistake," she muttered. "Forget what I said."

She retreated hastily. Nancy thanked the professor. Then, eager to leave, she quickly led the way to her car and drove out of town.

En route to Candleton, Bess opened the vial of *Mon Coeur* perfume she had bought. After she had sniffed the perfume, the girl gazed at her companions a bit sheepishly.

"I'm afraid I was swindled," she said. "This isn't as good as the sample."

"It's fragrant, anyway," Nancy remarked soothingly, as Bess held the bottle under her friend's nose.

Then George sniffed at the bottle and pretended to collapse on the cushions. "This would slay a man instead of making him propose, as Madame suggested. Take my advice and throw it away."

"And waste all my money?" Bess recorked the bottle. "No. I'll keep it."

The road no longer offered the monotonous scenery it had on the other side of Fisher's Cove. Instead, it ran lazily along moors carpeted with low-growing juniper, and at points the rocks split into colourful masses over which leaped the sea's filmy spray.

"We're not far from Candleton now," Nancy declared, as cliffs loomed in the distance.

Abruptly the car rounded a bend, and the girls caught their first glimpse of White Cap Bay. Never before had they seen such a stretch of beautiful water. Once only a fishing town, the little village of Candleton was now a fashionable summer resort with attractive cottages and fine hotels.

Mrs Chantrey's comfortable home stood at some distance from the beach, just beyond the business section of the town. Nancy drove the car up an attractive private drive and stopped in front of the house.

A young Negro maid opened the door, and smilingly said that she was Juno. She helped them carry their luggage to their rooms, and explained that her mistress was at the tearoom. Mrs Chantrey had left word that the girls were to make themselves at home.

"Let's go down to the tearoom," George suggested.

Presently the girls saw Mrs Chantrey's tearoom, the Salsandee Shop. Bright-coloured umbrellas dotted its outdoor dining-room and garden.

"What a clever name," Bess observed, as Nancy explained the tearoom specialized in salads and sandwiches. "What does the 'dee' stand for?"

"I don't know. We'll have to ask Mrs Chantrey."

A number of customers were seated in the outdoor dining-room waiting to be served, while others were waiting inside. A harassed waitress moved swiftly about, trying without success to take a dozen orders. Nervous and confused, she showed her annoyance as Nancy stopped her to inquire for Mrs Chantrey.

"She's in the kitchen," the girl replied, "but please don't bother her now unless it's important. Several of our girls failed to show up today, and we're nearly frantic trying to serve everyone."

Nancy and her chums might have gone away quietly to await Mrs Chantrey at her home, had not an idea occurred to Nancy.

"Why don't we pitch in and help her?" she demanded. "We've waited on tables before!"

"It would be fun!" agreed George.

Seeking their hostess in the kitchen, they found her frantically making dozens of salads. Bread in the toaster started to burn. With an exclamation of impatience, she switched off the current.

Mrs Chantrey, a woman in her mid-forties, was ordinarily a serene and attractively groomed person. Now a wisp of grey hair tumbled down over one eye, and a splotch of tomato ketchup stained her apron.

"Hello?" said Nancy cheerfully. "Do you need any help?"

Mrs Chantrey dropped a knife. Her face mirrored dismay. "Why, it's Nancy Drew, and these are your friends!" she gasped. "How ashamed I am to be found in such a state!"

"You need help and we're here to give it," Nancy offered with a smile. "Just tell us what to do."

"I can't put you girls to work the first moment you arrive! Why, you're my guests!"

"We'd like to do it," Bess spoke up. "Please let us."

"Then I won't protest any longer. You're a gift straight from heaven! If you can help out for an hour, the worst of the rush will be over."

Chatting excitedly, Mrs Chantrey tied aprons on the three girls. While George remained in the kitchen to make sandwiches, Nancy and Bess were sent to wait on tables. Seeking Dora, the waitress they had met a few minutes earlier, they requested instructions.

"You take the tables out in the garden," the girl directed Nancy, sizing her up as the more efficient of the two girls. "Bess and I will handle the inside dining-room. Here are your order pads. Don't try to carry too many dishes or you may have an accident."

"Waitress!" called an impatient voice.

"Everyone is in a dreadful mood," Dora whispered. "Some have been waiting nearly an hour for their food."

Nancy moved swiftly among the tables assigned to her. She took orders efficiently, learning the names of the dishes which made the Salsandee Shop so popular. A steady flow of food began to arrive from the kitchen, including the popular three-decker grilled lobster, cheese and tomato sandwich; the mixed green salad with minced ham and clam dressing; and the Dandee Tart, filled with steaming hot fish pudding topped with salmon-coloured meringue. The girls learned that the last syllable of the name Salsandee was derived from the "dee" in Dandee.

Customers, at first impatient and cross, soon began to smile at Nancy. After clearing one place she was amazed to find a dollar tip.

One of the last diners in the garden was a white-haired man with spectacles. He dawdled over a frosted glass of iced tea. Nancy hovered near, hopeful that he would leave, but instead he became talkative.

"Do you live here?" he inquired.

"No, I'm just a visitor, helping out," Nancy explained. "Actually, I'm not a waitress."

"Well, I'm a stranger to this town myself. Came here looking for a bell."

Nancy remained politely silent.

"Not an ordinary bell, but one that was made in a casting furnace in Boston during the Revolutionary War. A Paul Revere bell—that's what I'm after."

"Then you're an antique collector?" Nancy asked, becoming interested.

"Not exactly. Those old bells are valuable as antiques, but I want this particular one for another reason." The old man gazed at her with shrewd eyes. "They tell me there are any number of old bells to be had around this town."

"I wouldn't know about that," Nancy replied. "I arrived here only a few hours ago."

"I see, I see," muttered the stranger. Hurriedly drinking his iced tea, he dropped a coin by his plate and went down the path towards the ocean.

Wondering who the man might be, Nancy began to clear away the dishes. She dropped the coin in her pocket, intending to give it, and the other tips, to Dora.

As the girl picked up a plate, she noticed a folded piece of paper on the floor at her feet and brushed it aside. Then the thought struck her that the paper might be important. Perhaps the diner who had just left the garden dropped it.

Putting down her tray, Nancy picked up the paper. The handwriting on it was very old-fashioned. A puzzled look came over her face as she read the words, which were in French.

"Whoever finds this may become enormously wealthy," she translated in amazement. "In one of my XXX cast bells are embedded many jewels."

The paper had been torn in half, and the remainder of the strange message was missing!

·3· *Legend of the Cave*

As NANCY reread the mysterious words, Bess Marvin approached the table.

"Thank goodness, the last customer has gone!" she exclaimed, pulling off her apron. "Collect any tips, Nancy?"

"Uh-huh," her friend replied, her mind on the strange message.

"You're not listening!" Bess accused. "What is it you're reading, Nancy?"

"A paper I found on the floor after one of my customers left. He was an odd old fellow, Bess, and he told me he came to Candleton to find an antique bell made by Paul Revere!"

Offering the paper to her friend to read, Nancy waited expectantly for her comments.

"Jewels embedded in an XXX cast bell!" Bess translated. "Why, it's another mystery, Nancy!"

"Not so loud," the other warned with a quick glance around. "If the contents of this paper should become known, some dishonest person in Candleton might start buying up all the old bells around here and selling them at a fancy profit."

"What is an XXX bell, Nancy?"

"I don't know, but my guess is the three X's might be the trademark of the maker."

Mrs Chantrey dropped the paper into a desk drawer, instructing Dora to give it to the stranger, should he call. Then, grateful to the girls for helping her, she insisted they stop work and return to her cottage.

"I'll go with you," she declared. "Thanks to you most of the work is done. Dora will be able to take care of the few customers who may drop in between now and closing time."

The moon was coming up as the three girls walked along the beach with their hostess. Farther up White Cap Bay they glimpsed a lighthouse, and Mrs Chantrey pointed out Whistling Oyster Cove and Bald Head Cliff, two distinguished landmarks.

"Such picturesque names!" laughed George, stooping to pick up an odd-shaped shell. "Is fishing the chief occupation here, Mrs Chantrey?"

"I'd say the making of salt-water toffee is!" she chuckled. "And chewing it is the main pastime of the summer residents! But seriously, there is one interesting spot you must visit. Mother Mathilda's Candle Shop."

"Did those lovely ones at the Salsandee Shop come from there?" Bess inquired.

"Yes. You may have noticed they're slightly perfumed."

As Bess and George asked various questions about the village and its inhabitants, Nancy remained unusually quiet. She was thinking about her father, and wondering why he had not arrived. She was startled when her hostess suddenly asked:

"When will your father come to Candleton. Nancy? We were expecting him this morning."

"I thought he'd be here when we arrived," she replied. "He telephoned and said he was taking a plane from New York."

"Maybe he's at the house now," suggested Bess.

"I'm sure he's not." Nancy shook her head. "I left word for him to phone me at the tearoom." Her face became troubled. "I wonder if anything went wrong?" she said.

Although Mr Drew was a busy man, and Nancy understood that he might have been delayed by unexpected business, he had never failed to let his daughter know of a change in his plans.

"Now don't worry about your father," Mrs Chantrey said quickly. "He may have decided to come by train. Perhaps there's a telegram at home."

Nancy brightened at the suggestion. When they came to the cottage a few minutes later, however, she realized that the hope was a vain one. There was no message.

To relieve Nancy's mind, Mrs Chantrey telephoned the telegraph office and the airport. There was no word from the lawyer. Nancy decided that she could not allow worry over her father's absence to spoil the evening for Bess and George, so she pretended to dismiss the matter by saying that he surely would arrive the next morning.

"Tomorrow we must explore White Cap Bay," she declared. "Mrs Chantrey, you hinted at a mystery along the shore."

Her hostess smiled. "It concerns the cave at the base of Bald Head Cliff. My advice to you would be to avoid the spot."

"Please tell us why." Nancy moved forward in her chair.

"I've never been there myself," Mrs Chantrey continued, "but townspeople say it's spooky and dangerous. According to the story—"

"Yes?"

Mrs Chantrey laughed nervously. "I'm not sure I should repeat what I've heard," she said. "But then, I've never shared the superstitions of the local people."

By this time the girls were deeply interested, and begged her to tell them the story.

"According to the tale, Bald Head Cave is inhabited by a ghost," Mrs Chantrey revealed reluctantly. "I don't believe in ghosts, but the fact remains that some unhappy accidents have occurred lately in that area. Several persons nearly drowned, and one man did lose his life."

"How do the accidents happen?" Nancy questioned curiously.

"It's said the ghost causes water to rush out of the cave. It engulfs anyone in its path. He tolls a warning bell whenever reckless individuals venture too near his hideout, and if they don't leave at once there's trouble."

"How long has this been going on?" Nancy asked.

"I don't know exactly," Mrs Chantrey replied. "But not for long—at least, nothing of the sort occurred years ago. From what I hear, I judge the cave has always been here, but not the ghost nor the rushing water and the tolling bell."

"Has the cave been explored?" George asked practically.

"A few venturesome men have tried it but learned nothing. Evidently the ghost keeps close watch over his property."

The story excited Nancy's curiosity. She thought about it late into the night. Since she did not believe in ghosts, she concluded there must be some logical explanation for the phenomenon. As Nancy dropped off to sleep, she decided the only way to find out was to go there herself and investigate. Perhaps in the morning—

But in the morning Nancy forgot about exploring the cave, for no word had come from her father. Unable to hide her alarm, she called her home in River Heights.

Hannah Gruen had heard nothing from Mr Drew and she in turn became worried.

A call to the lawyer's office brought no reassurance. Mr Drew's secretary was on vacation, and the girl who was taking her place said she thought he had gone to Candleton.

"And there was no word from New York?"

"None at all."

Discouraged, Nancy thanked her and hung up. She became more and more worried.

"Perhaps he's been in an accident," she told her friends.

"Now do stop worrying, Nancy," Bess said kindly. "If your father had been in an accident, someone in River Heights would have been notified. Doesn't he always carry identification papers?"

"Yes, but—"

"Your father will be along any hour now, so stop building up gory pictures," George cut in. To get Nancy's mind off the matter, she added, "How about Bald Head Cave? Do we explore it this morning?"

"All right," agreed Nancy with forced cheerfulness. "I wonder how we reach the place?"

They learned from Juno that even at low tide the only safe approach to Bald Head was by motorboat. The maid's eyes rolled in fright when she learned the girls intended to go there, and she warned them not to venture near the cave. Nancy assured her they would be careful. She and her friends left the house and rented a sturdy craft from an old fisherman.

Under Nancy's guidance the little boat putt-putted slowly along the shore. Rising above the water, and stretching out for about two miles, were the colourful cliffs which had attracted artists from all parts of the country.

"I see a man up on that cliff with a telescope," George said, scowling. "He's looking at us. I hate people with telescopes. They have an unfair advantage!"

Nancy laughed as she steered nearer shore. "No doubt summer visitors are resented by the all-year inhabitants."

The man disappeared from view as the boat came into the shadow of the cliff.

"Look! The entrance to the cave!" George cried as they reached a secluded indentation about half a mile from the ocean. "It's rather large."

"Let's just look at it from the outside," Bess suggested nervously.

Nancy smiled as she switched off the boat's motor, allowing the craft to drift closer to shore. "We're safe enough so long as we stay in this boat," she declared. "But you know very well, Bess, we couldn't learn a thing without going inside the cave."

Bess, whose gaze had been focused steadily on the cave entrance, suddenly sat up so jerkily that she caused the boat to rock sideways. Glancing at their friend, Nancy and George were astonished to see that her chubby face mirrored terror.

"What is it?" George whispered.

For a moment Bess, badly shaken, could not speak. Then with a trembling hand, she pointed towards the dark mouth of the cavern, and said shakily:

"The ghost! I saw it in its white robe. It—it went back into the cave!"

·4· *Rushing Water*

STARTLED by Bess's words, Nancy and George gazed anxiously towards the cave entrance. They could see nothing but the dark opening framed by rocks and water.

"You must have imagined it, Bess," declared George. "There's no ghost—nothing white."

"Not now, but it was there!"

"What did it look like?" Nancy asked.

"I saw only a white blur. But then, ghosts aren't supposed to have a regular form."

"You probably mistook a sea gull for a ghost," George laughed.

Bess's lips drew into a thin, stubborn line. "It certainly was not a bird," she argued. "But forget it. Even if that cave were inhabited by twenty ghosts, I know I couldn't talk you two out of exploring it!"

Nancy had no intention of venturing farther in a reckless manner. As the boat drifted closer, she studied the entrance to the cave and listened intently.

"Hear any warning bell?" George asked jokingly.

Nancy shook her head. The only sound was the roar of the ocean in the distance.

"What's your plan?" George inquired after a moment.

"The cave is quite wide and if the water is deep enough we can row the boat inside," Nancy replied. From the bottom of the craft she picked up lead and line and began to take soundings at the entranceway.

"The water is nearly two feet deep inside the cave," she announced, measuring the wet section of the line. "Our boat shouldn't go aground."

Using the oars, the girls cautiously rowed through the cave entrance into the dark interior. Nancy, who always carried a flashlight in her bag, swept its beam over the jagged limestone walls.

The passageway in which the girls found themselves had a natural ledge on one side, etched from the rock by erosion. The walls were damp, and the temperature at least twenty degrees lower than it was in the sunny bay.

"It seems like a very ordinary cavern," commented George, relaxing. "No ghost. No bell. No water pouring out."

Nancy manoeuvred the boat to the ledge and fastened the painter securely to a jagged piece of rock.

"What are you going to do?" Bess demanded.

"I want to walk along the ledge for a short distance. This cave may have an inner room. It's too dark to tell from here, and if we take the boat much farther, we may have difficulty getting out."

Bess was reluctant to leave the boat, but when she saw that George intended going with Nancy, she too climbed out on to the ledge.

Walking ahead, Nancy flashed her light over the dark walls. "Hello!" she exclaimed, and her voice echoed weirdly. "Here's something!"

Bess and George moved closer to their friend. Over her shoulder they glimpsed a massive stone man whose half-closed eyes stared straight at them. Startled, Bess stifled a scream of terror.

"It's only a statue carved out of the rock," George scolded her. "Don't be a goose!"

191

Nancy's flashlight picked out the details of the figure. "My, it's large enough to be a real man!"

"It *is* real," whispered Bess in horror. "Look at his right hand! It's *moving*!"

Nancy started to say "Nonsense!" but the words froze on her lips. The stone man's upraised hand actually was moving! Even as she watched, it dropped to his side, rolled down the carven body, and fell with a splash into the water!

With a shriek of terror, Bess wheeled about and would have fled, but Nancy seized her wrist.

"It's only a piece of the statue chipping off," she reassured her. "For a second I was fooled too."

A moment later they heard a loud splash directly ahead of them. Focusing their eyes upon the spot, they were dismayed to see a dark object rise out of the water.

"That's no rock!" chattered Bess. "It's—it's something alive!"

The slithering creature, its sides glistening like satin, swam to the rocks, and pulled itself to the ledge.

"A seal!" whispered Nancy in relief. "I'll shoo him back into the water."

The seal, however, showed no interest in leaving his rocky perch. Instead, he rotated his head towards the girls, emitting a deafening bark which nearly split their eardrums.

"Do seals bite?" Bess asked nervously.

"I'm sure I don't know," Nancy replied. "The nearest I ever came to one before was at the zoo. This old fellow acts annoyed. He might do anything."

"I'm not going on!" Bess decided suddenly.

With that, she turned and hurried back towards the boat.

George picked up a small rock, intending to hurl it

at the seal. She raised her arm, only to let it fall to her side. So sharply did she draw in her breath that Nancy, who was standing beside her, heard the sound.

"What is it, George? What did you see?"

The seal had not moved. George's gaze was fixed upon a portion of the ledge far back in the cave.

"The ghost!" she whispered tremulously. "I saw it just then—a figure in white!"

Nancy had observed nothing, but George's fear increased her own growing uneasiness. A sixth sense warned her that they faced danger. For the first time since entering the underground passage, she considered turning back.

"Nancy, we'd better run!" George urged, unashamed. "I don't feel too happy about this place myself."

"It's not fair to leave Bess alone in the boat if something should happen," George said in a hushed voice.

"We'll go," Nancy agreed, her words hardly audible.

The two girls walked rapidly along the ledge towards the entrance. They had taken scarcely a dozen steps when a bell began to toll far back in the cave. Loud and full in tone, the pealing held a mournful note as if tolling for departed spirits.

Electrified by the sound, Nancy and George stopped suddenly. The same terrifying thought came to each of them.

"The warning bell Mrs Chantrey told us about!" cried George. "It rings just before water engulfs the cave!"

Nancy seized her by the hand. "Come on!" she urged. "We must get out of here—fast!"

It was too late!

"Listen!" George cried tensely. "That roaring sound —hear it?"

Both girls froze to the spot, for the sound they heard was the mad rush of a great wall of water plunging towards them with the speed of an express train.

"Run!" screamed Nancy. "Run for your life!"

The boat was still some distance away, tied to the jagged rock. Nancy knew what she and George could never reach it before the water struck them. But Bess, who stood on the ledge beside the craft, might escape.

"Get in the boat! Cast off!" Nancy shouted frantically.

It took Bess only a second to realize her great danger. She bent down to loosen the rope. Paralyzed with fright, her fingers became numb and would not unfasten the knot.

The next instant the great curtain of water raced through the cave, sweeping everything before it. Nancy and George, struggling desperately, were engulfed.

Instinctively Bess clung to the painter of the boat. As the water struck her, the rope snapped free of the rock. The craft raced towards the cave entrance.

Bess, holding fast to the rope, was carried face downwards through the torrent.

• 5 • *Nancy's Predicament*

ALMOST suffocated, Bess clung with all her strength to the rope as the boat shot from the mouth of the cave. Finally, when the speed of the craft lessened, she took a deep breath, and grasped the gunwale.

The motorboat was half-filled with water. Should she climb aboard? No, it probably would sink. Swimming with one hand, the girl tried to tow the boat towards shore. It was difficult going.

Frantically her eyes darted towards the cave entrance. Water still boiled from the cavern's gaping mouth. What had happened to her friends? She could not see them.

"Nancy! George!" she shouted.

There was no answer. Bess did not try to call out again. She concentrated all her efforts upon reaching the rocky beach.

Presently her feet struck bottom. Standing upright, she pulled the boat in so that it could not float away, and began bailing water. As she worked, the distressed girl kept scanning the bay, hoping she might see Nancy or George.

"They're both good swimmers. I'm sure they reached safety," she told herself hopefully.

But in a moment panic seized her again. What if the girls had not been swept from the cave. They might have been caught inside and drowned!

Her mind numbed by fear, Bess worked automatically on the boat, hardly taking her gaze from the water. She suddenly detected an object some distance away. Could it be a swimmer?

Leaping to a high rock, Bess shaded her eyes against the glare of the sun. Yes, someone was swimming feebly. Even as she looked, the person disappeared.

"Hold on! Don't give up!" she shouted, as the swimmer reappeared. "I'll reach you in a minute."

Rushing to the boat, Bess tried to start the motor. It was waterlogged and refused to catch. The oars had been washed overboard.

Kicking off her shoes, Bess plunged into the water.

"I'm coming!" she screamed. Then, "George!"

Bess reached her cousin not a moment too soon. George's strength was nearly gone.

"I'm—all—in," the girl gasped. "Hurt my arm."

Bess wasted no time in talk. She decided at once to use the swimmer's carry.

"Look into my eyes. Put your hands on my shoulders," she instructed quickly.

George obeyed, but at that instant a wave broke over the girls' heads. They were buried in an avalanche of water, and came up choking and fighting for breath.

"It's no use," gasped George, completely spent. "I can't make it. Save yourself."

Bess, realizing her cousin no longer could help herself, grasping her in the cross chest carry and pulled her through the water. But it seemed as if she could not possibly reach the shore. Burdened by George's weight, and with her own strength giving out, she found it harder and harder to keep going.

"But I *must* not fail," she told herself.

Then a wave, larger than any of the others, struck the two girls, lifted them up bodily, and wrenched them apart. It seemed impossible that they would ever reach shore.

But just as Bess was about to give up in despair, her feet came in contact with the beach. Standing up, she discovered that the water was only a little above her waist.

A short distance away George was being tumbled about in the breakers. Wading to her, Bess pulled the exhausted girl to safety. It was several moments before either one could speak. Finally George mumbled:

"Nancy— Is—she—safe?"

Fear for their missing friend drove Bess to her feet. Anxiously she looked about. Nancy was not in sight.

"Nancy—was—beside me—in the cave," she said brokenly. "That was the last I saw of her."

Tears rolled down the cheeks of the two girls. Each was silent with her own thoughts. Then suddenly Bess sprang towards the motorboat. She was just in time to prevent the rising tide from carrying it down White Cap Bay. As the girl tied the rope to a rock on the shore, she was startled to hear a faint "Hello" from the direction of the cliff above the cave.

"Nancy's voice!" she exclaimed joyfully. "She's safe! But where?"

Excitedly calling a reply, she and George waited eagerly for another shout. But it did not come. Bess waded into the water and looked up. Nancy was sitting high up on the cliff among the rocks.

"There she is!" Bess cried. "Thank goodness!"

George was so relieved, her strength returned at once. She got up, and together the girls shouted reassuringly to Nancy. But she did not seem to see or hear them. How were they to reach her?

"We'll have to use the boat," George decided. "Where are the oars?"

"Gone. And the motor won't start," Bess said forlornly. "But maybe I can dry it off."

In a watertight compartment under one of the seats she found a few dry rags which she used to wipe off the engine parts. After several sputters the motor finally started and they were able to get under way.

"Now where's Nancy?" Bess demanded, steering towards the mouth of the cave and looking up.

Their friend had disappeared!

Shouting her name several times, the cousins cruised back and forth near the base of the cliff. Nancy, however, did not reappear.

"She may have found a road up there and decided to hitchhike to the boathouse," George decided at length. "Let's go back."

Reaching the boathouse, the girls spied Nancy's roadster parked exactly where it had been left a few hours earlier. Their friend was not there, and the old fisherman from whom they had rented the motor-boat reported that she had not returned.

The man looked hard at the cousins. Although the hot sun had dried their clothing, they presented a very bedraggled appearance indeed. They replied to the old fisherman's questions briefly, but did not tell him of their mishap at Bald Head Cave. They thanked him for the use of the boat, paid him for it and the lost oars, and left.

"We must find Nancy," George declared anxiously. "Let's take the car and drive to the cliff. We may meet her on the road." Fortunately, she knew where Nancy kept an extra key to the automobile.

"But what about your arm?" Bess objected.

"It feels much better," George declared. "The numbness is gone now. I can move it."

Meanwhile, Nancy was making an effort to recover from her own frightening experience. The great rush of water had washed her out of the cave just behind George. Being a strong swimmer, she made her way back to the cliff and struggled for a handhold amid the rocks some distance from the entrance of the cave.

She pulled herself out of the water, and for a time lay panting on the rocks. Then, getting to her feet, she looked about in search of her friends. The uneven line of the cliff screened a good bit of the view, and she could see no one.

After shouting for her friends several times, Nancy

climbed higher. From this perch, she spied the motorboat and Bess and George on the shore. Relieved that
they were safe, she tried to figure out a way to reach
them. It seemed best to climb to the top of the cliff and
then scramble down the other side to her friends. When
Nancy reached the top, she stood still to look around.
Suddenly she began to feel light-headed and had to sit
down.

"I'm getting to be a cissy," she scolded herself. "I
must go on."

But Nancy seemed unable to move from the spot. She
became so drowsy she had to lie down. The warm sun
and a faint sweet aroma added to her drowsiness.
Delightfully comfortable, she lost all count of time.

Then, as if from a long distance away, Nancy thought
she heard voices. Two men seemed to be arguing
violently. Or was she dreaming?

Pulling herself up to a sitting position with great
effort, Nancy gazed about her. She could see no one.
She must have imagined the voices.

"Am I going out of my mind?" she asked herself.

Then she promptly fell back on the rock and drifted
off to unconsciousness.

·6· *Warning by Telephone*

DEEP in slumber, Nancy dreamed that she lay cushioned
upon a soft, sweet-smelling meadow. Nearby sheep
grazed peacefully, and the faint tinkle of bells came as
music to her ears.

Presently two little brown elves crept from beneath a

bush and stared at her as if she were an intruder. Nancy heard one of them say:

"We can't allow her to stay here."

"We certainly can't," agreed the other elf whose voice was deeper. "We must move her before she wakes up."

Nancy tried to resist, but the elves seemed to have cast a spell over her. Powerless to move, she attempted to open her eyes but the lids felt as heavy as stones.

Borne upon the shoulders of the elves, she was carried a long distance. Then they put her down, but the couch was not a comfortable one. Something sharp cut into her back. Nancy rolled over, and suddenly was wide awake.

Sitting up, she gazed about her in utter bewilderment. Her clothing had dried in the sun but was very crumpled, reminding her of the struggle she had gone through to keep from drowning.

Nancy listened for the roar of the surf but could not hear it. The only sound was a low, humming noise which she finally traced to a nearby telephone pole. Then she discovered that she was in a roadside ditch strewn with sharp rocks and pebbles. Bayberry and other bushes shielded her view of a narrow dirt road.

"How did I get here?" thought Nancy, rubbing her eyes. "I remember climbing the cliff, but how did I cross the field to this ditch? The last I remember—let me see. Yes, I stretched out on a rock on the cliff."

Dimly she recalled the dream in which elves had transported her from her resting place. Had someone actually carried her to the roadside? She dismissed the possibility as fantastic.

Scrambling to her feet, Nancy gingerly tested her arms and legs. They were stiff and cramped, but she did not have a single scratch. Long exposure to the bright sun had tinted her face a deep pink, and her skin had begun to smart.

Retreating to the meagre shade of a dust-laden pine tree, Nancy debated a course of action. The countryside was unfamiliar, and she had no idea how far she might be from Candleton.

"Who knows, I may have been lying in that ditch for an hour or longer," she reasoned, not trusting the time on her water-soaked wrist watch. "I wonder what Bess and George thought when I didn't show up. Probably they went home. I must find a phone and talk to them!"

The nearest cottage was a quarter of a mile down the sun-baked road. Though confused by her experience, and frightened lest another lapse of memory overtake her, Nancy tramped pluckily through the thick dust.

At length she came to a weather-stained shingled cottage. Seeing an old-fashioned well in the yard, she crossed a cinder path to draw herself a cool drink and bathe her burning skin. A woman, whose face was as faded as the gingham apron she wore, peered curiously at her through the screen door.

"Land o' goshen!" the housewife exclaimed, coming outside. "You look all tuckered out! Have you walked far?"

Nancy replaced the tin cup from which she had been drinking and considered her reply carefully.

"Yes, I've walked a long distance," she said quietly. "My friends and I had an accident with our boat. May I use your telephone?"

"Bless you, we haven't one. The nearest phone is at the Gladstone Dairy, half a mile down the road." Nancy looked so discouraged that the housewife added kindly, "But do come in out of the hot sun. Sit down and tell me what happened. Are your friends safe?"

"I think so. We became separated. Where am I now? Far from Candleton?"

The woman stared at the girl curiously. "Don't you know?"

Nancy shook her head, dropping into a chair near the kitchen door. "I'm a stranger here. After the accident, I became confused."

"You're about three miles from Candleton, and a quarter mile from the bay. You weren't by any chance near Bald Head Cave when the accident occurred?" The woman's eyes opened wide.

Nancy realized that she had revealed too much. If she should tell the true story of what had happened, the tale would be enlarged by the superstitious people who had already feared the cave. And Nancy wanted no publicity.

"Is Bald Head Cave near here?" she countered innocently.

"Over yonder." The woman pointed in a south-easterly direction. "Fishing's good thereabouts," she added, "but you've got to be careful. Once my husband was in his boat near the cave entrance when a flood o' water came rushing out. He was lucky to get away alive."

Bald Head Cave was a subject Nancy did not care to discuss any further. Declining the offer of a glass of lemonade, she asked if there was anyone at the farmhouse who could drive her to Candleton.

"I'll pay him well," she offered.

"Bless you, it's not a matter of money. My husband took a load of chickens to town and he isn't back yet. He'll likely drive in about sunset."

Nancy felt she could not wait. Even though a walk

to Candleton would mean gruelling punishment, she must attempt it.

Thanking the woman for her kindness, the determined girl started off. She felt much stronger now, and the sun did not seem so hot. Presently a car came speeding down the road towards her. It looked remarkably familiar.

"Why, that's my car!" she exclaimed.

Even as she shouted and waved, the driver braked and the car came to a halt. At the steering wheel was Ned Nickerson, a friend of Nancy's who was staying nearby and had stopped at Mrs Chantrey's to see her. Learning from Juno that the girls had gone to Bald Head Cave, he had driven to the boathouse intending to rent a boat and follow them. At the dock he had met Bess and George.

"Thank goodness, you're safe!" Ned cried, swinging open the car door and jumping to the ground.

Bess and George started to scramble into the back seat so that Nancy might sit beside Ned, but he vetoed this at once.

"Suppose you stay in front, and we'll climb in the back," he suggested. "I have a few questions I'd like to ask this young lady."

"Okay," said George, "but first I want to hear what happened to her."

Bess took the wheel and started for Candleton. Nancy, instead of telling of her adventure, asked eagerly.

"Has my father arrived?"

"Not yet," George shook her head.

"Any word from him?"

Again the answer was in the negative. Nancy's eyes filled with tears. She tried to brush them away before

Ned could see them, but she did not succeed.

"Please, Nancy," he said kindly, linking his arm through hers, "I'm sure your father is all right."

"But it isn't like him—"

"I know. Maybe he sent a message that never reached you."

"I hadn't thought of that," Nancy conceded. "You're probably right." She smiled up at the young man beside her. "I'm sorry you found me this way—"

"Well," he laughed, "you look all right to me. But suppose you tell us about your experience after you left the cave."

"You'll be amazed when you hear it."

Rather self-consciously Nancy related her strange dream and told of awakening in the roadside ditch. "I must have been completely out of my mind," she ended dismally. "I don't recall ever doing such a thing before in my life!"

"Perhaps you didn't wander in your sleep," Ned suggested. "You may have been carried."

"By elves? Oh, Ned!"

"By two man-sized elves. Notice anyone near the cave after the accident?"

"I wasn't in a state to observe anything." Nancy's blue eyes clouded with thought. "But I do recall—those voices—they sounded human!"

"Why do you suppose anyone would have carried you from the cliff?" George asked disbelievingly.

With a laugh, Nancy dismissed the subject, declaring, "All I know is that when I investigate Bald Head Cave again, I'll go prepared."

"And probably alone," Bess added darkly. "So far as I'm concerned, the mystery is welcome to remain forever unsolved."

Then seeing a roadside stand, she reminded the others that they had not eaten since breakfast. After a quick meal, which they all agreed could not compare with the Salsandee food, Bess drove on.

During the rest of the ride to Candleton, the three girls exchanged accounts of their strange and terrifying experiences inside the cave. All were sure that a warning bell had rung just before a flood of water rushed from within the cave.

"Why don't I try my luck there tomorrow?" Ned proposed.

"Don't even think about it!" Bess said, and was vigorously supported by George. "The cave is too dangerous!"

When they reached Candleton, Nancy, eager to learn if her father had written, asked that they stop at the post office. Quickly she fingered through the letters George brought from Mrs Chantrey's box.

"Nothing for any of us," she reported in disappointment. "Oh, now I'm sure something has happened to Dad!"

"Maybe there's a message at the house," Ned suggested kindly.

When they reached the Chantrey cottage, the young people heard the telephone ringing. As they walked up the porch steps, Juno, the maid, came to the door.

"Telephone for you, Miss Nancy," she announced. "A gentleman."

"There!" Bess exclaimed triumphantly. "It's your father, Nancy! All your worrying to no purpose."

Nancy raced into the hall.

"Hello, Dad?" she said eagerly into the transmitter.

But it was not her father who answered. The voice was that of a strange man.

"Listen carefully," he directed in clipped tones. "Your father requests that you meet him this afternoon at Fisher's Cove Hotel. Come as quickly as you can—alone."

"Who are you?" Nancy asked. "Why are you calling for my father?"

There was no answer. The stranger had hung up.

As Nancy turned slowly from the telephone, she found Ned standing behind her. Repeating the conversation, she asked for his advice.

"Don't go," he said instantly. "It's a trick."

"I'm afraid so myself, Ned. On the other hand, Dad may have a special reason for wanting me to meet him there. I must take a chance and go!"

"In that case I'll go with you."

"The man's instructions were that I come alone."

"Why alone, Nancy?"

"I had no chance to ask any questions. I only know I must obey instructions."

"If you insist upon going, I'll follow in my car," Ned decided.

While Nancy changed her clothing, he hastened to the village to have her automobile filled with petrol By the time he returned to the cottage, she was ready to leave.

Before Nancy could drive away, however, the telephone rang again. This time George answered it.

"Hello?" inquired an agitated femine voice at the other end of the line. "Has Nancy Drew started for Fisher's Cove yet?"

"Why, no, she's just leaving," George replied.

"Then stop her! Don't let her go!"

Before George could reply, the receiver clicked and the line went dead.

·7· *Suspicious Actions*

WITH mingled emotions, Nancy thought over the second telephone call. Common sense warned her she might be courting danger by driving to Fisher's Cove, but on the other hand, she was extremely anxious about her father.

"I'll carry out the first instructions, but I'll keep my wits about me," she decided. "If things look suspicious when I reach the hotel, I'll call the police."

Leaving Bess and George at the cottage to explain to their hostess what had happened, Nancy drove away. Ned kept close behind her in his own automobile, but as they approached Fisher's Cove he wisely put more distance between them.

Alone, Nancy drew up in front of a shabby, unpainted three-storey building which bore the name Fisher's Cove Hotel. A number of men, who were laughing loudly, sat on the front veranda. As she alighted from the car they eyed the attractive girl with an impolite scrutiny which embarrassed her.

"Dad never would have registered in a hotel such as this," she thought, hesitating.

Ned's car rounded the street corner. Reassured that she would not be alone, Nancy entered the building.

She walked up to the desk and asked the clerk for the number of Mr Drew's room. The clerk was about to reply when a flashily dressed man appeared. He rudely interrupted with a complaint that he had reserved a large room with bath and had been shown instead a small room with only running water. As she did not wish to call attention to herself by protesting against the man's rudeness, she sat down and waited for the clerk to finish. Much better dressed than the hotel guests who filtered past, she felt herself a target for all eyes.

To Nancy's great relief Ned soon sauntered into the foyer and seated himself on the opposite side of the stuffy, smoke-filled room.

At that moment, an elderly woman with a mass of grey hair and wearing a flowered print dress, pushed close to her chair. As she passed, the stranger dropped a scrap of paper into Nancy's lap. Without speaking or giving any sign that she had noticed the girl, the woman walked on quickly, vanishing through a side exit.

Nancy read the paper at a glance. It said, "Your father is **not** here. Leave at once before you get into trouble."

"This **is** the second time I've been warned," she thought. "I'd be crazy to walk blindly into a trap. The only sensible thing to do now is call Mrs Chantrey and see if there's a message from Dad."

Since it seemed best not to do this in the hotel, Nancy went down the street to a drug store. The call took longer than she had anticipated, and was discouraging. No word had come. Upon returning to the foyer, she glanced towards the chair where Ned had been sitting. It was vacant and the young man was nowhere to be seen!

"Now where did he go?" the girl thought uneasily. "Perhaps I should have told him I was going to phone. Oh, dear, I don't like the idea of staying here alone!"

However, she started towards the desk. Before she could speak to the clerk, a well-dressed man in a grey suit approached her.

"Miss Drew?" he inquired.

"Why, yes."

"I am Doctor Warren." The man's manner was flawless, but the expression in his dark eyes disturbed Nancy. "Will you come with me, please?"

Instantly the girl was on her guard, suspicious of a trick.

"Why should I?" she inquired, studying the man carefully.

"Your father is very ill upstairs."

"Oh!" The news stunned Nancy, but she did not accept it completely. "Then why hasn't he been taken to a hospital?" she asked.

"Your father did not want to be moved at this time."

"Then you were the one who telephoned me?"

"No, but I asked the manager to call you. You do not trust me, my dear?"

The question caught Nancy unawares. She did not answer.

"Your silence tells me that you are distrustful," the man declared. "I cannot blame you. Suppose I have myself properly identified at the desk."

"Please," the girl said quickly.

Desperately she glanced about the lobby, wishing Ned would put in an appearance.

"Expecting someone?" inquired Doctor Warren.

"I'm just nervous," Nancy said, and her manner confirmed the words. "Is my father seriously ill? Tell me what happened."

"In a moment." The doctor took her by the arm, guiding her to the hotel desk. "First, I wish to reassure you as to my identity."

The clerk, an unpleasant-looking fellow with shiny, heavily oiled hair, was scanning the comic page of a New York newspaper.

"Hi, Doc!" he greeted the stranger, lowering his paper and staring almost insolently at Nancy.

"I wish you would tell this young lady who I am, Mr Slocum," the physician said.

"Sure. You're Doctor Warren."

"Are you satisfied now?" the man asked. Without giving Nancy an opportunity to question the clerk about her father, he steered her towards the stairway.

"Surely you're not afraid to come with me now?" he asked in an amused tone as she hung back.

"Why—no," Nancy stammered.

The identification should have satisfied her, but somehow it did not. Ned had not reappeared. If she accompanied Doctor Warren upstairs, only the hotel clerk would know where she had gone.

"Of course, if you don't wish to see your father—" began the physician.

"I do!" Nancy broke in. Suddenly she made up her mind that she was being entirely too cautious. "Take me to him at once!"

As she followed the doctor up the dusty, creaking stairs to a dingy second-floor hall, she looked about warily. Despite his reassurances, she wondered if she might not be walking straight into danger.

"It's all so weird," she thought. "Those two tele-phone calls! Then that strange woman who dropped the note into my lap! Who was she, and why did she tell me my father is not here? And what became of Ned?"

Ned at that very moment was frantically searching for Nancy. He had observed the strange actions of the grey-haired woman in the flowered silk dress. He had seen her drop the note into Nancy's lap, and had noted the girl's agitation.

"It's a trick of some sort!" he thought instantly.

Alarmed when Nancy left the hotel, he jumped to the conclusion she had either accompanied or followed the elderly woman. Hastening to the street, he looked round to see where they had gone.

Nancy was not in sight. Some distance away, however, he saw the elderly woman enter a building.

Ned decided to follow her. Hastening down the street, he was somewhat disconcerted to note that the building she had entered was a beauty salon. Heavy blue draperies curtained the front windows, making it impossible to see inside.

"I wonder if Nancy went in there too?" he thought uneasily.

Posting himself across the street, Ned waited and watched. Minutes elapsed. No one entered or left the beauty shop. Finally the young man could bear the suspense no longer.

Recrossing the street, he rather diffidently opened the door of the shop. Two girls who were passing by at the moment stared at him and giggled. Ned's face turned red.

"The heck!" he muttered angrily, but did not retreat.

Inside the only persons visible were an attendant and a customer who sat beneath one of the hair driers. By no stretch of the imagination did either of them resemble the woman who had entered the shop.

"I beg your pardon," Ned said to the attendant who came to the desk. "I'm looking for a grey-haired woman who entered here a few minutes ago."

"No grey-haired woman came into our shop."

"But I saw her," Ned insisted. "She wore a flowered dress."

"Are you sure she didn't stop next door at the bakery shop?"

"Well—I was a good distance up the street, but I thought she came in here."

"Sorry, you must be mistaken," the attendant said with finality.

Ned apologized for having intruded and looked in the bakery. No one was in there but a salesgirl, so he walked back swiftly to the hotel. As he had feared, Nancy was not in the foyer.

At his wits' end, Ned questioned two strange men and a newspaper vendor. The latter offered him a slim clue.

"I saw a pretty lookin' blonde goin' up the stairway with a man. She acted like she was upset."

"That might have been Nancy!" Ned thought.

The hotel had no elevator. Climbing the stairs to the first floor, the young man peered up and down the deserted hallway. No one was in sight, not even a cleaning maid.

"There's only one way to find out if Nancy's here," he thought. "I may as well start knocking on doors."

He tapped firmly on Room 224. When no one answered, he pounded harder. The door flew open and a sleepy-eyed, heavy-set man in dressing-gown and slippers glared at him.

"What d'you want?" he growled.

"I'm looking for a friend of mine—" Ned began, but the man cut him short.

"I don't know you or any of your friends. I'm tryin' to sleep, so clear out and leave a guy alone!" He slammed the door.

Ned tried the room to the right. Apparently it had not been rented, for although he rapped many times, no one answered.

Room 227 proved to be Ned's Waterloo. Before he could explain anything, an excited female whose hair rollers stood out like the spines of a porcupine, grasped him by the arm and gave him a shove down the hall.

"Listen, please let me explain," Ned pleaded.

"You'll explain to the police!"

To the young man's distress, the woman began to scream. Before he could calm her or retreat, doors began to open all along the hall. In the midst of the confusion, the hotel clerk appeared, flanked on either side by burly assistants.

"Okay, boys," he ordered. "Throw him out! He's causing a disturbance."

Ned resisted, but the two men seized him roughly by the shoulders and pulled him towards the stairway.

· 8 · *A Mysterious Malady*

MEANWHILE Nancy had followed Doctor Warren up the creaking stairway to the second floor of the hotel. As the man paused at a doorway midway down the dark hall, she could not hide her uneasiness.

"My dear, you really do distrust me," he said quietly.

"No," Nancy denied, ashamed of her misgivings. "It's only that so many strange things have occurred. For instance, that note—"

"Note?"

Nancy told him about the woman in the flowered dress who had slipped a message into her hand.

"I begin to understand your reluctance in believing me," said the doctor. Opening the door, he stood aside for Nancy to enter. "You are not walking into a trap," he added reassuringly.

Nancy smiled at him, and without hesitation crossed the threshold. Instantly her eyes focused upon a walnut bed which had been pulled up near the windows of the tiny, stuffy room.

"Hello, Nancy," a weak but familiar voice greeted her.

She ran to the bedside and grasped the hand of the pale, weak man who lay there. It was her father all right, but so changed that his appearance shocked her.

"So—glad—you—came, Nancy," Mr Drew murmured.

He smiled at her, pressed her hand, then closed his eyes as if in slumber. Badly frightened, Nancy turned questioning eyes upon the doctor.

"Your father's case is most puzzling," he said in an undertone. "After he was found practically unconscious by one of the hotel maids, the manager called me here to examine him."

"But how did my father get to this hotel, Doctor?" Nancy asked.

"By taxi, I was told. Apparently he was ill when he arrived. I've not asked many questions, for he insisted that he did not wish to talk about it until you came."

"Why didn't someone get in touch with me sooner?" the girl demanded.

The physician shrugged. "I wasn't called till this afternoon," he replied. "When your father asked to see you, I insisted upon the management calling you immediately."

"Has he been in this drowsy state ever since the maid found him?"

"Oh, no. At times he rallies strongly, then has a

relapse. Frankly, I can't explain it. I recommend that he be taken to a New York specialist for an expert diagnosis."

The name of the city seemed to rouse Mr Drew. His eyes fluttered open and he gazed quite steadily at Nancy as she knelt beside him.

"New York," he muttered. "That's where I was."

"Yes," Nancy jogged his memory, and waited for the rest of the story.

But Mr Drew, though he seemed stronger, was not inclined to talk in front of the doctor. "I must talk to you alone—alone," the lawyer said to his daughter.

Doctor Warren picked up his black bag from the dressing-table. "If you need me, I can be reached by phone at Garfield 438," he told Nancy. "Your father may remain strong and able to talk for several hours. If he has another sinking spell, call me at once."

"Of course," the girl nodded.

She asked how much they owed for his services and paid him. Then, grateful for his kindness, Nancy extended her hand.

"I'm sorry I was—so distrustful," she smiled.

"You were very wise," he said, "and you are a brave girl. Don't worry about your father. He seems much better now."

After the doctor had gone, Nancy returned to the bedside. To her alarm, her father tried to raise himself to a sitting position.

"No! No!" she chided, pushing him gently back on the pillows. "You must lie quiet."

"Nonsense!" he exclaimed impatiently. "I have something important to tell you. I must do it while I have the strength. I asked you to come here alone, because what I have to say is not for others to hear."

"What is it, Dad?" Nancy bent closer for his voice was almost inaudible. "You saw those men who cheated Mrs Chantrey?"

"Yes. Then I took the plane. We landed at a small airport abóut ten miles up the shore."

"What happened after that?"

"Started here by taxi, intending to phone you to drive over and get me. A woman who couldn't get a cab, rodc with me."

"A woman?" Nancy inquired thoughtfully. "Can you describe her?"

"Stout—dark—not very talkative. Wore a big hat and veil. She left the cab at the outskirts of Fisher's Cove."

"Then where did you go?"

"Can't remember much after that. I became sleepy and must have dozed off. When I came to, I was in this bed. Some time later the doctor was called in. But this sickness is no mysterious malady, and I don't need any specialist to diagnose what is wrong with me."

"What do you mean, Dad?"

"I'm convinced I was drugged."

"Drugged! Not by the woman who rode with you in the taxi?"

"Probably by those two rascals I visited in New York. We had coffee together, and they may have given me a slow-acting sleeping powder. I recall when I told them I intended to prosecute to the limit unless they returned Mrs Chantrey's money, they left me alone for a while and went to another room to talk. When they returned they were very arrogant. I also remember—"

"Wait!" Nancy interrupted the story. "I think someone is at the door."

Crossing the room, she quickly jerked it open. No one was there, but she was positive someone had been eavesdropping.

Round the corner of the hallway, a woman crouched against the dingy plaster wall. A moment before, she had been listening at the keyhole of Mr Drew's room. Waiting until the door closed again, she noiselessly slipped away.

Descending the stairway to the first floor, the woman paused to see why a crowd had gathered in the hall. Ned Nickerson was protesting vigorously because hotel attendants were threatening to throw him out of the building.

"I'll not leave here until I find a certain girl and her father. If you put me out, I'll come back with the police!"

"Why didn't you say what you wanted?" the hotel clerk asked.

"You didn't give me a chance."

The woman who had descended from the second floor, pushed her way through the crowd to address Ned in a clipped, slightly nasal foreign accent.

"You search for bee-u-tiful blonde-head with eyes like ze stars?"

"Her eyes are blue, and she is—yes, she is pretty."

"Wearing ze dress of white?"

"Yes. You've seen her?"

"She left ze hotel long time past. She wait for monsieur in ze motor car perhaps?"

Thanking the dark-eyed stranger, the young man made his way downstairs to the street. But when he reached Nancy's roadster he did not find her waiting for him.

For a while Ned sat in the car, but as minutes elapsed

and still Nancy did not arrive, he became increasingly worried and restless.

"I was a fool to come down," he thought, suspicion springing up again. "I have a hunch that foreigner gave me a wrong tip."

At this very moment, Nancy, in the second floor room with her father, was trying to convince him that he should not get up and dress. In vain he argued that he felt strong enough to motor to Mrs Chantrey's home or at least to another hotel.

"I'm glad you've feeling better, but I doubt that the doctor would want you to get up so soon," Nancy said dubiously. "Why, you were practically unconscious when I arrived!"

"Just seeing you has helped me a lot, Nancy."

"I'll tell you what I'll do," his daughter offered, stalling for time. "Suppose I telephone Doctor Warren and ask his opinion? I also must settle your hotel bill."

"All right, but do hurry. I've had enough of this place."

"I'll be back as fast as I can. Don't stir from your bed until I return."

Nancy sped to the foyer. Doctor Warren's office did not answer her telephone call. As she left the booth, the hotel clerk motioned for her to come to the desk.

"You were asking about a Mr Drew a while ago?" he inquired.

"Yes. I found him on the second floor in Room 301."

"But we have no one here by that name," said the clerk, looking at the register. "Room 301 is assigned to Mr John Blake."

"May I see the register, please?"

Reluctantly the clerk pointed to an entry where a

John Blake had registered for Room 301. The handwriting was unfamiliar to Nancy.

"This isn't my father's signature!" she exclaimed. "Who brought him here?"

The clerk shrugged. "That I can't say," he said with a sneer. "I wasn't on duty. Maybe I'm all wrong."

Nancy was certain the man was lying. Nevertheless, she paid the bill, which was far in excess of what it should have been. Making no protest, she tried once more without success to reach Doctor Warren by telephone. Failing, she climbed the stairs to tap on Room 301.

"It's Nancy," she called, as Mr Drew did not answer.

Alarmed because there was no reply she pushed open the door.

"Oh!" she cried in dismay.

The bed was empty and had been remade. Mr Drew was not there!

Nancy rushed to the wardrobe, jerking open the door. Only a row of empty wire hangers greeted her gaze. Her father's clothing and overnight bag had disappeared.

· 9 ·   *A Frantic Search*

As NANCY gazed about the deserted room, she felt weak. Where was her sick father?

Badly frightened, and trying to decide what to do next, Nancy moved over to the window. Chancing to glance down into the courtyard, she was astonished to see a young man pacing slowly back and forth on the grassy plot.

Ned!

Her first impulse was to call out, but she thought better of this, and merely rapped on the windowpane. Hearing her, Ned glanced upwards. Nancy put her fingers to her lips and motioned for him to come up.

"Be right with you!" he silently formed the words, and noted the exact location of the room.

Nancy waited anxiously at the door for Ned. Several minutes elapsed. Then she heard footsteps in the hallway and angry voices.

"Now listen!" argued a man who the girl guessed was the hotel clerk. "Haven't you made enough disturbance around here?"

"Someone I'm looking for is in this hotel. I intend to find her!"

At that moment, Nancy opened the door and Ned rushed forward.

Nearly in tears, Nancy told him what had happened. The callous Mr Slocum listened coldly, and openly displayed annoyance as she suggested that Mr Drew might have wandered into an unoccupied room.

"Very unlikely," he tried to dismiss the matter. "In any case it's not our responsibility."

"You have a responsibility in helping me find my father, who is ill!" Nancy corrected him, her eyes flashing. "How many vacant rooms are on this floor?"

"I don't know without looking at the register."

"Are vacant rooms always kept locked?"

"They should be."

"But are they?" Nancy persisted.

"Not always."

"Then my father easily could have wandered into one of them. We must search for him."

"There's no sense in it," argued Slocum angrily.

"Perhaps you prefer to have the police do the investigating?" Ned cut in coldly.

The reference to police brought speedy results. Although the hotel clerk muttered beneath his breath, terming Ned a nuisance, he quickly produced his keys.

Beginning with the room directly across the hall, he tapped on doors and opened one after another. Dust stood thick on the furniture and beds had been stripped of linen.

"You see, it's a waste of time," Slocum grumbled. "Nobody here."

Nancy paid no heed. She had been examining faint footprints in the hall and now paused before a door at the end of the corridor. "Is this room occupied?" she asked.

The clerk could not remember. Without waiting, Nancy tried the door and found it unlocked. The room was dark, with curtains drawn at the windows. On the bed lay a man fully dressed, and sound asleep.

"He's probably been working all night, and is sleeping late. You'd better watch out!" Slocum said nastily.

But Nancy had recognized her father. With a cry of relief she darted to his side. Her first attempts to awaken Mr Drew brought no results.

Ned turned on a light. "Your father acts as if he's been drugged," he observed. Then he spied the overnight bag which stood by the door. "Wonder if all your father's things are in his bag?"

"I don't know," Nancy replied. "And there are several other things I don't know, too."

As she shook her father again, his eyes opened, and he yawned as if wakening from a pleasant slumber.

With an effort, the lawyer roused himself. "Why, hello, Nancy!" he greeted her. "Are we ready to leave?"

Then he turned over and went to sleep again.

Only after Nancy and Ned had tried for several minutes were they able to waken Mr Drew. He drank a glass of cold water, which seemed to revive him.

"Now tell me how you got in here," Nancy urged. "Did you dress yourself after I left?"

"Why, yes, I think so," he answered, trying hard to remember. "Then the girl came."

"What girl? You don't mean me?"

"No, the chambermaid. She wanted to make the bed and clean the room. I sat down to wait, and that's all I remember until you woke me up."

"You don't know whether you walked in here by yourself or were carried?"

"Now who would move him?" cut in the hotel clerk. "That's the craziest thing you've said yet."

"He was in 301," said Nancy.

"John Blake was in there. You said yourself you didn't recognize the signature in the register. Furthermore," Slocum added, turning to Mr Drew, "you're all mixed up about the chambermaid. The girls on this floor don't start work until just about now."

Mr Drew gazed at the man with sudden dislike. "That happens to be a point about which I am very clear," he said in a cold voice. "A dark-haired chambermaid entered my room to change the bed linen."

"You can identify her, I suppose?" the clerk asked insolently.

"I can if I see her again. How many girls work here as maids?"

"Four come on duty at this hour. Three others work the night shift, but they're not here yet."

"Send the girls to me, please. I should like to ask them a few questions."

Slocum looked annoyed for a moment, then a slightly sardonic grin played round the corners of his mouth.

"Okay," he muttered, "but you're making a lot of trouble round here."

A short time later four chambermaids, who could not understand why they were being summoned, came into the bedroom. Mr Drew asked each girl a few questions, then permitted her to leave. He had to admit he had never seen any of the maids before.

"Perhaps the woman who came to your room only posed as a chambermaid," Nancy suggested after the last girl had gone. "You may have enemies who followed you to this hotel."

Mr Drew nodded agreement. "Let's get away from here," he urged. "The sooner the better."

Nancy suggested that he should go to a hospital, but the lawyer assured her he was feeling much better.

"I want to go on to Candleton," he said stubbornly. "If I can walk to the car, a few days on the beach will make me as fit as a fiddle again."

To prove that he felt stronger, Mr Drew walked across the room twice. His steps were very uncertain. Nancy and Ned exchanged worried glances. At his insistence, however, they finally agreed to take him away. Nancy said she would telephone Doctor Warren and tell him of the change in their plans and bring the car to the rear entrance of the hotel.

"Your bill is paid so we can slip away quietly," she declared. "Ned, will you stay with Dad?"

"I shan't leave him a for second," he promised. "Signal with two toots of the horn when you're ready with the car."

Nancy told Doctor Warren of her father's improved condition and their decision to leave. She mentioned nothing of what had happened after his visit and hung up before he could make any objection to the arrangements.

Within five minutes Nancy had her roadster waiting at the hotel door. Not until her father was safely seated in the car did she relax.

"I'll follow close behind you in my car," Ned assured her. "I doubt that anyone will try to stop us now, but it's just as well to play safe."

Without further adventure, the two cars reached Candleton safely. Mr Drew, instead of showing signs of weariness or illness, actually seemed improved after the ride. And after he was settled in a downstairs bedroom of Mrs Chantrey's home, he insisted he felt as well as ever.

The next morning, before anyone was out of bed, Mr Drew dressed, slipped out of the house, and went for a long walk on the beach.

"Outwitted my keepers, didn't I?" he chuckled upon his return. "Now I've had enough of this invalid nonsense. Haven't you young folks anything to do?"

Satisfied that her father was his former self once more, Nancy joined her friends for a swim. The young people enjoyed an hour in White Cape Bay, then went back to the cottage to change their clothing.

Mr Drew was sipping a lemonade, deeply engrossed in a book. Nancy and Ned decided to go for a drive in the country for a few hours. Upon their return to Candleton, Ned parked the car on the main street and the two young people walked along looking at the shops. Ned paused before the window of a novelty jewellery shop.

"While I'm here, Nancy, I'd like to buy you a present. Something to remind you of your stay at Candleton."

Nancy blushingly shook her head. "I really don't need anything," she replied, smiling.

Just then the girl heard the familiar tinkle of a little bell. She turned her head quickly. Madame and her attractive cosmetic pushcart were coming up the street!

"Say, there's something!" Ned exclaimed, mistaking Nancy's intent scrutiny of the woman for an interest in her products. "Perfume and cosmetics! How about a pretty compact and some perfume?"

"I've seen these things before," replied Nancy, keeping her voice low. "Ned, they're very expensive and I believe not much good. I don't want anything that woman has for sale. Thank you, just the same."

Ned could not hide his disappointment. Glancing at the cart, he observed Madame with renewed interest. Her dark-skinned face was shaded by an elaborate flowered hat.

"Say, who is she?" he inquired. "I've seen her before somewhere, but I don't recall her pushing a fancy cart!"

"We might ask her where you met her," Nancy teased.

Madame, who was now opposite them, did not seem to recognize either the young man or the girl. She quickly pushed her cart past the couple and hurried down the street. Or was she only pretending not to know them?

"Maybe you're acquainted with her friend?" Ned questioned Nancy suddenly, his eyes twinkling.

A stocky man had emerged from the shadow of a nearby doorway, and joined the woman at the next corner. Both glanced back towards the young people.

"No, I never saw him before," Nancy replied, but she knew she would not forget his face. It was cruel and calculating.

225

The stranger made no attempt to buy any of the Frenchwoman's cosmetics or perfumes. Apparently they were well acquainted, for they conversed freely. They gestured angrily, and Ned and Nancy guessed he was trying to force the woman to agree to something against her will. Once Madame pointed towards the young couple. Wrathfully the man pulled down her arm.

"What do you make of it?" Ned asked curiously.

Nancy had no answer. Even as he spoke, Madame and her companion hurriedly walked away together, disappearing in the direction of the beach.

· 10 · *Story of a Bell*

NANCY and her father sat alone on the porch of the Chantrey cottage. Ned had left, Bess and George were at the movies, and their hostess had not returned from her day's work at the tearoom.

"It's wonderful to be here with you, Dad," the girl said affectionately. "But I'm getting a bit restless. You hinted at my being able to help you on Mrs Chantrey's case. You haven't given me my job yet."

"That's right, Nancy. But you must admit I was delayed in carrying on my own work. Thanks to you, though, I got out of that awful hotel. Now I can continue where I left off."

"Have you talked to Mrs Chantrey about the stock transaction, Dad?"

"Yes, and she took the news like a soldier. Harry Tyrox and his gang cheated her out of a lot of money and they must be prosecuted. I didn't tell her I'm afraid she'll never get any of her money back, but I believe she suspects it."

The lawyer went on to say that he regretted seeing Mrs Chantrey work so hard, and how deplorable it was that she had spent her savings so unwisely.

"The job I had for you concerns Mrs Chantrey herself, Nancy," Mr Drew went on. "I'm afraid if someone doesn't bolster her morale, she may break down."

"Oh!" escaped Nancy's lips. Then, "Sh, Dad, here she comes."

Mrs Chantrey walked up the porch steps, looking very tired. Nancy asked about her day at the Salsandee Shop, and she admitted she was having trouble again with her help. A waitress had given up her job without notice, and one of the shop's most reliable cooks had had an accident and was unable to work.

"I don't know what I'll do," the tearoom owner sighed.

"Since I didn't mix up too many orders last time, Mrs Chantrey, why not use me again?" Nancy volunteered. "I'd love to help, and I'm sure Bess and George would, too."

"It isn't fair to you girls," their hostess protested. "Didn't I invite you here for a vacation?"

"And we're having a grand one!" Nancy declared. "Why, it's fun at the Salsandee Shop. And I have another reason for wanting to work there," the girl added. "I'm especially interested in one of your customers."

"The odd old man who dropped the paper telling about the XXX bell with the jewels in it?" guessed Mrs Chantrey with a smile.

"That's right. Did he ever come to claim it?"

"No, he has never returned. The paper is still in the drawer at the shop."

Early the next morning, Bess, George and Nancy donned uniforms and once more took up their duties at the tearoom. The work was strenuous but they enjoyed it.

At noon Nancy watched for the odd old man who had sat at her table once before. But he did not come. Nancy wondered if she would ever meet him again. She was very much pleased, therefore, when late that afternoon she saw the man come in. He paused at the cashier's desk, and Nancy heard him say in an agitated voice:

"My name is Hendrick—Amos Hendrick, though I've been called A. H. all my life. Only this morning I discovered the loss of a certain paper. It's valuable, and I'll pay a good reward to get it back. I'm not certain I lost it here, but there's a chance it dropped from my pocket when I paid my bill."

"I'll ask about it, Mr Hendrick," the cashier replied.

"A. H., if you please," the eccentric man said firmly. "I don't like to be called Hendrick."

There was no need for the cashier to ask about the paper. Nancy identified the old man as the person who had sat at the table where she had found the strange paper.

"And you're the pretty little waitress who served me so nicely and asked so many questions about bells," the stranger chuckled.

As Nancy recalled she had merely listened attentively to his story and hadn't asked many questions, but she did not correct him. Instead, she said she would get the paper at once.

Nancy searched the desk drawer where the mysterious

message had been placed. She fingered through bills and invoices without coming upon it, then searched the other drawers. The paper could not be found. Neither Mrs Chantrey nor any of the employees was able to throw light on its disappearance.

Mr Hendrick plainly was distressed. "That paper is very old and valuable," he mumbled. "I wouldn't have lost it for a thousand dollars."

Equally troubled by the loss, Nancy did not know what to say.

"Don't you remember the contents of the message?" she inquired.

" 'Course I do. That paper was found in my father's safe when he died and I know the contents by heart. Thunderation! Do you think I want it to fall into the hands of a stranger?"

"Then you believe that some other person may be interested in searching for one of those XXX bells?"

A. H. gave her a quick, guarded look but did not answer. Edging towards the door, he muttered, "I do too much talking for my own good."

George, who had joined the group with Bess, intercepted the elderly man. "You're making a mistake if you don't tell Nancy Drew here all about your mysterious paper and get her to help you!" she exclaimed impulsively. "Why, she's solved more mysteries than you could count!"

The man paused. His eyes sparkled as he said, "Ganging up on me, eh? You girls are three peas in a pod, or I'm no judge. Now why are you so interested in that paper I lost?"

"Because we like mystery and adventure," Bess supplied eagerly. "Surely you've heard about Nancy Drew. After she solved the Crumbling Wall case, her picture was in half the papers in the country!"

"Bess!" remonstrated Nancy, embarrassed.

"Well, it's true!"

Mr Hendrick had not seen the articles, but his interest was roused. He asked many questions about the detective work Nancy had done. She was uncertain whether he was joking or serious when he inquired:

"Well, how much will you charge to take my case? It's a tough one, I warn you."

"I solve mysteries for the fun of it," Nancy laughed. "Suppose you tell me about your case, Mr Hendrick."

"Not here."

"We might go for a walk along the beach."

"Fine," agreed Mr Hendrick with enthusiasm. "Come along, all of you."

Walking a short distance down the shore, the girls led the old man to a seat on a half-rotted log amid the dunes.

"To make a long story short, I've been interested in bells all my life," he began. "So was my father and his father before him. Know anything about bells?"

"Only that they ring," giggled Bess.

"No two ring alike. Some are high-pitched, some low, some have beautiful tone quality, and others are so harsh they insult your ears. Bells are with us from the cradle to the grave; they rejoice in our victories and toll our sorrows. They have enriched historical moments, coloured romance, and struck terror in the hearts of the superstitious. They even tinkle from the ankles of dancing girls!"

Bess and George stole a glance at Nancy, for they thought the man who insisted upon being called A. H. was a trifle touched on the subject of bells. Their friend, however, was deeply impressed.

"My father was a bellmaker and so was my grandfather," A. H. resumed proudly. "They learned the art in Europe, where they had their foundry. Know how to make a big bell?"

Nancy replied that she had only a vague idea.

"First you make a mould, and that takes a good many weeks if the bell is to be a perfect one. Then you pour in the hot, liquid metal. You have to be very careful. If the mould is not properly constructed, or you don't wait until the metal sets properly, the bell will crack when you take it out. A large bell must be cooled for a week or two before it can be removed."

"Tell us about American bells," Nancy urged, wishing to draw Mr Hendrick into revealing more about the mystery.

"The first bell foundry in this country was established by the Hanks family, ancestors of Abraham Lincoln on his mother's side," Mr Hendrick related. "Then there was Paul Revere. After the Revolution, he built a furnace in Boston and cast small bells. He also made large ones for churches. During his lifetime he cast nigh up to two hundred bells."

"What became of them?" inquired Nancy innocently.

"Ah! There lies the story. Fifty were destroyed by fire, one hangs in King's Chapel, Boston, but most of the others are lost. By that I mean, they're scattered over the country, and the folks that own 'em probably don't realize what a treasure they possess."

"Do you collect bells?" Bess inquired.

"Yes, I do. I've toured the country up and down looking for them. Own maybe fifty bells of all types and construction, but the one I'm after eludes me."

"The XXX bell with embedded jewels?" Nancy supplied softly.

231

A. H. nodded. "That paper I lost was found in my father's effects and was written in my grandfather's hand. The bell was stolen from my grandfather's foundry. I've spent more than eight years searching for that bell."

"You've found no clues?" asked George.

"I found some, but nothing came of them. My search has been interesting, though. I've collected other valuable bells, and I've met a lot of nice folks. I use the Paul Revere story to get them to talk. Usually they end up by showing me all the worthless bells on the premises."

"There's one bell I wonder if you have seen," said Nancy thoughtfully. "According to the stories round here, it hangs somewhere deep within Bald Head Cave."

"Oh, I heard that story when I first came here," the old man answered carelessly. "Nothing to it."

"Why do you say that?"

"Because I went there and looked round."

"And you didn't hear the bell?"

"No bell rang and no ghost appeared to warn me," A. H. chuckled. "It's just one of those superstitious tales. Want to hear a yarn about the bells of Notre Dame?"

Nancy was far more interested in keeping the conversation centred upon Bald Head Cave, but she listened politely to the story the old man told. When he concluded, she said quietly:

"About Bald Head Cave. I can't understand why you didn't hear the bell. When my friends and I went there, we not only heard the warning bell, but we barely escaped with our lives."

Instantly Mr Hendrick became attentive, asking many questions.

"I must go there again!" he exclaimed. "Tomorrow, perhaps."

"You'd better take us with you," Nancy suggested. "After our experience I'm sure you shouldn't go there alone."

A. H. chuckled. "I can't swim a stroke, I admit. Maybe I could use the help of three athletic girls if I should get in a tight spot with that ghost!"

Arrangements were made to meet the old man the following afternoon at one of the boat rental docks. The girls arrived ten minutes ahead of time. Amos Hendrick soon ambled along.

"I want it thoroughly understood before we start," Bess announced as she climbed into the boat, "that we're not setting foot inside the cave. It's too dangerous! We can hear the bell without going inside!"

"Agreed," said A. H. "But I warn you, if I should hear a bell ringing, no telling what I'll do."

Nancy took the helm of the motorboat and they made a speedy trip to the foot of Bald Head Cliff. No fishermen were nearby, and the entire shore appeared to be deserted. Nancy shut off the motor, allowing the boat to drift close to the shore.

"Don't go any nearer the cave," Bess warned, becoming nervous. "It's dangerous."

A. H. said nothing, but from the way he smiled the girls knew he considered them overcautious. For half an hour Nancy kept the boat hovering near the cave entrance. Nothing happened.

"I'm getting tired," Mr Hendrick complained. "Why don't we go ashore and—"

He broke off, listening intently. Nancy and her frinds also had heard the sound. Deep within the cave a bell tolled mournfully.

"It *is* a bell!" cried the old man excitedly. "A mighty good bell, too, with fine resonance and tone quality! It sounds like those my grandfather made years ago!"

Forgetting the girls' warning, he seized an oar and started paddling the motorboat into the cave.

"No! No!" exclaimed Nancy, grabbing his arm. "We mustn't disregard the warning!"

"I must get that bell!"

A. H. climbed to the gunwale to jump out!

· 11 ·   The Deserted Cottage

WITH a mighty jerk Nancy pulled the eccentric old man back into the boat. A moment later a great flood of water rushed from the cave. The boat was buffeted wildly by the waves.

"The ghost must have seen us!" exclaimed Bess dramatically, gripping the side of the boat to keep from being tossed into the water.

Amos Hendrick, who a moment earlier had scoffed at the ghost tale, now was trembling like a leaf. As Nancy steered the craft into less turbulent water, he said with an attempt at composure:

"This brings to mind a story told me as a child. According to the tale, a worker in a bell foundry near the ocean set sail in a small boat equipped with a tolling bell. It was said he joined some pirates who hid their loot in a cave. Nothing was ever heard about him again."

"Perhaps he was drowned at sea," Nancy suggested.

"So it was assumed. Because for many years, on moonlight nights, other workers reported seeing his ghost walking on the water not far from the foundry."

"And you believe the story?" George asked.

234

"I do. Many persons vouched for the tale. The ghost finally disappeared, and it was said he went back to the cave."

Bess and George winked at Nancy. They were convinced A. H. was obsessed with the subject of bells. As if to confirm their suspicion, he quoted absently:

> "*A wizard of such dreadful fame*
> *That when in Salamanca's cave,*
> *Him listed his magic wand to wave,*
> *The bells would ring in Notre Dame!*"

"That's from 'Lay of the Last Minstrel,' " A. H. explained, and then added with a quick change back to the present, "I'd like to get my hands on that bell inside Bald Head Cave!"

"Please don't try," Nancy requested. "It's too dangerous."

"Let's go home," proposed Bess. "This place makes me feel uneasy."

"I have something I want to do first," said Nancy, staring speculatively at the cliff. "Who wants to go exploring?"

"I for one," replied George promptly.

Bess, less eager, said she would accompany her friends. But Mr Hendrick declined the invitation to go with them.

"I haven't enough of the goat in me to climb up and around rocks. You girls go along by yourselves. I'll stay here and watch the boat."

"Don't let the ghost get you," George said jokingly, as they stripped off shoes and socks before wading ashore.

Leaving the man behind, the three companions reached the rocky beach. There they put on their shoes again. Bess started up the cliff ahead of the others, unwisely choosing a steep trail. Suddenly she slipped, and with a scream began to slide down the incline.

Hearing the cry, Nancy looked up. Her heart jumped. Bess was headed for the sharp rocks below! She would be killed if something did not break her fall.

Nancy braced herself firmly and looked about for something to hold on to. Seeing an outcropping bush, she seized it firmly in one hand. As Bess slid against her, she put her free arm about the girl. The two teetered precariously on the edge of the cliff for a few seconds, then regained their balance.

"Wow! That was a close call!" Bess said trembling. "Thanks, Nancy."

George, who had been watching from below, hurried up the path to scold her cousin.

"Bess, you must be more careful!" she warned her. "Both of you might have been dashed to pieces!"

"I know it," Bess agreed. "No more rock climbing for me! I'll sit right here and wait until you girls get back."

Nancy and George left her and climbed swiftly but with caution. Reaching the top of the cliff they admired the view, and waved to A. H., who sat in the drifting boat.

"I came up here a much easier way the day we nearly drowned in the cave," Nancy said. "Want to see where I had that remarkable dream?"

"So that's why we made the climb!" scoffed George. "I'm curious to find out how the place looks, now that I have my wits about me."

Without difficulty Nancy spotted the general location where she had slept.

"I can't figure out how you reached the road from here," George commented. "If you walked in your sleep you were lucky you didn't fall off the cliff and kill yourself."

"I think so too," Nancy said soberly.

The two girls wandered about, seeking a trail which would lead to the road. Before they had gone many yards, George stumbled into a crevice between the rocks, severely twisting her ankle. Though she tried to walk, it was evident she could go no farther without great pain.

"I'll hobble back towards Bess," she decided. "You go on by yourself, Nancy."

Nancy hesitated, but George, who knew her friend wished to do some more exploring, would not permit her to give up the expedition.

Nancy went on alone, directing her steps towards a weather-beaten cottage nestled against high rocks. She did not recall seeing it the first time she was on the cliff, probably because of the drowsy state she was in that day.

"What a strange place for anyone to live!" she reflected. "No trees. No garden. It must be cold and windy in the winter."

Impulsively Nancy decided to call on the occupants. It was not until she was quite near the cottage that it suddenly occurred to her the men whose voices she had heard might live there.

Nancy was tempted to go back, but as she gazed at the house she began to feel sure that it was deserted. The curtains at the windows looked very soiled. A painted rocker stood on the porch, dust-covered and faded. It swayed gently to and fro in the wind as if occupied by someone invisible.

Nancy went to the door and knocked several times. No one answered. Convinced that the house was vacant, she tried the door. Finding it had no lock, she lifted the latch and went inside.

What Nancy saw caused her to draw in her breath sharply. Chills raced down her spine.

A dining table which stood in the centre of the room was set with two places. Food lay on the plates. But the food was mouldy and covered with cobwebs. A chair stood precisely at each place, as though the occupants had gone away suddenly just before sitting down to the meal.

"Some tragedy must have occurred here," Nancy reasoned. "And not recently, either. The owners must have left the cottage in a hurry, never to return. But why?"

Peering into the other rooms, the girl saw further evidence that the former tenants had fled quickly.

"It's strange they never came back to remove the furniture," she mused.

Deeply impressed, Nancy left quietly, carefully closing the outside door so that it would not bang back and forth in the wind. Reflecting upon the strange appearance of the house inside, she made her way slowly across the cliff. Midway to the spot where she had left George, she was startled to hear a scream.

"That was Bess!" Nancy thought, recognizing her friend's voice. "Now what has happened?"

She started to run. From afar she could see George, who looked greatly excited.

"Perhaps Bess fell again!" Nancy told herself.

Out of breath and thoroughly frightened, she reached the spot where George was standing.

"What is it?" she cried. "What's wrong?"

George answered by pointing towards the bay.

The motorboat, with only the eccentric old man

A. H. aboard, was chugging off rapidly in the direction of Candleton!

·12· *Stranded*

"WHAT's the matter with A. H.?" George cried furiously. "He can't go off and leave us stranded here!"

"Maybe he can't, but that's exactly what he's doing!"

Sharing George's alarm, Nancy cupped her hands and called to the eccentric old man. If he heard her, he gave no sign.

From some distance below, Bess also was shouting and waving. It seemed incredible that A. H. could not hear her.

"He's going off and leaving us on purpose!" George cried bitterly.

To be left alone on the cliff was a serious matter. There were no boats, and the nearest inhabited house was a long distance down the road. George, with an injured ankle, could not walk even a quarter of the way.

They watched, hopeful that the motorboat would turn and come back for them. Instead, it kept on steadily towards Candleton. Soon it was a mere speck on the water.

"There's only one thing to do," Nancy said. "You and Bess stay here and wait. I'll go for help."

"Where?"

"If necessary, to that house where I stopped the other day. Perhaps there's a cottage closer."

"Maybe I could walk." George gazed dubiously at her ankle, which had become badly swollen.

"You never could make it, George."

Telling Bess of the plan, Nancy overruled her offer to go along. "No, you stay with George," she urged.

The sun was still high overhead and beat down upon the rocks. As Nancy set off to bring help to her friends, she could not stifle a feeling of resentment towards Amos Hendrick. What had possessed the peculiar old man to leave them stranded?

"He must have had some reason," she thought. "I don't believe he would abandon us on purpose. When I see him again—Oh!"

Nancy stopped short. Unconsciously she had turned in the direction of the abandoned cottage. From afar she could see the door flapping in the wind.

"That's funny!" she thought. "I know I latched that door."

A dark shadow fitted round the side of the cottage. Nancy's eyes opened wide. Had someone left the house, or was the figure that of some animal?

"It must have been my imagination," she decided. "But just to make certain, I'll walk over there and find out."

The weather-stained cottage was as deserted looking as when she had seen it before. Again she knocked. Again no one appeared. Once more she pulled the door shut and tested the latch to be sure it would not open again.

Before leaving, Nancy hurriedly circled the house, but saw no one. Yet she was uneasy.

"The wind couldn't have opened the door," she reflected. "It isn't strong enough. And that shadow—"

In a hurry to reach Candleton, Nancy did not wait any longer. Striking out in what she judged to be the right direction, she was relieved to come upon a path which led out to a dirt highway. A quarter of a mile farther on Nancy reached the spot where she had awakened on her previous trip.

"How in the world could I have wandered such a distance in my sleep?" she asked herself. "It seems impossible."

Before long Nancy came to the same farmhouse she had visited before. This time a car stood in the yard, its engine running. A man, evidently the owner of the place, was about to start off.

"Wait!" Nancy hailed him.

He pulled up at the gate.

"Are you going to Candleton?" the girl asked breathlessly.

"That's right."

"May I ride with you?"

"Sure. Hop in." Dusting off the seat, the farmer swung open the door.

As the car bounced over the rough road, Nancy told him what had happened, explaining that she meant to hire another boat and return to the cliff for her stranded companions.

"By the way, who lives in the cottage on the cliff?" she inquired, hoping to pick up a little useful information.

"Why, nobody."

"I mean, who were the former occupants before the cottage was abandoned?" Nancy corrected herself.

"Sorry, but I can't tell you. My wife and I only came here a few months ago. We don't get around much or see any of our neighbours. Too busy trying to make a living from our farm."

They soon reached Candleton, and at Nancy's request the farmer obligingly dropped her off at the

241

waterfront. He would accept no pay for the drive, insisting that it had not inconvenienced him in the least.

Hastening to the wharf where she had rented the motorboat, Nancy saw that the craft in which A. H. had abandoned them had been returned. But where was he? Seeking the owner of the boat, she asked him if he had seen Mr Hendrick.

"Sure, he came in about an hour ago," the man replied.

"Did he leave any message or give any reason for going off in the boat and deserting my friends and me at Bald Head Cliff?"

"Why, no! You mean to tell me he deliberately left you girls in that forsaken spot?"

"He certainly did. I came to town for help. My friends are still there on the rocks, one with an injured ankle."

"That was a mean trick. I can't understand it. Take the boat and go after your friends. Do you need any help?"

"No, I can manage alone. Thanks just the same."

The boat owner filled the tank for Nancy, and to make certain she would be prepared for any emergency, tossed in an extra can of fuel, a bailer and a life preserver.

Although visibility was good on the water, late afternoon shadows were beginning to darken the shore line. At full speed she proceeded to Bald Head Cave, anxiously scanning the cliff for a glimpse of her chums.

To her relief she saw a flash of colour amid the rocks at the base. George and Bess were waiting for her on the beach.

Overjoyed to see her, they shouted and waved. Supported by Bess, George limped through the shallow water to climb aboard the boat.

"We thought you'd never get here," Bess sighed. "Did you see A. H. while you were in Candleton?"

Nancy shook her head.

"Just wait until I see him again!" George said angrily. "I'll tell him a thing or two!"

"I still think he must have had a reason for deserting us the way he did," Nancy said. "How did you get along after I left?"

"Okay," replied George. "It was hot on the rocks, but my ankle feels better now."

"No ghostly apparitions?"

"Not one."

"How about the bell inside the cave?"

"We listened for it," Bess said, "but didn't hear a sound. Apparently the ghost only goes into action when you're on the scene, Nancy!"

Without further delay the girls sped directly to the boat dock and took a taxi to Mrs Chantrey's cottage. Mr Drew, obviously upset, was restlessly walking about outside when they arrived.

"Why, Dad!" Nancy exclaimed, alarmed lest he might have had a recurrence of the strange ailment from which he had suffered while in Fisher's Cove. "Is anything wrong?"

"I'm disgusted! Thoroughly disgusted! Read this!"

The lawyer thrust a telegram into his daughter's hand. It had been sent from New York and was from one of the young assistants in his office. As Nancy read the message, her heart skipped a beat.

AS PER YOUR INSTRUCTIONS CALLED ON BROKERS AT OFFICE AND HOTEL. THEY HAVE SKIPPED. AWAIT FURTHER ORDERS.

"That's dreadful, Dad."

"Indeed it is! It ruins all my plans. I hardly know which way to turn," Mr Drew said.

"At least it proves they're dishonest. That will help strengthen your case against them, won't it?" Nancy asked, trying to soften the blow for him.

"Yes, dear, that's true. The mistake I made was in giving Tyrox and the others a chance to make good. They should have been told nothing until I was ready to prosecute. Now they've taken Mrs Chantrey's money and probably that of other investors as well and vanished!"

"You've never told me much about the case, Dad. What kind of stock was it Mrs Chantrey bought?"

"The stock has no listing on any exchange. In my opinion, the entire transaction was a swindle. I do wish Mrs Chantrey had asked my advice before she bought shares in a worthless perfume company."

"A perfume company?"

"Yes, a salesman showed her an impressive report of the firm's earnings which I'm sure was a fake. She thought she was buying into an old, well-established company dealing in exclusive French products of high quality.

"What's the name of the firm, Dad?"

"The *Mon Coeur* Perfume Company."

Nancy stared at her father, scarcely believing he had spoken a name so familiar to her. Mr Drew noted his daughter's startled expression.

"Don't tell me you know anything about that company!" he exclaimed.

"I've seen the *Mon Coeur* products," Nancy replied. "There's a woman right here in Candleton who sells them. And I've seen a man, whose looks I don't like, on the street with her!"

It was Mr Drew's turn to stare.

"He may be Harry Tyrox, one of the swindlers I'm after! He's the head of the company. Nancy, do you think you can find him for me?"

· 13 ·   *The Chemist's Report*

WHILE Nancy was telling her father everything she knew about Madame and her pushcart of cosmetics, Ned drove up and joined the Drews. He listened in amazement to the story.

"Did that woman speak with a French accent?" he asked suddenly.

"Yes."

"And was she dark-skinned, wore her black hair slicked back, and had a mole on her left cheek?"

"That's a very accurate description," Nancy agreed. "But I didn't know you were close enough to her to make such a minute observation when we saw her the other day."

"I wasn't!"

"Then don't keep us guessing. Where did you see her before?"

"At the hotel in Fisher's Cove. When we saw that woman with the pushcart I thought her face looked familiar. Ever since I've tried to remember where I had seen her before."

"She may have recognized you, Ned. That would explain why she hurried away so fast. Where was she in the hotel?"

"On the first floor when I was arguing with the

245

clerk. This woman came down from the second floor and told me you had left the hotel."

"From the second floor?" Nancy repeated thoughtfully.

"Yes. I should have been suspicious, but it didn't occur to me until later that it was a trick to get me away from the hotel."

"It certainly looks as if you've hit upon a good clue to locate the *Mon Coeur* crowd," Mr Drew reflected. "Let's take the car and see if we can find that woman with the pushcart."

For an hour the three searched high and low throughout Candleton, asking for Madame. No one had seen her for several days.

"She probably left town after she saw us, Ned," Nancy ventured. "Maybe she went back to Fisher's Cove."

"And you'd like to go there to find out," Ned smiled. "How about you folks having dinner with me there?"

Mr Drew declined, saying he expected a telephone call from his young assistant who was in New York. He knew Nancy and Ned were fully capable of handling any situation should they locate Madame.

The three returned to the Chantrey cottage. While Nancy bathed and changed her clothes, Ned talked with Bess and George, and politely asked them to accompany him and Nancy. They thanked him but refused, saying they had promised to help Mrs Chantrey, and left to have dinner at the Salsandee Shop.

"Shall we eat along the way or wait until we get to Fisher's Cove?" Ned questioned as he and Nancy drove off.

"To be truthful, I'm dreadfully hungry," Nancy confessed. "I haven't eaten for hours. There's an attractive place about five miles from here."

"I know the one you mean," Ned answered. "They have a good music group. We'il stop there."

It was nearly nine o'clock when they finished eating. Ned was reluctant to leave the good music and dancing, but finally they went on to Fisher's Cove and parked near the old hotel.

"Don't get into another fuss with the clerk," Nancy teased him as they went inside.

"If that fellow gets smart with you or me, I may have to."

The interview with Mr Slocum, who was on duty, started badly. When Ned asked if a woman answering the description of Madame had registered there, the man was as uncommunicative as before.

"I don't know who you're talking about," he retorted, "and furthermore, I don't care. All I ask is that you two quit bothering me."

"It should be of importance to you to know the kind of people who frequent your hotel," Ned said with dignity.

"I'll have no slurs on this hotel!" the clerk shot back. "The people who come here are all right—"

Ned bristled, but Nancy restrained him, saying:

"We're not accomplishing a thing this way. Let's go."

"Slocum knows more than he'll tell," said Ned as they walked away from the desk.

"Perhaps. But let's not make a scene."

Ned grudgingly acknowledged that Nancy was right. She told him that she had another plan for getting the information, and they left the hotel. Seeking a telephone, she called her father, telling him of Slocum's attitude.

"How about putting a plain-clothes man in the hotel to watch everyone who enters or leaves the place? Madame or Harry Tyrox may come in."

"Not a bad idea," agreed Mr Drew. "In fact, since we don't know the woman's name, it seems about the only way to spot her. I'll arrange it."

Nancy was not too hopeful that the plan would bring results. As she remarked to Ned on the way back to Candleton, it seemed reasonable that if the *Mon Coeur* crooks ever had made their headquarters at Fisher's Cove Hotel, they certainly had moved out by this time.

"Isn't it possible Madame is peddling her products in other small towns around?" Ned speculated.

"Very possible. I mean to do some investigating in them."

"And I'll make a date with you right now to help, Nancy."

The girl laughed. "But I want to start out right after breakfast tomorrow."

"That's okay with me."

"But can you get up that early?"

"I certainly can!"

"There's no putting you off I see," Nancy chuckled. "All right. Nine-thirty in the morning."

Ned was there promptly and they set off. The couple visited one seashore resort after another, but the trip netted nothing in their search for the promoters of *Mon Coeur* products. No one had seen Madame in days, although she had covered the countryside selling cosmetics.

"At least we're following her trail," Nancy said, refusing to be discouraged.

They were standing in front of a drug store window which prominently displayed *Mon Coeur* powder and perfume. "Perhaps we ought to warn this chemist not to buy any more of the products."

"These may be better than the stuff Madame sells from her cart," Ned suggested. "It's possible she gets good perfume and dilutes it to make a high profit for herself."

"I hadn't thought of that. Suppose I buy some of these and have them analyzed?"

"Good idea," approved Ned. "I have a college friend not far from Candleton who will make the report for us, and we can depend on it being accurate."

Nancy purchased a lipstick, a box of powder, and a small vial of perfume. Later that afternoon Ned took them to his friend, Bert Hamilton, who lived a few miles down the shore. Only two years out of Emerson College, which Ned now attended, the young man already had made a name for himself as a chemist.

"Bert promises us a report by tomorrow night," Ned told Nancy upon his return. "I took the liberty of suggesting he bring it over to Candleton. He's going to get hold of Bill Malcome—you remember him. We'll make it a sixsome and go over to the Yacht Club dance. Okay?"

"Sounds like fun," Nancy smiled. "I'm sure Bess and George would love it, too."

When the cousins heard about the date, they were very pleased. Both knew Bill. In fact he had escorted George to several parties in River Heights.

The following evening the girls were just finishing dressing when the boys arrived. Nancy ran downstairs ahead of the others to greet their guests, who already were talking with Mr Drew. Ned presented Bert, who seemed to be a likable person.

"Did you bring the report?" Nancy asked him at the first break in the conversation.

"I can give it to you in a few words," the chemist replied. "The sample of perfume was mostly water."

"I thought so!" exclaimed Nancy.

"The face powder contained chalk—the common schoolroom variety—mixed with a little ordinary rice powder to give it texture. The lipstick contains a cheap substance, which really is a poison to the skin. It's dangerous to use."

Nancy had asked Ned not to mention their suspicions regarding the *Mon Coeur* manufacturers. She herself merely said:

"Wait until poor Bess hears this! She spent a lot of money on those products."

Bess came downstairs at this moment and met the chemist. The truth of his findings was not easy for her to accept. She was ashamed to think she had not followed Nancy's and George's advice.

"I'd like to know what the perfume is like," Mr Drew spoke up. "Would you mind getting your bottle, Bess?"

The girl hastened to her room, and returned with the vial she had purchased from Madame. As she uncorked it, a strange, not too pleasant fragrance permeated the air.

"The dreadful stuff gets worse the longer it stands!" George declared.

"Why, how funny—" the lawyer started to say, then stopped. He put the back of one hand across his eyes.

"Mr Drew, you're not feeling ill again!" Bess exclaimed.

The lawyer sank into a chair, staring into space. Alarmed, Nancy darted to his side.

"Dad!"

"I'm quite all right, my dear," her father said. "But that perfume—"

"Cork the bottle," George ordered her cousin.

"No, no, that's not necessary," said the lawyer. "The perfume doesn't bother me. But I connect it with something unpleasant."

"In what way, Dad?" Nancy asked.

Mr Drew seemed lost in thought for several seconds. Then suddenly he snapped his fingers.

"I have it! I remember now!" he cried excitedly. "The woman in the taxi with me! She used that same perfume!"

· 14 ·   *The Candlemaker's Help*

As THE other young people went outside to get into the cars, Nancy and Ned hung behind to talk further with Mr Drew about the woman in the taxi.

"You're sure she had on *Mon Coeur* perfume?" the girl asked her father.

"Positive."

Nancy asked him to describe the woman again. The lawyer said he had not paid much attention to her, but recalled she was dark, had rather large features, and wore a veil.

"She could have been Madame," his daughter said excitedly. "Dad, you thought those *Mon Coeur* men in New York might have given you a slow-acting drug. Perhaps Madame was their accomplice at this end of the line."

"You're probably right," Mr Drew agreed.

"It's even possible—" said Nancy, then stopped.

"What were you going to say?" prompted her father.

"It seems fantastic—but then so do a lot of things that have happened lately—but maybe you weren't drugged in New York at all. Perhaps the woman in the taxi did it."

"But how? I didn't swallow anything."

"With the perfume."

"You mean the woman disguised something like— well, like ether, with that sweet-smelling perfume?"

"Yes."

At this moment an automobile horn began to toot loudly, and shouts of "Nancy! Ned!" reached their ears.

"You'd better go along," the lawyer urged. "I'll talk to you in the morning. Good night, Ned."

For several hours Nancy enjoyed the music and dancing at the Candleton Yacht Club. When they reached home, she, Bess, and George tumbled into bed to awaken rather late the next morning. As Nancy came downstairs, she heard her father telephoning the airport.

"You're going away?" she asked, when he hung up.

"I must leave at once for New York, but I'll return as soon as I can," he promised. "My assistant picked up what may be an important clue."

"About the *Mon Coeur* people?"

"Yes, Nancy. I haven't time to explain the details. A neighbour is taking me to the airport. Will you pack a few things in my bag?"

"Then I'm to stay here?"

"Yes, I've already talked with Mrs Chantrey. She won't hear of you or your friends leaving. You're to remain and work on the mystery. You don't mind?" he added, a twinkle in his eye.

"Maybe I'll have the whole thing solved by the time

you return. And the mystery of the tolling bell, too," Nancy countered, hugging her father affectionately.

She ran upstairs to pack his bag, and a few minutes afterwards he rode away. Bess and George appeared a little later and were surprised to hear of Mr Drew's departure.

"Hurry up and eat. We ought to get started," Nancy said suddenly.

"Started where?" Bess wanted to know.

"I want to go and talk to Mother Mathilda, the candlemaker Mrs Chantrey told us about. She's supposed to know everything that's happened round here for the past sixty years."

"And you think she can solve the mysteries?" George scoffed, finishing a glass of orange juice Juno had brought in.

"Maybe," Nancy grinned. "But seriously, Ned and I scratched only the surface in our search for Madame. If she's staying in some out-of-the-way place, Mother Mathilda may know where."

"Also, you'd like to find out from her who lived in that cottage on Bald Head Cliff, and why the people went away in such a hurry," Bess smiled.

"And learn a little more about the ghost in the cave," added George with a wink at her cousin.

The three girls set off on foot for the old section of Candleton. They exclaimed over the quaint houses and shops, declaring that walking down Whippoorwill Way was like stepping into another era.

Finally, passing a moss-covered stone church, the girls came to an old-fashioned dwelling of pounded oyster-shell laid brick. Attached to it at the rear was a fairly new wooden lean-to, which marred the otherwise picturesque lines of the house.

"This is the place," announced Nancy, noting a wrought-iron sign which said "Màthilda Greeley. Hand-poured, perfumed candles for sale."

They rang the doorbell. When no one came, the girls circled the building to investigate the lean-to at the rear.

"Why, it's the shed where the candles are made!" exclaimed Nancy, peering through the open doorway.

From the ceiling hung hundreds of gaily coloured wax candles of all lengths and sizes. Near the door were bright scarlet ones, and beyond blue, yellow, pink and green.

"Doesn't it remind you of a rainbow?" gasped Bess in delight.

At the rear of the room, a bent-over old lady with white hair and crinkly skin stood with her back to the girls. She was stirring a kettle of hot, green-coloured wax.

"Oh, dear! What shall I do?" the woman mumbled to herself.

Nancy tapped lightly on the door before crossing the threshold. At the sound of footsteps, Mother Mathilda turned and nodded for them to walk in.

"We're staying with Mrs Chantrey," explained Nancy, smiling. "She suggested we come here."

"Oh, yes, I have heard of you." The old lady went on stirring. "Look around. You don't have to buy."

Nancy and her chums became aware of a familiar but faint odour. Nancy asked what it was.

"I have been making perfumed candles," Mother Mathilda replied, "but they are a failure. The entire lot is ruined! Not in thirty years have I had such a loss."

"Are they bayberry candles?" Bess asked, since the colour of the liquid was green.

"Oh, no, my bayberry candles are the only ones which turned out well this week."

The old lady pointed to a rack of delightfully fragrant tapers, explaining they had been made by cooking berries, skimming off the wax, refining it, and pouring it onto strings suspended from nails.

"Isn't that a rather unusual way of making candles?" Nancy asked. "I thought they were always made in moulds, or else the wick was dipped into hot wax."

"You're right," agreed the old lady. "But years ago my family perfected the method of pouring the liquid onto the wick. When one layer hardens, we put on another coat. But I was the one who added the perfume," she announced proudly. "And never in the thirty years that I've been making sweet-scented candles have I had a failure until now."

Mother Mathilda explained that after she had added a newly purchased perfume to her "batter," it not only did not hold well to the wick, but the candles did not have the fragrance they should.

Nancy noticed three large empty bottles on a shelf above the kettle. They bore the *Mon Coeur* trademark.

"Did you use the perfume from these bottles?" she inquired.

"Yes. I bought them from a woman who claimed her products were superior to any other on the market. But I am burdening you with my troubles! You came to buy candles, or to see how they are made."

"We do want to buy some of the bayberry variety," Nancy replied. "What really brought us here though is to ask you about that very woman who sold you the perfume."

Mother Mathilda looked surprised. Then she said, "There is little to tell. The woman, a foreigner, came here and gave me samples of a lovely oil. It seemed exactly what I needed for my candles, so later I bought a large supply. But the perfume was inferior to the oil."

"What a shame!" murmured Bess. "That woman is a fraud and a cheat. She has sold worthless perfume all along the coast."

"Have you any idea where she is?" Nancy asked Mother Mathilda.

"No. I asked several of my neighbours, but no one knows."

"It won't be easy to trace her, I'm afraid," Nancy said, worried. "Once she cheats a person, she's wise enough not to return."

She and her friends could find little to say to comfort Mother Mathilda. They were afraid she never would recover a penny of the money she had given to Madame for the worthless perfume.

"It must have been only Madame's perfume that was of poor quality," the old lady went on in a more hopeful voice. "Ordinarily, *Mon Coeur* products are of the best."

Nancy stared at her curiously. "Why do you say that? Have you used them before?"

"No, but Monsieur who sold me stock in the company showed me testimonials signed by a dozen film stars praising their products."

The words stunned Nancy and her friends.

"You also bought *Mon Coeur* stock?" the Drew girl asked, hoping she had misunderstood.

"Twenty shares. Monsieur Pappier, president of the company, sold them to me himself. Oh, he was a fine, elegant gentleman! He kissed my hand and made very pretty speeches." Mother Mathilda blushed as she said this.

"Can you describe him?" Nancy asked.

"Monsieur was a stout man with plump, apple-red cheeks. He wore a velvet jacket with braid. His voice sounded husky as if he had a sore throat."

"My father may know the man. The description fits a certain Harry Tyrox, wanted in New York for a similar sale of *Mon Coeur* stock."

"You don't think the man is an impostor?"

"I am afraid he is, Mother Mathilda. Did anyone else in this neighbourhood buy stock?"

"Oh my, yes! Maude Pullet, my next door neighbour. And Sara Belle Flossenger, the seamstress, took forty shares. Then the tailor, Sam Metts, bought some."

"What a day for Monsieur Pappier!" commented Nancy grimly. "I'm sorry to tell you that the stock he sold has no value."

"Oh, it can't be true! There must be some mistake! Almost all my life savings were given to that man!" gasped the woman, sinking into a chair.

As Mother Mathilda wept softly, Nancy told her who she was, and attempted to comfort the woman by saying Mr Drew was trying to trace the stock swindlers.

"Nancy is working on the case, too," added George. "I'm sure those awful men will be caught."

After some time the girls succeeded in cheering up the old lady a little. They bought several dozen bayberry candles, and changed the subject of conversation.

"Who used to live in the cottage on the top of Bald Head Cliff?" Nancy asked the candlemaker.

"Oh, you mean the old Maguire place!"

"Is that the name of the people who lived there? Did they leave suddenly for some reason?" Nancy pursued the subject.

The question seemed to surprise Mother Mathilda. "Why, not unless you'd call going to their heavenly re-

257

ward suddenlike," she commented. "Grandpa Maguire and his wife died from old age. But so far as I know, the son and his wife are still there."

"The place is deserted."

"Then the report that they moved away must be true. I couldn't believe it," remarked the old lady.

"You knew the Maguires well?"

"As well as I knew my own mother. Grandpa was quite a character!" The old lady chuckled. "He had a flowing white beard that reached to his knees. And how he did like to spin yarns! He was a lookout in the old days."

"Lookout?" Nancy questioned.

"Grandpa Maguire had a powerful telescope," Mother Mathilda explained, "and he'd sit on his porch, watching the sea for returning fishermen in their boats. Whenever he'd spy one, he'd scramble across those rocks nimble as a goat, and drive to town to tell the women. Then they'd come down to the sea to meet their menfolks."

"What became of the telescope?" Nancy asked, recalling the man who had gazed at them through one the first time she and her friends had gone to the cave.

"I don't know," the candlemaker replied. "Do you want me to find out for you?"

"Thank you, no," Nancy answered. "I was just wondering."

Actually she was wondering whether the man on the cliff might have been using the Maguire telescope, and if so, where it was. She had not noticed it lying anywhere in the cottage during her hurried inspection of the place.

Nancy discussed her idea with Bess and George as they walked home. George thought the man with the telescope might have been Mr Hendrick.

"He's a strange old fellow," she declared. "I'll bet he knows the secret of that cottage."

"I agree," said Bess. "When he saw us climb the cliff and head towards the deserted cottage he went away in the boat. Perhaps he thought that would distract us from our investigations. He might have been afraid that we'd discover something he didn't want us to know."

"But he may have enemies, too," added George. "Who else would have stolen the paper he dropped in the tearoom?"

Nancy had to admit there was something to her friends' theory. She was determined to find A. H. and learn what she could from him. Even if he said he had never been on the cliff, at least he owed them an explanation for running off with the boat.

But Amos Hendrick seemed to have vanished from Candleton. The girls inquired at the boat rental dock, stores, and boarding houses. No one had seen the man. Finally the three friends went to the Salsandee Shop and ate an early luncheon. Mrs Chantrey, learning they were there, asked if they would go on an errand for her.

"I've just had a phone call from Maplecrest Farm," she said. "They were to bring me a crate of berries, but their truck has broken down. Will you drive over and get the berries for me?"

Nancy said they would be very glad to and got her car. She headed for Maplecrest Farm which was situated about two miles out of town on the shore opposite the cliffs. As she sped along, Nancy passed a parked car. No one was in it, but down by the water, a hundred yards away, two men stood talking.

Their backs were turned to the girls, and it was not until Nancy drove into the farm lane a few minutes later that she suddenly thought she recognized the men.

"A. H. and the fellow I saw talking to Madame!" she cried aloud.

"Honestly?" exclaimed George.

"I'm going to find out!" Nancy declared.

"How about the berries?" Bess asked. "Mrs Chant—"

"I'll get them. Take the money out of my bag for me, will you, Bess?"

Nancy accomplished the errand in less than two minutes, much to the amazement of the owner of the farm. She quickly turned the car round and raced out of the lane to the highway.

·15· *Minnie's Awakening*

As NANCY sped back to the spot where she had seen the two men talking, she kept hoping they were still there.

"I wish I'd stopped before," she said to Bess and George. "Probably they've gone by this time."

They were gone. There was not a sign of the men nor the car. Bess tried to console Nancy by saying she doubted the men could have been A. H. or Madame's friend. George, meanwhile, had spied a boat chugging slowly away from the shore.

"Look, Nancy, maybe the fellow in there is one of the men you saw!" she suggested. "He's going towards Candleton. Let's find out!"

Nancy put on more power and they skimmed along the road. Reaching the Salsandee Shop, the girls left the crate of berries at the kitchen door and hurried off again.

"Now where are we going?" Bess asked. "That man at the dock told us A. H. hadn't rented a boat, so he won't come in there."

Nancy felt that the old bell collector probably had hired a boat from one of the fishermen.

"I suggest we go over to the wharves where the fishermen are and find out," she said.

Upon their arrival, Nancy made inquiries and learned that her guess was right. Mr Hendrick had rented a dory only an hour before.

"What a surprise he's going to get when he sees us," George laughed. "Three detectives ready to pounce on him!"

When A. H. reached the wharf, the girls expected him to try to avoid them, but the eccentric man greeted them with a smile and said:

"Well, I'm glad to see you. That saves me a trip. I was going to call on you and offer my apologies."

"We did expect to hear from you and learn why you took our boat and left us stranded on the cliff," Nancy told him.

Amos Hendrick hung his head. "I'm right sorry about that," he said. "The truth is, I suddenly remembered I had an appointment. I couldn't wait for you girls any longer."

"Was it with the same man you saw today?" Nancy shot at him.

The bell collector looked surprised and asked how she knew that. Nancy explained vaguely.

"Yes, it was the same man," A. H. answered. "The other time Mr James didn't show up."

"Mr James who?" George interposed.

"James is his last name." A. H. leaned forward and whispered confidentially, "He has a bell I might buy."

"Oh!" said Nancy. Then she asked, "What does the man look like?"

"Oh, kind of red-faced. Has a stocky build and dark hair. Why?"

Nancy evaded the question. "I might want to talk to him myself sometime about bells," she answered noncommittally.

Inwardly she was very excited. The description definitely fitted the person with whom Madame had been talking! Mr Hendrick started to move off, but Nancy was not through questioning him. She wanted to know about another matter also. She asked him when he had last driven to the cliff above Bald Head Cave.

"Cliff?" the man repeated. "I've never been up on those rocks and don't intend to go. Nothing there worth going for that I know of."

"We thought we saw you up there looking through a telescope," said Bess.

"Not me. And where would I get a telescope? Well, I must go now," he smiled. "Hope you've forgiven me for running off with the boat."

After he had left Nancy felt that the interview had not been entirely satisfactory. Either Amos Hendrick was hiding some facts for reasons of his own, or else he was the victim of some hoax. She was sure the man who called himself Mr James and said he had a bell to sell to the collector was the one she had seen talking with Madame.

"You thought that man was Harry Tyrox," George reminded her. "He's connected with the *Mon Coeur* scandal, not bells."

Nancy shrugged. "I may have been mistaken," she said.

"What's next on the programme?" Bess asked. "Pleasure or mystery?"

"Couldn't the two go together?" Nancy laughed. "But seriously, what's next isn't going to be fun. I'm afraid it will be heartbreaking."

"Gracious, what is it?"

"I want to call on the people who bought stock in the perfume company from Monsieur Pappier."

Nancy had written down the names of the victims mentioned by Mother Mathilda. Because of her father's connection with the case, she felt she ought to see them and learn what she could. At least one of them might be able to give a clue to the whereabouts of the swindler who had taken their money.

"Do you want us to go with you?" Bess asked.

Nancy nodded. After learning from Mrs Chantrey where the people lived, the girls set out.

As Nancy had predicted, the calls were anything but pleasant. Maude Pullet wept on hearing the news. The little seamstress declared she felt too discouraged to try to save even a penny of money again. Sam Metts, white-faced and grim, told the girls that the swindle would cost his son a college education. At each home Nancy acquired the names and addresses of additional persons who had been cheated by Monsieur Pappier.

"This swindle is rolling like a snowball," she said excitedly to her friends. "Unless we check it, there's no telling how many others will lose their savings!"

Nancy kept hoping she might uncover a clue to the present address of either Monsieur Pappier or Madame. Such information was not forthcoming. The only one given by the people she interviewed was the New York office, vacated several days earlier.

Learning that several persons in the little country town of Branford had bought stock, Nancy motored there in the late afternoon with Bess and George. Interviews with two purchasers brought only the familiar story of fabulous profits which had been glibly promised by Monsieur Pappier and a companion salesman.

Discouraged, Nancy was leading the way to the parked car when she noticed a girl standing on the opposite side of the street.

"Isn't that the girl who bought some cosmetics from Madame?" she asked. "The one whose mother tried to have me arrested?"

"Yes," agreed George. "And look at the get up! Where did she find such outlandish clothes?"

The girl's face was made up heavily with lipstick and rouge. She wore a scarlet, sleeveless dress. It was unfashionably cut. High-heeled slippers with rhinestone buckles fitted her badly. As the girl walked down the street, she kept pausing every few steps to readjust the buckles.

The three crossed the street.

"Hello," Nancy greeted the girl with a friendly smile. "Aren't you a long way from home?"

"Not half far enough!" the girl retorted, tossing her head. "But I'll never go back, not even if Ma takes a horsewhip to me!"

"You've run away from home?" Nancy guessed.

"So what? I couldn't stand it on the farm another day. I've changed my name from Minnie to Hortense, and I have a fine job already!"

"In an office?" inquired Bess, wondering who would employ such a gaudily dressed person.

"No, as a model."

The three girls were speechless.

"I demonstrate *Mon Coeur* cosmetics for thirty dollars a week," Minnie went on proudly. "Madame is going to give me a bonus, too."

This information excited Nancy, but she was careful to keep her voice even as she asked, "Where do you give the demonstrations?"

"We'll have one tonight at nine o'clock in front of the Branford Hotel."

"Oh, not until tonight?"

"We never have our demonstrations until late," Minnie explained innocently. "Madame says the night light makes everyone look better." The girl giggled. "You ought to see me. I pretend to look awful, and then she fixes me up grand."

"I see," said Nancy, hiding a smile. "Well, I wish you good luck with your new work." Then she added carelessly. "I can see you like working for Madame."

"She's a fine woman!" Minnie retorted. "She gave me enough money to buy these clothes, and she lets me have all the perfume and cosmetics I want without charging me a cent!" Minnie teetered away on her spike heels.

"It's too bad we can't notify that girl's mother where she is!" exclaimed George, when the model was beyond hearing.

"I'll try to persuade her to go home," Nancy replied, "but not until after the demonstration tonight. Girls, do you realize Minnie may solve the mystery for us!"

"Will you notify the police to be on hand?" asked Bess.

"I may. How I wish Dad were here!"

"You have a date with Ned tonight," Bess said. "Why not talk it over with him?"

Nancy said she would. When Ned arrived and heard the news, he assured Nancy he was all the police force she needed.

"I can handle Madame," he laughed. "And Minnie, too. There's bound to be a constable not far away, if we want him to make any arrests."

Nancy was not completely satisfied. But she admitted to herself that the presence of the police might forewarn Madame or her accomplices.

She and Ned started off, and shortly before nine o'clock they reached the Branford Hotel and waited near the entrance. Soon Minnie appeared looking very unattractive in a black dress, her face pale, her lips colourless.

"She's certainly carrying out her part of the bargain," Nancy smiled.

"By the way, where is the pushcart woman?" inquired Ned, glancing towards a clock in the square. "It's ten minutes past nine now."

The seller of *Mon Coeur* cosmetics had not appeared. Even Minnie showed signs of increasing restlessness. She glanced uneasily up and down the street.

"I have a feeling Madame isn't going to show up!" commented Nancy presently, beginning to be fearful her plans would fall through.

"I have the same idea," said Ned.

At nine thirty-five Minnie suddenly lost patience. With an angry exclamation she started away from the hotel, convinced that her employer would not appear. This was the cue for Nancy and Ned to saunter forward and intercept her.

"Isn't there to be a demonstration?" Nancy inquired innocently.

"I can't give it alone!" the girl snapped. "And I haven't anything to sell. Oh, why doesn't Madame show up?"

"Maybe you'll never see her again," suggested Ned.

"I will so! Something must have kept her. I'll go to her home."

"You know where Madame lives?" Nancy could barely keep her voice calm.

In reply, Minnie took a paper from her purse and read the address aloud.

"We'll drive you there," said Nancy firmly.

· 16 · *A Thwarted Scheme*

DURING the ride to the house where they hoped to find Madame, Minnie Glaser kept up a chatter which exhausted both Nancy and Ned. But as the car drove up in front of an old, dark house, Minnie suddenly became silent. Not a light shone from any of the windows.

"It looks as if it's deserted," Ned observed. "You two wait in the car while I find out."

He was gone over ten minutes. Nancy had started to wonder what had happened, when he returned and shook his head.

"No one there?" she inquired.

"No one except a caretaker. The owners have gone away for the summer."

"Madame has gone away!" exclaimed Minnie. "I know better than that!"

267

"I didn't say Madame was the owner of the house," Ned corrected the girl impatiently. "No such person has ever been here. The woman gave you a false address."

At first Minnie Glaser refused to believe the truth. When it finally dawned upon her that she had been tricked, the girl burst into tears. She had no place to go, she declared. Her last dollar had been spent on clothes.

"You could go home," Nancy suggested. "We'll take you there."

"And have my family laugh at me? Or whip me?"

"Isn't it better than having no place to sleep or eat?"

Because she had no choice, Minnie finally consented to being driven to her parents' farm. But as they neared the place, Nancy became more and more fearful of the reception they would receive.

"Suppose you go in alone," Nancy urged Minnie.

"Oh, no!" she exclaimed, clinging to Nancy.

As the car stopped, the door of the farmhouse flew open and Minnie's parents rushed out to see who was in it. When they saw their daughter they cried out in happiness, and as she stepped from the car Mrs Glaser took her child in her arms.

"Oh, Minnie, don't ever go away again!" she sobbed. "I know I've been harsh, but from now on you kin have more freedom."

Tears flowed freely down Minnie's cheeks. Then suddenly she remembered Ned and Nancy!

"These—these people made me come home," she said. "You can thank them."

Mr Glaser put out a gnarled hand, and his wife wiped her tears and said:

"Please excuse me. I've been so upset these past few days I forgot my manners. Thank you kindly for bringing Minnie back." She did not recognize Nancy, and the girl was rather glad of this.

Nancy and Ned left the Glaser family happy in their reunion. As they rode back towards Candleton, Nancy became very quiet.

"What's the matter, Nancy? Worried about something?" he asked.

"Just disappointed. I had such high hopes for solving part of the mystery tonight, but—"

"But instead, you helped a poor girl who needed help badly, and I admire you for it, Nancy."

"Thank you, Ned," Nancy smiled. Then she added, "You know what I mean, this mystery is so important."

After she reached home, Nancy continued to think about the strange puzzle. She wondered how her father was making out; where Madame had gone; how they could find Harry Tyrox; and when the mystery of the tolling bell would be solved.

The next morning Nancy was her usual cheerful self. But Bess and George knew she had something special on her mind, for she fairly raced round doing all sorts of unnecessary chores. With her friends she went to the Salsandee Shop early, and speedily helped Mrs Chantrey arrange garden flowers on the tables and prepare fruit before any of the regular employees arrived.

Soon patrons began coming in to breakfast. The first man to seat himself at Nancy's table was a dwarf-like fellow she had seen in the tearoom before. He gave his order in a gruff voice, then became absorbed in the morning paper.

As Nancy went back and forth from the kitchen, she kept stealing glances at the man. Where had she seen him before? To satisfy herself, she asked Mrs Chantrey about him.

"I don't know his name," the tearoom owner replied. "He's one of our most unfriendly customers. Never so much as says hello, although he comes here regularly. Evidently his wife is an invalid, for he always takes food for her when he leaves."

That night after the shop closed, Mrs Chantrey invited Nancy, Bess and George to a concert. The cousins accepted, but Nancy begged off, saying she would rather stay at the house as her father might telephone or even return. Juno was out and it was very quiet at the cottage. Nancy picked up a book, but instead of reading she sat lost in thought.

"Who *was* that man at the tearoom?" she asked herself over and over again.

Presently a car pulled up at the kerb outside the house. Thinking her father might have arrived by taxi, Nancy ran to the porch. But she was wrong. A stocky man with a dark moustache alighted, pulling his felt hat low over his eyes. Seeing the girl, he asked gruffly:

"Are you Nancy Drew?"

"I am."

"Then you're to come with me."

"For what reason, please?" The man's manner had made Nancy suspicious.

"Your father needs you. He's in trouble."

"I don't believe it and I won't go!"

"Oh, you won't, eh?" the fellow growled, losing his temper. "Well, listen to me! You and that snooping father of yours had better mind your own business, or it'll be the worse for you both! Understand?"

The stranger advanced towards Nancy. Frightened, she ran into the house, slamming and locking the door. Turning off the lights, she stood behind the living-room draperies and watched the man from the window.

He started towards the door, but changed his mind. Returning to the parked car, he drove away, keeping close to the kerb as he disappeared down the street.

Nancy picked up a flashlight and ran outside to look around. Tyre tracks were plainly visible in the sandy road. As she examined the pattern left by the rubber tyres, her roving light revealed a small bundle lying close by.

"Here's something!" she thought, picking it up. "This must have fallen from the car when that man opened the door!"

Inside the cottage Nancy examined the package under a bright kitchen light. A crude sketch of three chiming bells in a cluster had been pencilled on the plain brown wrapping paper.

Puzzled, Nancy unwrapped the bundle. Hundreds of labels bearing the *Mon Coeur* trademark fluttered to the table and floor.

"So that man was one of the *Mon Coeur* crowd!" Nancy thought excitedly. She stared at the sketch on the paper. "I wonder if they're going to change their design from hearts to bells?"

The idea so intrigued Nancy she decided to try getting in touch with her father by telephone. At that moment the doorbell rang. Startled, Nancy tip-toed to the hall and peered through the window. Careful not to open the door, she called to the man on the porch. Then, she snapped on a desk light in the living-room and hastily penned a note to her friends. Leaving the message in plain view, the girl let herself out of the back door.

But in her haste to get away from the cottage, Nancy neglected to close a side window in the living-room. Scarcely had she gone, when a strong gust of wind caught her note and carried it beneath the couch.

Some time later, Mrs Chantrey, George and Bess came home to find Nancy absent and not a word to explain what had become of her. As the minutes became hours and she did not appear, they grew uneasy.

"Shouldn't we notify the police?" Bess asked anxiously. "Something must have happened to Nancy!"

George was inclined to agree to the proposal, when Mrs Chantrey called from the kitchen. She had just spied the package of *Mon Coeur* labels.

"How did these get here?" she asked in amazement. Bess and George had no answer.

"Nancy must have had a visitor while while we were away!" Bess exclaimed fearfully. "Maybe she's been kidnapped!"

· 17 ·   *A New Trademark*

MRS CHANTREY could think of no reason for Nancy's long absence, but she was inclined to believe the girl was too resourceful to allow herself to be kidnapped.

"Why not wait a while longer before calling the police?" Mrs Chantrey suggested, and finally the girls consented.

When another hour passed, they were confronted with a new worry. A glance at the falling barometer warned of an approaching storm. The wind began to moan through the trees surrounding the house.

"I'm going to call the police," Mrs Chantrey said with sudden decision.

As she started towards the telephone, the storm broke

in full force. A mighty gust of wind swept through an open window, blowing a sheet of paper from beneath the couch.

"What's this?" exclaimed Bess, picking it up. "It's a note from Nancy!"

The others ran to her side. The brief message said:

"Have gone out with Ned on important business."

"Maybe they've eloped," giggled Bess, glad the strain was over.

Not feeling entirely relieved, Mrs Chantrey closed the open windows and wiped the spattered woodwork. Rain fell in torrents. The water was running like a river in the streets.

"Wherever Nancy is, I hope she's not out in this storm," Mrs Chantrey said, pacing the floor.

George was inclined to believe that Nancy had gone with Ned to investigate a clue in connection with the *Mon Coeur* case. In this supposition she was right.

Earlier in the evening when Nancy heard the doorbell ring, she called through the window and discovered it was Ned. Briefly she told him of the strange man's visit and the package he had dropped.

"We must trail that man if we can!" she added. "But someone may be watching the house, so I'll slip out the back way and meet you over on the next street."

Ned was waiting in his car when she reached the appointed place.

"This may be a wild, useless chase," Nancy said breathlessly. "But I saw the man's car turn down this street when it left Mrs Chantrey's."

"Notice the make?"

"No, it was too dark to see the car plainly."

"Then how can we trace it?"

Playing the beam of her flashlight along the roadway

close to the kerb, Nancy did not answer.

"What are you looking for?" asked Ned, puzzled, as he got out of the car.

Nancy pointed to tyre tracks plainly visible in the sandy road. She explained that they were of the same pattern as those she had found in front of the Chantrey house after the man's car had pulled away.

"I noticed that the driver hugged the kerb," she added, "so we may be able to trace him."

"It's worth trying," Ned agreed, springing into the car again.

The tyre tracks led to a small print shop in an alley. There the car had turned in, apparently parked near the side entrance, and then had gone on.

Inside the building a light burned brightly. A man in a printer's apron could be seen working over one of the presses.

The thud of a hand press deadened the sound of their footsteps as Nancy and Ned entered the cluttered little shop. Not until they shouted did the stooped old man with grease smeared over his apron whirl round to face them.

"We may want some stationery printed," Nancy said as an excuse for the interruption. "Would it be possible for you to do it soon?"

"Miss, I couldn't even touch it for six weeks! Why, I'm wallowin' up to my ears now in commercial orders. That's why I'm puttin' in extra time tonight—trying to get caught up."

"Do you do much label printing?" Nancy asked casually.

"Makes up about fifty per cent of my business. Been doing a lot of work for the *Mon Coeur* people lately."

Nancy was careful not to show her elation at the

information. "Oh, yes, I understand they're putting out another line, too. What's their new trade-mark? Is it three bells or—"

She purposely hesitated, and the old man completed the sentence for her.

"You mean *Sweet Chimes*."

"Are you going to do the work for the firm?"

"No. I'm too rushed. Anyhow, that fast-talkin' foreigner, Monsieur Pappier, said he'd rather give the job to another printer who is closer to where the products are goin' to be made. Said it wouldn't pay him to have any more work done here."

"Where is the place?" Nancy asked, trying to keep down the excitement in her voice.

"Let me see. Was it New York—no, that wasn't it. Yorktown! Or maybe it was Yorkville. All I remember is, that it had a York in the name."

"Did Monsieur Pappier call on you tonight?"

"Yes, just before you came. This morning he picked up a package. He started talkin' about that *Sweet Chimes* idea, and he drew a sketch of the design on the wrapping paper. Tonight he came back saying he couldn't find his package. He thought maybe he'd forgotten to take it, but I guess he lost it."

"I think I've seen Monsieur Pappier," Nancy said. "Does he wear a moustache?"

"No," replied the old man. "Must be somebody else you have in mind."

"Probably," said Nancy. "I'm sorry we kept you so long from your work. Goodnight."

Nancy was excited as she and Ned returned to the car.

"It must have been Monsieur Pappier who called on me!" she remarked. "He put on a moustache for a disguise! And he didn't have a trace of a foreign accent. I'm convinced he's Harry Tyrox!"

"Maybe he changes his nationality at will," suggested Ned.

Although it was now after eleven o'clock, Nancy had no intention of abandoning the chase. Consulting a road map which she kept in the car, she discovered that a small city named Yorktown was less than thirty miles away.

"Ned, I have an idea that is where Monsieur Pappier went! It's too late for a printing shop to be open, but he may be staying at a hotel. Let's follow him!"

"All right, if you want to, Nancy. But it's a long drive. Won't the folks at home be worried about you?"

"I'll telephone Mrs Chantrey and tell her our plans," Nancy declared. "We'll stop at the first drug store."

When Nancy called the Chantrey cottage, she was unable to reach her friends. She assumed the group had not returned from the concert and decided to drive on and call from Yorktown.

Forty-five minutes later, she and Ned entered the Yorktown Hotel. While Nancy tried again without success to get an answer at the Chantrey cottage, Ned checked the register. Monsieur Pappier had not registered for a room there that night, nor had the clerk seen anyone remotely answering his description.

"Perhaps he went to another hotel," Nancy said uncertainly.

The young people went the rounds, but learned nothing. Nancy had known the trip might end in failure, but even so, she was bitterly disappointed. At the last place, the Koven House, she placed another telephone call. Again there was no answer from the Chantrey home.

"Surely they're back by now!" she thought nervously·
"I hope nothing has happened to them!"

Ned tried to allay Nancy's fears by telling her that a
strong wind which had sprung up might mean there
had been a bad storm at Candleton. The wind could
have affected the telephone wires.

"It's going to storm here," he added. "Shall we wait
until it's over or get started?"

Nancy thought they should leave. But as they walked
towards the entrance, she stopped to look into the
restaurant where there was dancing, and spoke to the
hat-check girl. When she joined Ned her eyes were
sparkling like stars.

"Ned, I just learned something interesting! A Spanish
Señora who sells cosmetics has been in here tonight!
She hasn't registered, but she said she was coming back."

"We're not trailing a Spanish woman, Nancy."

"We may be after tonight! Oh, I'll bet Madame and
Monsieur change their nationality whenever the police
get warm on their trail!"

"The police!" exclaimed Ned. "That's the ticket!
Let's dump this in their laps, and start for home before
that storm breaks."

A stop was made at the Yorktown Police Headquarters where the night inspector assured the couple a
close watch would be kept for both Monsieur Pappier
and the mysterious Señora.

Trees were cracking in the wind as Nancy and Ned
drove out of town. Before they had travelled five miles,
the storm broke in all its fury. Lightning zig-zagged
across an inky sky and deafening claps of thunder
seemed to shake the lonely, seldom-travelled road.

The wiper was chugging back and forth, but water
pelted down so fast the glass could not be cleared. It

was impossible to see three yards ahead.

"We'll have an accident if we keep on in this!" the young man declared as the car swerved and nearly went off the pavement. "What do you say we pull up somewhere and wait until the worst is over?"

Ned removed his foot from the accelerator pedal and started to ease on the brakes. Before he could do so, the couple heard the screech of rubber tyres directly behind them.

The next instant their car was rammed violently from the rear!

·18· *Danger in the Storm*

NANCY and Ned were thrown against the windscreen. The car skidded, but fortunately did not overturn. Though stunned by the force of the impact, Ned put on the brake and switched off the ignition.

They heard loud exclamations and screams from the car which had caused the accident.

"Are you hurt, Nancy?" Ned asked anxiously.

"Just shaken up," she managed to say jerkily. "How about the people in the other car?"

Ned craned his neck to peer out of the rear window into the pelting rain. He saw that the driver was slumped over the steering wheel. But someone was climbing over from the back seat to push the man aside and take his place.

"They're going to get away!" Ned exclaimed. "Hey, you!"

He tried to open his door, but it had jammed. The

new driver of the other car backed quickly down the road. Before Nancy and Ned could get out, he had turned into a side road and sped off.

"Let it go," said Nancy weakly.

"We'll have to let it go," agreed Ned in disgust, looking at the rear of his automobile.

A tyre was flat, and the mudguard was jammed tightly against it.

"Those men fled from here so that they wouldn't have to pay damages!" he exclaimed. "We didn't even see who they were. Now we're stranded!"

"Maybe not." Far down the road Nancy saw the headlights of an approaching vehicle. "Maybe we can get a lift."

Ned signalled the approaching truck and the driver pulled up.

"Havin' trouble?" he called cheerily.

"Yes!" replied Ned with emphasis. "My car's out of commission. Any chance of a lift into Candleton?"

The trucker, who was hauling a load of chickens to a city market many miles away, assured the young people it would not be out of his way to drop them off at Candleton. In fact, he insisted upon driving them directly to Mrs Chantrey's house.

"Glad to have done it," he said, as they bade him good-bye. "I don't have to be at market until six o'clock."

Lights blazed in the cottage, telling Nancy that her long absence had worried the members of the household, and that they could not sleep. Mrs Chantrey, George and Bess greeted the couple joyfully, asking what had happened.

"We'll tell you everything," Nancy promised, sinking into the nearest chair. "But first, is anything the matter with the telephone? I called and called."

Investigation revealed that the instrument was out of order for outgoing as well as incoming calls. Nancy and Ned related what had occurred at Yorktown. Then, at Mrs Chantrey's insistence, Ned accepted an invitation to stay overnight, and everyone wearily went off to his or her room for a much-needed sleep.

It was nearly noon the next day when Nancy was wakened by her friends, who told her that Mr Drew had arrived from New York. Dressing quickly, she ran downstairs to greet him with an affectionate kiss.

"Did you find out anything about those swindlers?" she asked eagerly.

"No," he reported in disgust. "Our leads were worthless. Not only Harry Tyrox, but all the rest of his gang have disappeared completely. But I hate to give Mrs Chantrey this bad news."

"Why not wait for a few days?" Nancy suggested.

She told her father about all that had happened since he had left, including the two times she thought she had seen Tyrox; her experience in Yorktown; the new clue which she hoped might lead to the arrest of the perfume seller; and what she had learned from the people in Candleton who had bought *Mon Coeur* stock.

Although Mr Drew was shocked to hear about the number of investors in town, he was delighted at his daughter's progress with the case. The lawyer decided to motor to Yorktown himself to learn what luck the police were having in tracing the mysterious Señora, and set off in Nancy's car. Ned had gone off a short while before to see about having his damaged automobile repaired.

Left to themselves, Bess and George insisted Nancy relax and go for a swim. They rented a motorboat and went to Whistling Oyster Cave. After a delightful hour in the water, the three friends lay on their backs in the soft, warm sand. Suddenly Nancy sat bolt upright.

"Why didn't I think of that before!" she exclaimed, springing to her feet. "It may explain everything!"

"You might try doing a little explaining yourself," drawled George, tossing a pebble into the water. "What's rolling round now in that clever little mind of yours?"

"The best idea I've had in a week! Girls, you must go to Bald Head Cave with me at once!"

"Not inside," objected Bess. "As a matter of fact, I don't even want to go close to the entrance."

"It's low tide now—just starting to change," Nancy declared excitedly. "I want to make an experiment. You take me round the point of the cliff and drop me off. Then hurry back to the cave."

"And if we do drop you off, what are your plans?" asked George.

"That depends upon what I find among the rocks on the ocean side. But please hurry. I want you to drop me off and get back to the cave entrance as soon as possible."

"Your scheme sounds risky to me," Bess complained. "Anything else you have in mind?"

"Yes, you're to watch the mouth of the cave closely. If the bell tolls or water rushes out, note the exact time, then return to the beach for me."

"You've certainly worked out your little blueprint in minute detail," George said. "Just what do you expect to discover among those rocks on the ocean side?"

"I'll tell you later, after I'm sure I'm right," Nancy grinned. Catching a hand of each of her friends, she pulled them towards the boat. "Come on! The tide is starting to come in, and there's no time to lose."

The boat presently slipped round the point into the ocean. As Nancy started to dive out, George seized her by the wrist.

"Maybe you'd better not do this. At least, not unless you tell us exactly what you have in mind."

"All right. I have a theory that as the tide comes in on the ocean side of the cliff, it may rush through a tunnel in the rocks and gush out of the cave entrance."

"You mean before the tide is very high on the White Cap Bay side?" George asked, turning the matter over in her mind.

"That's my idea. You recall that when we heard the bell toll, the tide had not turned in the bay."

"There may be something to it, Nancy. But what about the tolling bell?"

"I'll know more after I've made my investigation, George. Now will you let me go?"

"All right," her chum agreed, "but do be careful. We'll keep watch at the cave entrance and return here for you."

Diving out of the boat, Nancy swam off and easily reached the shore. As the rocks were sharp, she put on her beach shoes which she had tied round her neck. Up and up she climbed, clinging tightly to precarious holds.

The tide was coming in fast. Waves licked greedily at Nancy's heels, only to fall back in angry froth and foam.

Above Nancy, a fisherman who had been seining with a large net and now was on his way home, saw the girl. He signalled to her, but she was so engrossed searching for a narrow opening in the rocks that she did not see him.

"The tunnel must be lower down," she decided and started to descend. "I believe I see the place!"

Nancy slid towards a pile of debris deposited by the

incoming waves. Crossing this, she went over to a definite opening in the rocks. Only then did she hear a shout from above.

Pausing, the girl glanced up at the ledge where the old fisherman was motioning frantically to her. His words sounded like "High tide!" but she did not catch the rest, because the wind was blowing away from her.

Nancy hesitated, then advanced again in her search for an opening amid the rocks.

But before she could move, a net weighted by sinkers was slung over her. The next instant, Nancy was swept from her feet.

Enmeshed in the dripping net, she was swung up towards the top of the cliff!

•19• *Confidential Information*

FOR several seconds, Nancy swung precariously in the net above the dashing waves. The old fisherman struggled to lift her the remaining few yards to the rocky shelf, but as he puffed and strained she began to fear that he lacked the strength for the task.

"If he drops me now, I'll never get out of this net alive!" she thought in terror. "I'll be dashed on the rocks, or so tangled in these meshes that I won't be able to swim!"

With one last effort, the old fisherman brought the net almost to the shelf. Nancy, forcing an arm up through the opening above her head, clutched at a small tree which had grown from a crack amid the rocks. She had just caught hold of it, when the fisherman lost his grip on the net!

Desperately Nancy grabbed for the tree with her other hand, and got a toe hold among the rocks. The old man pulled her to safety. Both were breathless and so shattered by the narrow escape that for a moment they could not speak. Then the fisherman gasped in apology:

"I thought I could swing you up easylike! You never should have been foolin' around down there! More than one person's been drowned when the tide comes in!"

"But I knew what I was doing," Nancy defended her actions. "I came here searching for an opening in the rocks. I know about the cave with its tolling bell and rushing water. I thought I could find an explanation for them over here."

Nancy explained her belief that strong waves, dashing through a small opening, might be responsible for the rush of water through the big cave.

"Could be," the fisherman agreed, drawing on his pipe. "But I've lived hereabouts for well on sixty years. I've never heard tell of any such hole in the rocks."

"Did you ever see the ghost or hear the bell?" asked Nancy.

"I've never seen the ghost, and don't want to. But I've heard that mournful bell," the old man replied. "Jim Wester, a young fisherman who was caught out in a heavy fog, lost his life. Him and his boat was never found. Folks figure maybe it's his spirit that's come back to prowl in that cave. Leastways, the bell sounds powerful like the one he had on his old dory."

"A boat with a bell on it might be caught somewhere in the cave," Nancy said thoughtfully. "Has no one ever investigated to find out?"

"Folks hereabouts got too much common sense. Anyway, what good would it do for a body to go in there and fetch the bell? Long as it tolls a warning, it keeps a lot o' people out o' trouble."

Nancy talked for a while longer with the fisherman, but soon was convinced he could contribute nothing to a solution of the baffling mystery. Observing George and Bess on their way back, she signalled to them.

"If you're agoin' down to join your friends, I'll show you a safe path on the bay side," the fisherman offered.

He pointed out a well-worn trail which Nancy followed without difficulty. Reaching the beach, she found George and Bess waiting for her a hundred yards from shore. After knotting her shoes about her neck, she plunged in and swam out to the boat.

"What happened at the mouth of the cave?" Nancy demanded as soon as she was in the boat. "Did the bell toll?"

"Exactly on the hour," George replied. "We didn't see the ghost, but the water did rush from the cave the same as before."

"Then I'm sure I'm right," Nancy said excitedly.

Relating her experience and her conversation with the man, Nancy said she thought it possible that an old, wrecked boat with a bell attached might be lodged somewhere deep within the cave.

"You mean when the water comes through, it makes the bell ring?" Bess asked. "But, Nancy, how do you explain the ghost?"

"So far, I can't. The ghost must be a person. But where does he come from and where does he go? Frankly, I can't guess who would have a reason for hiding there or dressing up in white robes. The only way to solve the mystery is by thoroughly investigating the cave."

"Not today!" said Bess emphatically.

Nancy smiled as she turned to start the motor of the boat. "No, I promised Dad and Mrs Chantrey I wouldn't venture in there even at low tide. But that promise certainly hinders me."

"It may save your life, though," declared George. "This is one mystery I feel we should leave unsolved!"

Nancy did not debate the matter. Her silence as the trio returned to Candleton told Bess and George more clearly than words that she had not the slightest intention of abandoning the enigma of the tolling bell cave.

Nancy had no opportunity to discuss the matter with her father that night. On reaching the Chantrey cottage, she learned that he had sent word he planned to remain another day in Yorktown.

"That means he must have run into some interesting clues!" Nancy thought. "Perhaps the police have traced those scoundrels we're after!"

At Nancy's suggestion the three girls spent the evening at the Salsandee Shop, assisting their hostess. While George and Bess helped prepare Dandee Tarts, Nancy waited on table, hoping she might see Amos Hendrick again. But the old man did not dine there that evening.

Among the customers she saw the same dwarf-like stranger who made a practice of carrying food to his wife. He ate rapidly, with a display of very bad table manners. When he finished, he ordered the usual package of food, and departed. Though Nancy questioned several of the waitresses, no one could tell her the man's name nor where he lived.

"I've certainly seen that man somewhere before," she thought. "It wasn't in the theatre, and yet he seems like someone acting a part."

"He reminds me of a brown-skinned elf," one of the waitresses contributed. "Only he has such mean, cruel eyes!"

"An elf!" exclaimed Nancy. "Why, that's it! I mean—" she amended hastily, "—he does have that appearance."

The waitress's words had recalled to Nancy the strange dream she had experienced many days before on the cliff above Bald Head Cave. In a flash she knew that the characters in her dream were not visionary but actual persons! Now she had identified one of the "elves"!

"I didn't walk from the cliff by myself," Nancy reasoned excitedly. "I was carried by two men. But why?"

Realizing that such a theory might sound fantastic to the others, she was careful to say nothing about it, not even to Bess or George. Nevertheless, she determined to learn more about the stranger.

Hoping that he might lunch at the Salsandee Shop, she made a point of working there the next day. The man did not come, but to her delight, Amos Hendrick strolled into the tearoom. As usual he had a startling remark to make before Nancy could speak.

"Well, well, my favourite waitress again!" he greeted her with a chuckle. "You bring a fellow bad luck, though."

"What do you mean, Mr Hendrick?"

"A. H., if you please," he corrected her. "Remember that man I was telling you about who was going to sell me a bell?"

"You mean the one you met on the other side of the bay, a Mr James?"

"I haven't seen him since, and he was going to bring the bell for me to look at," A. H. reported. "Now I'm afraid maybe I'll never see him again, and I believe he has something I've been hunting for all over the country."

"Not the jewelled bell?" Nancy asked excitedly.

"Mr James didn't tell me much, but I have a sneaking suspicion that it might be," Mr Hendrick confided.

Nancy was startled at the information. She instantly concluded that if Mr James were Harry Torox, he had not secured the jewelled bell by honest means. Perhaps he did not even have it, but knew where it was and was trying to get hold of it. This might account for his not contacting A. H. again.

"Unless his reason is because he has left this part of the country permanently," she thought.

Nancy hoped this was not true, and asked the bell collector to let her know the minute he heard from Mr James. Mr Hendrick promised to do this if possible. Then she inquired what kind of a tone the jewelled bell had.

"Oh, a very pleasant musical sound, almost like one in the middle register of a set of chimes."

"Then your lost bell couldn't possibly be the one in Bald Head Cave?"

"Oh no, that one has a deep tolling sound." A. H.'s eyes brightened. "I'd give a lot to get my hands on it just the same," he declared, "but I value my life too much. Can't figure a way to keep from drowning, or you can bet your last dollar I'd be inside that cave this minute!"

"Perhaps I can help you," Nancy said.

While the old man listened with rapt attention, she told him of her theory that the cave was flooded for only a few hours each day, and that the period of danger could be clocked accurately.

"Say! Maybe I'll go there sometime!" the old man exclaimed. "You really think it's safe?"

"I have an idea that if a person doesn't venture into the cave after the tide has started to come in, he won't be bothered with the rushing water. I'll let you know later."

Because Mr Hendrick was so pleased at the information she had given him, he talked more freely as he ate his luncheon. As she served his dessert, he surprised her by saying:

"I've been thinking things over since I've been sitting here. I have a hunch that man James may be mixed up with the thief who has the jewelled bell."

"How?" Nancy asked, trying not to show her eagerness to hear his answer.

"Didn't I tell you I traced it to a son of the original thief? His name is Grumper. He's an ornery little fellow with a misshapen back. Haven't actually seen him, but I've been told he's around here."

"You think Grumper still has the bell after all these years? Wouldn't he have been tempted to sell it, or at least the jewels?"

"Not Grumper. He's a strange sort of fellow, not much concerned with money. They tell me chemistry is his main interest in life. He got into a jam with the chemical company where he worked, and disappeared. I've good reason to think he's skulking round here somewhere."

"How did you learn Grumper had the bell?" Nancy asked curiously.

"From that note found in my father's possessions. You saw only part of the message."

Nancy would have asked many more questions, but just then another customer sat down at a nearby table. A. H. immediately became silent. Soon he left the tea-room, so the girl had no further opportunity to talk with him.

"He certainly didn't tell me all the story," Nancy thought. "I must see him again and learn the rest."

Later that day she and Ned went to the boat dock with the intention of renting a motorboat to do some further exploring at Bald Head Cave. There they learned that Amos Hendrick had rented a boat and had gone alone to Bald Head Cave.

"He may get into trouble there!" Nancy said anxiously. "I'm afraid he took a theory of mine too seriously. I should have warned him not to enter the cave until I've had a chance to prove my idea about the tides. If I should be wrong, he might drown!"

"Then we must go after him, and we've no time to lose!" declared Ned.

With Ned at the wheel of the motorboat, they raced up the bay. Nancy peered nervously ahead, hoping to catch a glimpse of the elderly man. But he was not in sight.

"Oh, Ned, I'm so afraid we may get there too late!" she exclaimed.

·20· *An Identification*

WHEN Nancy and Ned reached Bald Head Cliff in the motorboat, they could not find a trace of A. H. They had no way of knowing whether or not he had ventured into the cave.

"Say, who is that up there on the cliff?" Ned demanded suddenly. He pointed to a short figure on the high rocks, peering intently at them through a telescope. It was not Mr Hendrick as George had thought the time she and her friends had seen a man on the cliff with a telescope.

"He certainly looks familiar!" Nancy remarked. "Why is he watching us, I wonder?"

Her attention was distracted by a flash of white near the cave entrance. Distinctly she saw a ghostly figure retreat into its dark interior. Within a few moments a bell from within the cave started to toll.

"The warning!" Nancy exclaimed. "Oh, what if A. H. is inside!"

Should this be true, it was too late to do anything to save the man. Fearfully, Ned and Nancy watched as water began to boil from the entrance. A box floated clear, but to their intense relief, no body or overturned boat was washed from the cave.

Convinced that A. H. could not have been trapped by the flood waters, Nancy sighed in relief, and suggested that they climb the cliff to question the man with the telescope.

"He may be able to answer a lot of questions about this place," she said.

Accordingly, Ned anchored the boat, and the couple waded ashore. They climbed the rocks, using the path up which Nancy had gone before. But when they reached the top, the man had disappeared. They walked round, but could not find him.

"Show me the place where you went to sleep that time," Ned suggested.

Nancy ran ahead, searching for the exact spot. When she thought she had located it, the girl paused to catch breath. Presently she began to feel a trifle dizzy from her exertion. The blue sky above seemed suddenly misty, as if a film had dropped over her eyes. Vaguely she recalled that the same symptoms had overtaken her the first day she had visited the cliff.

"Ned!" she called in a weak voice. "Ned!"

He ran quickly towards her. One glance at her face told him something was seriously wrong.

"It's probably the climb," he said solicitously. "I'll carry you to the beach and you'll feel okay."

He quickly lifted her up in his arms and worked his way down the steep slope. By the time they reached the beach, Nancy seemed better.

"Why, I don't know what came over me," she apologized, deeply embarrassed. "I've never had spells like this before!"

Ned insisted upon their going home at once so she could rest, but after he had left Mrs Chantrey's, Nancy subjected herself to a severe athletic test. She raced up and down stairs four times without pausing. George and Bess, who entered the cottage unexpectedly, stared at her in amazement.

"I'm not crazy!" laughed Nancy. "I'm only trying to determine if I get fainting or dizzy spells after strenuous exertion."

"You're a star athlete, if you ask me!" retorted George. "Why, you're not even breathing very hard."

"I feel fine! This test certainly proves I'm all right. But there was something weird about the way I nearly fainted while on Bald Head Cliff! Twice while up there I became very drowsy—almost as if I'd been drugged!

Do you suppose some gas could have escaped from crevices in the rocks where I was standing?"

She had noted no unusual odour other than a sweet one like that of the wild flowers on the cliff, and was unable to offer a satisfactory theory for the strange symptoms she had experienced.

Later that afternoon, at Nancy's suggestion, the three girls called upon Mother Mathilda to ask her if she knew anything about the cliff that might throw some light on the girl's experience. To their disappointment the woman could offer no explanation. So far as she knew, no gasses or deadly fumes had ever exuded from crevices in the rocks.

"I'm glad you dropped in," the elderly candlemaker said. "When you were here the other day, I forgot to tell you about Amy Maguire."

"A daughter of the Maguires who lived on the cliff?" Nancy inquired.

"Yes. She was an adopted daughter. Amy was a wild one, and not really a Maguire, although she took the name. As long as Grandpa Maguire was alive she behaved herself pretty well. After his passing, she made her adopted Ma a heap o' trouble, running off to marry a no-good."

"Someone you knew?"

"No, and I never did hear his name, nor what became of the couple. But I know her adopted Ma was heartbroken. And her Pa took it kind of hard, too. They never mixed with other folks after that."

As the girls rose to leave, the old lady timidly inquired if any progress had been made in tracing Monsieur Pappier, the *Mon Coeur* stock swindler.

Nancy assured her that Mr Drew was working on the case. "We have good reason to think both he and

Madame may be caught within the next few days," she added.

"I hope he's sent to jail for at least twenty years! And that she's punished, too! Will I get my money back, do think, or will the scamp have spent it?"

"No one can tell that until they're caught. But let's hope you'll recover part of it, at least."

Nancy's words cheered the old lady. Grateful to the girls for taking so much interest in her troubled affairs, she insisted upon presenting each of them with a dozen delicately perfumed candles.

"I used good perfume this time, and the entire batch turned out perfectly," she declared proudly.

A little later, at the Chantrey cottage, Nancy learned from Juno that during her absence she had received a telephone call from Yorktown. Knowing that it was from her father, she stayed indoors for the next hour, and as she had expected, he telephoned her again.

"Nancy, I've been trying to get you," he began in an excited voice. "How soon can you reach Yorktown?"

"Why, I don't know," she replied. "You have my car, and Ned's is in the garage being fixed."

"Then catch the first train you can," the lawyer instructed. "The police are holding that Señora you eard about. She may be the seller of *Mon Coeur* perm∋. You're needed to identify her."

"I'll come as fast as I can," Nancy promised.

With the assistance of George and Bess, she packed a few belongings into an overnight bag and consulted time-tables. The only train to Yorktown that evening was a local which stopped at every station.

"I have no choice but to take it," Nancy sighed. "It will be a tiresome trip."

As it developed, the journey was not tiresome, but

proved to be both pleasant and profitable. Soon after the girl had settled herself in a carriage, Bert Hamilton sauntered in.

"Hello," said the young chemist who had analyzed the *Mon Coeur* cosmetics, as he sat down beside her.

During the trip the young people kept each other company. The chemist displayed keen interest when Nancy steered the conversation to her recent experience at Bald Head Cliff. He looked serious when she revealed her theory that her drowsiness might have come from inhaling some strange fumes.

"I could mention several kinds which have no noticeable odour, and others with a sweet odour," Bert said. "But I've never heard of any near White Cap Bay."

The slow train finally reached Yorktown. With reluctance, for she really had enjoyed the long chat, Nancy said good-bye to Bert. Descending from the coach, she looked about for her father. He was not at the station to meet her, so she went directly to Police Headquarters.

As Nancy entered the building, she saw the lawyer talking to the desk sergeant. He turned, and seeing her rushed across the room.

"I'm glad you're here, Nancy!" he exclaimed. "If you're able to identify the prisoner we may crack the case!"

"Where is the woman, Dad?"

"She's in a cell now. But you'll have to select her from a line-up. Think you can do it?"

"I'll try."

"The woman will not be wearing a costume, which may confuse you," Mr Drew warned.

"If I've ever seen the woman before I think I'll

recognize her," Nancy said quietly. "Tell the police I'm ready."

· 21 ·   *A Dust-Covered Bible*

As NANCY, her father and two police officers stood behind a screen, other policemen escorted five women across a small stage which was brilliantly lighted.

All were heavy-set, dark-complexioned and wore street clothing. Blinking under the bright lights, they stared straight ahead.

Nancy gazed at each woman in turn. Then, without the slightest hesitation, she said, "The one in the centre is the perfume seller. She is known to me only as Madame."

"Good!" praised Mr Drew. "That makes the identification positive."

After the prisoner had been led away, he told Nancy that previously he had identified the same woman as the one who had accompanied him in the taxi to Fisher's Cove.

"The woman who drugged you!" Nancy cried.

"I'm convinced of it. We'll place charges against her."

Nancy learned that Madame, who had been posing as the Spanish Señora while in Yorktown, had been caught by the police as she sought to sell *Sweet Chimes* perfume to the proprietor of a beauty parlour. She had denied knowing Mr Drew or having anything to do with the *Mon Coeur* firm.

"She refuses to tell us anything about her confederates," the lawyer added. "Fortunately, a number of names and addresses were found in her wallet when it was searched. The police are checking them now."

As Nancy and her father stepped into the corridor, they came face to face with Madame, who was being escorted to her cell by two policewomen. Seeing the girl, she suddenly halted to glare at her.

"Your meddling did it!" she cried furiously. "You're responsible for me being held here! But just wait until I get free! Just wait!"

Nancy made no reply, and the woman, still muttering threats, was led away.

"Madame speaks English without an accent," Mr Drew observed. "The truth is, she hasn't a drop of foreign blood. She was born in New York City and her name is Mary Smith."

"Monsieur Pappier hasn't been found yet?"

"No, but the police are hard on his trail. They think he's in hiding around here, but I shan't be able to stay in Candleton to await his capture. I must return to my work at River Heights tomorrow. I have an important case up in Federal Court."

"Oh!" murmured Nancy, unable to hide her disappointment. "Then that means we must leave the case entirely to the police?"

"Not unless you've lost interest," he smiled meaningly.

"Oh, Dad! You know how much solving the mystery means to me! I hope those men are still around here."

"I hope so too, Nancy. We are not letting it be known Madame has been caught. In fact, we planted information here and there that she went back to the vicinity of Candleton. I believe she and Harry Tyrox work hand in glove, and he'll trail her there. I'd like to have you stay at Candleton a few days longer to keep in touch with the situation. If anything develops that you think you can't handle alone, I'll try to fly back."

The next morning Mr Drew took the train for River Heights. He had barely left when Nancy asked Bess and George if they would go out to Bald Head Cliff with her again.

"And have you go to sleep on our hands?" George cried. "And maybe be put to sleep ourselves? I should say not!"

"I don't fancy being carried off by a man even if he is an elf!" said Bess. "Anyway, I promised Mrs Chantrey I'd help her unpack a lot of gifts which arrived yesterday."

Nancy finally prevailed upon George to make the trip by promising to go by car and avoiding the cave.

"But I thought you were supposed to stay here to catch a certain Harry Tyrox who is posing as Monsieur Pappier," George reminded her friend.

"I am. Dad and the police set a trap to get him back to Candleton to look up Madame, but they don't think Harry Tyrox will come out of hiding until nightfall. If he's caught, then I'll probably go home and maybe never solve the mystery of the tolling bell, so I want to work on it now."

"How do you expect to accomplish that on top of the cliff?"

"I think there may be some connection between the ghost in the cave and the disappearance of the Maguires. Another thing, I've been giving a lot of thought to that queer dream I had while lying on the cliff. I've decided one of those little elves may have been Grumper—the misshapen man A. H. told me about."

"Oh, Nancy!" scoffed George. "How could he be?"

"A. H. said he thought Grumper was around Candleton. The answer may lie in the Maguires' deserted home," Nancy decided. "Anyway, I'm going to look for a clue there."

Nancy drove to the footpath which led to the cliff, and parked. The girls walked the rest of the way to the deserted house, gazing about in all directions to find out if they had been seen. Apparently, no one was near to observe their actions.

"This place does have a spooky look," George said uneasily, as they went up to the door.

Nancy pushed it open. Everything appeared exactly as she last had seen it. The mouldy, cobwebby food remained on the dining-room table, and the two dust-covered chairs stood at each end.

"I never saw such thick cobwebs in all my life!" George gasped.

A worn Bible on a marble-topped table drew Nancy's attention. Blowing off the dust, she slowly turned the pages until she came to the family birth and death records.

"This is what I hoped to find!" she exclaimed, and pointed to a notation in faded ink. "Amy's marriage is recorded here. Oh!"

"Now what, Nancy?"

"Amy married a man named Ferdinand Slocum! Why, Slocum is the name of the hotel clerk at Fisher's Cove."

"But Slocum is a fairly common name. He may not be the same person."

"True," Nancy acknowledged. "Let's see what else we can find."

The other records were of no interest to Nancy, but she did find among the pages of the Bible a letter which had been written by Amy to her parents. Obviously, it was sent soon after her runaway marriage two years before. In the letter she disrespectfully referred to her mother and father as being far behind the times.

"Maybe I don't love Ferdie," she had written flippantly, "but he's a big hotel man and we'll have a lot of fun together. Ferdie is a man of the world. He's a big business man, not like those boys at Candleton who only think about following the sea. I'll write again after Ferdie and I are settled in our own hotel."

"I'll bet they never were in any better one than the Fisher's Cove Hotel," George guessed after hearing the letter.

"This note explains a number of things that puzzled me," Nancy cried elatedly. "George, our case is closing in!"

"Find anything else of interest?"

"Yes, here's something!" Nancy cried an instant later.

George, however, did not hear her, for she had made an important discovery of her own. "Nancy, look at these cobwebs on the table!" she exclaimed. "They're real enough, but they're not attached to anything!"

"Just put there, you mean?" Nancy bounded across the room to look. "You're right. Someone is using this cottage as a hide-out!"

"But why would anyone go to so much work just to make this place look weird and deserted?" George asked. "We ought to call the police!"

"I agree with you." Nancy spoke quietly as she stooped to pick up a torn sheet of paper from the floor.

"What's that?" her friend asked.

"Mr Hendrick's torn note that was stolen from the Salsandee Shop!" Nancy replied.

George started to cross the room to see the paper for herself. But as she took a step, a masculine voice from directly behind the two girls said coldly:

"Don't make a move, either of you! Put up your hands and march straight ahead!"

· 22 ·   *Behind the Fish Nets*

AT THE command, Nancy did not turn round. As she slowly raised her hands, she saw in a dusty wall mirror the reflection of the man who had given the terse order.

He was a short, dark-skinned little fellow with an elfin-shaped body. Instantly she recognized him as the man who came frequently to the Salsandee Shop—one of the elves in her dream.

"Step lively and don't try to turn round," he snapped.

Perhaps the man held a weapon, but Nancy could see none in the mirror. She decided to take a chance. Whirling around, she swung her arm directly into his startled face, causing him to lose his balance. As he stumbled backwards, Nancy gave him a push, and over he went! From his hand fell a telescope!

Instantly the two girls followed up their advantage. George plumped herself on the man's chest and held his arms. Nancy searched him but found no weapon.

"You're the one who helped carry me from the cliff!" Nancy accused him. "You and your friend put me to sleep with a gas which oozed up through crevices in the rocks!"

Nancy and George took the precaution to tie the

301

man's ankles together with the belt from George's dress and then released their hold. They stood him upright against the wall and placed themselves between him and the outside door. Nancy supposed they ought to take the man to the police station, but she was eager to continue her investigation of the old house.

The man muttered some unintelligible words. He leaned against the wall, his hands behind him. Suddenly, from far away and seemingly from deep beneath the house, a gong sounded.

Nancy was startled. A sardonic grin spread over the elfin man's face.

"It was a signal!" Nancy thought instantly, observing his pleased expression. "He must have an accomplice somewhere!"

Recalling how the little man had many times bought food at the Salsandee Shop for his "wife," she reasoned that was who his accomplice might be. Then, too, there was the possibility no wife existed, and that actually the food had been carried to another man.

"Perhaps he carried the food to that second elf I thought I saw in my dream!" she reasoned. "Grumper! If he is anywhere near here, then George and I must be on our guard!"

Nancy was convinced that the man before her had managed to sound the warning gong by pressing a button or pulling a hidden cord. Even at this moment his accomplice might be coming to his aid.

The door behind Nancy creaked on its hinges. Frightened, she turned swiftly. A shadowy figure loomed large in the entrance.

Nancy laughed aloud in relief. It was not Grumper! Instead, Ned Nickerson stood there!

"Hello, Nancy, are you girls safe?" he called

anxiously. "Bess told me you came here. I was afraid—"
He stopped short and stared at the girls' prisoner.
"Who—?"

Briefly Nancy told him what had happened. The
story was cut short by the sullen little man.

"It's a lie! You'll not take me to the police station!"
he shouted. "I won't leave this house!"

The elf-like figure flayed out with his fists, losing his
balance. As he went down, Nancy said:

"Ned, can you take this man to the police station
alone?"

"With one hand!"

"Then go as quickly as you can and come right back.
George and I will stay here."

"Not alone!"

"Yes. I must find out more about this place."

Ned was reluctant to leave the two girls. However,
at their repeated urging, he finally agreed to drive the
prisoner to Candleton and return immediately.

He bound the man's hands behind him, released his
feet, and ordered him to walk to the car. The fellow
had no choice as Ned prodded him from the rear.

George felt somewhat uneasy when she and Nancy
were alone. As Ned and the prisoner disappeared, she
glanced nervously about her.

"That gong—" she whispered to Nancy. "Don't you
think it means someone else is in here? Perhaps in the
basement?"

"Yes, I'm sure it was a signal. He must have pulled a
wall cord to sound a warning."

Nancy began to explore the wall inch by inch. She
found a tiny cord, smaller than her little finger, not far
from where the fish nets hung. As she pulled on it, a
gong sounded far off.

"That's how he did it!" Nancy cried. "But where is the gong? It sounds so muffled—as if it were underground!"

Apparently the house had no basement, for the girls could find no steps or passageway leading downwards. The only outside door seemed to be the one through which they had entered.

Puzzled, Nancy wondered how the elfin man had entered the house. Certainly not through the front door. She recalled the sudden manner in which he had appeared and his terse order, "March straight ahead!"

"Why, to march straight ahead would mean I'd have to walk through a solid wall," she thought. "Or at least through those fish nets!"

Nancy stared speculatively at the wall, almost completely covered with old cord nets to which dried seaweed still clung. On a sudden inspiration she tore away a portion of the covering.

"What are you doing?" George asked curiously.

"Look!"

Nancy had uncovered a door hidden behind the netting. George stared in amazement.

"The house must have a secret room or passageway!" she whispered. "We've found the entrance!"

Cautiously Nancy twisted the knob, making no sound. The door was not locked. Slowly it swung back on its hinges.

"Oh, Nancy!" shivered George, huddling at her elbow. "Someone may be hiding down there! Let's not leave this room until Ned comes back!"

STONE steps led down to a dark, narrow tunnel beneath the old house. Even Nancy hesitated as she thought of the risks involved in venturing below unprotected.

"George," she whispered, "you have my flashlight, don't you?"

"Yes, but it's dangerous for us to go down there!"

"Let me have the flashlight," Nancy replied. "I'll investigate alone. You stay here and watch the outside door."

"Oh, Nancy, please wait until Ned returns!"

"I don't dare. Our prisoner must surely have an accomplice. I'm convinced there's some tie-up between the *Mon Coeur* crowd and the little man we found here. At this very minute one of the gang may be destroying valuable evidence downstairs."

Disregarding George's protests, Nancy took the light and slowly descended the stone steps. Fearfully, the other girl stood guard at the door in the wall.

"Oh, Nancy!" George called nervously. "Do come back!"

"Sh! Everything is all right," her chum insisted.

Nancy moved deeper into the dark passageway until her light could be seen no longer. Above, George waited with growing uneasiness. After twenty minutes had passed, she could not endure the suspense a moment longer.

"Nancy!" she called softly. When there was no answer she shouted her chum's name again.

George became frightened. She was convinced Nancy was lost or in serious trouble somewhere below.

"I'm going down!" she determined.

On the old buffet stood an antique candlestick with a half-burned candle in it. Beside it lay a match. George lighted it, and holding the candle before her, descended the steps.

Reaching the bottom of the stairway, she groped her way along the passage until she glimpsed a closed door a short distance ahead. Just then her light began to flicker violently and suddenly went out. George had no way to relight it.

As she was about to turn back, she suddenly became aware of footsteps. The tread seemed too heavy to be Nancy's!

George flattened herself against the wall just as a figure brushed past her in the dark. A moment later a man was silhouetted in the doorway at the top of the stairs. He went through, closing the door behind him.

Stumbling up the stairway, George tested it. Her worst fears were confirmed. The door was locked! She and Nancy were prisoners underneath the cottage!

Giving way to sheer terror, George kicked and pounded on the door, shouting for release. No one came to free her.

"That man, whoever he is, has probably left the house," she thought. "Oh, why did I ever let Nancy get us into this mess?"

Nancy! George recalled with alarm that she had come below to find her friend. Remembering the other closed door, the girl groped her way to it. At her touch it readily moved inwards. Nevertheless, she hesitated on the threshold, sniffing the air.

George could see nothing, for the room was dark, but she did notice a strange, sweet scent. As she breathed deeply, a dizzy, giddy feeling took possession of her.

"Why, Nancy had these sensations just before she fell asleep on the cliff!" George recalled. "Oh, I'm being drugged!"

With all the strength she could muster, George pulled the door tightly shut. She felt so weak her limbs barely could carry her away. Through sheer will power she stumbled along the passageway and up the stairs. Dropping to the floor, she pressed her face close to the crack under the door and sucked in great gulps of fresh air.

At once George felt better. Her head cleared and she no longer was weak or drowsy. Then, realizing that she had barely escaped being drugged into unconsciousness, a feeling of panic for Nancy's safety came over her.

What had become of her? She surely had disappeared beyond the closed door because there was no other place to go. At this moment she might be lying unconscious in the dark, sweet-scented room!

"I'll have to do something!" George thought desperately. "But what? Oh, why doesn't Ned come?"

Nancy truly was in need of help. After leaving George, she too had reached the closed door, and cautiously opened it.

A dim light burned overhead in the room, revealing a strange sight. Shelves along the walls were filled with bottles, vials, and flasks of coloured liquid. There were quantities of perfume, lipstick, and face powder.

"It's a cosmetic factory!" Nancy thought excitedly. "And yes, they make *Mon Coeur* products!" she added, as her gaze roved to a wooden bench upon which lay scattered samples of both *Mon Coeur* and the newer *Sweet Chimes* labels.

Hanging above the door was a gong. At this instant she became aware of men's voices.

Desperately the girl sought a hiding place. Wooden benches against a wall offered the only possibility. Quickly she crawled underneath one of them.

Barely had Nancy hidden herself than she heard the voices again. To her alarm, the sound seemed to come from behind the very wall where she crouched.

"I'll have to go now," she heard one of the men say, "but you have your orders, Grumper! I arranged for that old fool Amos Hendrick to come to the cave. All you have to do is get his money, and if you're wise you'll keep him there until the tide comes in!"

"That won't be hard to do, Boss," was the reply. "She's due to turn in about twenty minutes."

The voices became more distinct. Lying beneath the bench, Nancy was startled to see that close by, another bench was slowly moving inwards! Evidently it was attached to a secret door which now was being opened by the approaching men.

A rush of cool air struck her face. As she lay motionless, the door behind the bench opened wider and two men with lighted lanterns tramped in. Before the opening closed, Nancy caught a glimpse of stone steps, and guessed that they led directly to the interior of the tolling bell cave.

One of the men was grotesquely misshapen, his head disproportionately large for his little body. Nancy was certain he must be A. H.'s old enemy Grumper. From her position Nancy could not see the other man's face but his stocky figure was like that of Harry Tyrox, alias **Monsieur Pappier!**

Nancy listened eagerly as the men conversed in low tones. Just then, from outside the room, her own name was shouted in a loud voice.

"Nancy! Nancy! Where are you?" It was George, searching for her friend in the dark passageway.

The two men heard the cry.

"Get to work, Grumper!" the dark-haired one ordered in a whisper. "We have visitors!"

The misshapen fellow pulled a can of blue powder from one of the wall shelves, and with a little water he quickly mixed it into a solution. Dividing the liquid equally into two containers, he jammed one of them into a tiny niche in the stone ceiling and left the other standing uncovered on the floor.

"Now I'll take care of Amos Hendrick!" he muttered.

Slipping noiselessly through the bench door, he closed it behind him. The man with the lantern extinguished the overhead light. Nancy heard him tiptoe towards the other door. There was no further sound, but she was sure he had gone out.

"I must follow him and help George," she thought vaguely. "He may harm her!"

Despite the need for haste, Nancy could not seem to hurry. As she crawled from beneath the bench, a sweet-smelling scent began to fill the room. She became lightheaded.

"The drug!" she thought in panic. "Unless I get out of here quickly, I'll never make it."

Nancy pulled herself to a standing position, but she could not walk. Her feet seemed to weigh a ton.

She knew she never could reach the passageway. Her only hope of escape was through the door behind the adjoining bench. Could she make it?

Using all her strength, she tugged at the bench. It

would not move. Feeling so dizzy that she scarcely knew what she was doing, she made a last desperate attempt to force the door.

"Oh, please open!" she whispered. "Please!"

· 24 · *Trapped in the Cave*

THE DOOR from the fume-filled room suddenly moved outwards. Nancy staggered through and closed the opening behind her. Then she collapsed on the stone steps.

It was several minutes before her head cleared enough for her to think.

Her flashlight had fallen from her hand. After groping about in the darkness, Nancy recovered it and focused its rays upon the dial of her wrist watch.

"Only ten minutes until the tide is due to turn!" she thought in panic. "Where is Grumper? If he carries out his orders, Amos Hendrick will surely drown!"

Without considering her own safety, Nancy started down the steep descent to the cave. When halfway down, she heard the tinkle of a beautiful, sweet-toned bell. Switching off the flashlight, she paused. Some distance below her she saw a faint flash of brilliant light.

Making no sound, Nancy swiftly descended the stairs. The passageway veered slightly to the right. As she rounded the corner, she saw a white-hooded figure seated on the ledge inside the cave. The "ghost" was swinging a small bell which gave forth a sweet, musical sound.

"Just as I thought!" Nancy told herself as she hugged

the damp wall to keep from being seen. "This is the interior of the tolling bell cave! And that ghost can be only one person—Grumper!"

As the bell swung back and forth, it gave off flashes of iridescent fire. Only priceless diamonds of great size could provide such a rainbow of colours!

"The jewelled bell!" Nancy thought excitedly.

She had not the slightest doubt that she was gazing at the stolen Hendrick heirloom. Even as she watched, the ghost raised his hood to peer eagerly towards the mouth of the cave.

Suddenly she heard the splash of oars and realized that someone in a boat had ventured deep into the cavern.

At intervals, Grumper tinkled the bell. When the boat came quite close, he suddenly stripped off his disguise and flung it aside. Then, still clutching the precious bell, he crept forward.

Nancy now could see that the man in the boat was Amos Hendrick. Presently he tied up the boat and stepped on to the rocky ledge. As he did so he saw the half-crouched figure.

"Grumper!" he exclaimed. "So we meet at last!"

"Yes, you trailed me to Candleton, but it will do you no good!" cackled the deformed little man.

"You're wrong about that," retorted A. H. His eyes gleamed as he looked at the bell. "I won't haggle over price, but you'll sell it or go to jail!"

Grumper chuckled evilly. "That's impossible. You couldn't get the police if you tried. It's too late! The hour of doom is upon you! The bell is mine, and I also will taste revenge for what your father did to my father!"

"Grumper, you're crazy! My family always treated

your father with more respect and consideration than was his due. The truth is, he robbed my grandfather while working in his forge! Give me the bell or I'll take it from you. I have three times your strength."

"You may seize the bell, but you'll drown! Any moment now the waters from the ocean will rush through this cave!"

Nancy, who knew the threat was no idle one, called frantically from the stairway:

"A. H.! A. H.! It's true! The tide will turn any minute! We must all get out of the cave before it's too late!"

The old man looked at the girl as if she were a ghost. "Nancy Drew!" he exclaimed. "How did you get here?"

"Never mind! We're all in danger!"

"Oh, yes, the tide!" exclaimed A. H. in a startled voice. "I forgot!"

"Come with me up these stairs!" the girl ordered. Grumper snarled at the girl and barred the man's path.

"You'll have to fight me to get past here!" he chortled. "Anyway, it's too late! I can hear the water now!"

Hopping about gleefully, the crazed fellow swung the bell. A. H. pushed him aside and dashed for the steps. Grumper indulged in a fit of sardonic laughter.

"The waters of the cave will swirl to the very top of the stairs!" he chuckled. "You can't open the door without a key, because it locks itself from this side."

"Quick, you fool!" Hendrick cried. "Give us the key!"

"I threw it away! We'll all die here together!"

Nancy and A. H. were frantic. Although it seemed utterly useless, they started up the stairway. Grumper trailed them, gloating over his enemy's predicament.

"Why don't you try to save yourself?" Nancy asked, hoping that the crazed fellow might know of some other way out of the cave. "Your boss didn't ask you to give up your own life."

"That guy who calls himself Monsieur Pappier, and Mr James, and half a dozen other names? He'll be my boss no longer." Grumper laughed mirthlessly. "His real name is Harry Tyrox, and he's a trickster and a cheat. Why, he even tried to steal my jewelled bell and sell it to A. H. When I found him out, he bargained with me to share the money I'd get for it. But I've outwitted him! I'll take the bell with me to the bottom of the sea!"

"So that's what upset you?" Nancy asked soothingly. "You thought Monsieur intended to take the bell? Just lead us out of this trap and we'll have the police put that man behind bars."

' It's no use," Grumper replied in a calmer voice. "I have no key. Even if I could open the door, we could not escape through the fume-filled laboratory."

"Then we really are trapped here?" Nancy asked, losing heart for the first time.

"Yes, we're trapped. You're young and pretty. I'm sorry you have to go, too. I tried to warn you. When you first came to the cave I tried to frighten you away, and later I tried to scare you with sleeping fumes. But you would not leave me alone, so you must suffer the consequences."

The trio had reached the head of the stairs. Below, in the cavern, they heard a faint, gurgling sound.

"The water is starting through," Grumper said. "In a moment now the water will come in with a rush!"

In desperation, Nancy pounded on the heavy door, trying to smash a panel. She succeeded only in bruising her fists.

"Help! Help!" she called weakly.

Then Nancy was certain that her mind was playing a cruel trick on her. From behind the door she fancied she heard footsteps and a muffled voice!

· 25 ·   *The Secret Revealed*

AGAIN Nancy pounded on the heavy door. Again she heard the muffled voice on the other side, but she could not make out the words. Maybe the person was asking where the door was.

"The bench!" she cried. "Pull on the bench!"

An eternity elapsed, and the water was coming very close. Then slowly the door was pushed open. The dreaded fumes rushed out, but Nancy, holding her breath, staggered forward. Behind her came A. H. Grumper, paralyzed with fear, cowered on the step.

Nancy caught a glimpse of their rescuer, a young man in a gas mask which protected him from the fumes. She was amazed to recognise Ned!

"Water coming!" she gasped. "Man still below!"

"Go on!" he shouted to Nancy.

Nancy assisted Amos Hendrick to the passageway where the air was comparatively fresh. Ned darted down the stairway. After much prodding he was able to get Grumper to the door. Barely in time to prevent the laboratory from being flooded, Ned pushed the bench door shut.

Then he turned to Grumper. The man had collapsed on the floor, a victim of the very fumes he had concocted!

Ned picked him up in a fireman's carry. As he staggered into the cottage with his burden, he pulled off his gas mask. Nancy's first question was:

"Where's George?"

"She went down to the cave entrance with a trooper," Ned replied. "Nancy, you owe your life to George," he said soberly.

"And to you!" Nancy said.

He waved aside the remark and continued:

"When I delivered your prisoner to State Police Headquarters, I asked one of the troopers to return here with me. We couldn't find anyone inside the cottage. After a while we shouted, and heard George pounding on the secret door behind the fish nets."

"Then she must have trailed me down into this passageway!"

"Yes, she did. George was convinced you were lying unconscious in the fume-filled room. Fortunately, the trooper had a gas mask, a flashlight and other equipment in his car. That's about all there is to tell, except that when I couldn't find you in the laboratory I became desperate. Just as I started upstairs again I heard you pound on the door."

Nancy was too shaken to say much. At this moment George rushed into the cottage wild-eyed. Seeing Nancy, she flung her arms about her friend.

"Oh, you're safe!" she cried. "And I thought—"

Ned turned Grumper over to the State Trooper. "Anyone else downstairs?" he asked.

"No," Nancy spoke up, "but the worst scoundrel of the lot—Harry Tyrox, who also calls himself Monsieur Pappier—escaped," Nancy revealed.

"Just give me a description of him and we'll find the crook," the policeman said confidently. "I'll notify

Headquarters over the short-wave radio in my car."

He was true to his word. Within an hour Harry Tyrox was captured on the road while attempting to flee in a stolen car.

Nancy and her friends had returned to Mrs Chantrey's cottage. A telegram was sent to Mr Drew, telling of the arrests.

"Good work, Nancy," the lawyer replied by wire. "Knew you would not need me to clear up the case."

The next day Nancy and the others were given permission to talk to Grumper and Harry Tyrox. Little by little the entire sordid plot was pieced together.

As Nancy had expected, the confessions of the two men implicated Ferdinand Slocum, the hotel clerk in Fisher's Cove. He, too, was brought in for questioning. At first the man maintained his innocence, but finally admitted his part in the swindle.

"Tyrox and I were friends. He offered me a cut in the perfume business if I would let him use the hotel for some of his shady deals," he confessed to Nancy. "After your father saw Harry in New York, he wired me that Mr Drew was coming to Candleton and something had to be done to delay him at Fisher's Cove. So I told Amy we had to get busy."

"Your wife?"

"Yes."

"Go on with your story."

"I might as well tell it from the beginning. Soon after we were married, my wife Amy mentioned the secret door and passageway leading to the cave. Her foster father had a workshop down there."

"Surely he didn't build the tunnel himself?"

"No, it was there when the Maguires bought the cottage. Old Grandpa Maguire discovered the closed-

316

up entranceway one day when he was repairing the wall, and the secret always was kept in the family.

"The cave originally was used as a hide-out by pirates," Slocum resumed. "The stone carvings are believed to have been their work."

"Tell me about the cosmetic factory," Nancy urged. "Whose idea was that?"

"Harry's. I foolishly told him about the workshop above the cave, and right away he thought he saw a chance to make big money. First, he got the Maguires out by telling them Amy had committed a crime and they would be disgraced when the townspeople heard about it. They packed up and moved away immediately."

"How did Grumper figure in the scheme?"

"Harry knew about him and some crimes he'd committed. He promised Grumper a lot of money if he'd come in with us and work as our chemist. Grumper thought he could use the money to go away some place where no one knew him, so he agreed. But he didn't figure on Amos Hendrick."

"He upset Grumper's plans?" Nancy inquired with a smile.

"He turned them upside down. Grumper was in terror that A. H. would find him and reclaim the stolen jewelled bell."

"How did he learn Mr Hendrick was in Candleton?"

"Through his cousin Franz, who served as a lookout at the cliff. Whenever people came near the cave, he sounded the gong and Grumper, hearing it in the laboratory, rushed down and tried to scare them away with his ghost act."

"And the rush of water had nothing to do with his appearances," said Nancy. "Nor the tolling bell?"

"No, but they sometimes happened close together," Slocum replied. "Whenever Franz spied someone on the cliff, he would run down to the laboratory and have Grumper send up sleeping fumes through that opening in the rocks."

"Then Franz was the second little elf I thought I saw in my dream!" Nancy exclaimed. "He was the one who came so frequently to the Salsandee Shop and carried away food. I suppose he also stole the note A. H. lost there!"

"That's right. Franz knew A. H. by sight and happened to see him drop the note in the tearoom. Later he took it from the drawer where somebody had put it. Before Franz could show it to Grumper, Tyrox got hold of it and then the cat was out of the bag. He tried to get the bell, but Grumper wouldn't let him have it. Tyrox was afraid of him because he could put people to sleep with his drugs."

"You haven't told me how my father was drugged," Nancy reminded the prisoner.

"When your father told Harry he intended to prosecute, he knew we had to do something quick. Harry followed him to the airport, then telephoned Madame that Mr Drew was on his way here. We were ordered to see that he conveniently disappeared for a few weeks. Grumper made up a vial of sleeping fumes, and gave it to Madame. She managed to get into a taxi with your father, and just before leaving it, broke the bottle and dropped the liquid on the lapel of his coat."

"Then how did my father reach Fisher's Cove Hotel?"

"The driver of the cab had been paid by our men and knew what to do. He took your father there. I

318

registered him under another name, and then kept an eye on him."

"It was Madame, I suppose, disguised as a chambermaid, who moved my father from his room."

"Right. Every so often when he was getting better, she gave him another dose and put him to sleep. My wife Amy threw a wrench into the machinery by warning you not to come to the hotel. She was afraid I was getting in too deep, and wanted to spike the entire plan."

"Your wife was far wiser than you, Mr Slocum."

"I wish now I had listened to her," the hotel clerk said miserably. "My wife works in a beauty parlour. The day you came for your father she borrowed a wig from there, dressed as an old lady, and looked for you in the lobby."

"Then she was the one who dropped the note into my lap!"

"That's right."

"Were you in a car that bumped into an automobile I was in one rainy night?"

"Yes, Tyrox and Amy were with me. I was driving and rammed your car by accident. Tyrox recognized you and was afraid we'd be identified. So he grabbed the wheel and drove off."

Nancy and her friends were happy when they learned that Harry Tyrox, alias Monsieur Pappier, still possessed a portion of the money he had fleeced from innocent victims. Mrs Chantrey, Mother Mathilda, and the others who had bought the worthless stock recovered a good proportion of what they had put into it.

"What will become of Amy?" George speculated, as the girls were sitting on the Chantrey veranda one day discussing the case. "Her husband will be sentenced to prison, and she'll be left alone."

"The Maguires are taking her back," Nancy replied. "Mother Mathilda told me the news today. They're all moving to the cottage in a few days—which reminds me, we should go there this minute!"

"But why?" asked Bess in surprise. "All the crooks have been caught."

"True, but the mystery of the cave is only half solved. Mr Hendrick recovered the jewelled bell from Grumper. But we know it wasn't his bell that frightened people away from the place. Another bell must be somewhere in the cave. I intend to find out now." Nancy sprang to her feet. "Anyone going with me?"

"How about me?" inquired a voice from the driveway.

Turning quickly, the girls saw Ned Nickerson approaching the porch. It was his last day in Candleton, and Bess and George generously declined an invitation to ride with the couple to the Maguire home.

"Why this trip to the cottage?" Ned inquired, as he and Nancy sped along the road. "Anything special in mind?"

"I want to clear away the mouldy food and artificial cobwebs Tyrox and his men left there. The Maquires would be shocked. Then, there's something else."

"What?"

"The bell."

At the deserted cottage, the two spent half an hour cleaning away the debris. Then Nancy looked at her watch.

"The tide won't be coming in for nearly two hours. We'll have time to make a complete investigation of the cave."

"I thought that would be on the schedule," the young man chuckled. "Well, I came prepared! I have a gasoline lantern in the car, and it gives off a brilliant light. We'll really be able to see what's down there."

Equipped with the lantern, the two descended into the passageway. They took the precaution of placing a block of wood in the secret door.

"We don't want to get locked in the way George was," Ned stated. "Even if all those crooks have been captured, this place is still dangerous."

The cosmetic factory bore only a faint trace of fumes. Passing quickly through it, Nancy and Ned descended the stone steps into the cave. With the tide out, it was possible to walk on the ledge to the entrance.

But Nancy turned the other way, and asked the youth to focus the light in that direction. Almost at once she found the gaping hole through which the water rushed. To Ned's astonishment, she reached her arm far back into the gap.

"What are you looking for?" he demanded.

Nancy did not answer, but a moment later she asked his help to draw forth a rusty, corroded bell. As it swung slowly, a doleful tolling echoed in the cave.

"The warning bell!" Ned exclaimed. "How did you know it was hidden back there?"

"I didn't, but I got to thinking about the story of the pirates and the loot they hid here."

"Yes, but the bell never rang until recently," Ned protested. "How can you explain that?"

"My guess is that at the time the pirates hid their loot in this cave the opening was very small and only a little water trickled through when the tide changed. Perhaps they placed the bell where it would be tapped lightly when water struck it, and they'd know the tide had changed. But as the years went on, the rushing waters carved a deeper hole, and more and more water poured into the cave. And just recently the violent action of the water caused the bell to toll loud enough to be heard outside the cave."

"That bell must be very old," Ned commented. "Maybe it has been in this cave since Revolutionary War times."

"I'm sure of it, Ned." Nancy peered at the trade-mark, then excitedly she said, "This is a Paul Revere bell! Just what A. H. is looking for!"

"Wouldn't you like to keep it? Mr Hendrick already has his jewelled beauty, thanks to you. This could be your own trophy—a souvenir of your successful solution of the mystery of the tolling bell."

"I should like to keep it," Nancy admitted. "A. H. said yesterday he wanted to reward me for recovering the jewelled bell, so perhaps he won't mind my having this one."

"No one could dispute your claim but the pirates," Ned laughed, as he assisted Nancy up the stairway. "And they're not likely to cause you any trouble after all these years!"

"It must have been very exciting in the old days," Nancy said wistfully. "How I wish I could have been here when the cave was a pirates' hide-out."

"They'd have elected you their leader!" chuckled Ned. "You are a little pirate, you know!"

"Why, Ned!"

"You're a *Mon Coeur* stealer yourself. I know some people who would like to carry you off!"

Nancy opened the door into the Maguire cottage. Laughing, she said teasingly:

"Why, Ned! If anyone should carry me away, how could I solve more mysteries?"

"Mysteries!" he exclaimed, turning out the lantern. "Haven't you had enough of them?"

Nancy was sure she never would have. Already she was longing for another, and it was to come in the form of *The Clue of the Black Keys*.

"Anyway," said Ned, "there's one mystery I know never will be solved."

"What is it, Ned?"

"Why you always change the subject when I try to talk to you about something that isn't a bit mysterious!"

Nancy merely smiled sweetly, and walked out into the sunshine.

The Clue of the
Black Keys

·1·

An Urgent Request

NANCY DREW'S eyes sparkled as she and Bess Marvin stepped from the afternoon plane.

"Wasn't it a grand weekend in New York?" Nancy said. "But it's good to be back in River Heights. There's your mother, Bess."

Mrs Marvin kissed the girls and offered Nancy a ride home.

"Thank you," she answered, "but I left my car here."

As the slender, titian-haired girl walked towards the car park with her small suitcase, a young man in a grey coat signalled her to wait. His worried look and the urgency of his pace gave Nancy the feeling that something was wrong.

"You are Nancy Drew?" he asked. When she nodded he said, "Your father—"

"Is Dad—is something the matter?" Nancy interrupted fearfully.

"I'm sorry. I didn't mean to frighten you. Your father is all right. But I'm concerned about a friend," the stranger went on. "I consulted your father about him this morning. Mr Drew said my case sounded more like a mystery for a detective than for a lawyer!"

Nancy studied the eager young man. He was not

331

more than twenty-five, tall and attractive, with serious, blue eyes and reddish hair.

"Perhaps I should introduce myself," he said. "My name is Scott—Terence Scott, but my friends call me Terry. I'm on the faculty of Keystone University. You may think it's strange, my coming to meet you here. But when I learned how clever you are at solving mysteries—"

"I'll do what I can," Nancy promised.

Though still in her teens, Nancy had earned a reputation as a clever sleuth.

"It's quite comfortable in the waiting room," she said. "Suppose we go in there and you tell me your story."

As soon as she had locked her suitcase in her car, they found a secluded bench in the main building beyond a group of waiting passengers. Terry Scott removed his coat, folded it, and placed it on the bench between them.

"The story," he said, "begins in Mexico. I was with a group of professors working there last summer to unravel an ancient mystery. Our search led us to an unexplored area, where we planned to dig for a treasure."

"Yes?" Nancy said, her interest aroused.

"According to old legends, something of great benefit to mankind is secreted with the treasure. We professors —Dr Graham, Dr Pitt, Dr Anderson and myself—are as interested in finding out what this is as we are in finding the treasure."

"You have no idea what it is?" Nancy asked.

"No. After weeks of excavating, Dr Pitt and I came

across a clue which the four of us were sure would lead to the treasure."

Terry Scott leaned forward, his face tense. "It was a stone tablet. We knew at once that all we needed to do was translate the cipher on it, and the secret would be ours. But then something terrible happened."

"What?"

"The night of the day of our find, Dr Pitt and the stone tablet disappeared!"

"He stole it?" Nancy asked, shocked.

Terry Scott frowned. "I don't know. Dr Pitt was pretty secretive. He is a bachelor, and close-mouthed about his work. But he's a fine teacher, and all the professors would swear he's honest."

"Perhaps he was the victim of foul play," Nancy suggested. "Did you call in the police?"

"Yes. They haven't turned up a thing, but I feel that Dr Pitt is alive."

"Being held captive somewhere?"

Terry Scott shrugged. "Whatever it is, I mean to get to the bottom of it. Dr Pitt must be found. And I don't intend that anyone else shall get the credit for something that belongs to us professors!" The young man's eyes blazed.

"I can't blame you," Nancy agreed. "Have you any clues to help solve this mystery?"

"Yes. After Dr Pitt disappeared, I found a couple of things in his tent that I believe are important. Here is one of them."

He reached deep into a pocket of his overcoat and brought out an object wrapped in tissue paper. It was

333

the bottom half of a large, ancient key, black in colour and of an unusual lustre.

"There were three of these keys originally," he explained, "all made of obsidian."

"That's glass, isn't it?" Nancy asked.

"Yes, a kind of volcanic glass," Terry Scott answered. "The other keys disappeared when Dr Pitt did."

He held the curious half-key up to the light for Nancy's examination, then returned it to the pocket of his coat.

"We'll need the other half of the key before we're through," he stated. "But, in the meantime, I figure what we ought to do is find a man named Juarez Tino."

"Why?" Nancy asked.

Terry Scott said that he suspected the man and his wife of being the thieves. They had been working near the Mexican camp-site for some time before the stone tablet had been found.

"The Tinos passed themselves off as scientists, but my guess is they're fakers. The same night that Dr Pitt, the cipher stone and the keys disappeared, the Tinos vanished."

"You think Dr Pitt went off with them?" Nancy remarked.

"Either with them or after them. I believe if we can trace Juarez Tino and his wife, we'll find Dr Pitt as well as solve our ancient mystery."

"Oh, I hope so," said Nancy. "Did any of you make a copy of the cipher on the stone tablet?"

The young man shook his head ruefully. "We found the tablet at the end of the day when we were tired.

We never thought it might be stolen before morning!"

Suddenly Terry Scott glanced at his wrist watch. "I almost forgot!" he exclaimed. "I promised Dr Graham I'd phone him. The old man gets very upset if he's kept waiting. Excuse me for a moment, please."

Leaving his coat at Nancy's side, Terry Scott dashed off to a telephone booth round the corner. Nancy waited, pondering the events he had related.

A dark, swarthy man sauntered over and took Scott's place on the bench. Out of the corner of her eye, Nancy saw the man fingering the professor's overcoat.

"What are you doing?" she cried, jumping up and snatching the coat from him.

The man stood up hastily and hurried towards a side door. Just as he disappeared, Terry Scott returned. He noticed Nancy's look of apprehension.

"Is something wrong?" he asked anxiously.

"I'm not sure," Nancy answered. "A man who came to sit here acted as if he wanted to steal your coat."

A frown came over the young professor's face. "What did the man look like?"

"Dark, short," she replied. "Sort of a crooked mouth and beady eyes."

"That sounds like Juarez Tino, the man I was telling you about!" Terry Scott snatched up his coat and plunged a hand into the inner pocket. "It's gone!" he gasped. "Juarez has the black key!"

"We'll go after him!" Nancy rushed for the door through which the man had gone.

Terry dashed after her, and they hailed a policeman, who Nancy recognized as Sergeant Malloy of the River Heights police force.

335

"Sergeant," she asked excitedly, "did you see a short, dark man come out of the waiting room?"

"You mean the one that was running, Miss Drew? He just drove off in a blue saloon with another fellow." Malloy waved towards a departing car.

"He's a thief! We must stop him!"

The policeman and Terry Scott followed Nancy as she raced for her car. The two men piled in beside her, and they sped off.

Nancy drove northwards along the main highway towards River Heights, and at last came close enough to note that the saloon ahead had a Florida licence plate. Then, at a busy intersection, she was stopped by a traffic light and lost sight of the other car.

"Keep pushing," Malloy directed her when the light changed. "They're up ahead some place."

A few minutes later Terry Scott pointed excitedly. "They just passed us—going the other way! They're heading back to the airport!"

Nancy manoeuvred her car in a neat U-turn and took up the chase again. The saloon was well ahead, but Nancy kept gaining. Another quarter of a mile and they would overtake Juarez Tino.

But just as she approached the far side of the airfield, the blue vehicle suddenly swerved from the road. Swaying dizzily, it swung across a rough field and on to the runway. Nancy started to follow, then jammed on her brakes. Her car screeched to a stop, but the car kept on directly in the path of an incoming plane.

"There'll be a crash!" Nancy cried out.

·2·

A Suspect Escapes

NANCY covered her face with her hands, expecting to hear the ripping, grinding sound of a collision. Instead, she heard Terry Scott shout:

"They've made it!"

Looking up, Nancy saw the plane taxiing along the runway.

"That crazy driver just missed being killed by the skin of his teeth!" Malloy exclaimed.

"Somebody's getting out of the car," Nancy remarked.

"I'll get him," the sergeant said, opening the door.

"I'll go with you," Nancy offered.

"You two stay here," the officer ordered. "It's too dangerous on the runway."

Nancy bit her lip in vexation. From her first mystery, *The Secret of Shadow Ranch*, through her most recent, *The Mystery of the Tolling Bell*, Nancy had shown that she possessed courage and daring beyond her years. But she always paid heed to the wisdom of her father and others of his generation. Now she obeyed Sergeant Malloy's order and waited in the car.

The officer reached the saloon on the runway. A second man stepped out of the car.

"Must be the driver," Terry Scott commented. "He's too tall for Juarez."

The policeman leaned inside. Apparently Juarez was not there.

"Juarez must have escaped!" Nancy gasped.

"With my key, the rat!" Terry fumed.

Nancy frowned and turned to her companion. "Are you sure Juarez was in the saloon when it passed us on the road?"

"Yes. Both men were on the front seat."

"Then Juarez must be here at the airport," Nancy declared.

With one hand shielding her eyes from the glare of the sun, she studied the tall grass that fringed the far side of the runway.

"Look!" she cried. "He's running towards the airport building!"

Nancy backed her car on to the road, and headed for the building. Traffic was heavy, and she chafed at the delay, but finally she made it.

As Nancy parked, she and Terry heard the roar of an outgoing plane. A crowd of onlookers were waving good-bye.

"Must be that Florida Special I saw chalked up on the flight board," Terry remarked.

Florida! An idea flashed into Nancy's mind. The plane was bound for Florida—and the licence on the blue saloon was Florida! Was there a connection?

"Let's go to the ticket office and inquire about the passengers," she said excitedly. "Juarez Tino might be on that plane!"

Nancy quickly gained the attention of a clerk. "May

I see the list of passengers who boarded the Florida plane?" she asked.

"Certainly."

She was handed a typewritten sheet. Six passengers had boarded the plane at River Heights. Juarez Tino was not one of them.

"Did all the passengers with reservations claim their seats?" Nancy asked.

The girl at the counter chuckled. "Yes, all the passengers got on. But one of them almost didn't make it. He came rushing up at the last minute, out of breath."

Nancy leaned forward excitedly. "What was his name? Please tell me. I have a particular reason for wanting to know."

The clerk tried hard to remember. Then she pointed to a name on the list. "Conway King. His wife kept fidgeting, worrying where her husband was and commenting in a loud, brassy voice."

"Did you see her husband when he came in?"

The clerk shook her head. "He went right out to the plane. Somebody said he made it all right. That's all I know."

"Thank you," Nancy said, and turned away. When she and Terry Scott were alone, she said quietly, "Do you think Juarez might be using the name Conway King?"

"It's quite possible. And that 'brassy voice' certainly sounds like his wife. I think we should inform the police so that Juarez can be questioned at the next stop."

Nancy looked at the flight schedule which had not yet been erased from the board. "The plane won't land for another two hours. Before we tell the police, I think we should make a thorough search for the key."

Her companion looked puzzled.

"When you didn't find the key in your pocket, we both assumed Juarez had stolen it," Nancy reminded him. "But maybe—"

She did not finish the sentence. Beckoning him to follow her, Nancy walked over to the bench which they had occupied earlier. It was possible, Nancy thought, that Juarez had dropped the key in his haste to leave. He might even have hidden it, intending to come back later.

Hurriedly Nancy looked along the top of the bench. No key there. And it was not on the floor underneath. Finally she turned to Terry Scott, who was also searching.

"Are you sure you didn't take that key into the phone booth with you?"

"I'm quite certain. But I'll look just the same."

While he was gone, Nancy examined the floor from the bench to the side door through which Juarez had made his exit. She looked on the ground outside the door. No key.

Disappointed, she returned to the bench and sat down. Suddenly Nancy realized that the dark wooden seat was not solid, but built of strips about half an inch apart.

With renewed hope she felt along the cracks of the smooth wood. Her little finger discovered something. Looking closely, Nancy saw an irregular black object wedged between the boards!

Terry Scott's antique half-key! Nancy thought exitedly. Taking a nail file from her purse, she dug out the relic and presented it to the young man upon his return. He could hardly believe his good fortune.

"You're a cool detective! I'm sure that from now on our case will prosper."

Nancy was amused by the word "our," but merely said, "I'm afraid I haven't been very helpful so far. I was only two feet from the man you want to catch, and I let him get away!"

"But you proved something," Terry Scott insisted. "I know now that Juarez is on my trail. He probably has learned about the half-key and means to steal it. Also, you discovered that he's on his way to Florida with his wife, and that they travel under an assumed name."

"We don't know that for certain," Nancy reminded him. "We're only guessing."

The young professor laughed. "Now I'm sure you're a lawyer's daughter. That careful, logical mind! Well, how about it? Will you stay on the case and help me solve my puzzle?"

Nancy's curiosity was thoroughly aroused. But nice as Terry Scott seemed, she must check on him first. Nancy decided to talk the matter over with her father.

"If you'll tell me where you're staying, I promise to let you know soon," she replied.

Reluctantly the young man accepted her decision, saying he was staying at the Claymore Hotel. Then, after thanking her, he went to call a taxi.

As Nancy walked across the parking area towards her car, she heard a shout. Sergeant Malloy was sternly leading an angry, gesticulating man. Nancy recognized

341

him as Juarez's companion—the man who had driven the blue saloon.

"Arrest me, will you?" he roared. "It's this girl—you said her name's Nancy Drew—she's the one you ought to arrest!"

·3·

Clue in a Triangle

NANCY looked at the heavy-set man in amazement. Sergeant Malloy protested, "Come, now. What do you have against Miss Drew?"

"Plenty," he answered, his grey-green eyes flashing. "She sent you to embarrass me. Look how everybody's staring at me, as if I was going to jail. She's hurt my good name. I've been doing business in River Heights and people know me. My reputation is worth money. My business—"

"What kind of business?" interrupted the sergeant.

"I sell citrus fruit for the Tropical Sun Fruit Company of Florida."

Sergeant Malloy grumbled, "Let's see your driver's licence and car registration."

The man thrust them under Malloy's nose. Nancy and the sergeant studied them together. The licence and registration were made out to Wilfred Porterly on a street in Miami, Florida.

"All right, Mr Porterly," said the sergeant. "Tell me one thing. Where's your friend?"

"Juarez Tino," Nancy added.

Porterly blinked and hesitated, then said, "I don't know any Juarez Tino."

"How about the man who rode in your car? Is his name Conway King?" Nancy asked.

The man's eyes narrowed. "I never saw him before. He begged a ride. Told me he'd left some important papers at his hotel. Couldn't find a taxi, so he asked me to take him back to town.

"After he picked up his papers, I drove him here to the airport. He made me drive on to the field so that he wouldn't miss his plane."

"And you nearly killed yourself and all the plane passengers just to accommodate a stranger?" Malloy said sarcastically.

"It wasn't my fault. He grabbed the wheel."

Nancy pretended surprise. "You say Juarez took the wheel?"

"Sure. I mean—I don't know what his name was."

Porterly must have felt that his words had trapped him. He turned his fury on Nancy.

"You're responsible. If there'd been a crash, you'd have been to blame!"

"Nancy Drew," stated a firm, angry voice from the crowd, "is a very fine girl. You'd better be careful what you say about her."

Nancy turned in astonishment. An athletic-looking dark-haired girl was striding towards her. She was Nancy's friend, George Fayne. With her was pretty Bess Marvin, her cousin.

"What is it all about?" Bess whispered when they reached Nancy's side. "I found I'd left my hatbox, so I asked George to drive back here with me."

"Tell you later," Nancy said in a low voice.

"You'd better quieten down," the sergeant was telling Porterly, "or I'll arrest you for disturbing the peace. Sell all the grapefruit you want, but behave yourself. I'll be watching you."

Porterly hesitated. Then, with a baleful look, he turned and walked rapidly towards his saloon.

Sergeant Malloy spoke to the crowd. "All right, folks, break it up." With a wave of his hand at Nancy and her friends, he strode off.

George Fayne watched the disappearing figure of the blustering Porterly.

"Gosh, Nancy," she scolded, "you do get mixed up with the strangest characters."

"Nancy, you aren't involved in another mystery before you even get home!" Bess exclaimed.

"Well," Nancy confessed, "I'm not sure."

The three girls walked together to Nancy's car and she stepped in.

"We have company," George whispered.

Nancy looked through the rear window of her car. Terry Scott was hurrying towards her and waving an arm. Nancy introduced him to Bess and George.

"I'm sorry about that rumpus with Porterly," Terry began. "I was in a booth trying to call a taxi. I heard shouts, but I hadn't any idea you were involved."

"No harm done," said Nancy. "My friends here came to my defence."

"And we mean to keep on defending you until we get you safely home," George promised.

Terry grinned. "Since your friends protect you so well, perhaps you'll drive me to my hotel. Every public taxi in this town seems to be busy."

"I guess it'll be safe." Nancy laughed.

As the car rolled towards River Heights, Bess and George followed close behind. When she pulled up in front of the Claymore Hotel, Terry reached into his pocket and brought out the tissue-wrapped half-key.

"I want you to keep this for me," he said to Nancy, "both as a pledge of my integrity and because I no longer dare keep it myself."

"You mean someone like Juarez may try to steal the key?" Nancy asked.

Terry nodded and said, "This must never get into the hands of the wrong people. Please take my case," he went on. "I believe that you are the person who can solve it."

Nancy hesitated to take the key until she knew him better, but decided to show it to her father when she asked his advice about the case. Aloud she said, "You'll hear from me tomorrow."

Nancy slipped the relic into her shoulder bag. As Terry entered his hotel, Bess and George pulled up alongside her.

"Lucky you!" Bess called out.

"He's charming," George teased. "I'm sending an application to Keystone University!"

"Stop it, girls," Nancy pleaded, then added with a grin, "But he *is* handsome, isn't he?"

Without waiting for a reply, she started her car, waving good-bye to Bess and George. Nancy threaded her way through the heavy traffic.

When she arrived home, her father and the house-keeper, Hannah Gruen, greeted her at the door. Mrs Gruen had taken care of the home and reared Nancy since Mrs Drew's death many years before. After kissing them both, Nancy led the way into the attractive, comfortable living-room.

Carson Drew said with a chuckle, "Nancy, from the grip you have on that bag, you must have brought a treasure from New York."

"It may lead to one," his daughter declared.

She showed him the half-key, asking if he had ever seen anything like it.

"No."

"Dad, do you know a Terence Scott?"

"I just met him this morning. He was at my office. What made you ask?"

"This key is his. He met me at the plane."

Mr Drew's eyes widened. "I did tell him you were arriving by plane, but I had no idea—"

"How much do you know about him?"

"Practically nothing."

"Dad, please phone Keystone University and ask what he teaches and what they think of him?"

"Gladly, Detective Drew." Her father smiled.

Nancy gave him a hug. "Oh, Dad, there's so much to tell—"

"But not now, please," said Hannah Gruen. "I've been saving dinner for you, and if you don't sit down soon, it'll be ruined."

"Dinner!" cried Nancy. "That's a lovely idea. I'll be ready in two jiffs."

She hurried upstairs. Before she even smoothed her hair, Nancy took the key from her bag and hid it among scarves and handkerchiefs, in a drawer of her dressing table.

During dinner Nancy told about her weekend and

the exciting events that had taken place at the airport.

Mr Drew said that he knew the elderly Dr Pitt with whom Terry Scott claimed to have been in Mexico. "I'll call Keystone now."

After a slight delay, Mr Drew was connected with the president's home, and presented his questions. In a few minutes the conversation was over.

"The report is, Nancy, that Terence Scott is an outstanding young professor, who has a leave of absence this year. He went to Mexico last summer on an exploring expedition."

"Then his story is true!" Nancy exclaimed. "Dad, is there any reason why I shouldn't help him on the case?"

"I can't give my answer to that question until I make a further investigation." Mr Drew could not be dissuaded from this decision.

Nancy retired, still trying to account for the strange happenings of the day. But her head was hardly upon the pillow, before she fell fast asleep.

It was past midnight when she awoke with a start. The light on her bedside table was on. Hannah Gruen was gently shaking her. The woman's face was drawn and white.

"What's the matter?" Nancy asked in alarm.

The housekeeper put a finger to her lips, then whispered, "Burglar!" She signalled Nancy to put on a robe and follow her into the hall.

Mr Drew was on the stairs. In his hand he held a golf club ready to use as a weapon.

"Hannah," he ordered, "stay close to Nancy. You

two look round the rooms up here. I'm going down-stairs. Yell if you find anyone."

She and Nancy looked through each room, searching closets and peering under beds. Everything seemed to be normal.

"Dad's calling us," Nancy said a few minutes later.

They hurried downstairs. Mr Drew was in the living-room, looking at the open window next to the piano.

"It's been jemmied," he said.

"Do you suppose somebody's still in the house?" Mrs Gruen asked.

"I think that whoever it was got away," Carson Drew concluded, pointing outside the window. In the soft earth close to a rose bush, they saw a man's foot-prints.

"Has anything been stolen?" the housekeeper asked.

"No. I checked," Mr Drew said.

"The black key!" thought Nancy.

She turned and raced upstairs. The key was where she had put it.

"I'm glad I didn't leave it downstairs," she told her-self with a sigh of relief.

Every place that had not been searched before was investigated, in case the intruder had an accomplice hiding in the house. But there was no stranger on the premises.

"It's too bad Togo wasn't here, Nancy," Hannah said. "He would have taken care of the burglar!"

Togo, Nancy's terrier, was with Mr Drew's sister, who was spending a three-weeks' vacation at her summer home.

When Nancy came downstairs at nine o'clock the

next morning, she found Bess Marvin waiting for her. Bess sat at the table and chatted excitedly while Nancy ate breakfast.

"Mrs Gruen told me all about last night," Bess began. "If you take Terry Scott's case, something awful is bound to happen."

Nancy raised her eyebrows. "But what?"

"Well, it seems so dangerous. And Ned Nickerson won't like it a bit. He'll be so worried, Nancy, especially when he takes a look at your professor!"

"Bess!" exclaimed Nancy, smiling. "Ned won't think anything of the sort!"

As she finished a glass of milk, the telephone rang. "Nancy, it's for you," Hannah announced.

The caller was Terry Scott. His voice sounded hoarse and excited. "Is everything all right?" he asked.

"Oh yes. Quite safe," she assured him, thinking he meant the key. "Has something happened?"

"Yes. Something serious. When I came up to my hotel room last night, a visitor was waiting for me in the closet. He struck me on the head and I didn't come to until six o'clock this morning."

"How dreadful!" Nancy gasped. "What did he look like?"

"I don't know. All I saw was a mask."

"Did he steal anything?"

"He certainly did. Took most of my notes on that Mexican expedition. I planned to use them for a lecture I'm giving soon."

"Did he take anything else?"

"Apparently not. He did a thorough search job,

though, on my suitcase. Dumped everything on the floor."

Terry decided he had better say no more on the telephone. "I'll come over later and talk to you," he suggested.

"All right. I'll be here."

When Nancy told Bess what had happened, the girl's eyes grew wide with fear. "Maybe he's the same thief who came to your house last night," she said.

"I've thought of that. I ought to tell Dad," Nancy added, going to the telephone. As she started to dial, Carson Drew himself walked down the stairs.

"Good morning, girls," he said.

"Dad!" Nancy exclaimed as the lawyer bent down to kiss her cheek. "I thought you'd gone to the office."

"Not this morning," Mr Drew replied, smiling. "I have news for you."

"I have news, too," she said, and related what Terry Scott had told her over the telephone.

"Too bad," the lawyer remarked.

"Now tell us your news," Nancy urged him.

"It's about the same young man," her father explained. "What you have just told me complicates matters still more. You recall that I hinted to you on the phone just before you left New York about doing a little detective work for me?"

"Yes, Dad."

Before he could continue, they heard a car enter the driveway. A taxicab pulled up.

"My news will have to wait," he said.

Nancy hurried into the hall. "It's Terry Scott," she called, and opened the door.

The pale young man, a bandage on his head, entered the living-room and smiled wryly. "Good morning," he said. "I'm afraid I don't look very presentable."

"Oh, it was dreadful, that man assaulting you," Bess spoke up.

"Sorry to hear it," added Mr Drew. "Any clue to your attacker?"

"No," Terry replied. "The hotel detective and the police checked my room."

"Any idea who the man was?" Nancy asked.

Terry shrugged. "If Juarez Tino hadn't gone to Florida, I'd suspect him. But I can't think of anyone else."

Bess decided to change the subject to something more pleasant. "Terry, do you speak any of the Mexican languages?" she asked.

"Why, yes, I do. Spanish, and a couple of Indian dialects. That's one of the reasons Dr Pitt and the others chose me to go to Mexico."

"Nancy says you almost found a fortune down there," Bess said. "What was it?"

Terry smiled. "I suspect the treasure will be one or more frogs."

"Frogs?" cried the two girls together.

The young professor nodded. "In certain ancient civilizations the frog was sacred, just as the cow is sacred in many parts of India today. Because of its religious meaning, the frog symbol was used frequently by craftsmen.

"Many of these frogs were made of silver, some of them inlaid with precious stones. A collection of such jewelled pieces would be worth a fortune."

"How did you learn about the—the frogs?" Bess asked.

"An ancient monument in Mexico carries a message in an unknown language," Terry answered. "It's all in pictures. The Indians call it the Mystery Stone, and say it tells where a fabulous treasure is buried. It is called the Frog Treasure, and according to legend, it is locked away in silver by three 'magic' obsidian keys."

"And I have half of one?" Nancy asked.

Terry nodded. "I'm hoping against hope that the treasure can't be unlocked without this missing piece, even if someone else locates the place."

"Please tell the whole story from the beginning," Bess begged. "Couldn't any Mexicans read the Mystery Stone?"

"No. They knew only the legend. Late one afternoon Dr Pitt and I dug up a small stone tablet—the one I told you about, Nancy. From photographs we had of the Mystery Stone monument, we saw that one side of the tablet had the same picture writing as the monument.

"On the reverse side of the tablet, the ciphers had been translated into one of the ancient Indian dialects, which I know. With the help of the tablet we could solve the mystery! But, as you know, the tablet vanished."

"What about the three keys? Where did you find them?" Nancy asked.

"They were on a silver ring. This was fastened to the tablet through a hole bored in one end of it. I knew at once that they were the 'magic' keys of the legend."

"But the cipher stone was stolen—and the keys with it!" Bess exclaimed.

"And what's more important, Dr Pitt vanished at the same time. It's his fate that's worrying me more than anything else. This morning I began to wonder if there might be some superstition about the Frog Treasure which the natives fear and are afraid that we will discover. This might be a reason for holding the doctor."

"Have you any idea what the superstition might be?" Nancy asked.

From an inner pocket Terry Scott pulled out a crude drawing. "I found this in Dr Pitt's tent the next morning," he said.

There were actually three drawings which formed a triangle: at the lower left, a frog; at the right, what appeared to be the prostrate figure of a man; and at the top, a symbol representing the sun.

"What do they mean?" Bess asked.

Terry said he had not figured it out. But he was sure the riddle could be solved and Professor Pitt found.

"You see why I need the services of a good lawyer, Mr Drew," he said, "and also the help of a good detective like your daughter. Can't we start work at once?"

Carson Drew was thoughtful a moment. "It looks as if solving this mystery will have to be done in Mexico," he mused.

Turning to his daughter, he said, "I'm afraid, Nancy dear, that in this case you've started something you can't finish at this time—unless you go to Mexico. I can't spare you as far away from home as that, and besides, I have some work of my own for you to do in the next few days."

·4·

Suspicion

NANCY looked at her father in surprise, but did not argue the point. She knew he would not have asked her to turn down Terry Scott's case without good reason.

The young man showed his disappointment, but smiled politely. "Well, you can't blame me for trying, sir," he said, getting up from his chair. "Your daughter seemed to be the very person I needed to help me."

Nancy gave the mysterious drawing a last-minute look. "Have the other professors any idea what these signs mean?" she asked.

"No, none," Terry replied. "Well, I guess I'd better get back to my hotel."

"I must go, too," Bess added, rising.

After saying good-bye to the callers, Nancy followed her father upstairs to his study.

"Dad, if I can't work on Terry's case," she said, "shouldn't I give back the half-key?"

"The lawyer smiled quizzically. "That depends on something. I know one thing Terry Scott may or may not know. And that's why I asked you not to continue trying to solve the mystery until certain things can be proved."

Her father explained that Joshua Pitt's will left everything he owned to Terry Scott, and it was a sizeable sum of money.

"Dad! How did you learn that?"

"Because," he replied, "I drew up the will. Dr Pitt and I have a mutual friend who recommended me to him last year."

Nancy was astounded. Instantly she guessed what was in her father's mind. There was a chance Terry's whole story was a fake. The truth might be very ugly. For some reason best known to Terry, Dr Pitt might never return and the young man would inherit the money!

"Oh, Dad, I just can't believe Terry's that kind of person," she declared.

"He probably isn't," her father said. "But it's something to keep in mind."

Nancy nodded. "Why did he come to you for help, Dad?"

"Terry quoted old Pitt as saying, 'If you're ever in trouble, go to Carson Drew. He'll get you out of it if anybody can.' "

"And you would," Nancy remarked loyally.

Her father made a mock bow. "Don't misunderstand. I like Terry, too. But my first interest is to protect Dr Pitt. That's why I want you to take on a little investigation job."

Nancy leaned forward expectantly.

"I want you to go and see the other members of the team—Dr Graham and Dr Anderson," Mr Drew proposed. "Find out what you can about the expedition, and what they think of Terry."

Nancy was eager to begin her work. "I'll start with

Dr Graham. Terry says he's at Jonsonburg College. Maybe George will drive over there with me this afternoon."

Nancy telephoned Dr Graham's office to arrange an appointment. Next, she asked George to accompany her.

"Gosh, Nancy, I don't know how to talk to a doctor of archaeology! But I'll go."

A few minutes before quarter past three, George and Nancy knocked at a door marked *Professor Graham*. A small, stooped man with wrinkled, leathery cheeks opened the door. He eyed the two girls briefly. When Nancy introduced herself and George, the professor looked at his watch.

"I see you're punctual, Miss Drew. I like young people to be on time." He stepped back from the door and invited them in.

Nancy told Dr Graham that she was acquainted with Terry Scott, and through him had learned of the expedition to Mexico and the disappearance of Dr Pitt.

"My father is a friend of Dr Pitt and is much concerned about him," Nancy added. "He suggested that I come and talk to you."

The little man fixed his sharp, calculating eyes on the girl. "I suppose young Scott told you *he* found the cipher stone," the professor remarked coldly, ignoring the reference to Dr Pitt.

"No," Nancy replied. "He said, 'Dr Pitt and I.' Terry has a very high respect for your work, too, Professor," she added hastily.

She could see the old man relax under this compliment. "Humph! He's an arrogant young fellow. But he has a good mind. I suppose you want my opinion of the case."

Nancy nodded.

"About Pitt, now." Dr Graham leaned back in his chair. "I don't mind saying his disappearance hardly surprised me. I like Pitt, but he's secretive. He'll listen; he'll find out what others have on their minds, but he'll never tell what he has found out."

"Do you believe, Dr Graham," Nancy spoke up, "that Dr Pitt went off by himself to find the treasure?"

Graham shrugged. "It's possible." Then he added, a half-smile on his face, "Some of us scientists are a bit selfish, not in acquiring money, but we want recognition; we want to discover things for ourselves. We're not always generous when we work together."

"But I'll give credit where credit is due," he added testily. "Terry Scott found that half-key and I agreed to let him take charge of it."

"Where do you think the lost keys are?" Nancy asked.

The professor said he was working on an idea. He did not care to reveal it then. "But Terry will never be able to solve the mystery alone."

"Have you any theories about the drawing he found in Dr Pitt's tent?" Nancy asked.

Dr Graham compressed his lips and shrugged. Did he know something he was not telling? Or was he too proud to admit that he could not explain the secret message?

Nancy knew it would be difficult to find out whether or not he had any suspicion about Terry in connection with Dr Pitt's disappearance. At last she broached the subject. Dr Graham stood up dramatically and pounded his desk.

"The idea!" he stormed when he got the full import of her question. "Maybe we four did have our differences about what we ought to do on that expedition, but I want to tell you this: not one of us would harm another for all the treasure in Mexico!"

"That's just what I wanted to hear," Nancy said, rising. "Thank you for letting me come."

Much relieved, she and George left Dr Graham's office. On the way home, George suggested with a sly grin. "Ned will be surprised when he learns about your interest in professors. When are you seeing him again?"

Nancy grinned back. "This weekend."

After supper that evening Ned Nickerson telephoned from his fraternity house at Emerson College.

"You're not forgetting our date this weekend?" he asked anxiously.

"Of course I haven't forgotten," Nancy assured him. "I've a marvellous memory for dates—especially when they're for house parties. Bess and George are just sunk because they couldn't accept Burt's and Dave's invitations."

"Yes, it's too bad. Nancy, I have a favour to ask of you. There's a professor visiting River Heights—a fraternity brother of mine. He needs a lift to Emerson."

Nancy laughed. "Why, Ned, are you asking me to drive over with another man?"

Ned snorted. "That stuffy codger? He's probably sixty if he's a day. He's due to give a lecture here, and you know those weekend trains. I thought you wouldn't mind bringing him with you Friday."

"Glad to. Where's he staying?"

"At the Claymore Hotel. The professor's name is Terence Scott."

·5·

The Highway Trap

TERRY!

Nancy gasped in surprise and amusement.

"What's the matter?" As she hesitated in her reply, Ned asked, "You're not backing down, are you?"

"Oh no," Nancy assured him. She was tempted to reveal Terry's age but decided the joke was too good to spoil. "I'm sure Professor Scott will be very pleasant company," she added. "See you Friday, Ned. Goodbye now!"

Immediately Nancy telephoned Terry and told him about Ned's call. The young professor laughed heartily at the joke. He said he would be delighted to drive to Emerson with her on Friday.

Nancy now spoke of the obsidian half-key, saying that perhaps she should bring it along. Terry begged her to keep it.

"I haven't given up hope you'll agree to help me solve the mystery," he said.

After she had hung up, Mr Drew confided to Nancy that he was fast losing any suspicion he might have had regarding Terry. But there were still points about Dr Pitt's disappearance which needed explaining.

361

"Maybe I'll learn more over the weekend," Nancy said hopefully. "I'll call on Dr Anderson. He's not far from Emerson."

On Thursday Nancy busied herself with preparations for the weekend party. The next day proved to be a warm, sunny day, so Nancy decided to put down the top of her convertible. Promptly at eleven o'clock she pulled up in front of the Claymore Hotel. Terry was waiting.

Soon they were rolling along the wide highway towards Emerson College. It was not long before they found themselves once more discussing the mystery in Mexico.

"You've never told me much about Juarez Tino," Nancy said.

"That's rather a long story," Terry answered. "Mind if I tell it while we have lunch? I'm starved."

Nancy parked at an attractive roadside restaurant, near the brow of a hill, and they found a secluded table.

"I disliked Juarez Tino," Terry told her, "the first day I saw him. He was a shifty sort of fellow. According to his story, he was exploring a ne ghbouring site. But he was always coming over to see what we were doing.

"He asked hundreds of questions, and prowled around our excavation ditches after dark to see if we'd left anything around. I was sure he was up to some devilry."

"Did the other professors distrust him, too?"

"They didn't suspect him in the same way I did. Dr Pitt told me to ignore the fellow. I didn't agree. It seemed to me that if we let Juarez hang around, sooner or later we'd have trouble on our hands."

"Did you?"

"One day I lost my temper. I told Juarez to keep out out of our excavation. We had a regular set-to, and the upshot was that I ran him off the place."

"Did you find out anything about him?"

"Nothing very conclusive. He'd taken a few courses somewhere and had a smattering of this and that. His specialty was supposed to be ancient gems. But his reputation wasn't good. There were rumours that he'd once tried to pass off some fake pieces."

Nancy asked if Juarez had ever come back after he was chased away.

"Yes. Although he stayed out of my sight, he did plenty of snooping when he thought I wasn't around. Once in a while I would get a glimpse of his wife."

"What was she like?"

The young man frowned. "You wouldn't like her, Nancy. She wears loud clothes and always makes herself conspicuous. She has a bold manner, and her voice is harsh. In fact, her whole personality suggests just one thing to me—cruelty."

Nancy thought, "This couple sounds equal to taking on almost any underhanded work!"

As she and Terry stepped outdoors into the sunshine, she was not thinking of the dinner party at Emerson. She was wondering about Mrs Juarez Tino and her husband. If Professor Pitt were in their clutches, he was not being treated well, she felt sure.

Nancy was about to step into her car when Terry touched her arm. "Look!" he said in a low, tense voice. "Those two men up the hill—I think they're spying on us."

When Nancy turned her head to look, the pair, with

hats pulled low over their faces, stepped hurriedly into a black saloon. The car quickly got under way and passed out of sight over the top of the hill.

"Those men ran the minute we looked at them," Terry said. "I wonder why they did that."

"Did you recognize them?" Nancy asked.

"No."

"We'll watch out for them, just the same," Nancy decided.

"I'll feel better when we get to Emerson," Terry replied a bit nervously. "Perhaps you'd better speed up."

Nancy shook off her sombre mood and grinned mischievously. "Do you suppose your elderly nerves can stand the strain, Professor?"

"Give them a try!"

They stepped into her car and she started it rolling once more towards Emerson. The speedometer crept steadily higher, but Nancy did not overtake the two sinister-looking strangers in the black car. Finally she and Terry began to enjoy the flying landscape, the swift rush of wind, the dips and curves of the road.

Then suddenly—too late—they saw disaster just ahead. They had rounded a bend. Beyond was a wide repair ditch. Desperately Nancy wrenched the wheel to the left.

But she could not make it in time. There was a hurtling impact as the car nose-dived into the ditch! Nancy blacked out.

·6·

New Challenge

WHEN Nancy regained consciousness a few minutes later, Terry Scott was bending over her.

"Nancy!" he whispered anxiously.

"I'm all right," she managed to say, but her head ached badly. "You're not hurt?"

"A few bruises. But we're lucky."

The couple got out and surveyed the car. It was tilted precariously on its front end.

"There should have been a warning sign," Nancy said grimly.

Terry pointed. "There was a sign—but not where it should have been."

Lying at the side of the ditch was a long board. " 'Danger. Road Repairs. Drive Slowly,' " he read aloud. "A lot of good that does us now! The road gang shouldn't have been so careless."

"Don't blame the road gang," Nancy said. "I believe that sign was deliberately removed just before we got here."

"Nancy, that would be murder!"

"It very nearly was murder," she answered. "And by those two men who were watching us at the restaurant, I'll bet."

Terry dragged the sign round the bend to warn other motorists. He had just returned to Nancy when they heard the squeal of brakes.

Nancy and Terry relaxed as they saw a kindly-looking, middle-aged couple in the car that came round the bend.

"Oh, my dears!" the woman cried, getting out of the car. "Is anyone—"

Terry said no one else was involved in the accident. Nancy added that they were all right except she had a headache.

The man offered the young people a ride, but Nancy preferred waiting until a break-down wagon could come. The friendly strangers promised to stop at the next town and send back mechanics, as well as a state trooper.

A few minutes later a tow truck arrived and two men in overalls stepped out. In a short time they had Nancy's car on the road and were checking it for damage.

Both mechanics grinned. "Some car!" one commented. "She's got a few dents and scratches. But no real harm done by her tumble. No reason why you two can't keep goin' under your own power. 'Course, you'd better check again when you get where you're goin'."

As the men were leaving, a state trooper rode up on a motorcycle. Nancy and Terry told him their story. He said that a watch would be set for the two men whom the young people thought were responsible for the removal of the road sign.

Then Nancy and Terry started off once more for Emerson. Terry took the wheel.

"You relax and pamper that head of yours," he told

Nancy, "or you won't be able to show up at the dance tomorrow. I'm counting on at least one dance with you, young lady."

"Are you going?" Nancy asked in surprise.

"Well, that depends on whether or not I get an invitation."

"I'll be looking for you," Nancy said.

When they reached Emerson College, Terry got off at the president's home, where he had been invited to stay. Nancy drove on to meet Ned Nickerson at the Chi Omega Epsilon fraternity house.

Tall, athletic Ned saw Nancy drive up and ran out to greet her. When he noticed the dents in the car, he gasped, "What happened? Were you in an accident?"

When she told him what had occurred, Ned's tanned face took on a look of deep concern. He insisted she call Hannah to say she had arrived at Emerson. Then he drove Nancy to the college infirmary for a checkup. To his relief she was pronounced all right.

On the way back to the fraternity house, Ned asked, "How did you and the prof. hit it off? Was he much bother?"

Nancy smiled demurely. "He was a lamb. He even insisted on driving part of the way himself. And you know what I think you should do, Ned? Invite him to the fraternity dance. As your fraternity brother, he'd be immensely flattered."

"All right," Ned agreed reluctantly. "I'll see that he gets an invitation."

At dinner she mentioned that her father wished her to call on Dr Anderson, a professor of geology at Clifton nearby.

"It would be nice if you could drive me over," she said. "How about Sunday?"

"Look here, Nancy. Is this some more of your detective work?"

Nancy admitted that she had become interested in a fascinating mystery and would tell him more about it on the drive over. For the time being, she was just going to enjoy the house party.

Next afternoon there was a football game. It was a close contest with Harper. Emerson pulled ahead only in the last quarter to win by a score of 14 to 7.

Ned played a spectacular game as quarterback. He scored the first touchdown on a brilliant dash around the Harper end, and threw a pass to the left halfback for the winning touchdown. Nancy cheered until her voice was hoarse.

Later, when they were dancing at the fraternity house, Ned remarked that he had not seen any elderly men. "I guess Professor Scott decided not to come."

Nancy suppressed a smile. A few minutes later she saw a tall young man on the fringe of the crowd. As she and Ned reached him, Nancy stopped and said:

"Hello! I'm glad you got here. Ned, I'd like you to meet Professor Terence Scott. Terry, this is your fraternity brother Ned Nickerson."

Terry put out his hand. Ned's jaw dropped and he gave Nancy a sidelong glance. The name Scott had hit him like a delayed-action bomb.

"You're Professor Scott who's giving a lecture here tomorrow?" he exclaimed.

Terry grinned. "I guess I am, Brother Nickerson!"

Ned shot Nancy an "I'll-get-even" look, then burst

out laughing. "Well, you two kept your secret well," he
said.

He immediately introduced Terry to his fraternity
brothers and the girls with them. Terry became popular
at once.

When the dance ended, he told Nancy and Ned, "I
haven't had so much fun since my own college
days."

The next day, directly after lunch, Nancy and Ned
set out for Clifton Institute. Nancy kept her promise to
tell Ned about the mystery of the black key, and the
strange events that had taken place in connection with
it.

"That's why I want to talk to Dr Anderson," she
concluded. "He may give us a clue."

They located the robust, forty-five-year-old professor
seated in a garden behind one of the faculty houses. He
wore comfortable tweeds and was puffing on a briar
pipe.

"Never find me indoors, weather like this," he told
his callers after Nancy had introduced herself and
Ned.

Dr Anderson went on to say that he felt he could teach
his students more on field trips than they could possibly
get out of books. "On the ninth of this coming month
I'm taking a group of special students from various
colleges on a field trip to Florida."

"How exciting!" exclaimed Nancy.

"Great country, Florida," the professor said. "Fascinating history."

Nancy manoeuvred the conversation to Mexico, and
explained that her father knew Dr Joshua Pitt. "Dr

Anderson, do you have any theories about where Pitt might be?"

The question seemed to annoy the professor. With a frown he replied, "I'm interested in facts, not theories, Miss Drew."

He further astounded her by saying that Juarez Tino had called on him a few weeks before. He had offered to tell where Pitt and the missing cipher tablet were if Anderson would pay him for the information.

"You didn't do it?" Nancy asked excitedly.

"That rascally scoundrel?" the professor exploded. "I should say not. I threatened to call the police, and then threw him out of my office!"

Nancy asked a few more questions, but Dr Anderson became evasive. Realizing she could get no more information from him, she thanked him for the interview and left with Ned.

As they drove back to Emerson, Nancy remarked, "If I had been in Dr Anderson's place, I would have tried to find out where Juarez Tino went."

Ned agreed. "Do you think he might be holding Dr Pitt for ransom?"

"If so, there's no telling what might happen to the poor man," Nancy said. "I must find Juarez Tino just as soon as I can!"

"Sounds too dangerous," Ned retorted. "Remember, I like you all in one piece!"

"Don't worry," Nancy replied laughingly. "So do I!"

That afternoon she and Ned attended Terry Scott's lecture at the college auditorium. The young scientist thrilled his audience with a story about a Mexican jungle, where there had once lived an ancient race of

THE CLUE OF THE BLACK KEYS

people quite unlike any of their neighbours. From statues that had been found, it was thought they might have been pygmies.

"But they were people of a high culture," Terry said, "who made many beautiful objects. These are just beginning to be uncovered. I had some colour pictures of them, but unfortunately all of my slides, as well as my notes, mysteriously disappeared a short time ago."

Nancy whispered to Ned that this was when Terry was assaulted at his hotel. Towards the end of the lecture, the young professor mentioned his own work in Mexico and the cipher stone.

"Some day I hope to come back here and tell you that the cipher stone has solved a great mystery," he remarked, looking straight at Nancy.

When the lecture was over, his listeners applauded loudly.

"Never heard people so enthusiastic over this kind of lecture," Ned declared as he and Nancy left the auditorium.

"Terry's really good, isn't he?" Nancy said.

The couple had dinner that evening at a popular steak house, and discussed plans for Ned's Thanksgiving vacation.

They said goodnight at ten, since Ned had classes the next morning and Nancy planned to start early on the drive home.

Terry drove most of the way back to River Heights on Monday. "I'm glad this trip was uneventful," he declared laughingly as he said good-bye at his hotel.

"I'll be in touch soon about the mystery," Nancy promised as she waved, and headed home.

"Well, I'm glad you're back, and safe and sound," said Hannah Gruen as she met Nancy at the door.

"Any news here?" Nancy asked.

"Yes. Your father left town. Didn't say when he'd be back. And call Bess or George right away."

"Important?"

"If you could hear them, you'd think so!"

Nancy hurried to the telephone and called the Marvin house.

"At last!" Bess gasped. "Wait there. George and I will be right over."

A few minutes later the cousins arrived in the Marvin car. They joined Nancy in her bedroom where she was unpacking.

"Did you have fun?" Bess began.

George cut her short. "Let's tell Nancy our news first. She might want to report it to the police."

"Yes, please do," Nancy begged.

The girls said that they might have a clue to the person or persons who had caused the car accident, about which they had already heard from Hannah.

"It all started in Cliffwood," said Bess. "Remember that terrible man who said all those awful things to you at the airport?"

"You mean Wilfred Porterly?"

"He's the one." George took up the story. "Bess and I were shopping on Friday in Cliffwood when we spotted him."

The cousins were so sure that he had not been telling the truth about himself at the airport that they had decided to follow him and see what they could find out.

"We trailed him to a hotel, where he went into a

phone booth," George reported. "He dialled a number and talked to somebody named King."

"Conway King?" Nancy asked excitedly.

"I don't know. He just said King. But he was talking about you, Nancy. We heard him say, 'That Drew girl and Scott are acting too smart. You know what to do.' "

"Then what happened?"

"King must have answered quickly and to the point, because Porterly said, 'That sounds all right.' Then he hung up."

Bess said the girls had expected Porterly to go upstairs, and were planning what to do next, when he suddenly went out of a rear exit.

"We followed him," said George, "but he disappeared. I think he caught a glimpse of us."

"The hotel clerk said nobody was registered there under the name of Porterly," Bess added.

"Was there a Mr King listed?" Nancy asked.

"No," George replied.

"What time did Porterly make the phone call?"

"A little after ten," George declared. "It must have been, because we left home at nine."

Nancy was thoughtful. It was unfortunate that she had caught only a brief glimpse of the men's backs when they had jumped into their parked saloon near the restaurant. Had the shorter one been King—alias Juarez Tino—back from Florida? Had the taller man been Porterly?

Nancy told the girls about the two strangers who had been watching the restaurant.

"Nancy, you might have been killed!" Bess said with a shiver.

George agreed. "Those villains are plotting trouble for you as well as for Terry. Since one plan didn't work, they'll try another."

All the time Nancy was relating details about the house party, her mind dwelled on George's remark.

"I ought to warn Terry!" Nancy decided after the cousins left to return home.

She hurried into her father's study and telephoned. Nancy quickly related the story and her suspicions.

Terry whistled in surprise. "Well, that clears up the mystery of the road sign," he remarked.

"When they find their scheme didn't work," Nancy said, "they'll try something else. Terry, you're the one they're really after. I think you should leave town for a few days."

"Oh, I'll be all right," the young professor replied reassuringly. "But how about you? Does your father know what happened?"

Nancy told him her father was away for an indefinite stay.

"That settles it," Terry said. "You and Mrs Gruen should not be in that house tonight. Stay at some hotel."

"Nonsense," Nancy told him. "We'll be perfectly safe, especially if Juarez Tino thinks I'm scared off the case. But why do you have to stay in River Heights?"

"I have no choice. You know I'm a bit of a linguist.

A woman here engaged me just this afternoon to translate an old diary for her, and I've accepted. It belonged to her grandfather, a sea captain. It's sort of a puzzle and she has persuaded me to decipher it for her."

"Can't you do your translating somewhere else, while you're in hiding?" Nancy asked.

Terry said the woman considered the diary a priceless relic and would not permit it out of her sight. That meant he would have to work on it at her home in River Heights.

"But here's an idea," he said. "She and her husband have invited me to stay with them while I'm doing the work."

"Well, that might be safer than staying at the hotel," Nancy said. "I'd suggest you go there immediately. But please do it quietly. Don't let Juarez Tino or Porterly know where you are!"

"All right," Terry agreed. "If you want to get in touch with me, I'll be at the Earl Wangells'. They're in the phone book."

A sudden look of alarm came into Nancy's eyes. "Terry, did you say the Wangells? On Fairview Avenue?"

"Yes. Do you know them?"

Nancy's voice was excited now. "Terry, listen to me. I beg you, don't go there and stay. Don't even take the job!"

Terry was astounded. "Why not?" he asked.

"I can't tell you over the phone. But Dad would say the same thing if he were here. Please don't go there, Terry."

For a minute he did not reply. When he did speak, the young man's voice was kindly but determined.

"Thanks for warning me. But I've just got to run the risk. I must see that diary again," he said. "I believe it will help solve the mystery of the black keys."

·7·

A Mysterious Diary

VARIOUS thoughts raced through Nancy's mind. Her father distrusted the Wangells. Why had they contacted Terry? And why did he think the diary would aid in solving the mystery of the black keys?

"Please," she said, "let's talk about this some more before you go to the Wangells' again. But not on the phone. I'm having dinner at George Fayne's. Could you come there afterwards?"

Terry agreed. At eight o'clock he arrived. After she had introduced him to George's parents, the Faynes went off to watch a television programme in the recreation room.

"The first thing I want to know," the young professor said, once he was seated, "is why you distrust the Wangells."

Nancy explained that several years before, the Wangells had done some travelling in Europe. "When they came back, they set themselves up as experts on rare, old pictures."

"Fake art dealers?" Terry suggested.

"Yes. They convinced a widow that they had some rare French paintings. She paid a fancy price for them, only to discover later that the pictures were worthless."

377

"Did she sue?" Terry asked, with a worried frown.

"Yes. But the Wangells claimed they had bought the pictures from a young man named DuPlaine, and had been duped themselves—that DuPlaine had painted the pictures and forged a famous artist's signature."

"How did you hear of the case?" Terry wanted to know.

"A friend of Dad's defended DuPlaine," Nancy replied. "DuPlaine admitted he had painted the pictures but said they were only copies he had made, as a student, in the museums. He had sold them as copies for practically nothing."

"What was the Wangells' answer to that?"

"They acted injured and indignant. Mr Wangell had a bill of sale and all sorts of documents to prove they had paid a high price."

Terry asked how the case had been settled. Nancy said the court had decided there was insufficient evidence, and had dismissed the case.

"But my father always believed that the Wangells had forged the bill of sale, the documents, and the signatures on the paintings."

"Nice people," Terry commented.

"You see why I'm convinced they're up to something dishonest in this diary business," Nancy said. "It seems odd that Mrs Wangell won't let you borrow it."

"She says she can't run the risk of losing it," Terry replied.

"I wonder if that's the real reason," Nancy mused. "And by the way, you haven't told me what Mrs Wangell's diary has to do with the mystery of the black keys."

"From skimming through it, I gather it is full of unpublished legends which I suspect may have some bearing on our case."

"How?"

"Mrs Wangell's sea-captain grandfather retired in Florida, but he'd picked up stories everywhere, especially in Mexico."

"I see why you want to read the diary." Nancy smiled. "But I still don't like your dealing with the Wangells. Promise you won't stay there. How about going to a small hotel tonight and sending for your baggage so no one will know where you are?"

"I'd like to please you," Terry replied, "and be safe besides." He grinned. "I'll go to the Parkview and ask a porter to take my things over there. Ever since that attack, I've kept everything locked in my bags, so the move will be easy."

"I believe we ought to check the story of Mrs Wangell's grandfather being a sea captain, and the valuable diary belonging to him," Nancy said.

Terry lifted his eyebrows. "I never thought of that. It's a good idea."

Nancy and Terry went to the recreation room and Nancy thanked the Faynes for dinner. "I'm sorry I haven't been the least bit sociable since dinner. And now you'll think me rude, but would you mind terribly if Terry and I go? I want to stop at Mrs Prescott's on the way home."

George groaned. "Goodness, Nancy, don't you ever take time off from a mystery?"

Nancy shook her head laughingly as she and Terry said good-bye.

While driving to Mrs Prescott's, Nancy explained that the woman's business was tracing family trees.

"She has studied the history of every family in this area, and is president of the local historical society. She has stacks of records."

Mrs Prescott was at home and welcomed her two guests at once into the library. She seemed delighted to have Nancy ask a question on her favourite subject.

"Mrs Wangell? Let me see," she mused, squeezing her pince-nez on to her nose. "She was Lillian Webster before she married."

The woman's eyes studied the shelves. "This will take a little while, my dear. Do you mind waiting?"

"Not at all," Nancy replied.

At last Mrs Prescott turned away from her books and records, and took off her glasses.

"I have checked both of Mrs Wangell's grandfathers," she said, "and neither of them was a sea captain."

Nancy and Terry pretended surprise.

"It's all in the record," Mrs Prescott insisted. "Neither of them followed the sea at any time."

"I guess I have the story confused," Nancy murmured.

She thanked Mrs Prescott for her help and hurried out to the car with Terry.

"You see, Mrs Wangell isn't to be trusted," Nancy said. "I think you should insist upon taking that diary to the hotel and translating it before she becomes suspicious and changes her mind."

"She'll never agree to my taking it," Terry objected.

Nancy thought for a moment. Suddenly she remembered a small camera her father had presented her on her last birthday. She kept it in the glove compartment of the car. Now she took it out and gave it to Terry.

"Put this in your pocket and take it to the Wangells' tomorrow. The camera's loaded with self-developing film. Ask to borrow the diary, and if Mrs Wangell refuses, take pictures of the pages you think may be especially important."

Terry promised to do as she suggested. Then, making sure they were not being followed, Nancy drove him to his new hotel, the Parkview.

"Sure you'll be all right?" he asked. "I hate to think of your spending the night in that big house without your father."

"Nonsense! I'm not the least bit worried," Nancy said with a laugh.

Though Nancy was not alarmed over the situation, it was quite apparent, when she reached home, that Hannah Gruen was. The faithful housekeeper was waiting at the front door.

"Thank goodness you're back!" she exclaimed.

Nancy put an affectionate hand on the woman's shoulder. "You're a lamb to be so concerned. But here I am, safe and sound. And maybe tomorrow Dad will come home."

Nancy went up to her room, undressed, and slid into bed. As she dropped off to sleep, she could hear Hannah still busy in the kitchen. "What a clatter!" Nancy thought in amusement.

When she awoke, it was in bewildered alarm. Somewhere in the darkened house there was loud banging and jangling. Simultaneously, something crashed heavily and there was the thud of footsteps.

Springing out of bed, Nancy pulled on a dressing-gown and rushed into the hall. There was no further sound. The entire house was in darkness.

Her first thought was of Hannah Gruen. She stepped quickly into the housekeeper's bedroom and flicked on the light. The room was empty, the bed not turned down.

Suddenly Nancy heard a moan from the floor below. She dashed to the head of the stairs and turned on the lower hall light.

Close to the front door lay Hannah Gruen!

·8·

A Lesson in Sleuthing

NEAR Mrs Gruen's right hand was a rolling pin. Evidently she had dropped it. Stretched across the hall between chairs was a homemade burglar alarm— a clothesline strung with tin pans and kitchen utensils. Nancy ran down the stairs.

"Hannah!" she cried, bending over the housekeeper. "What happened?"

The dazed woman opened her eyes and whispered, "Get him! Get him!"

Nancy looked out of the hall window but saw no one. She helped the housekeeper to a sofa, then raced through the ground floor, peering into closets and behind doors. There was no sign of any disturbance except in the hall. Evidently the burglar alarm had scared off the intruder.

Nancy notified the police. Then she hurried back to Hannah.

"Shall I call a doctor?" she asked anxiously.

The woman shook her head. "All I've got are bruises —and a bump on my head."

"Did he hit you with something?"

"No. I heard him trying the front door lock, so I waited in the dark. I thought if he got in, he'd run into

383

that line, and I'd nab him. But I wasn't quick enough. When he hit those pans, one of them caught me on the head and dazed me a bit. That's why I didn't see where he went."

Nancy brought a cloth wrung out in ice water and bathed Mrs Gruen's swollen forehead.

"My, that feels good," the housekeeper said.

Nancy asked why the strange burglar alarm had been put up.

"I had an idea someone might visit us," the woman confessed. "I rigged an alarm at each door and window on the ground floor."

Nancy slipped into the hall to remove Hannah's alarm system. Her eye caught a small sheet of paper lying just inside the front door and she picked it up. Printed boldly in pencil was a warning message. It read:

NO MORE INTERFERENCE OR THERE WILL BE
TROUBLE FOR YOU

"What are you doing?" Hannah asked.

Nancy returned to the living-room and read the message aloud. She remarked that the note might have been written by Juarez Tino. Not wishing to alarm the housekeeper, however, she added quickly, "It may not be for you or me. Dad makes enemies in his legal work, you know. Some crank could have written it."

Hannah started to speak, but Nancy patted her arm and continued, "You were a darling—and brave, too—to rig up that burglar alarm and lie in wait. You almost caught him!"

Just then the shriek of brakes and tramping footsteps

told her that the police had arrived. Nancy ushered Sergeant Malloy and two of his men into the hall, explaining what had happened. She showed them the note.

While the police busied themselves taking footprints and fingerprints, Nancy decided to look outside. Taking her pocket flashlight, she went to the porch and peered over the railing.

The beam of her light revealed two slips of paper caught in a barberry bush. Undoubtedly the intruder had dropped them. Excitedly Nancy examined them. One contained the number 74772. On the other was printed "5 x 7 and one."

Nancy returned to the hall and copied the notations, then handed the slips to the police.

"I'll work on them. They're a good clue," Sergeant Malloy said.

When the officers had concluded their investigation, the sergeant told Nancy and Hannah he would send a plainclothesman to watch the house.

After the police left, Hannah and Nancy returned to bed for a few more hours of sleep. The following morning Nancy was wakened by the ringing of the telephone. She was delighted when she recognized the deep voice of her father.

"How's everything?" he asked.

When Nancy told him what had happened during the night, Carson Drew expressed concern.

"My plane will get in this afternoon," he said. "In the meantime, I advise you not to go out of the house alone. And look after Hannah. That experience must have been a severe shock to her."

Nancy promised to do as he suggested, and as soon as she had dressed, insisted upon preparing breakfast alone.

Hannah protested at first, but at last gratefully sat down to read the morning paper. After eating, Nancy tidied the dining-room and kitchen. She was just putting away the last plate when Bess Marvin popped into the kitchen.

"I can't believe my eyes! You in that apron—and Hannah sitting on the sun porch reading at nine o'clock in the morning!"

Nancy grinned. "Did she tell you about the excitement last night?"

"Yes," Bess said. "And do you know what I think? You ought to have a bodyguard."

Leading her friend to a window, Nancy pointed to a slender man in a grey suit and a soft hat walking near the driveway entrance.

"One of the plainclothesmen the police sent. It makes me feel very important."

Bess giggled. "As if you were an heiress with a pile of diamonds in your bureau drawer."

"It's a black key, instead," Nancy countered. "And only half of one, at that."

"When's your dad coming home?" Bess asked. When she heard he would arrive that afternoon, she added, "That's good news. You should celebrate. I'll help you get dinner. Let me make a pie."

Shortly before noon Bess was established in the kitchen beating up the meringue for a mountainous lemon pie. Nancy was seated on a stool beside her, but was not watching the pie-making. She was studying the mysterious numbers she had found in the shrubbery the night before.

The "5 x 7 and one" completely stymied her. It suggested nothing at all. The 74772 was easier. The 7 she thought, might be a River Heights telephone exchange. Whose number could 4772 be?"

Suddenly she had an idea. With an excited gasp, Nancy jumped off the stool and rushed into the hall. Quickly she thumbed through the River Heights telephone directory to the W's.

Her hunch was correct. River Heights 7-4772 was listed as the Wangells' number! She rushed back to the kitchen and told Bess.

"How on earth did you figure that out?" the plump girl gasped.

Nancy said she had wondered ever since hearing about the diary why Mrs Wangell had picked Terry to translate it. The whole thing was clear now.

"There's some connection between the Wangells and at least one of Terry's enemies," Nancy explained.

"The one who came here last night and dropped the pieces of paper!" Bess exclaimed. "Oh, Nancy, this is awful!"

"I must warn Terry," Nancy said. "I hope he's at the Parkview."

Her heart was pounding excitedly as she telephoned the hotel.

"I was just going to call you, Nancy," Terry said. "I worked all morning on Mrs Wangell's diary, and..."

"Then she let you borrow it?"

"No, but I took some pictures with your camera. The

C

black keys we found in Mexico are mentioned in the diary!"

Nancy was so surprised at Terry's news that she forgot to mention her own discovery.

"I want to see the pictures," she cried. "Bess and I are having lunch here in half an hour. Will you join us?"

Terry thought this a splendid idea. Nancy asked him to try covering his tracks so that his enemies would not know where he was going. Half an hour later he arrived.

Lunch was a merry affair, but directly afterwards Nancy talked to him seriously about the scraps of paper she had found. Terry could make nothing of the "5 x 7 and one" notation.

"So your would-be burglar had the Wangells' number." The young professor whistled. "I can't stop going there now," he continued. "I'm just beginning to get some valuable facts from the diary. Wait until you see what I have brought."

He opened a briefcase and laid several photographs and carbon copies of notes on the table.

"At your suggestion, Nancy," he said, "I left my notes with the diary. Mrs Wangell doesn't know I have these copies."

"Good."

Terry said that most of the diary was a puzzle to him.

Nancy picked up several of the pictures and studied them. "Will you leave them with me for a while?" she asked. "Perhaps I can find the answer."

"I'd certainly like to have you try," Terry replied. "But here's one I did figure out," he said, handing it over.

The photograph was of page seventy-six in the diary. The upper half of the sheet was covered by handwriting. On the lower part was the rough drawing of a key. Nancy read the strange text:

"In this sodden wilderness I met a curious character, a Swamp Indian. He told me of the hiding place of Treasure, and of three Black Keys that would unlock the Secret of the Ages."

Nancy could not make out the next sentence. It seemed to be in a foreign language. When she asked Terry about it, he said it was in Indian dialect. When translated, it meant:

"If Fortune be kind, the Sun and Raindrop keys will help me find this secret myself."

Underneath the text was the faded outline of a key. Examining it carefully, Nancy could see a design on the stem. One of the symbols in the design looked like the sun. The other could symbolize rain.

"I'll get your half-key, Terry, and we'll compare them."

Nancy got the key and placed it beside the one in the photograph. The lower half of the one in the picture and the relic Terry had brought from Mexico were identical!

"Are there any other references to the black keys?" Nancy asked excitedly.

Terry nodded and picked up a page of notes he said had come from pages ninety and one hundred.

"Here is something I translated from the Spanish. It

says, 'Today I heard another story about the Keys of Sun and Raindrop. Whoever finds the secret may be Ruler of Mankind,' and listen to this! 'Look for the Frog.'"

"It's the same Frog Treasure mentioned on the Mystery Stone!" Nancy exclaimed.

"It looks that way," Terry agreed.

Bess was re-reading the text above the key drawing. "Where is the 'sodden wilderness'? And who is the 'Swamp Indian'?" she asked.

Terry said he wished he knew. If it were true that a sea captain owned the diary, even though he was not Mrs Wangell's grandfather, there was no way to prove it. If a name had ever been in the book, someone had torn it out, along with several other pages.

"I suspect Mrs Wangell did the tearing," Bess decided. "She probably didn't want to be caught lying about the diary's owner."

Terry said the rest of the notes he had made that day were interesting, but he doubted if they had any bearing on the mystery.

"Terry, it's important you go on with what you're doing. Only now, translating and deciphering the diary is just part of your job."

"What do you mean?"

"I mean you're to become a detective."

"A—what?"

Nancy nodded her head seriously. "The Wangells are dishonest. That's been proved. They need you for translating the diary. But once you've given them what they want, you won't be safe."

Terry stared, unbelieving. Nancy went on to say that

it was necessary to find out more about what they were up to, before the work on the diary was finished.

"It isn't hard to do some simple sleuthing," she said encouragingly. "You see, it's not just the big things—like the diary—that are important. If you want to solve your mystery, you should start noticing the little things, too. For instance," Nancy went on, "did you notice the mail in the hall as you came in?"

"Good grief, no! Am I supposed to?"

"Of course. Postmarks and return addresses are important clues. How about the pad on the telephone desk? Any messages?"

"That's snooping."

"I'm afraid a good detective has to snoop," Nancy said.

Suddenly the young professor remembered something. His eyes widened, and he leaned forward excitedly.

"Maybe I do notice things after all," he said.

"What?" both girls asked at once.

"This morning at the Wangells'," Terry said, "while I was in the study, Mrs Wangell made a telephone call. I just happened to overhear part of it."

"Who was she calling?" Nancy asked.

"I don't know. But she said, 'I won't forget. The name's King.' She laughed with a sort of a sneer, and added, 'Some king he is!' Then she hung up."

"You *are* a detective, Terry!" Nancy praised the young professor. "The 'King' Mrs Wangell mentioned must be Conway King—the name Juarez Tino uses!"

·9·

Terry Disappears

TERRY smiled. "That seems to prove the Tinos and Mrs Wangell are in league."

"Keep your eyes open and make sure of that," Nancy begged him. "Try to find out how the Wangells got that diary."

Later that afternoon, when Terry and Bess had gone, Nancy again studied the photographs of the drawings. When her father arrived, she put them aside and went to greet him.

"Oh, it's so good to have you back!" Nancy exclaimed, giving him a hug and a kiss. "You should see the pie Bess made to celebrate your homecoming."

Carson Drew sighed. "In that case I'll have to stay home and not leave until tomorrow."

"Leave?" Nancy cried. "But, Dad, I have so much to tell you about Terry's mystery. I saw Dr Anderson, and I think we've found another clue in an old diary."

She accompanied the lawyer to the living-room sofa, then proceeded with her story.

"Well, you have been busy," her father said. "Good results, too. I guess there's no reason now why you shouldn't work on Terry's case. And I have news of my own," he added.

Upon returning to his office, Mr Drew had found a letter from a man in Baltimore. Caswell P. Breed claimed to be a cousin of the missing Dr Pitt and demanded a share in any money he might have left.

"Dad!" Nancy exclaimed. "How did he know you're Dr Pitt's lawyer?"

Mr Drew said this was exactly what he intended to find out. "Since I have to go to Baltimore anyway, in connection with another case, I'll look up Breed," he said.

Nancy strongly suspected that Breed was not really Pitt's cousin, and told her father so.

"Well, real or not," he said, "I'm going to Baltimore. I'd like you to go along and help me, and also meet some friends."

"I'd love to. But first, I want to tell Terry about this Breed person. Maybe he knows him, or Dr Pitt might have mentioned him."

Nancy quickly telephoned Terry. He was amazed to hear about the letter. The young man had never heard of Breed.

As Nancy put down the telephone, a thought struck her. "Dad," she said, "what gave Breed the idea that Dr Pitt is dead?"

Mr Drew looked at Nancy admiringly. "That's something I must find out."

The lawyer wired ahead for hotel reservations. After dinner he and Nancy boarded an evening plane for Baltimore. On the way Nancy told her father that plainclothesmen were watching the house.

"Just the same I brought the mysterious pictures with me, and the half-key."

"Good idea," the lawyer said to her approvingly.

At nine-thirty the next morning Nancy and her father taxied to a ramshackle dwelling situated next to a factory. *C. P. Breed* was inscribed on a card nailed above the knocker.

The door was opened by an old man. Mr Drew introduced himself and Nancy, saying he was the lawyer from River Heights and would like to hear more about Mr Breed's claim.

The man stroked his whiskered chin, and limping, led the way into the sitting-room. "I'll talk to y'all," he said in a high-pitched voice, "but I won't give up the claim. Doc said not to."

Nancy glanced at her father. "When did you last see your cousin?" she asked Mr Breed.

The old man scratched his head. "He ain't no cousin o' mine. He's my doc, an' a good one, sure enough. Fixed my broken leg what I got at the factory. An' he told me not to give up my claim to any o' you lawyers."

"There must be some mistake," Mr Drew said. He took the letter from his pocket and handed it to the old man. "Did you write this?"

Mr Breed pulled a pair of spectacles from his vest pocket, adjusted them on his nose, and peered at the letter.

"This is me an' it ain't me," he said. "Breed's my name, but I don't know Dr Pitt an' I ain't his cousin, an' I didn't write this."

"Do you know who could have sent it?" Nancy asked.

The man said he did not have the slightest idea,

adding testily, "But I'd like to get hold o' the person who used my name!"

As his callers rose to leave, he accompanied them to the door.

On a hunch Nancy asked him if he knew any people named Scott, Graham, Anderson, Tino, King, Porterly, and Wangell. The answer was "No" in each case.

"You didn't leave out one," the lawyer teased his daughter as they rode off. "But I know what's in your mind; that one of them wanted to work some scheme while we were away, and sent that letter to get us out of town. Which one do you suspect?"

"Juarez Tino," Nancy replied quickly. "I'm sure he's the ringleader of that group. We'd better phone home and see if anything has happened."

"You take over while I go to the courthouse," Mr Drew suggested.

For the next three hours Nancy was kept busy at the hotel. First she telephoned Hannah Gruen to be sure everything was all right.

"Yes," the housekeeper replied. "Now stop worrying, honey."

"Be extra careful," Nancy warned, and told Mrs Gruen about the fake letter.

Nancy next turned her attention to the photographs Terry had made of the diary pages. There were nine of them, and not one of the strange drawings suggested a picture.

Then Nancy had an idea. She bought a pad of thin tracing paper, and cut nine sheets to the exact dimensions of the photographs. On each sheet she made a careful tracing of one of the drawings, using indian ink.

Laying aside the original photographs, Nancy began to juggle the sheets around. She shuffled and rearranged them.

Very soon she began to make discoveries. The meaningless lines on three of the drawings, placed one beneath another, suddenly became a picture. Nancy could see a tangle of trees, a large pool of water, and a winding path.

It was the picture, Nancy thought, of some remote tropical wilderness!

She searched for other clues. One of the trees seemed lopsided. It was fan-shaped, like a traveller's palm. But the palm had been neatly split in half!

Was that half-tree a clue? Nancy excitedly searched through the rest of the drawings. At last she found what she was looking for—the other half of the fan-shaped tree.

Edging the two sheets together to complete the tree, she made another discovery. The sheets placed together completed another picture.

And among the trees and branches was the distinct outline of three keys!

At another spot, where the sheets joined, Nancy found symbols representing the sun, a prostrate man, and a frog. The same figures on the note Terry found in the tent in Mexico!

"The person who wrote this diary somehow learned the directions to the Frog Treasure," Nancy thought wildly. "He didn't dare draw just one picture for fear somebody else would find out the secret!"

Feverishly she worked to decipher the whole picture message. Two other drawings, viewed separately, were nothing but irregular oval blobs. When the drawings were placed one beneath the other, however, the blobs suddenly appeared in pairs.

Footprints!

Six pairs were leading—where? With painstaking care, she traced the footprints on another sheet of transparent paper. Then she laid them over the drawing of the tropical wilderness.

The result was just what she had suspected it might be. The circle was no longer empty. The footprints led to the rim of the large pool!

Then she placed the sheet over the second drawing, which revealed the keys and the symbols of frog, prostrate man, and sun.

This time the footprints led to the symbol of the frog!

She could hardly wait for her father to finish his work at the courthouse. She wanted to get home and talk to Terry Scott and show him her discovery.

When Mr Drew came in, Nancy exclaimed, "Dad, I've pieced together the treasure map!" She added quickly, "Maybe Terry will recognize the location."

"Great work," the lawyer said. "You're really hot on the trail, but we must stay here until the day after tomorrow."

On Friday the Drews caught an early plane for River Heights.

Mr Drew went directly to his office. Upon reaching home, Nancy immediately telephoned Terry at his hotel.

"Mr Scott hasn't been in for two days," the desk clerk informed her.

"Did he check out?" Nancy asked in amazement.

"No, miss. He just hasn't been around."

Worried, Nancy asked Hannah if she had heard from Terry. When she learned no message had come, Nancy wondered if he had changed his mind about staying with the Wangells. She dialled the number, River Heights 7–4772. There was no answer.

Alarm for Terry's safety now made Nancy's heart beat faster. She telephoned George.

"I'm picking you up in five minutes," she told her startled friend. "I need your help on a search expedition."

Nancy quickly returned the obsidian key to her dressing-table drawer and locked the photographs in her desk, then hurried to her car. Within ten minutes she reached George Fayne's house. George was waiting at the kerb.

"What's on your mind, partner?" she asked as they drove off.

"Worry," Nancy replied, and told about the disappearance of Terry Scott. "We're going to the Wangells'."

"Ugh!" George commented. "I see trouble ahead."

"We'll soon know," Nancy said.

She parked round the corner from the Wangells' house. Nancy rang the doorbell and they could hear creaking footsteps inside. But the footsteps hesitated and the person waited until Nancy rang again. Then the door flew open.

A red-faced woman with bleary eyes, her hair uncombed, stared out at them. Was this Mrs Wangell? Nancy wondered.

"What do you want?" she asked suspiciously.

"We're looking for a friend," Nancy stated. "Terence Scott."

"Scott? Must be another house," the woman said and slammed the door. They heard a bolt slipping into place.

George grinned. "Seems as if we're not wanted."

"Wanted or not, I'm staying here until I do some investigating," Nancy decided. "Did you see those suitcases in the front hall?"

George nodded. "Maybe the Wangells are leaving town."

"If they are, it's for no good reason. George, I saw Officer Riley back at the intersection. Would you mind asking him to come here quickly?"

While George hurried away on her errand, Nancy circled the house. The blinds were drawn and all the windows were closed with the exception of a small, first-floor one at the side. When she looked up at it, Nancy saw a curtain move, as if somebody were watching her.

Then suddenly her attention was directed to the top floor. Fluttering from an attic window was what looked like a man's white handkerchief!

Was it a signal of distress?

·10·

Nancy's Search

WHILE Nancy stood staring upwards, she heard a car stop in front of the house and ran to see who was coming. It was a taxi. A man and a woman, each carrying a suitcase, hurriedly jumped into it. The Wangells were leaving!

"Wait! Stop!" cried Nancy, darting across the lawn.

Before she could reach them, the driver started off. Either he had not heard her, or he had been told not to pay heed to her call. The taxi gathered speed and disappeared round the corner.

Nancy dashed to her own car. She was determined not to let the Wangells get away.

When she turned the corner, the taxi was not in sight. Nancy drove on for several blocks, looking up and down the intersecting streets, but in vain.

"I'll try the railway station," she said to herself and drove to it. Again no luck.

Her next stop was at the bus station. The Wangells were not there, and waiting passengers said no taxi had stopped at the place for over fifteen minutes.

"Maybe they went to the airport," Nancy thought. But a stop there gained her no information about the Wangells.

She decided that they must have engaged the taxi to take them out of town. The young detective hurried to the office of the Winfield Taxi Company. Perhaps someone on duty could communicate with the driver by radio. As Nancy dashed in, the girl at the desk looked up.

"One of your drivers had a call to 619 Fairview Avenue. Has he returned?" Nancy asked.

"No."

"Then please talk to him over your radio," said Nancy. "I must find out where his two passengers are going."

"And why should I do that?"

"Because it may save a man's life."

"Say, who do you think you are? An FBI agent?"

Nancy knew it was useless to waste any more time arguing with the girl. It would be better to get back to Fairview Avenue. George would be there with the police.

When she returned to the Wangell house, Nancy saw that George had arrived with Officer Riley, who said he had telephoned headquarters for help, since he could not leave his traffic post for long.

George burst out, "Gosh, Nancy, I've just about had heart failure. I thought you'd been kidnapped!"

"Have you tried to get into the house?" Nancy asked.

Riley nodded. "I rang the doorbell, but there was no response."

Nancy told them about seeing the couple leave the house, and that she was sure they were the Wangells.

"Did you notice the fluttering handkerchief?" she asked.

"Where?" Riley queried with sudden interest.

"I'll show you."

She led the way to the side of the house. The wisp of white cloth was no longer in sight!

"It was there. I saw it. Someone was waving it out of that attic window!" Nancy exclaimed, pointing excitedly. "I suspect someone is imprisoned in that house. I'm going to call and see if he answers."

Nancy cupped her hands to her mouth and made a yodelling sound. Then she called as loudly as she could: "Terry! Terry Scott! It's Nancy. Can you hear me?"

The three held their breath, but not a whisper came from the shuttered house.

"Let me try," said George. She in turn called Terry, but there was no response.

Riley smiled tolerantly. "You sure you haven't been imagining things, Miss Drew?"

Nancy was indignant. "Of course not!" Once more she shouted, "Terry!"

There was no answer from the Wangell house. But next door a window was flung open and a stout woman leaned out.

"What is it?" she cried. "Is there a fire? Has something happened?"

At the same time an old man, with spectacles resting across his forehead, came bustling out.

"Say, why are you shouting?" he asked crossly.

Riley said, "These young ladies think someone they know is imprisoned in here. Have you seen the Wangells lately?"

The old man snorted. "Them? I don't pay them no mind. Don't like 'em. Phonies."

"What do you mean?" George asked immediately.

"Just what I say. Not decent folks. Not neighbourly. Not nice."

"But haven't you noticed anything?" Nancy persisted. "Your house is pretty close to the Wangells'. Are you sure you haven't heard any disturbance?"

The old man suddenly straightened. "Yesterday. I'd clean forgot," he said. "I thought it was my radio."

"Go on, mister," Riley prodded him.

"I was upstairs yesterday morning, taking my pills. And I heard somebody calling, 'Help, help!' Feeble and far away, you know. I thought, 'I've got interference. One of those stations cutting in and spoiling my music.' That's what I thought."

"Didn't you investigate?" Nancy asked.

"No, young lady. I just went downstairs and fiddled with my radio a bit and I didn't hear anything else."

"Oh, it was Terry! I know it was," cried Nancy. "Officer, we must go into the house."

The policeman still seemed doubtful. He was about to ask a question, when George gasped, "Look!" and pointed upwards.

From the attic window the white handkerchief was once more flying its signal of distress. Riley, as well as the old man, stared wide-eyed.

"We won't wait any longer," Riley stated.

The stout woman who had yelled from the upstairs window now appeared on the scene. She was carrying an axe. Riley grasped the heavy tool and nodded his thanks.

He strode towards sloping double doors which

led to the outside cellar steps. Testing the doors, he found they had been firmly barred on the inside.

"Stand away, everybody!" he ordered.

Riley took a mighty swing with the axe, and the heavy door shivered and splintered. Something on the other side fell away with a clatter. Riley prised one side of the door open and swung it wide.

"Stay outside girls. There may be trouble," he commanded.

The officer descended the stone steps. Nancy and George could see the beam of his flashlight as he played it into the dark corners of the cellar. A moment later they heard the warning siren of an approaching police car.

Nancy turned to her friend. "George, I'm going inside with the officers."

"I'm with you," George declared.

They ran to the front of the house in time to see the police car stop at the kerb. Four officers climbed out hastily. Two of them dashed to the rear of the house.

The girls met the other two at the front porch. One of these was Sergeant Malloy, who grinned at Nancy. "You still on the job?"

Officer Riley appeared at the front door and let them in, then left to go back to his post. Nancy hurried up the stairway, with George and two of the police following.

"Terry! Terry, are you all right?" Nancy called.

She expected an answer, but it did not come. The first floor was in semi-darkness. Nancy felt along the wall for a light switch. At last her fingers touched a button. She pressed it, and light flooded a narrow hall.

"Terry!" she called again in alarm.

This time she heard something; not a voice, but a muffled tapping sound. It was an answering signal and it came from above.

Nancy, George, and the policemen climbed to the second floor and began opening doors, but each one led to a closet or bedroom. Presently Nancy tried one which she found locked.

"This must be the attic door," she called excitedly. "And Terry Scott's up there. I know he is. Oh, hurry and open the door, officers. Please!"

Sergeant Malloy and Officer Trent braced their shoulders against it.

Several swift crashes of their bodies against the door broke the lock. With a splintering sound the door gave way.

· 11 ·

A Grim Story

NANCY was the first one up the narrow stairway to the attic. At her heels was Sergeant Malloy, his flashlight beaming the way ahead. The attic seemed to consist of a single storage room, low-roofed and windowless.

But among the shadows Nancy noticed a small door, the key still in the lock. While the police searched behind trunks and dust-covered chests, Nancy went towards the door and unlocked it.

As she did, there came a tap from the inside. Quickly she pulled the door open. A figure, bent over, stumbled towards her.

Terry Scott!

"Terry! Are you hurt?" Nancy gasped.

Though he shook his head, his face was deathly pale and his eyes looked dull and sunken. He tried to smile. One hand wandered feebly to his throat.

"You're ill!" Nancy cried.

The policemen carried him to a chair. Sergeant Malloy reached into a pocket and brought out a tiny glass phial. Nipping off the end with his thumbnail, he held the phial under Terry's nostrils and ordered him to take a deep breath.

406

Soon the colour flooded back into Terry's face. His eyes brightened. He moved one hand to his throat.

"Lost my voice yelling," he whispered. "Thanks. You saved me from starving to death."

"Let's get him out of here," Sergeant Malloy ordered.

"I'll take him to my house," Nancy offered quickly as they assisted Terry downstairs.

"All right. Then I'll stick around here for a while," Malloy said. Turning to Terry, he added, "I'll get your full story later. Anything special you can tell us now?"

"Look for an old diary," the young scientist managed to say.

Nancy and George drove Terry to the Drew home. Hannah Gruen was concerned when she saw him. After learning that he had been without food for two days, she announced firmly:

"You leave him to me. I know what he needs."

Hannah insisted that Terry lie down on the living-room sofa. She put some chicken broth on the stove and made toast.

"How can I ever repay you, Nancy?" the young professor murmured over and over after George had gone home.

"By resting and getting your voice back, so that you can tell me what happened." Nancy smiled.

When Hannah returned with the food, Nancy announced that she had an errand downtown but would be back as soon as she could.

Nancy hurried out to her car and drove once more to the office of the Winfield Taxi Company. This time the blonde girl at the desk was co-operative. She said to Nancy:

"Our driver Johnson just phoned in. He's at a farm-house a couple of miles this side of Kirkland."

The driver had told her his two passengers from Fairview Avenue had forbidden him at gunpoint to turn on the car radio. They had ordered him to drive to Kirkland.

When they reached a lonely stretch of woodland, about three miles from Kirkland, Wangell had forced Johnson to stop, get out, and walk in the opposite direction.

"We're going to use your cab for a while, buddy," Wangell had said. "If you want it back, you'll find it parked in Kirkland."

Nancy asked the girl if the driver had notified the police. She did not think so.

"Johnson just called the office a minute ago."

Nancy leaned over the desk, picked up the telephone, and dialled the Wangells' number. Sergeant Malloy answered. Nancy reported what she had just heard.

"I'll relay that to the police in Kirkland," he said, "and tell them to scour the town for the taxi, and the Wangells, too."

"Have you found out anything about them at the house?" Nancy asked.

"Not a thing. No sign of that diary the professor mentioned, either. By the way, the Wangells don't own this house. They only rent it furnished."

Nancy was disappointed. "Well, I'll appreciate your letting me know if anything turns up."

She was glad to learn, when she returned home, that Mrs Gruen's care had worked wonders with Terry. He looked like himself again.

Nancy pulled a hassock and sat down beside him. "Don't strain your voice," she cautioned, "but please tell me in a few words what happened at the Wangells'."

"They must have suspected what I was doing and planned to imprison me until they could get away," he replied.

"How did they manage to get you to the attic?"

"As you know, there were several pages missing from the diary. Mrs Wangell said that they might be in the attic with some other old papers. So I went with her to look."

"And Mr Wangell sneaked up after you and locked you in?" Nancy asked.

Terry nodded grimly. "Yes, but before he locked the door we had a scuffle. Wangell gave me a knockout punch. I don't know how long I was unconscious. When I started coming to, my brain seemed very foggy."

"Drugged," Nancy guessed.

"I think so," Terry answered. "Wangell was standing over me, laughing. It was an awful feeling. He kept asking me questions about the cipher stone. I knew I mustn't give him any information."

Terry went on to say that he had found out a few things about the Wangells, however, before his capture.

"They hate each other, for one thing. I'm sure of that. Listening to them talk was like waiting for an explosion. There was constant tension between the two, even when they weren't quarrelling. Mrs Wangell seemed to be afraid of her husband."

"Why?"

"I couldn't figure out why, but every time she started

to find fault with him, he would stop her with a stunt that would send her into a panic. I'll show you."

Terry walked over to the Drews' piano. Clenching his right hand into a fist, he ran his knuckles along the black keys, hitting them in a loud, quick glissando.

"How strange!" Nancy murmured.

"After Mr Wangell did that, he'd laugh uproariously," Terry explained. "It had the strangest effect on Mrs Wangell. She'd clap her hands to her ears and scream, 'No, Earl, no!' as if she were in pain."

"Go on," Nancy urged.

"Here's something a bit more definite," Terry continued. "I think Mrs Wangell and Mrs Porterly are sisters."

Nancy was amazed. She praised Terry's detective work and asked, "How did you find out?"

"I listened, the way you suggested. Mr and Mrs Wangell talked a lot about Miami and a couple down there named Will and Irene. I deduced that Will was short for Wilfred Porterly."

"And his wife?"

"That was easy. Once when the Wangells were arguing, I heard her say, 'You should have listened to Irene and me. We Webster girls at least have common sense.' "

Terry said he had remembered Mrs Prescott saying that Mrs Wangell was Lillian Webster.

"Oh, Terry, this is wonderful!" Nancy exclaimed.

"Glad you think so," he replied, grinning.

"I wonder if the Wangells are on their way now to join the Porterlys in Miami," Nancy mused.

She told Terry about the Wangells' treatment of the

taxi driver, and also that the police had searched the house but had failed to turn up the diary or any other clues.

Suddenly Terry remembered Nancy's trip to Baltimore. He asked what she had learned there.

"That was just a trick to get us out of town," Nancy answered. "I came back a little too soon for the Wangells. Or did I?" She smiled ruefully. "They got away."

"But you saved me," Terry whispered. His voice was giving out again. "You saw my handker—" The rest was lost.

Nancy insisted he rest again, promising a big surprise at dinnertime that evening. Terry Scott slept for three hours, awakening just as Mr Drew walked in. The lawyer was deeply concerned when he learned what had happened.

"I had no idea your enemies would go to such lengths," he said to Terry. "It's amazing what evil men will resort to in trying to acquire a treasure."

This reminded Nancy of her promise to Terry. She brought out the photographs of the diary pages and the tracings she had made from them. Terry was intrigued by the footprints leading to the travellers' palm; the symbols of the frog, the prostrate man, and the sun; and the three black keys.

"Amazing!" he murmured.

After studying the complete drawing which Nancy had made, Terry shook his head. "I've never seen a spot that looks like this one," he said. "Too bad it has no directions or points of the compass on it. If I could only locate the cipher stone—"

Nancy brought out her copy of the slip of paper she had found in the shrubbery with its mysterious notation "5 x 7 and one." Terry could make no more out of it than he had the first time.

Mrs Gruen announced dinner and they all went to the table. As soon as the meal was over, Mr Drew drove Terry to his hotel. He promised to retire at once.

At eight o'clock the next morning Terry called Nancy on the telephone. For a moment she feared something had gone wrong, but he soon reassured her.

"I did a lot of thinking last night," he said. "I feel I should return to Mexico. The Mexican police haven't sent me any report. Maybe they have given up the search for Dr Pitt. I must find out."

Terry said that he had a nine-o'clock plane reservation, and was leaving for the airport at once.

"I hate to say good-bye this way," he added. "You've been such a good sport, Nancy. But I hope next time I see you, I'll have good news."

Terry said that if she did not hear from him soon, she would know that he was deep in a Mexican jungle looking for his scientist friend.

"Don't you want to take the half-key with you?" Nancy asked.

"No. I might lose it. If I need the key, I'll send for it. Anyway, I feel that I'm not going to solve this whole mystery in Mexico. There will be many things you'll have to clear up if you will. I'm depending on you."

"Terry, are you sure you'll be safe?"

"Now don't worry," he said, laughing. "Well, I must say good-bye now."

After she had put down the telephone, Nancy sat lost in thought. No matter how she looked at it, she had a strong hunch Terry's sudden decision to start for the jungle was unwise. What could he do alone against ruthless enemies?

·12·

A Hard Decision

AFTER Mr Drew had been told of Terry's decision, and had left for his office, Nancy reviewed in her mind the swift-moving events of the past twenty-four hours. What was there she could do to help solve the mystery, now that Terry was returning to his explorations in Mexico?

"I can still try to find out where the Wangells went," she decided. "That may lead to the Porterlys and then to Juarez Tino, and—"

Her thoughts were interrupted by the ringing of the telephone. Sergeant Malloy reported failure in locating the Wangells.

"The Kirkland police thoroughly searched the town. No clues to where those folks went. You got anything else to suggest?"

"Florida."

"What?"

"My guess is," Nancy replied, "that the Wangells will join the Porterlys in Florida."

Malloy seemed to be intrigued with the idea that the two wives might be sisters. He said the police would communicate with Florida authorities to try to find the couples.

414

"We have a report on Wilfred Porterly," the officer went on. "His driver's licence is okay. But according to the records, he hasn't owned a car for years, so the car registration was forged and the licence plates stolen."

"Did the Miami police find him at his home?" Nancy asked.

"No, but they'll keep an eye out for him. Remember the Tropical Sun Fruit Company that Porterly talked about? There's no such business in Florida."

"What is his business?"

"A lot of pretty fancy rackets. At one time, for instance, he was connected with some art dealers."

"The Wangells," thought Nancy. After she had thanked the officer for calling and hung up, she said to herself, "And now the 'fancy racket' is cashing in on an old treasure."

When Bess and George dropped in a few minutes later, Nancy was improvising idly on the piano in the living-room.

"George told me all about yesterday," Bess said excitedly. "She says Terry left town. Oh dear, I wish I'd been home for the excitement, but I suppose I'd have been scared green."

Nancy smiled, but made no comment.

"You wouldn't be feeling lonesome for Terry, would you?" George asked slyly. "Or is it the plainclothesmen you miss? I notice they've left."

"They're on duty only at night now," Nancy answered. "But I'm not lonesome. I'm trying to puzzle something out. Bess, do you know what five times seven and one are?"

"Why, thirty-six," Bess replied in surprise.

"Yes. And I've just been counting, Bess. There are exactly thirty-six black keys on the piano."

She told the girls about Mr Wrangell's method of frightening his wife. "Like this." Nancy illustrated by running her knuckles over the black keys as Terry had done the day before.

"Nancy, are you trying to say there's some connection between that slip of paper you found in the shrubbery and Wangell's trick of scaring his wife?" George asked.

"I don't know. But that stunt at the piano must have reminded Mrs Wangell of something very unpleasant. Maybe some sort of a threat."

"Nancy, you make me positively shudder!" Bess declared.

"How would you two like to take a trip to Florida?" Nancy asked her friends suddenly.

"Love to," George declared. "But my bank account would never stand the strain."

"Neither would mine after that trip to New York." Bess sighed.

George changed the subject. "How about a little tennis to take your mind off the mystery?"

"Not now," Nancy replied. "I have some heavy scheming to do!"

"Well, we're off to the courts," Bess said.

"Don't think *too* hard!" George teased as the girls waved good-bye.

But Nancy was soon deep in thought about the mystery. She was more eager than ever to carry on a search in Florida. After lunch she broached the subject to her father.

"Dad, do you suppose you could manage a Florida vacation next week?"

"I'm afraid not," he replied. "I must be in court on Wednesday."

"Then how about my taking that field trip with Dr Anderson? It sounds interesting. If he lets me join his students, will you give me money for the trip?"

The lawyer's eyes twinkled. "If I furnish the capital, seems to me I deserve a statement of some kind. Are you really so fascinated by Indian culture—or do you want to keep your eyes on Dr Anderson?" he teased.

"All right, Dad. I'll own up. You'd never let me go to Florida alone."

"And?"

"You see, it's not just Dr Anderson who is heading for Florida. My guess is that Wilfred Porterly is there this minute. And the Wangells are on their way."

"I see, ' Mr Drew said. "But what made you think of getting to Florida by trying to join Dr Anderson's group?"

Nancy said there were several reasons. She believed it was not just his duties as a teacher that were taking Dr Anderson to Florida. It might well have to do with the mystery of the black keys and the Frog Treasure.

"Maybe we can work together," she said. "Anyway, if I locate the Wangells, I may need a man's help."

"Right you are," the lawyer agreed. "Well, if you go

with the class, I'll give you the money. But I'm wondering if Dr Anderson will permit it. You're not a student of his, my dear."

Nancy smiled confidently. "No. But several who are going on the trip are specials. They come from various places." She gave her father a hug. "Thanks a million," she said. "I'll phone for an appointment to talk it over."

When Nancy faced the professor in his office the following Monday morning, she did not feel so confident, however. Dr Anderson was not very cordial.

"I suppose you know, Miss Drew, that you are a bit late. The students who have registered for the trip have already completed their preparatory work."

"I know it's highly irregular, Dr Anderson. But I've done some reading about American Indians, ancient and modern. And I was hoping you'd accept me as a sort of special student."

The professor narrowed his eyes. "Isn't your interest in this field trip a bit sudden?"

Nancy could not help smiling. "I'll be honest with you, Dr Anderson. It's not only interest in your subject that prompted my visit. I want to do some research of my own in Florida. And I need you as a sort of— bodyguard."

Perhaps it was Nancy's smile or her show of honesty that brought about a change in the professor's manner. He softened. There was a suggestion of compromise in his voice when he spoke again.

"As you say, it is highly irregular. But I'll tell you what I'll do."

"Yes?" Nancy asked hopefully.

"I'm giving my students here a quiz on the work we've covered so far. If you can pass that quiz, you may accompany us to Florida."

Nancy's pulse quickened. "I'll try it," she said. "Thank you."

D

·13·

Smoke Screen

"WHEN is the quiz?" Nancy asked Dr Anderson.

"This afternoon at three," the professor replied.

Nancy looked at her watch. It was ten-thirty. She had a few hours to study!

Eager to use her time to advantage, Nancy hurried to the college library. There the librarian pointed out the books used for Dr Anderson's course in American Indian Culture.

"And this should help you," the woman said, giving Nancy a typewritten sheet. "It's an outline of the work covered each month."

The syllabus stated that the subjects assigned for the past month were *The Aztecs of Mexico* and *Early Indian Tribes in Florida*.

Fortunately, Nancy had brought a notebook and her fountain pen. She read all the chapters on Florida Indians, and made notes on the facts which seemed most important about the ancient Aztecs.

She hardly took time for lunch, studying her notes while she ate a sandwich in the cafeteria. After lunch she returned to the library and did more reading until it was time to go to class.

As the students flocked in to take their seats, Dr Anderson rose from behind his desk.

"Please remember that none of you will be given special consideration," he said, looking straight at Nancy. "If you know the subject, you will pass. If you do not know the answers, you will fail."

He gave out the quiz sheets and the blue notebooks in which the students were to write their answers. Nancy's hours in the library, she discovered, had been well spent. She was able to answer all the questions except the last: *Who were the Zapotecs? Where and when did they live?*

She did not remember having read anything about the Zapotecs. Terry Scott had never mentioned them.

She had to leave the question blank!

At the end of the period, Professor Anderson asked the students to put their quiz books on his desk. When Nancy left hers, she hoped he would speak to her. But his only response to her smile was a stern nod.

"He'll be a hard marker," Nancy thought woefully.

"How did you make out?" a friendly girl asked.

Nancy sighed. "I couldn't answer the question about the Zapotecs."

"Anderson's a mean old crow for asking that one. It wasn't in the lectures—he just said we could look it up."

"Pretty shrewd," Nancy commented, then introduced herself.

The girl said that she was Frances Oakes, and she introduced her two friends as Marilyn Maury and Grace James.

"Are you coming to Florida with us?" Grace asked hopefully.

Nancy said that she planned to go if she passed the test.

"That's the big 'if' for all of us," Marilyn said with a sigh.

"I'll never stand the strain of waiting until tomorrow!" Fran groaned. "That's when the quiz grades will be posted."

"What time?" Nancy asked.

"Dr Anderson said they'd be posted by five o'clock," Fran answered. "I'll call you as soon as I know them myself."

That night was a restless one for Nancy. Next morning, she decided to look up the answer to the question she had missed. From the encyclopaedia she learned that the Zapotecs were an important tribe of Mexican Indians. They had resisted invasions by the Aztecs and their culture had been one of the highest in that country.

After reading the article, Nancy's hopes sank. "That does it," she thought. Her ignorance would seem inexcusable to Dr Anderson. She would flunk the quiz.

"And Dad will never let me go to Florida alone." She sighed.

At lunch Carson Drew noticed that Nancy was not eating with her usual appetite. "Is that quiz on your mind?" he asked kindly.

Nancy admitted that it was. Then she changed the subject and tried to act cheerful. But after her father had left for his office, she looked at her watch anxiously. How could she spend those four long hours, waiting for Fran to call?

Nancy had just settled down to a new novel when,

shortly after one-thirty, the River Heights fire siren blasted. Mrs Gruen came hurrying from the kitchen.

"It's our district," the housekeeper announced. "That fire must be right in this neighbourhood."

She and Nancy rushed out to the front porch. Black smoke was pouring from the Hackley house, two doors up the street.

Nancy and Hannah raced across the lawns, reaching the scene just before the fire engines. From somewhere in the rear of the house, Nancy heard a woman screaming. Leaving Mrs Gruen, she ran to the back door. Mrs Hackley came staggering out, carrying her year-old baby. The woman and her infant were crying hysterically.

"Let me help you," Nancy offered and did her best to calm them.

Meanwhile, the firemen had gone inside the house. Presently one of them ran out of the cellar carrying a bucket full of black, smouldering rags.

The fireman approached Mrs Hackley. "Here's your trouble," he said. "Know anything about this?"

Mrs Hackley stared. "N-no. Where did you find that?"

"These rags were stuffed into a duct from your furnace. They've got oil on them and some sort of chemical. That's what made the terrible smoke in your house."

"Mercy!" cried Mrs Hackley. "Whoever would do a crazy thing like that?"

Nancy shuddered. The Drews' front door had been left open. The firebug might have gone into their house!

Not seeing Hannah, Nancy hurried home alone. Quickly she went to the kitchen and opened the cellar door. There was no sign of smoke. She was breathing a sigh of relief when she heard a stifled cough.

Nancy's heart pounded. Was the man who had started the fire at the Hackleys' starting a fire here?

Then another thought came to her. Had he set the Hackley fire to lure her and Hannah away so he would have time to look for something—and steal it?

Nancy thought with regret of the plainclothesman who had been on guard during the day. If only he had not been dismissed!

She tiptoed through the kitchen, and cautiously crept across the lower hall and up the carpeted stairway. As she reached the upper hall, Nancy saw a man emerge from her bedroom.

The intruder turned, saw her, and stiffened. Juarez Tino! He was clenching something black in his hand.

Terry Scott's half-key!

·14·

Danger and Diplomacy

J<small>UAREZ</small> T<small>INO</small> gasped in astonishment. He stood irresolute, then wheeled round and started for the back stairs.

"Oh, no, you don't!" Nancy cried. With a lightning lunge she was after him, reaching for his clenched right hand.

"Give me that key!" she demanded.

"I will not!" Juarez muttered.

Nancy was desperate now. She tore at his right hand with both of her own and managed, for a moment, to wrest the key from the man's grasp.

But not for long. With an angry oath, Juarez wrenched his arms free and pushed her violently through the bedroom doorway. Prying her fingers loose, he once more took possession of the key, dropping it into his breast pocket.

"Help! Help!" Nancy screamed, hoping Mrs Gruen was near the house.

"That won't do you any good." Juarez leered triumphantly, and forced Nancy to her knees. "I'll teach you," he sneered.

His knee against her back, he sent her sprawling

face downwards. Then he seized both her hands and pinned them behind her. With his tie, he quickly tied her wrists together.

Nancy twisted and thrashed away from him. Though she was powerless to escape, the struggle delayed him a few seconds. She tried to scream again, but Juarez clamped a hand over her mouth.

"When I get through with you, you won't be able to talk," the swarthy man threatened.

He whipped a handkerchief from his breast pocket to gag her. Nancy saw the half-key fly through the air. Then he gagged her, and she did not see the key land. Juarez, apparently, did not know he had lost it.

Next, he tore a blanket from her bed and stretched it on the floor. He rolled her over and over until it encased her from toes to shoulders. Then he tied it with a sheet.

At that moment the front door slammed, and Hannah Gruen called, "Nancy, are you home?"

Muttering to himself, Juarez pushed Nancy out of sight under the bed.

"You should have stayed at the fire a while longer, Detective Drew," he sneered.

Creaking footsteps told Nancy he was sneaking down the back stairs. If only she could scream Hannah's name! She could barely moan.

Nancy desperately tried to roll out from under the bed. She heaved against the bedside table and shook the lamp. The noise brought Mrs Gruen to her side immediately.

"Nancy!"

Hands trembling, she removed the gag from the girl's

mouth. As Hannah untied the sheet, Nancy explained what had happened.

"Juarez Tino started that fire and tied you up?" Hannah Gruen cried. "If I ever get my hands on that —that—!"

She flew to the window. Not seeing him, she rushed to the telephone. As Mrs Gruen dialled police headquarters, she stormed:

"They shouldn't have let that daytime plainclothesman go. Leaving you here at the mercy of that maniac!"

Nancy got to her feet stiffly, rubbing her arms to bring back the circulation. She stood deep in thought, wondering about the key. It was not in sight. Had Juarez discovered his loss and retrieved the key?

Hopeful that he had not taken the precious relic with him, she examined every inch of carpet. The key was not in sight.

Hannah called, "Nancy, I have Sergeant Malloy on the phone. He wants to talk to you."

The officer asked a number of questions about Juarez Tino. He said he would put several of his men on the trail immediately.

"We'll comb this town," he declared. "I'll be up to see you later."

After Nancy had hung up, Mrs Gruen joined in the search for the missing obsidian key. When neither of them could find it in Nancy's room, they were forced to conclude that Juarez must have taken it with him.

Nancy was blaming herself for not having chosen a safer hiding place, when she heard a car in the driveway. Glancing from the window, she saw Sergeant

Malloy step out. Hannah admitted the policeman and brought him upstairs.

"You found Juarez?" she asked hopefully.

"Not yet, but the men are out looking. I stopped in to get a full report on what happened, and to tell you we heard from Savannah, Georgia."

"About the Wangells?"

"No, the Porterlys. The police there say a couple who swindled a garage attendant, and rode off just before the police got our message, were probably the Porterlys. The Savannah police are trying to track them down."

"I thought they were already in Florida," Nancy said. "I wonder when the Wangells expect to meet them."

The officer said he wished he knew. Malloy made an examination of the premises. He was just leaving when George and Bess came in. When Nancy walked outside with him to conclude her conversation, Mrs Gruen told the two cousins the story.

"Gosh!" said George when Nancy returned. "Talk about a cat having nine lives! This must be your forty-ninth!"

"That awful man!" Bess wailed. "He might have killed you!"

George gave her friend a searching glance. "You don't seem very happy," she remarked. "Aren't you glad to be safe?"

"I'm afraid Juarez took the key with him. Terry will never forgive me!"

George and Bess made Nancy tell everything that had happened, moment by moment. They ended reenacting the drama together, with Nancy's bedroom key substituting for the black half-key.

George suddenly had an inspiration. "Which blanket did Juarez use?"

"The dark navy one from my bed."

George spread the blanket on the floor. Caught in the fleecy wool was the black half-key! It was hardly noticeable against the navy colour.

"George! You found it!" cried Nancy, delirious with joy.

In the midst of the excitement, the telephone rang. Hannah answered, then called up the stairway, "It's for you, Nancy. The girl says her name's Frances Oakes."

Nancy sobered at once. On the way to the telephone in her father's study she tried to calm herself.

This was a decisive moment. She was about to learn whether she had passed Dr Anderson's quiz. Upon this call would depend her chance of a trip to Florida to continue her quest for the black keys and the Frog Treasure!

"Hello, Fran," Nancy said into the telephone, her heart thumping. "What's the news?"

"Nancy, you made it! I don't see how you did it without going to class. But you passed!"

Nancy had to giggle, she felt so relieved. "I was lucky, I guess. How did you girls make out?"

"We passed, and we're thrilled you're going to Florida with us."

Nancy asked when the trip would start.

"Dr Anderson has chartered a morning plane for the day after tomorrow. It leaves from the airport near the

Institute," Fran replied. "Why not spend the night at my dorm?"

"Wonderful!" Nancy exclaimed. "I'll be there. Any special clothes I should bring?"

"A few cotton dresses, slacks or dungarees, and high-laced boots for trips in swampy terrain. The going will be rough in some places, Dr Anderson says. Snakes and things."

"Mm! What else?"

"Bring a bathing suit—naturally. Say, do you like to water ski?"

"Love to."

"My cousin Jack Walker who lives in Miami has a motorboat," Fran said. "When we're not working, maybe we can go out with him."

Nancy promised to meet Fran at her dormitory for dinner the next evening. Then she said good-bye, and hurried to tell the good news to Bess, George, and Hannah.

"I don't envy you one bit!" exclaimed Bess. "I'm afraid of snakes."

"When I was about ten years old," said George reminiscently, "my family took me to Key West." Suddenly she snapped her fingers. "Maybe the treasure is buried on one of the Florida Keys!"

"What treasure?" Bess asked.

"The Frog Treasure. The ancient secret which Terry thinks is hidden in a silver frog."

"I thought it was in Mexico," Bess said. "You mean Juarez Tino found out where it's buried?"

"Or buried it there himself after he brought it from Mexico," George replied. "Remember how Wangell

scared his wife, striking those black keys on the piano?
Maybe it was a sort of pun."

"You mean," Nancy spoke up, "that Wangell knew
the story from Juarez and might have been reminding
Mrs Wangell of something that happened on a *Black
Key* in Florida?"

"Exactly."

"The way the reminder bothered her, the happening
must have been pretty bad," Bess declared. "Burying a
treasure isn't so awful."

"That's right," Nancy said, frowning. "There must
have been something more to it than just that. But
anyway, if Juarez Tino had the treasure, why would
he still want the half-key?"

"I didn't think of that," said George.

Nancy decided to look at a map of the area to which
she was going. Perhaps an answer to the problem would
present itself. She went to the bookcase for an atlas. She
quickly flipped the pages to a detailed map of the
Florida Keys.

As the cousins looked over her shoulder, Nancy ran
her fingers along the many Florida islands, scanning
them quickly for their names.

She sighed. "No Black Key yet."

"Here it says 'Ten Thousand Islands,'" Bess remarked. "I wonder if all of them have names."

Once more Nancy ran her finger along the fine print
of the map. No Black Key listed. But probably many of
the small islands had names known only locally, she
concluded. As soon as she reached Florida, she would
find out if there were an island called Black Key.

It was possible that such an island might be uninhabited and unexplored. A perfect spot for hiding a captive—like Dr Joshua Pitt!

Long after Bess and George had left, Nancy continued to brood over this possibility. Alternately she was excited about the prospect of finding the elderly professor hidden there, and afraid he might have been starved or tortured by Juarez Tino and his friends.

A voice from upstairs brought her back to reality. "If you don't come and see about your clothes, Nancy, you won't be ready to go."

"Coming, Hannah."

Nancy went upstairs and picked out a few summer dresses, skirts, slacks, and sweaters. Then as Hannah started the packing, Nancy went downtown to buy heavy, high-laced boots.

Upon her return, Hannah told her that Ned Nickerson had telephoned. Hearing of Nancy's plan to join Dr Anderson's expedition at Clifton Institute, he had decided to come down and drive her there.

"He's expecting to take you to lunch and spend part of the afternoon with you," the housekeeper reported. "That means you'll have to be ready early."

Next morning, after kissing her father good-bye and promising to write often and not take dangerous risks in her sleuthing, she and Hannah went to Nancy's bedroom to finish the packing. As the housekeeper opened the young detective's handkerchief drawer, she found Terry Scott's half-key.

"While you're away, it seems to me you ought to put this in a safer place," she advised.

"You're right," Nancy admitted. "From now on, I'm going to know where it is every minute."

She fastened the half-key securely to a narrow but strong, flesh-coloured ribbon. Then she tied the ribbon and slipped it over her head, hiding the key inside her blouse.

"I should have thought of this before Juarez came here," she told the housekeeper.

Nancy was ready to leave. Bess and George arrived and wished her a wonderful trip. Ned came and they drove off.

The hours sped by pleasantly. Before Nancy realized it, the time had come for Ned to leave her at Frances Oakes's dormitory.

"Good-bye and good luck," he said. "Wish I were going to Florida."

After a leisurely evening and breakfast with Fran and her friends, Nancy taxied with them to the airport. Dr Anderson was there and most of the students who were taking the trip.

When they were taking seats, Nancy selected the one next to Dr Anderson. She said, "Do you mind?" and pretended not to notice when the professor gave her a cold, unfriendly stare.

The engines roared and the plane sped down the runway and lifted gently into the sky.

Nancy waited for the professor's face to unfreeze in a smile. But he stared straight ahead.

"I'll have to use diplomacy if I'm ever to win his friendship," she thought.

Aloud she said, "I looked up the answer to the question I missed on the quiz. About the Zapotecs." The professor merely nodded.

Then Nancy mentioned the Indian tribes in Florida.

She spoke guardedly of a diary which described their legends. It had been written, she said, partially in an Indian tongue.

"Might have been Timucuan," growled Dr Anderson. "At the time of the conquest, Timucuan was the language known all over Florida."

After he said that, his face flushed and his eyes got fiery.

"Look here, Miss Drew, why don't you admit you've been working for Terry Scott—that you still work for him? Are you meeting him in Florida?"

"No," Nancy said quietly. "Terry has gone to Mexico."

Dr Anderson exclaimed, "Mexico! What has he found out? Why has he gone back there?"

When Nancy did not immediately reply, he burst out petulantly, "I suppose he took that half-key with him. He has no right to it!"

·15·

The Helpful Fisherman

NANCY winced. Terry had no right to the obsidian key? Who had a right to it if Professor Scott did not?

If Dr Anderson only knew that the key was not two feet from him, he might feel even more disgruntled and suspicious than he was!

"Terry Scott has no more right to it than Dr Graham and I have," Dr Anderson continued in an angry tone.

Nancy breathed easier. Smiling, she said, "Perhaps not. But someone has to keep it."

"Well," the professor said testily, "Terry Scott is acting mighty secretive about the whole thing. Why didn't he inform me that he was going to Mexico?"

Nancy tried to keep her voice calm and unruffled. "As you know, Terry is on leave from his classes at Keystone this year. While you and Dr Graham are busy with your teaching, he naturally feels that he ought to be trying to solve the ancient mystery."

"He'll make certain that he appropriates the honour and the glory, too," Dr Anderson complained bitterly.

"I'm sure that's not his intention, Professor," Nancy said, assuring him that Terry's main concern was the disappearance of Joshua Pitt. Both she and Terry were fearful the doctor was being held a prisoner.

435

Dr Anderson did not agree. He still had a feeling that the elderly professor was hunting for the treasure by himself.

"Anyway," Nancy went on, "I'm sure that as soon as Terry learns anything definite, he'll tell both you and Dr Graham."

"That old fuss-budget!" the professor scoffed.

Nancy laughed. "You know what I think, Dr Anderson? You're all jealous of one another. Talk about Terry being secretive! I'll bet right now you have a secret you're not telling either Terry or Dr Graham."

A slow flush came to Dr Anderson's face, and Nancy pressed her advantage.

"For instance, this trip to Florida. You have chosen that spot for the field trip because you think that something—or someone—is hidden there. Haven't you?"

The professor was taken by surprise. He turned to peer at her, a startled look in his eyes.

"For a girl of your age, you seem to know a lot of answers." He sighed. "I may as well admit the truth. I suspect the treasure may be buried in Florida, and Dr Pitt and Juarez know this."

"Why?"

Dr Anderson told her that during Juarez Tino's call on him at Clifton, the man had accidentally dropped a hint. He had mentioned the fact that the ancient Indians of Mexico and Florida had a great deal in common in their state of civilization.

"I'm sure he didn't figure that out himself," Dr Anderson said. "He got it from Pitt. Right away I suspected he'd been with Pitt in Florida and was double-crossing him."

"Did you accuse him of that?" Nancy asked excitedly.

The professor nodded. "Juarez swore he hadn't been near Florida. But I knew he was lying."

"Wouldn't he tell you anything about Dr Pitt?"

"He was so furious at me for guessing it, that he raised his price. That was when I threw him out of my office."

"I can't blame you for that," said Nancy. "And it fits right in with a theory of mine." She told about Terry and the Wangells and the trick on the black piano keys. "But I'm positive Dr Pitt and Juarez are enemies, not friends."

She also told him about the warning message at the Drew house, and of her recent encounter with Juarez, when he had bound and gagged her, and shoved her under a bed.

"He'd probably treat a man even worse," she added.

Dr Anderson's eyes widened. "I don't mind saying I admire your spunk," he remarked. "And I like the way you think things through. What would you say to our joining forces in Florida? Terry can't object to that, while he's in Mexico."

Nancy agreed willingly, and the professor told her that the study group would have their headquarters at the Southern Skies Guest House in Miami. From there, they would take trips to museums and Indian villages to study the culture of present-day Seminoles.

"Of course I'll do a bit of detective work on the side," he told Nancy, and added slyly, "I suppose you'd like permission to do the same."

Nancy was thrilled. Everything was turning out so well!

"And now that I've let you in on my secret, young lady," Dr Anderson said, "how about telling me yours? What is your special project in Miami?"

"I'm afraid it's not very definite," Nancy admitted ruefully.

She told him about her discovery that the Wangells and Wilfred Porterly were heading for Florida. She also showed him the diary drawings which might possibly have a connection with the treasure.

"Of course it's just a hunch," Nancy said. "But if there is a Black Key down there, I think it may be the hiding place we're seeking. I'd like to hunt for it."

The professor stared in horror. "Explore the Keys—by yourself?"

Nancy laughed. "Not exactly. I was hoping you'd give Fran Oakes and me a separate assignment. We could study Indians too—the ancient Indians on the Keys."

Anderson shook his head. "That would still be unwise. Two girls alone!"

"Fran has a cousin, Jack Walker, who lives in Miami," Nancy explained eagerly. "He has a boat, and knows the bay. He could act as guide and protector."

Dr Anderson smiled. "That's different," he said. "I'll talk to Miss Oakes's cousin when we get to Miami, and if he seems the proper sort, I think we can arrange things."

After that, the professor yawned a few times and began to doze. Even Nancy, excited as she was, at last went to sleep. When she awakened, the other students were excitedly scanning the view far below them. Nancy left her place by the professor and walked back to take the vacant seat beside Fran Oakes.

"Pines and lakes and palm trees," Fran said. "We must be over Florida."

Nancy told her new friend that Dr Anderson might allow them to go exploring together on a field trip of their own.

"Do you think Jack Walker would take us in his motorboat?" she asked.

"He'd love to!" Fran declared.

After a hearty lunch on the plane, the travellers landed in Miami. The Southern Skies Guest House, where Nancy and five other girls were to stay, proved to be a very attractive place. Its palm-studded yard sloped to the edge of a pleasant inland waterway.

"Jack can bring his motorboat right to our door, Nancy," Fran Oakes cried happily.

Mrs Young, the guest-house owner, showed Nancy and her friends to two double rooms, then told them to make themselves comfortable. The girls thanked her, unpacked, then went for a swim.

That evening the student group assembled in the dining-room of a hotel up the street. Professor Anderson outlined some local points of interest, then gave the students their assignments for the following days.

Nancy was awakened the next morning by Fran, who told her that Jack Walker was coming to the hotel at eight o'clock. They took quick showers and dressed.

Jack proved to be a good-looking man in his early thirties, serious-minded and athletic. Dr Anderson seemed to take a liking to him.

"Miss Oakes and Miss Drew want to arrange their own field trip," he said. "If you can give them some time, I'll grant permission."

"I'll take the job—my boat's in A-1 shape." Jack grinned.

They skimmed over the blue water for two hours. Nancy tried to map out in her mind the complicated waterways of the area, but admitted defeat. At last they returned to the dock.

"I wish we could do our research on water skis." Fran sighed.

Jack wanted to know what the research was. "It had better be interesting," he teased.

"Nancy is treasure hunting," Fran explained. "She's looking for an island called Black Key. Know where it is?"

"Never heard of it. But I know the right man to tell her. His name is Two Line Parker."

"What a funny name!" Fran giggled.

Jack took them to see the bearded old fisherman, who lived in a tiny white cottage on the waterfront. His eyes twinkling, he told them how he had received his curious nickname.

"I kin manage two lines at once," he boasted, "just as easy as most folks handle one. Tell you 'bout the time I got me two big fish, one on the left side o' the boat, one on the right side. They was tuggin' so hard, I thought they'd pull me clean apart."

"Did you bring both fish in?" Nancy asked.

"Sure did," said Two Line. "I just tied those two lines together and let the fish fight it out. When they got tired, I pulled 'em in easy."

The old fisherman laughed uproariously and winked at Jack. Then he asked what he could do for them.

"This young lady," said Jack, indicating Nancy, "is looking for treasure on the Florida Keys. Have you any ideas, Two Line?"

The old man became thoughtful. "I don't rightly know where to lay my hands on any at the present. But a heap o' treasure has been buried time and agin on the Keys."

"What kind of treasure?" Fran asked.

"Smugglers' stuff. The Keys used to be a great place for smugglers. And then there was the pirates. They'd make raids on the cargo ships that passed this way."

"Didn't our Navy try to capture the pirates?"

Two Line Parker chuckled. "Sure, but for a long time they couldn't catch 'em. Those pirates was smart. They used shallow boats so they could sneak into the narrow channels of the Keys. They'd hole up there, after they'd made a raid. The big ships couldn't follow 'em. They'd have grounded if they had."

Jack asked who finally got rid of the pirates.

"Commodore Parker, back in 1824. He built a fleet o' barges and some light-draught schooners. Went after them pirates and cleaned 'em out in no time."

"And that was the last of the pirates?" Fran asked.

Two Line Parker smiled wryly. "I wouldn't say that. Ever hear of the Florida reef wreckers?"

The girls shook their heads.

"I used to know a couple of 'em myself. Wrecking captains, they was called. Here 'em talk, you'd think they was kind and honest. They'd keep boats ready.

When there was a wreck, they'd sail out and rescue the folks on the doomed ship."

"What was wrong with that?" Jack wanted to know.

Two Line Parker snorted. "It wasn't just the folks they wanted to save, Jack. It was the cargo. Why, there was plenty of wreckers in the old days, what would lure ships on to the reefs at night with false signals. Wreck 'em on purpose, for the cargo."

"How horrible!" Nancy cried indignantly.

"So you see, all sorts of things have happened on the Keys. Treasure hid and treasure stolen, I reckon. Any special Key you were thinkin' of, young lady?"

"Do you know of a Black Key?"

Two Line Parker scratched his head. "Never heard tell of that one. I could name you hundreds. But Black Key—"

Then suddenly the old fisherman remembered something. "I tell you what, though. There's that Key where the *Black Falcon* was sunk, back in the eighties, in a hurricane. I never heard a name for it, but Black Key'd be a good name on account of the *Black Falcon*."

Nancy was very excited now. This might be the place for which she was searching!

"But if I were you, young lady, I'd—" Two Line paused, shaking his head.

"You'd what?" Nancy prompted him.

"I'd stay away from there—I'd stay as far away as I could get!"

·16·

A Burned Letter

INSTEAD of being frightened by the fisherman's warning, Nancy found her curiosity aroused about the island. She asked Two Line Parker why he had advised her to stay away from it.

"Stories they tell," he answered. "The place is haunted, some folks think. Take that ship, the *Black Falcon,* the night she sank. I've heard Indians talk about it. They say a fire rose up out of her even when she was under water. And after that it rained frogs."

"Frogs?" echoed Jack Walker, and Nancy wondered if the old man' mind was not wandering.

"You don't believe me," Two Line said. "Well, it ain't just me that says so. It's writ down, sure enough, in a book."

"Who wrote it down?" Nancy asked suspiciously.

Two Line nodded his head wisely. "Old sailor down here. Dead now. Lived on the Keys for years, just writin' everything down. Stories the Indians told mostly. He knew their language like his own, and Spanish, too."

The old man's final sentence caught Nancy's attention.

"Who was he? What was his name?" she queried.

"Evans, they called him. Never knew his first name. He went everywheres listenin' to stories and writin' 'em down."

"Had he been a sea captain?" Nancy asked excitedly.

"I don't rightly know. Never talked about himself. When I knowed him, he'd lived around here for years."

"And he kept a diary?"

"Maybe that's what it was. He made drawin's, too. He'd fool hours away, adrawin' and ascribblin'. But he'd never show that book of his to nobody."

The old man babbled on about Indians, pirates and shipwrecks, but Nancy kept thinking about Evans, and the "book" he kept. It could very well be the diary Mrs Wangell had in her possession!

"What happened to the diary?" she asked.

Two Line had no idea.

"Would you please show us, on a map, where the *Black Falcon* was sunk?" Nancy requested.

Jack Walker had a map of Florida in his pocket. He unfolded it and handed the flattened sheet to the fisherman.

Two Line Parker squinted at the shoreline, and pushed a calloused forefinger over a scattering of small Keys.

"About here. There's a Key nearby, I seem to remember, that's called Storm Island."

Nancy marked the spot on the map with her pencil, and decided to ask Dr Anderson to accompany her there the following day.

But the professor had other plans for Saturday. He told Nancy that he had chartered a bus for a visit to a

Seminole Indian reservation. Fran and Nancy, he insisted, were to join the other students on the trip.

Though she was reluctant to spend the time this way, especially since the next day was Sunday and Dr Anderson had ordered a day of rest, Nancy found the trip a fascinating one.

Sunday evening, while eating supper with her friends in a tearoom, Nancy decided to make a start on her detective work. She took a notebook from her purse and found the address Wilfred Porterly had given to Sergeant Malloy at the River Heights airport.

Fran Oakes groaned. "Watch out, girls. Nancy has a plan. I can see it hatching."

Nancy laughed. "How would you three like to go on a manhunt with me?"

"With bloodhounds?" Grace James grinned.

"No. Just with our own wits."

"Who are we going to hunt?" Marilyn asked.

"A man named Wilfred Porterly and his wife Irene," Nancy replied. "Not respectable, I warn you."

"Let's go!" said Fran. "It's a better game than just sitting around at Mrs Young's."

In high spirits, the girls left the tearoom and hailed a bus which carried them north on Biscayne Boulevard. A few minutes later they got off and after a short walk reached a neat, Spanish-style bungalow.

The four girls walked up the steps and Nancy rang the doorbell. They heard footsteps inside, and the door was opened by a woman with a mop in her hand. She looked surprised to see her four callers.

"Good evening. Are you Mrs Wilfred Porterly?" Nancy asked, eyeing the mop.

The woman smiled. "Mercy, no. I guess you're looking for the former tenant."

Nancy showed her disappointment. "Did the Porterlys move out recently?"

"Two weeks ago yesterday."

The woman set down her mop. "You'll have to excuse me. I'm busy cleaning. I have to clean day and night, they left the place so dirty. I guess they moved out in a hurry."

She took a slip from her apron pocket. "I found this on a nail in the kitchen. I guess it's their forwarding address."

Nancy read the notation: "Porterly, c/o General Delivery, Florida City."

"I suppose you don't know the Porterlys personally?" she asked.

The woman threw up her hands and made a face. Then she looked embarrassed. "I hope you're not friends?"

"Not exactly," said Nancy. "We came on business."

She and the other girls said good night and walked back towards the boulevard.

"Florida City," said Grace. "That's too far away for tonight."

"Any other criminals we can hunt? In Miami that is," Fran teased.

"Perhaps," said Nancy. "If I can find his address."

While the other girls waited, Nancy stopped at a drugstore telephone booth and looked for the names Juarez Tino and Conway King in the Miami directory. They were not listed. When she called Information, the operator said that neither person had a telephone.

"The missing persons," Nancy told her friends, "will have to stay missing until tomorrow. Let's go back to Mrs Young's and get some sleep."

Next day Dr Anderson promised Nancy that he would accompany her and Fran on their trip to find Black Key. But he could not start, he said, until after lunch.

"Would it be all right if Fran and I spent the morning in Florida City?" Nancy asked. "It's only a few miles from here and we could rent a car."

The professor gave permission, and shortly before ten she and Fran were speeding through the picturesque area south of Miami.

Parking their hired car along the palm-lined main street of Florida City, Nancy and Fran went in search of the post office. But no help was to be gained from that quarter.

"Sorry," said the clerk. "We can't give you any information."

"I might have guessed," Nancy told her friend. "We'll just have to do our detective work the hard way."

Someone, somewhere, Nancy hoped, would have seen or heard of the Porterlys. She asked a policeman, but he shook his head.

She tried a drugstore, a garage, and a snack-bar, but none of the personnel had heard of the Porterlys. After that, she visited a market and a sweet-and-stationery shop, again to no avail.

"I don't see how you can be so persistent," Fran said. "I'd have given up ages ago."

Nancy chuckled. "That's the fun of being a detective.

You look and look and keep on looking. And suddenly, when you least expect it, you find a clue."

They next inquired at a small souvenir shop selling Florida shells and curios of various kinds. Nancy repeated her usual question.

"I'm trying to locate a man and his wife who, I understand, are staying in Florida City. Their last name is Porterly."

As had happened so many times, the proprietor shook his head. But a young boy who was sweeping the shop spoke up politely.

"I think I can help you, miss. I delivered a package to a Mrs Porterly just last week. She was staying at the Sunland Tourist Home."

He gave directions for reaching the house. The two girls hurried to their car and drove away quickly.

"Now we're getting somewhere," Nancy said triumphantly.

But her triumph was short-lived. They found the tourist home boarded up and deserted. Nailed over the Sunland sign was a neat card which read: *Closed Temporarily. Will re-open December* 15.

"What do we do now? Go back to Miami?" Fran asked gloomily.

"Not yet," Nancy replied. "Let's look around."

She went to the porch and peered into the mailbox. It was empty. Then she and Fran walked towards the back yard.

In the middle of the driveway stood a wire incinerator. Evidently it had been in use recently, for it smelled faintly of smoke. Upon investigation Nancy found that a pile of letters had been burned. Some of the envelopes had not been entirely consumed by the flames.

"It won't hurt to look," Nancy told Fran. "Here—hold my shoulder bag, please."

She turned the incinerator on end and upset the contents in the driveway. Then she singled out the letters which had partially escaped the fire. Seating herself on the back steps, she began to examine them.

Most of the scraps proved valueless. But one envelope excited her interest. It read:

"Mr W. Port—" The rest of the address was seared.

Nancy looked inside the crumbling folds of paper. Only a scrap of the letter had survived. But its contents startled her.

Drew girl and
the trail. Cover you
Will meet you at B
the fifteenth.

Nancy's heart thumped wildly. *Drew girl!* Were the Porterlys and their friends plotting some new evil against her?

'The fifteenth is the day after tomorrow!" Nancy cried. "Oh, Fran, if only more of that letter hadn't burned, we'd know where Porterly and someone else—probably Juarez Tino—are going to meet. And why!"

Nancy put the scraps of paper in her purse, and the girls returned home.

"Nancy, it all sounds as if you were in dreadful danger," Fran said worriedly as they went to lunch.

"I admit I must be very careful. But if a lot of us stick together, no harm can come to me," the young detective assured her. Fran perked up. By two o'clock they were out on the bay in Jack's boat with Dr Anderson.

On the way to the spot where so many years before the *Black Falcon* had sunk, Jack pointed out various sights to the girls.

"Over there is what's called a sea garden," he was saying. "It's very pretty. Grasses, coral, ferns, starfish, and conch shells."

The roar of a speedboat, passing a few yards at their left, almost drowned out his words. Nancy looked up curiously—and her back stiffened.

In that brief moment, as the boat rushed by she had glimpsed the dark, sinister face of someone she knew. Nancy caught Dr Anderson's arm.

"That man in the boat!" she cried, pointing excitedly. "He's Juarez Tino!"

·17·

The Elusive Island

As THE speedboat passed, Juarez Tino turned to look back. Had he recognized Nancy?

"Follow that boat!" Dr Anderson ordered.

Jack opened the throttle and his boat leaped ahead, its prow out of the water.

"Glad to speed. But why?" he asked. "Is that man ahead someone you know?"

"We think so," Nancy answered. "Keep him in sight if you can."

An idea suddenly came to her. The note in the incinerator had said "Will meet you at B—" Was Juarez heading for Black Key?

They raced after his speedboat, following its zigzag course. Then Juarez disappeared behind a palm-fringed islet. When the others rounded it, he was not in sight. They cruised in the vicinity for a while, searching for him, but he had vanished.

"We'd better not waste any more time," Nancy said. "I think Juarez went straight on to the Black Key. Let's look on the map for Storm Island."

After studying it, Jack headed the motorboat west, but could not find the Key which Two Line had vaguely pointed out on the chart. After an hour he changed his

E

451

course. "You'd have to be a wizard to know this place thoroughly. Shorelines keep changing. New Keys building up."

"How does that happen?" Fran asked.

"Tides, storms, shifting sands. And the busy mangrove tree. That's the great land builder in these parts."

He pointed to the junglelike growth edging the Key they were passing. "Mangrove roots grow fast and spread faster. They catch drifting plant life and debris. And so the shoreline keeps building up."

About twenty minutes later, Nancy asked, "Are we nearing the place where the *Black Falcon* sank?"

Jack shrugged. "That Key we just passed is Storm Island. And out there near one of those Keys, according to Two Line Parker, lies the *Black Falcon*." He pointed towards a vista of islets.

"But don't ask me which one," Jack added with a grin. "You'll have to figure that out yourself."

He wound in and out among the islands. But since Two Line had told them nothing specific about the surrounding Keys, it seemed hopeless to identify Black Key.

They watched for Juarez, and listened for the drone of his speedboat. But all they heard were the cries of cranes and the lonely wail of limpkins.

"It's lonesome out here," Fran said. "We must be miles from civilization."

Dr Anderson looked at his watch. "I think we'd better start back."

Nancy felt frustrated as Jack headed his boat towards Miami. The hunt had certainly been disappointing.

"But," she told herself, "I'll come back. The fifteenth isn't until Wednesday."

Nancy told Dr Anderson about the charred letter she had found in Florida City that morning.

"According to that, Porterly and his friends are meeting on the fifteenth at some place beginning with a B. It may be Black Key," she declared.

"Sounds reasonable," the professor agreed. "Perhaps we should come back tomorrow and continue our search. We may be able to pick up Juarez's trail."

Nancy was delighted that he had expressed her own desires. "But let's get an early start," she said. "In the morning."

Dr Anderson frowned. "You forget that I have other students. I'm taking my class to a museum in the morning. We'll have to wait until afternoon."

"How about Fran and me going out in the morning with Jack?" Nancy proposed.

The professor shook his head. "Now that I know Juarez is around, the answer is No. Two men in your party is the absolute minimum."

When they reached the dock of the Southern Skies Guest House, a familiar figure came to meet her.

"Terry Scott!" Nancy was dumbfounded.

The young man grinned. "Like a dutiful daughter, you wired your dad. So when I talked to him on the phone, he told me where I might find you."

Nancy introduced him to Fran and Jack. "And of course you and Dr Anderson—" she added.

The older man gave Terry a long, cautious stare. Then, smiling, he held out his hand.

"I guess we may as well be partners," he said. "I've

been using the services of your young detective on my own."

Terry laughed boyishly. "With the three of us working together, we can't lose."

"What have you been doing, Terry?" Nancy asked as they walked to the house. "We haven't heard a word from you."

"I'll tell you at dinner," he promised. "How about you and Fran and Dr Anderson eating at my hotel?"

Half an hour later they gathered in the big dining-room. Terry picked up the menu card and smiled.

"Ummm. Pompano steak, corn bread, and papaya!" He sighed appreciatively.

After a waiter had taken their orders, Nancy said, "Now tell your news."

"First of all," Terry began, "a good lead came from the Mexican police. They told me about an old woman —an aunt of Juarez—who lives a few miles from the site of our excavations. They have a signed statement from her."

She admitted that Juarez had stolen the cipher tablet and Dr Pitt had trailed him. She knew this, because Juarez had stopped at her place for food to take on a journey and had told her the story.

"Did she know where Juarez was going?" Nancy asked eagerly.

"No. She had no idea where either Pitt or Juarez might be found."

Nancy smiled impishly. "Dr Anderson and I can do better than that. *We* know where Juarez is."

Terry looked at her in amazement. "In Florida?"

Nancy told about the pursuit of Juarez and their fruitless search for him in Jack's motorboat.

"I'd like to go out myself and hunt for him," Terry declared. "Do you suppose, Fran, that your cousin would take us all out tomorrow morning?"

Nancy threw Dr Anderson a demure look. "I'm sure Jack will go, but the professor is conducting class tomorrow in a museum."

Early the next morning Jack Walker moored his boat at the guest-house dock. Terry and Nancy were waiting, and Fran hurried to join them at the last minute, pencil and notebook in hand.

"The prof is making me write a report," she said. "Otherwise, I can't go with you."

Jack started the motor and the boat sped off on it mission.

"What's the subject?" Terry asked. "Maybe we can help you."

"The Florida Keys—Their Character and Their History."

Terry smiled. "All right. Let's start with their character. The Keys are small coral islands stretching some two hundred miles beyond the mainland. At one time they were probably part of the land link to Yucatan."

Fran looked at Terry thankfully. "Gracious, I didn't know that!"

Nancy reminded the girl of Two Line's stories about pirates and wreckers, and Fran wrote busily in her notebook.

At last the searchers reached the group of Keys they

had visited the afternoon before and started cruising around. Finally Jack let the motor idle.

"Hopeless," he said.

"It's a maze, all right," Terry agreed. "But let's not give up."

Nancy pointed towards a small craft near one of the islets. "Could that be Juarez?"

Jack headed his boat in that direction, and they soon overtook the other boat. It proved to be a small fishing cruiser, and Juarez was not aboard. Its only occupant was a sun-tanned fisherman, obviously intent on the day's catch.

Nancy addressed him with a smile. "Good morning. We're doing a little exploring. Would you please tell us how to find the Black Key?"

"Black Key? Never heard of it, miss."

"Perhaps you know where the *Black Falcon* was sunk many years ago?" Nancy asked hopefully.

The man in the cruiser grinned. "It's fishing I like, not history," he said. "It's enough if I know the Keys by their shape, so to speak, and how they're arranged. It helps me remember where the catch is good."

"Well, thank you, anyway."

Jack Walker was about to pull away from the other boat, when Nancy remembered something—the slip of paper she had found in the shrubbery at home, with the notation "5 x 7 and one."

"I have one more question, if you don't mind," she called to the fisherman. "You spoke of knowing how the Keys are arranged. Is there any place where they're in groups of five and seven—and then one Key lying alone?"

456

The man frowned, and thought about this. "Five and seven. Well, I'll be switched! That's the way they are, though I never figured it out before."

He pointed with his rod.

"There's five of them over that way, spreading south and eastward. They're in a kind of half-moon. And yonder there are seven more of those Keys, sort of chain-like. They run north."

"And the single island?" Nancy asked.

"I'm not sure about that one," the man answered. "There might be a single one in there somewhere. I don't remember."

Nancy told the fisherman he had been very helpful, and Jack turned his boat in the direction the man had pointed out. Soon they reached the five half-moon Keys and the chain of seven Keys.

"Now let's look for that odd island," Terry said. He was becoming intrigued, too, by the possibility of solving the mystery of Black Key.

Jack cruised slowly around the inside of the half-moon. There, overshadowed by the larger Keys and at an equal distance between the two groups, was a tiny islet.

Nancy was so excited she could hardly speak. "This must be Black Key!" she whispered.

Viewed from the boat, the spot looked like a small jungle of mangroves. But as they approached, its extent proved to be greater than they had supposed. Searching its shadowy rim, they at last found an opening in the dense growth.

Jack guided his motorboat into the narrow inlet.

Sheltered by the trees, they were completely out of sight of passing boatmen.

"A wonderful hideaway for pirates like Juarez!" Terry commented.

Nancy spotted a path that wound off among the trees and suggested that Jack stop. "Let's get out here," she said in a low voice, "and do some exploring."

The group disembarked and cautiously moved inland. For a short distance the path wound and twisted among the mangroves. Then it suddenly ended at an open, sandy knoll.

Nancy and her companions stood still and gazed around them. In a moment Nancy pointed through a tangle of bushes across the clearing.

"Look!" she whispered.

Almost concealed by the surrounding trees was a low grey hut. As they dashed across the open space towards it, the searchers heard a plane overhead. It was flying low.

"Hide!" Terry commanded. "We don't want to be seen."

·18·

The Hidden Hut

EVERYONE ducked beneath the concealing shelter of mangroves, but Nancy was afraid her group already had been spotted.

"If Juarez was in that plane, there may be trouble for us," she declared.

The seaplane circled the island several times, then droned off.

"Looks bad," Terry said. "We'd better hurry and see what's on the Key before the plane returns."

Once more he and Nancy crept towards the hut, with Fran and Jack following. Fran was frightened and nervous.

"Is this what detective work is like?" she asked. "Why, you take your life in your hands!"

Terry said nothing, but he agreed. He had not forgotten the episode at the Wangells'!

The hut ahead was about the size of a two-room bungalow and built of heavy weather-worn timbers. "Driftwood from wrecked ships," Nancy mused. There was one small window in the front and a low door.

Terry knocked. No answer. He put his hand on the latch and pushed. The door opened. The four walked inside.

459

They stood in a small room, unfurnished except for two canvas deck chairs. In one corner lay a pile of newspapers and magazines—most of them in Spanish—and a box of tinned goods.

"Somebody's been here recently," Fran Oakes whispered. She pointed to the window sill.

A half-eaten choc bar was being consumed by black ants. Beside it stood a bottle of soda, half empty.

Suddenly they heard, from somewhere in the hut, a shuffling sound. Terry motioned towards a heavy door with an old-fashioned, primitive bolt. It apparently led to an inner room, and someone was in there!

"You two girls stand back," Terry whispered.

As he started to open the door, a hoarse voice cried out:

"Go away! I won't tell you!"

Nevertheless, Terry swung the door open. Jack followed him inside. Then came Terry's astonished voice:

"*Dr Pitt!*"

Nancy and Fran dashed forward. Seated on a camp bed was a haggard, elderly man, his eyes sunken but with a determined, fiery light in them.

"Thank goodness you found me," he said, deep emotion in his voice. "But I don't know how you did it."

Eagerly Terry introduced the old man to his friends. Joshua Pitt gave them a sad, wry smile.

"Welcome to my prison cell on Black Key!"

He pointed to a small hole in the roof, too small for escape, and the meagre furnishings in the room—the

460

bed and two packing boxes which served as table and chair. One of them held several tins of food.

Dr Pitt explained that Juarez and two other men had held him captive, trying to make him tell them where the Frog Treasure was hidden.

"Were the other men named Porterly and Wangell?" Nancy asked.

"Yes. Porterly was here twice, Wangell only once. But I wouldn't tell them a thing," the elderly professor said proudly, "no matter what they did."

Terry asked eagerly, "Dr Pitt, did you learn the ancient secret we were trying to find out?"

Dr Pitt's eyes flashed defiantly. "I know. But I won't tell anyone—not even you," he announced. "No one shall ever force the secret from me."

"But why not?" Nancy asked, astonished.

"Because it would mean the destruction of mankind," the archaeologist replied.

The two men helped the elderly professor to one of the deck chairs in the outer room.

"At least tell us," Terry begged, "how you came to be captured."

Joshua Pitt said that the night following the afternoon he and Terry had found the cipher tablet, he had translated the message on the Mystery Stone. He had learned that the secret was one of evil. The professor refused to say more about it.

Terry asked, "While you were making your translation, did you drop a paper with notes on it?" He described the symbols of the frog, sun, and prostrate man.

"Yes. Those symbols are the clue to the secret." Joshua Pitt frowned. "Because of that I decided to keep the three black keys. But in removing them from their ring, I broke one of them."

Nancy said that she had the half-key with her. Fingering the ribbon at her throat, she explained that Terry had entrusted it to her.

"How did Juarez steal the cipher tablet?" Terry asked.

"After I made the translation," Dr Pitt said, "I hid the stone tablet under a blanket. Juarez must have been watching me. As I dozed off, I heard a noise. It was Juarez making his escape. I knew at once what had happened and I started after him."

"Why didn't you yell?" Terry asked.

Dr Pitt admitted that was where he had made his mistake. Thinking he could handle the situation alone, he had not awakened the others.

"But Juarez turned the tables," he said wryly. "I followed him to some old woman's house—she was a relative of Juarez. He and a Mexican pal ambushed me, packed me into a plane, and brought me here."

"And the cipher tablet, too?" Terry wanted to know.

"Yes. It is buried on Black Key," came the startling announcement.

"Do you know the spot?" Nancy inquired excitedly.

"I have no idea," Dr Pitt replied.

Nancy asked when he expected Juarez back.

"Tomorrow."

The fifteenth! But he might come sooner, Nancy decided. If the man in the plane were a spy, Juarez would come as soon as he got the word!

Dr Pitt's eyes smouldered. "Juarez said tomorrow would be my last chance. He was bringing friends here to make me tell my secret by torturing me in some devilish way."

Fran Oakes shivered, and Terry, frowning, looked at his watch. He turned to Jack Walker.

"See here, Jack. We can't leave the cipher tablet on the island. How about you and Fran taking the boat and getting the police? Bring them here as soon as you can. In the meantime, Nancy and I will hunt for the tablet."

Jack nodded. He and Fran hurried from the hut.

Joshua Pitt turned to Terry. "Now that I've told my story, how about yours? I'm curious to learn how you knew I was here."

"The credit belongs to Nancy." Terry smiled. "She did a smart bit of detective work."

At Dr Pitt's insistence, Nancy told the story herself. At the end she asked, "Why did Juarez bring you to Black Key?"

"He knows this area well. Used to come here years ago, looking for pirate gold. I fancy Juarez is a bit of a pirate himself."

"But why Black Key?"

"A friend of his owned an old diary. That must be the one you were translating, Terry. Don't you remember about the *Black Falcon*? There was something in the story about frogs, and Juaree got the idea it might mean the Frog Treasure and it was hidden here. But they won't find it on Black Key because it's buried elsewhere."

Terry looked puzzled. "Wait a minute," he said slowly. "The Wangell diary made no mention of the *Black Falcon* nor any frogs in connection with it."

463

"Juarez showed me the pages. He must have torn them out of the diary before you saw it."

"That's the answer!" Terry exclaimed. "When Mrs Wangell showed me the diary, several pages were missing."

Pitt went on with his story. "Juarez has the two good obsidian keys, and the broken half. Heaven help the world if he ever finds the other half, and becomes master of the secret!"

Nancy longed to know the nature of the secret, but the stern look on the scientist's face warned her not to ask. Instead, she decided to go outside and look around for clues to the buried cipher stone.

As she reached the doorway, Nancy heard a step outside. Before she had time to slam the door, a woman rushed in. Her strong arms encircled Nancy's neck in a stranglehold and forced her back into the hut.

"Now I've caught you!" she yelled at Nancy. "We saw you and your boy friend from the plane."

Terry reached for her arm, but he was too late. Three men sprang at him. While two pinioned his arms to his sides and bound them with rope, the third stood by dumbfounded, as if he had seen a ghost.

"Will! Juarez!" he cried. "It's Professor Scott!"

"Yeah," Porterly said in disgust. "You thought you'd fixed him for good, didn't you? Get to work!"

Nancy was bound hand and foot, then Earl Wangell tied up Joshua Pitt.

The woman pushed Nancy roughly against the wall. "I'm Mrs Juarez Tino," she snarled. "Does that mean anything to you?"

Nancy did not answer.

"Think you're clever, don't you?" the woman cried. Mrs Tino started to drag the girl to her feet, then changed her mind.

"I'll search you first," she said in her brassy voice. "You still have the key we want."

Seeing the ribbon round Nancy's neck, she tore off the obsidian relic with a savage wrench.

"Now we have everything!" Juarez exclaimed triumphantly. "The fortune is ours!"

·19·

Threats

PORTERLY, Wangell, and the Juarez couple dragged their prisoners from the hut, and through some dense underbrush to a clearing.

The captives were ordered to sit side by side. Juarez began to dig in the earth with a shovel.

Nancy's heart sank, but she was determined not to show it. There was one gleam of hope. Only two of her group had been spotted from the plane. These people did not know that Fran and Jack had gone for the police!

"It won't do you any good to dig up the tablet," Dr Pitt said. "You can't translate the message."

Juarez gave him a sneering look. "You'll tell us. We'll use Nancy Drew as a new means of persuasion," he said meaningfully.

"The police know all about you," Terry warned him. "For instance, they know it was Porterly who knocked me out at the hotel, stole my papers, and then broke into the Drew home."

"And they know, too," Nancy added, "that Juarez calls himself Conway King. That's how we found out you caused our accident on the road to Emerson!"

"Count me in on that." Wangell smirked.

466

Nancy wished she could look at her watch. It seemed a long time since Jack and Fran had left to go for the police.

"They ought to come any minute," Nancy thought. "We must play for time." Aloud she said, "You tried to break into our home in River Heights one night, Juarez."

"That old woman of yours with her home-made burglar alarms!" Juarez growled. "If it hadn't been for her, I'd have got the key that night."

"But we have it now!" Mrs Tino cried, showing it to her husband.

Juarez's face broke into a smile. He signalled Wangell to take over the digging. Then he came and stood in front of Nancy.

"Even if you hadn't walked into this trap, I had plans for taking care of you."

"I know," Nancy said quietly. "You sent a note to Wilfred Porterly. But he didn't do a thorough job when he burned that letter in Florida City."

Just then Wangell's shovel made a ringing sound, and a moment later he lifted a large stone slab from its hiding place. It was decorated with grotesque carving and mysterious symbols.

Nancy's heart was pounding. Now that these thieves had the tablet, they might leave the island and take their prisoners along. And the police had not arrived! She must delay these people if she could.

"Well, I guess we're ready for our trip," Juarez said. "First my boat, then the plane."

Even seconds counted now! Nancy asked calmly who

had mailed the fake letter from Baltimore, using an innocent old man's name.

"A friend." Juarez smiled in satisfaction. "But nobody could ever prove it."

Juarez made a sign to his companions, picked up the stone tablet, and proceeded down a narrow path. The Tinos, Wangell, and Porterly followed with their three captives.

The path led to the opposite side of the island from the one where Nancy's party had landed. A cabin cruiser was anchored a short distance out.

The prisoners' ankle bonds were removed, and they were forced to splash through the water and go aboard. They were crowded into the cabin, then the ropes were replaced and tightened securely. Wangell started the motor.

"You know where to head," Juarez said. "Porterly's place."

As the cruiser pulled away from Black Key, he chose a seat on a bench between Nancy and Dr Pitt.

"Now, Joshua Pitt," Juarez sneered, "tell us what you know. Where's the ancient treasure?"

Nancy cried out, "Don't tell him! Don't tell—"

Juarez raised his hand as if to strike Nancy.

"Stop!" Dr Pitt cried. "I'll tell you. Go to Mexico. You'll find the treasure in Mexico." He named a site near the centre of a little-known jungle region.

Juarez got up and stood over Dr Pitt. "You're going with us to Mexico. Tomorrow morning we start looking for the treasure! If your directions are wrong, Professor —*you'll be to blame for what we'll do to Terry Scott and Nancy Drew!*"

By this time the boat had reached another Key. A red-faced, nervous woman, whom Nancy recognized as Mrs Wangell, met them. She cried out in astonishment upon seeing Terry.

"It can't be! It can't be!" she wailed.

"Shut up!" Mrs Tino commanded. "Help me take the girl."

Nancy was half dragged, half carried through a grove to a yellow cement bungalow. Terry was brought in by Juarez and Wangell, while Porterly remained on the boat to guard Dr Pitt.

An evil smile contorted Juarez's face as he turned to leave. "My little wife, you know what to do with these prisoners."

He and Wangell left, closing the door behind them. A few minutes later Nancy and Terry heard the cruiser churning away from the dock. They were lined against the wall, while the women surveyed them.

"See here," Terry said. "Be reasonable. Those ropes are cutting Miss Drew's wrists."

Mrs Tino's face set grimly. "We'd better separate these two." Motioning to Mrs Wangell, she said, "Take the girl into the bedroom."

Mrs Wangell did as she was directed. The door swung shut behind them.

"Maybe I can get her to talk," thought Nancy. "She's not cruel like the others." Smiling disarmingly, she said, "I know you don't want to do things like this, Mrs Wangell."

The woman looked at the floor. "No, I don't. But Earl makes me. Oh, I don't know what to do. He and

Juarez shouldn't have kept Dr Pitt a prisoner. It might have killed him."

"It's a serious offence," Nancy said. "By the way, Mrs Wangell, where did you get that interesting old diary?"

The woman became silent, as if listening for eavesdroppers from the other room. Then she whispered, "Juarez stole it from a man named Evans. After he tore out some pages, he gave it to me."

"And asked you to have Terry Scott figure out from it where a certain fortune was?"

Mrs Wangell admitted this, saying he also wanted to keep Terry busy, so he would not hunt for Joshua Pitt.

Nancy heard an aeroplane. It came closer, flying so low over the bungalow that the walls vibrated. Mrs Wangell ran to the window.

"There they go!" she exclaimed. "Oh, I hope Dr Pitt's wrong that something dreadful is going to happen when they find the fortune! Earl is so foolish!"

Nancy pressed her advantage. "Mrs Wangell, why are you so afraid of your husband?"

The woman hung her head. "I once stole something. But only Earl and Juarez know about it."

"I see," Nancy said. "Nevertheless, I advise you to turn state's evidence when the police round you all up. You'll get off easier."

Mrs Wangell looked frightened. "Earl didn't mean to be bad after he got caught once."

"About the paintings?"

"Yes. It's just that he hooked up with Juarez. Juarez knew Earl had me in his power. He used to play the black keys on the piano to remind me of Pitt being a prisoner. Then Earl took it up. It was awful—"

The door burst open.

"You'll pay for this, Lillian, you tattletale!" cried Mrs Tino. "I'm going to fix you and the Drew girl after I've taken care of Terry Scott!"

·20·

The Three Keys

WHEN Mrs Tino rushed to attack Mrs Wangell, she screamed and dashed into a cupboard. Quickly Juarez's wife sprang to the lock and turned the key.

Almost simultaneously, Nancy saw Terry in the doorway. He had finally succeeded in loosening his bonds.

As Mrs Tino flew at him in a rage, she tripped over a chair and fell to the floor, stunned. Terry rushed to Nancy's side and untied the rope on her hands. With her hands free, she wrenched at the knots around her ankles. Then while Terry tied the woman's ankles together, Nancy bound her wrists.

Nancy looked at him gratefully. "Thanks for rescuing me. I'll never forget it," she said. "But we mustn't delay here."

"You're right," Terry agreed.

He noticed a fishing rod in a corner. "Nancy, give me a white handkerchief. I'll rig up a distress signal."

It took only a few seconds for him to attach. Then he and Nancy ran from the house.

"I see a boat out there," Terry called. "It looks like a police launch."

He waved the fishing pole wildly. The boat came towards them.

There were six figures on deck—Fran, Jack, and four policemen!

"That white flag handkerchief did it," one of the officers said when the boat docked. "We couldn't find you."

"Oh, we've been frantic!" Fran cried. "We went to Black Key and there wasn't a sign of you. We've been searching everywhere."

Nancy knew there was not a moment to lose. Hurriedly she and Terry explained what had happened and said they must get back to Miami at once.

"We'll take care of those women at the house," the sergeant in charge said. He radioed a report to headquarters, then told one of the men to take the young people to the Key where Jack had left his boat.

The fastest possible speed was made. When Nancy and her friends transferred to Jack's craft, Terry urged him to use all the power it had, saying:

"Nancy, Dr Anderson, and I have a date in Mexico. We must reach the treasure spot before Juarez gets there with Joshua Pitt."

Dr Anderson met them at the dock in Miami, anxiety on his face at their long absence. While Terry telephoned to charter a plane, Nancy told the professor what had happened. His eyes were wide with amazement.

"Do you think we can get there in time?" he asked.

"We'd better," Nancy said grimly. "We have several hours. The others won't begin work before morning."

Dr Anderson dashed to a telephone and got in touch

with a retired friend. After a few minutes' conversation he returned to the others.

"Miss Oakes, please tell my students that Dr Lewis White will take over the work while I'm gone. And," he added, "will you get in touch with Dr Graham long-distance at Jonsonburg and tell him the developments here? Ask him to come to Miami if possible. We'll be in touch with him here."

Fran promised, then fearfully said good-bye to Nancy. "Oh, do you have to go? Something dreadful might happen to you!"

Nancy assured her friend she would be in safe hands. Then she hurried to the waiting plane with Terry and Dr Anderson.

About dusk the three alighted at a small airfield in the interior of Mexico. Three uniformed police officers hurried to meet them, and spoke in Spanish to Terry.

"They'll have a car waiting for us at the crack of dawn," Terry told the others. "We'll go by a short cut the men know to the spot where Juarez is heading."

Nancy and the professors were escorted to a hacienda by the police. After a late supper they retired immediately in order to be fresh for the task of the following day.

They were awake before daybreak, and by the time the red sun shone over the jungle, the party was on its way.

Nancy, Terry, and Dr Adamson climbed into a mud-spattered station wagon, while the police took the car ahead. They rode into the jungle until the path dwindled to a one-man trail.

Terry consulted the police, then translated, "The officers say we can ambush Juarez at Diablo Point."

Single file, Nancy and the five men hurried along the trail. At a fork in the trail, the police halted. They told Terry that Juarez and his friends would have to pass there, to reach the site mentioned by Joshua Pitt. It was suggested they all hide in the undergrowth, and nab Juarez and his accomplices as they came by.

For a long time nothing happened. The jungle air was hot and oppressive. Trailing vines tickled Nancy's neck where she lay, and gnats and mosquitoes attacked her ankles.

She began to worry. Perhaps they were too late. What if Juarez and his cronies had already reached the treasure spot! Perhaps, at that very moment, they were torturing Joshua Pitt—

Then she heard the distant tramp of feet, the sound of a voice. Peering through the dense growth, she saw men approaching. Joshua Pitt was in the lead, head bent, feet dragging. He seemed to be in the last stages of exhaustion.

Behind him came Juarez and his pals. Wangell had several tools in his hands. Porterly held a shovel and a large canvas bag.

As they came near, Joshua Pitt said in a cracked, weary voice, "I don't know the exact location. Anyway, the secret will destroy mankind, I tell you!"

Wangell sneered, "Then that power will be ours. And we'll have the treasure, too!"

"Professor, you're lying about not knowing!" Juarez

snarled. "Do you want Nancy Drew to be tortured?"

Terry and Nancy glanced at each other. Any second now Juarez would learn that his chances to torture Nancy or anyone else had come to an end forever.

At that moment the police leaped from the bushes, followed by Terry and Dr Anderson. There were astonished cries, a fight, but it was over quickly. Juarez and his two accomplices were handcuffed, then the police went through their pockets.

"The black keys!" Terry cried as one of the policemen held them out. "And the half-key, too!"

Joshua Pitt's gratefulness at finally being rescued was overwhelming. Tears trickled from the elderly man's eyes.

"You are truly my friends," he said. "I should have shared the secret with you from the start."

"We understand," Terry said. "Let's forget that, and find the treasure. Where is it, Dr Pitt?"

The professor said he had been unable to figure out the exact site, because from his translation he had learned the landmark was a tall stone shaft. According to the Indians that Juarez had consulted the evening before, this no longer existed, nor any of the other clues on the Mystery Stone.

"It may take years of digging to find the Frog Treasure," he said sadly.

Suddenly Terry snapped his fingers. "Maybe not," he said. "I believe Nancy has solved the mystery for us. She pieced the story together from the photographs I took of some drawings in that old diary which the Wangells had. Let's see—what were they, Nancy?"

Excitedly Nancy told about the footprints leading to a large pool, with a split palm tree along its edge. Terry translated this to the police.

"*Si, si!*" one said, and told them to follow him.

Presently the dense growth gave way to a small lake. There were many palm trees growing near it.

"Look for a marker," Dr Pitt said, new enthusiasm taking hold of him. "Maybe that stone shaft is only covered up. The top of it might be showing."

Everyone searched eagerly. It was Dr Pitt who finally located the marker. The top of the narrow stone monument was barely visible among the leaves and undergrowth. Into it was roughly cut the symbol of a frog!

"This must be it!" he cried excitedly. "Let's dig here!"

Terry took the shovel and quickly set to work unearthing the shaft. One of the policemen stepped forward.

"Let the prisoners dig!" he ordered.

Juarez was given the shovel. When he seemed to be lagging, the officer prodded him with his boot. Wangell and Porterly had to take their turns. The hole grew deeper and wider.

At last, several feet underground they came upon a tarnished but waterproof chest of solid silver, richly ornamented. Terry lifted it out. The chest had three separate locks, on the front, the back and the bottom, for each of the obsidian keys.

"I hope they work," Nancy thought fervently as Terry inserted the first one.

Terry turned it. The lock yielded. The second gave

way. Fortunately, the break in the half-key was not in a vital spot and also worked.

Terry swung open the lid. The Mexicans crowded close, their eyes round with wonder.

Inside was indeed a Frog Treasure. There were frogs of various sizes, made of silver. All but a very large one were set with precious jewels: emeralds, sapphires, and turquoise.

Juarez was beside himself with rage. "It would have been our treasure," he screamed, "if it hadn't been for Nancy Drew."

Dr Pitt eyed him contemptuously. "The treasure belongs to none of us. It is the property of the Mexican government."

"But where is the secret, Dr Pitt?" Nancy asked. "The fabulous secret of antiquity that you say can destroy mankind?"

"It will be found," the professor replied, "inside this large silver frog."

Taking the finely carved relic in his hands, he showed the others the tiny marks where one foot of the frog had been attached. Joshua Pitt pulled off the foot. A greenish powder trickled out. He plugged the hole quickly.

"This substance," he said, "has a terrible power. We must destroy it forever."

Terry Scott was thoughtfully taking a paper from his pocket.

"Perhaps so," he said. "But I hope and believe, sir, that you are mistaken."

He showed the paper to the other scientists. It was the cryptic note containing the symbols of the frog, sun, and prostrate man.

"As you know," Terry continued, pointing to the figure of the prostrate man, "this symbolizes death. But it can also mean disease or human weakness. It must be considered in relation to the other symbols, particularly the symbol of the sun."

Joshua Pitt's eyes now had an excited, happier gleam. "Go on," he said.

"According to my interpretation," Terry said, "the frog represents the sacredness of the secret rather than a motive of evil. The secret is that this green powder can heal mankind."

"I think you're right," Dr Anderson agreed.

For a long time Joshua Pitt studied the three symbols. At last he nodded.

"You've convinced me. This powder must be an ancient herb remedy. We'll have it analyzed."

He replaced the silver frog in the chest. Dr Anderson picked up the treasure, and the little procession started back to civilization, where Juarez and his friends would be imprisoned, and where the scientists would announce their find to the world.

Terry took Nancy's arm. "How does it feel," he asked, smiling, "to be such an important person? After all, it was you who finally solved this mystery."

Laughing, Nancy said she was glad that the case had ended so happily. Now she wondered when a new mystery would challenge her. In fact, in a short time she was to be involved in *The Clue of the Leaning Chimney*.

"But *The Clue of the Black Keys* is not yet finished," Dr Anderson spoke up, a twinkle in his eye. "Not until Nancy Drew has visited my classes at Clifton. I want you to tell my students, Nancy, that the best way to discover treasure is to have an observing eye and a brave heart.

"I wish all my students were live wires like Nancy Drew!"